THE LETTERS OF WILKIE COLLINS

Wilkie Collins photographed for *Men of Mark* (© Andrew Gasson, source APG)

The Letters of Wilkie Collins

Volume 2
1866–1889

Edited by

William Baker

and

William M. Clarke

First published in Great Britain 1999 by
MACMILLAN PRESS LTD
Houndmills, Basingstoke, Hampshire RG21 6XS and London
Companies and representatives throughout the world

A catalogue record for this book is available from the British Library.

ISBN 0–333–67466–9 Volume 1: 1838–1865
ISBN 0–333–73246–4 Volume 2: 1866–1889
ISBN 0–333–73247–2 two-volume set

First published in the United States of America 1999 by
ST. MARTIN'S PRESS, INC.,
Scholarly and Reference Division,
175 Fifth Avenue, New York, N.Y. 10010

ISBN 0–312–22343–9 Volume 1: 1838–1865
ISBN 0–312–22344–7 Volume 2: 1866–1889

Library of Congress Cataloging-in-Publication Data
Collins, Wilkie, 1824–1889.
[Correspondence. Selections]
The letters of Wilkie Collins / edited by William Baker and
William M. Clarke.
p.   cm.
Includes bibliographical references and index.
Contents: v. 1. 1838–1865 — v. 2. 1866–1889.
ISBN 0–312–22343–9 (v. 1). — ISBN 0–312–22344–7 (v. 2)
1. Collins, Wilkie, 1824–1889—Correspondence.   2. Novelists,
English—19th century—Correspondence.   I. Baker, William, 1944–
. II. Clarke, William M. (William Malpas)   III. Title.
PR4496.A4   1999
823'.8—dc21
                                                          99–19642
                                                          CIP

This book is printed on paper suitable for recycling and made from fully managed and sustained forest sources.

10   9   8   7   6   5   4   3   2
08   07   06   05   04   03   02   01   00

Printed and bound in Great Britain by
Antony Rowe Ltd, Chippenham, Wiltshire

For our wives

Contents

List of Illustrations

Preface

As was indicated in Volume 1, this two-volume edition of the letters of Wilkie Collins will shed light on the life and activities of one of the few remaining major Victorian creative personalities whose letters and papers remain uncollected and unpublished. Although Collins has been the subject of recent biographies, these works only quote brief extracts from the limited correspondence already available to biographers.

Now that permission has been given to examine and publish the whole correspondence – one of the editors, William Clarke, is the husband of Collins' great-granddaughter and author of a revealing biography of Collins *The Secret Life of Wilkie Collins* (1988, 1996) – this two-volume edition will illuminate an extraordinarily rich and varied Victorian life. It will shed light on Victorian literature and publishing, music, art and many other areas of intellectual, cultural and artistic endeavour.

As explained in Volume 1, there are two main sources for Collins letters: those which survive in institutional holdings or in private hands; and those which have disappeared but survive in printed form. In *Letters of Charles Dickens to Wilkie Collins*, published by Harper Brothers in New York in 1892, Laurence Hutton collected the letters Dickens sent to his close friend Collins. In his preface to *Wilkie Collins* (1952) Robert Ashley wrote of "the huge bonfire at Gad's Hill to which, irritated at the invasion of his privacy by the press, Dickens consigned the whole of his correspondence". Consequently, he concluded, "although we have many of the letters Dickens wrote to Collins, we have none of those which Collins wrote to Dickens". Ashley also noted that "another loss was occasioned when Collins himself burnt the greater part of his correspondence before moving from Gloucester Place to Wimpole Street in the closing years of his life".

Two recent biographies have drawn upon some of the many extant letters throughout the world in university libraries and private collections. William Clarke's intention in his biography is to unravel the secrets of Collins' complicated private life. Clarke's pioneering research revealed the identity of Collins' copyright holder and identified 18 institutions whose libraries held Collins' letters and the names of some private holders. Catherine Peters in her *The King of Inventors: A Life of Wilkie Collins* (1991), building upon Clarke's foundation, interweaves Collins' complicated life with her subject's literary achievements. Clarke's biography prompted Sir John

Lawrence to reveal the existence of letters sent by the ageing Collins in the last years of his life to an eleven-year-old girl and her mother.

The largest institutional collections of Collins' letters are to be found at the Pierpont Morgan Library in New York, at the Parrish Collection at Princeton and at the University of Texas. The Pierpont Morgan has over 300 Collins letters. These include 117 revealing letters to his mother, 86 to his close friend Charles Ward, and letters to publishers such as Harper and Brothers and William Henry Wills (1810–1880,) the general manager and proprietor of *Household Words* and *All the Year Round*. There are also many letters, not included here, by other members of Collins' family – his mother, his father and his brother Charles. The Parrish Collection has upwards of 250 letters including those to Collins' close friends the Lehmanns, to his physician Dr Frank Beard, to his various publishers and a host of other correspondents. The University of Texas has been adding to its Collins holdings edited by Coleman in the 1970s and now has just under 300 letters.

These three repositories alone yield upwards of 850 letters. There are also significant Collins holdings at the Berg Collection, New York Public Library, including letters to the publishers George Bentley (94) and George Smith (21), at Harvard, the Huntington Library, the University of Illinois at Urbana, the Beinecke Library, Yale University, and elsewhere including Kansas and Stanford.

Interestingly, there are fewer Collins letters in institutional holdings in the British Isles. The largest of these, over 140 letters to Collins' solicitor W.F. Tindell is at the Mitchell Library in Glasgow. There are smaller collections at the British Library, the National Library of Scotland, the National Art Library (the "V and A"), the Bodleian Library, Oxford, the John Rylands University Library of Manchester, the Manx National Heritage Museum and elsewhere. These holdings numerically do not compare with those in the United States. The most extensive collections of Collins' letters (more than 300) in the United Kingdom are in private hands owned by his descendants or by private collectors who inherited them or purchased the letters at auction. Thanks to the generosity of these collectors, some of whom wish to remain anonymous, we have been able to utilize their holdings.

Collins' letters are emerging almost daily at auction and in dealers' catalogues. A world-wide search reveals Collins letters on three continents including Australia. There are also Collins letters scattered in printed sources too, many of which belong to the last years of the nineteenth century and the early years of the twentieth century. Various memoirs by actresses such as Kate Field and Mary Anderson, actors such as Frank Archer and Squire Bancroft, literary figures such as William Winter, publishers such as Bernhard Tauchnitz, included lengthy and interesting Collins letters. Collins' letters are scattered throughout the world and found in diverse locations and sources.

Our researches have uncovered upwards of 2000 letters written by Collins in institutional and private holdings. Some of these letters are social notes – Collins was invariably polite – for instance declining invitations to dine. Others are brief notes to his publishers or business letters. Some repeat what has been previously written, for instance to his agent A.P. Watt. Some letters are polite responses to people he doesn't know who for one reason or another have made contact with him. Others are of importance and contain details of his personal or artistic life, political, religious, or other opinions. Some are found only in summarized form.

We have decided to publish full transcriptions of what we consider to be the most important Collins letters, with annotations and linking commentary. Pressures of space have forced us to partly summarize others in a manner which retains the flavour of the originals while omitting redundant matter. Each volume, in addition, contains an Appendix setting out the date, recipient, present source and a one-line summary of all the remaining letters in date order. In this way, the letters in these two volumes should provide researchers with a comprehensive guide to contents and show the diverse nature of Collins' letters. While Volume 1 contains letters dated from 1847 to 1865, Volume 2 contains letters dating from 1866 to the year of his death, 1889.

With two exceptions, Collins' letters appear in the order of their composition. A letter that can be dated only approximately is placed at the earliest date on which the editors believe it could have been written. Letters with the same date are printed in alphabetical order of the addresses, unless the contents dictate an alternative order. Letters to which it has not been possible to assign a day or month are placed at the end of the year. We have made an exception to our chronological order in the case of Collins' correspondence with Nannie Wynne, which extended from 1885 to 1888, because it forms such a unique exception to all his other letters. We have therefore put these particular letters in a separate section of their own in Volume 2.

As well as being arranged in a general chronological order, the letters have also been divided into ten groups that reflect major stages in Collins' life. Each of these sections is introduced by a brief summary overview which also gives background sketches of crucial events for the benefit of those who wish to read the letters sequentially. Readers interested in particular correspondents or subjects treated in the letters can find access through the various indexes. Each letter is preceded by a brief head-note that identifies the addressee, the date, the manuscript location or other source for the text that follows, and other pertinent information. Collins' letters have been transcribed literally for the sake of fidelity to the originals and in the interest of keeping their special flavour as cultural and historical documents. Nevertheless, some minor regularizations have been made. This is a diplomatic transcription: for instance, Collins' punctuation is very inconsistent and has been regularized. We indicate below exactly which editorial procedures have been followed in preparing this edition.

1. Ampersands, cancellations, abbreviations, and Collins' often idiosyncratic spelling, *are retained*. Uncertain readings, textual cruxes, and material cancelled by Collins but still legible, and other editorial insertions, appear in square brackets. Collins' word spacing and line division are not reproduced, but to conserve space, line divisions in addresses, headings, and complimentary closes are indicated by a vertical rule (|).

2. Paragraphs are sometimes not clearly indicated in the letters. Collins at times marked a change of subject by leaving a somewhat larger space than usual between sentences; sometimes Collins started a fresh line. In both of these cases, a new paragraph is started in the transcription.

3. Collins' signature is conveyed in its various forms. It has not been practical, however, to reproduce his inconsistent underlinings of his name. Sometimes Collins signed his letters with his initials "WC", and the "C" of his final name is often much longer than his "W": it has not been possible to reproduce such flourishes. Collins extensively underlined words or parts of words, including his name, sometimes using a single line, or double or treble underlining. Double and treble underlining is noted in the explanatory notes, as is marginal lining when conceivably useful to the reader.

4. Collins often uses both single and double quotation marks inconsistently within the same letter. Here, double quotation marks are used throughout, and punctuation at the conclusion of quotations follows current conventions.

5. Return addresses at the top of each letter are taken from the letter itself. If Collins did not write an address, then wherever possible it has been supplied in square brackets. Complimentary closes are brought to the right-hand margin; names of recipients, when Collins wrote them in, appear after his signature. WC used a variety of printed stationery. In order not to confuse the reader a standard address style has been used.

6. Less familiar foreign words and phrases are translated, in square brackets, within the text of the letters. Explanatory notes, which for convenience follow the text of each letter, briefly identify references, whether these be personal, historical or contextual. We have tried to identify every person or title mentioned, usually at the first occurrence. The sources of quotations and literary allusions have similarly been given when possible. Many names, titles, and allusions have, however, eluded us, and we shall be grateful to readers for suggestions and

corrections. In reference to printed books, when no place of publication is given, London is understood as the place of publication.

7. Postmarks and watermarks have been recorded when conceivably useful in any way; for example when they are evidence for the date or address of the letter.

Part V
The Moonstone to the Death of his Mother

1866–1868

Introduction

Early 1866 sees Wilkie still involved with *Armadale*. Then he writes ecstatically to his mother six weeks before the final instalment is due to appear in *The Cornhill*: "I have Done !!!" [12 April 1866]. Dickens and Forster heap lavish praise upon the close of the novel: "I [Dickens] think the close extremely powerful" [4 June 1866]. In between the dramatization of the novel, the preparation for a limited edition, and his preoccupation with a revival of *The Frozen Deep*, which played at the Olympic from 17 October to 15 December 1866, Wilkie keeps recurring illness at bay and is "getting cured without Colchicum" [4 July 1866].

He goes yachting off Ryde with Pigott in early July 1866. Before leaving for Italy with Pigott in mid-October 1866, he visits his mother in Tunbridge Wells and his relatives in Reading. A characteristically revealing, lengthy letter to Nina Lehmann is written from Milan [26 October 1866], the subjects ranging from the theatre, sights and fashions to the "ever-lasting business of unbuttoning and going to bed".

Wilkie visits Paris in February 1867, to collaborate with Régnier, the producer and director on the theatrical adaptation of *Armadale*. He goes to the theatre and opera and breakfasts on "pig's trotters" [26 February 1867] and return to London in early March 1867. His letters to George Smith begin a pattern of correspondence over business matters, copyrights and practical literary matters which is to continue for the next few decades. May 1867 sees him dividing his father's "pictures and sketches" with his brother, Charles, and negotiating with Smith Elder and *All The Year Round* – "bargaining for my book" [11 May 1867].

The second half of the year brings two important developments. He writes to his mother: "I am in a whirl of work" [18 July 1867]; and in the second week of August he completes the purchase of a house at Gloucester Place, Portman Square. Returning from a brief Ryde yachting expedition with Pigott, he stays in town the whole of August, working without interruption. During September and October, in order to continue work on *The Moonstone*, he takes refuge at Dickens' House at Gadshill and with the Lehmanns in Highgate, while his new house is being prepared. The start of an important set of correspondence begins with William Tindell, his solicitor.

The New Year ushers in what is to be a momentous year. Wilkie writes to tell Holman Hunt [18 January 1868] that his "dear mother is ... sinking" and that "all the leisure I can spare from my mother, must be devoted to my book" [28 January 1868]. Returning only briefly to London in February, he stays with his mother near Tunbridge Wells until the end, finally writing to Hunt [19 March 1868], "one line to tell you that my dear mother died at 3 this morning". Wilkie is too ill to attend her funeral and writes on black-edged mourning paper for at least the subsequent year. He tells "Padrona" [Nina Lehmann] of his "shattered nerves" and the next two months are taken up with tangles over his mother's will. He completes *The Moonstone* full of grief.

Early August sees Wilkie attempting to recuperate with Rudolph Lehmann and his elder son in St. Moritz and Baden Baden. As usual Charles Ward is left to deal with the business side of things. Wilkie returns in better health and begins the electric bath treatment. About this time Caroline suddenly leaves him and marries someone much younger. Wilkie attends the wedding, but remains silent in his correspondence.

To Mrs Harriet Collins, 26 March [1866]

MS: PM

9, Melcombe Place | Dorset Square | NW[1] | Monday March 26

Summary:

He is "wonderfully well", considering the work he has got to do. He is "better than half way through the last number". He would have "been nearer the end", if he had not "encountered difficulties in reconciling necessary chemical facts, with the incidents of the story. But Wills has helped" him "nobly, and the difficulties are vanquished". Hopes to have written the last lines early in next month. Asks about the preparation for moving. Charley (whom he saw yesterday at the Benzon's) tells him he will be with her on the 31st. Mrs Lehmann is much better – able to get out for a drive. Lehmann begins to talk of Paris again. Has no news. He refuses most invitations, and sticks to his work. Has sent her the "Saty Review".[2]

Notes

1. Envelope postmarked: "LONDON–NW | 7 | MR 26 | 66".
2. *Armadale* was reviewed in the *Saturday Review*, 16 June 1866, 726–7.

To Mrs Harriet Collins, 1 April 1866

MS: PM

[9, Melcombe Place | Dorset Square | NW] | Sunday April 1

My dear Mother,[1]

A line to keep you going. I shall be done – barring accidents – in a week more. I have also bought in £[300] [more] – and am now possessed of £1500 [indecipherable word] the Funds.[2] About as much saved from "Armadale" as Marshall & Snellgrove make in a quarter of an hour by the brains and industry of other people. If I live, I will take a shop – and appeal to the backs or bellies (I have not yet decided which) instead of the brains of my fellow creatures.

I am reported "dead" in France – and a Frenchman writes to say that he has betted ten bottles of Champagne that I am alive – and to [beg] I will say so, if I am!

Give my love to Charley if he is with you – and send me a letter. Ever yours affly | W.C

You will have the Saty tomorrow and the next day. Did you get the Cornhill? Was there ever such a dull Magazine? I wonder anybody reads it.

Notes

1. Envelope postmarked: "LONDON.N.W | 7 | AP 2 | 66".
2. i.e., Government stock.

To Mrs Harriet Collins, 12 April 1866
MS: PM

9, Melcombe Place | Dorset Square | NW | Thursday April 12th

My dear Mother,[1]
   Here is something to start you pleasantly on your move tomorrow:
   I Have Done[2]
! ! !

It has been a tremendous job – nearer 50 pulls than 30 – and we have had to enlarge the 19th number which you have read. But done it is – and done well, though I say it that shouldn't!

I shall see Lehmann about Paris tonight or tomorrow &c. If [and: erased] you don't hear from me again assume that I have gone – and that my next letter will be from Paris.

We shall not be away more than ten days – and then I can see the new lodging.

Yours ever affly | W.C
I will tell them to send you the proof when ready, at Mr Pott's.

Notes

1. Envelope, postmark obscured, but endorsed "TUNBRIDGE WELLS | AP 13 | 66".
2. Written in bold. WC finished writing *Armadale* on 12 April 1866, six weeks before the final instalment was published in *Cornhill*.

To Mrs Harriet Collins, 22 April 1866
MS: Private Possession

Hotel du Helder Paris | Sunday [22 April 1866]

Summary:
WC there with Lehmann. "Paris more dissipated than ever ... A grand morning concert today – and races at the Bois de Boulogne among other Sunday amusements the heavens smile on these anti-Sabbatarian proceedings ... warm, sunny, everybody smartly dressed and in charming spirits. It may all be very wrong – but it is indescribably pleasant to a man who has just got rid ... of a heavy responsibility. I am quite content to idle about in the open air, without going anywhere or seeing anything in particular. And yet, such is the perversity of mankind, I am half sorry too to have parted from my poor dear book."

WC and Lehmann will be there no more than a week. "Lehmann wants to get back to his wife, improving at Broadstairs and I must see if I can turn 'Armadale' into a play before the book is published in the middle of May ... to pre-empt thieves. ...

My own idea is that I have never written such a good end to a book ... at any rate I never was so excited, myself, while finishing a story ... Miss Gwilt's death quite upset me."

To Mrs Harriet Collins, 4 June 1866
MS: PM

9, Melcombe Place | Monday June 4

My dear Mother,[1]
I send you by today's post two reviews. "The Athenaeum" in a state of virtuous indignation.[2] "The Reader" doing the book full justice, and thoroughly understanding what I mean by it.[3]

Dickens and Forster have both written to me about the last chapter. Here is Dickens: –

– – – "I think the close extremely powerful. I doubt the possibility of inducing the reader to recognise any touch of tenderness or compunction in Miss Gwilt after that career, and I even doubt the lawfulness of the thing itself after that so recent renunciation of her husband – but of the force of the working out, the care and pains, and the art, I have no doubt whatever. The end of Bashwood I think particularly fine, and worthy of his whole career."

And here is Forster: –

"It is a masterpiece of Art which few indeed have equalled to bring even pity and pathos to the end of such a career as hers. You certainly have done this – and this single page in which it is done is the finest thing in the book."

=

This is of course only for y<u>our</u> eye. You wanted news of "Armadale" – and here it is.

Poor dear Billy Grant (of whose illness I told you) died on Saturday at his father's house. Another old friend gone! His brother wrote to me with very little hope a week since. The malady was a tumour – and the weakness following the dispersion of it has been fatal.

I saw Mrs Elliot yesterday. She sends her love, and is resolute to [see: erased] pay you a visit, when I go next to Prospect Hill.

Ever your affly | W.C

Henry Bullar is going abroad, and takes Edith with him. They go with William to Wildbad. Henry wants me to join him afterwards in Switzerland.

Notes

1. Envelope postmarked: "LONDON.W | 7 | JU 5 | 66", and endorsed "TUNBRIDGE WELLS | B | JU 5 | 66", and addressed to: "Mrs Collins | Prospect Hill | Southborough | near Tunbridge Wells".
2. See H.F. Chorley's unsigned review, *Athenaeum*, 2 June 1866, pp. 732–3.
3. See *The Reader*, 2 June 1866, pp. 538–9.

To Mrs Harriet Collins, 4 July [1866]
MS: PM

9, Melcombe Place | Dorset Square | N.W. | July 4

My dear Mother,[1]

I send you "The Argosy"[2] by this post.

How are you? Any more [Whitlows]? Write and tell me.

As for <u>me</u>, I have had the gout plaguing me again. All my engagements have had to be put off or declined. I am living by rule, and getting cured <u>without Colchicum</u> and in a week's time, I hope to come to you – before going to the seaside.

I shall bring you a copy of the play. A provincial manager is already in treaty with me for the right of acting it in the country at the opening of the "winter season" – and <u>after</u> it has been produced in London. The manager in London I shall communicate with, before I see you next week.

"Armadale" (the book) has, I hear, fully satisfied the publishers in the matter of Sale thus far. [erasure] The numbers are not "returned" yet to the West-End Department in Pall Mall. But a great pressure was put upon "Mudie" by my faithful public – and an unexpectedly large demand was the consequence.

Charley has been complaining a little – but is better again. I saw them both yesterday, in very good spirits – just back from a visit to Mrs Sartoris. The sudden change in the weather from hot to cold has been trying everybody in London. Yesterday, it was cold enough here, for some people to have fires – and I found it necessary to shut the window! This is July!!!

Ever yours aftl | W.C

Notes

1. Envelope, postmarked: "LONDON – W | [obscured] | JY 4 | 66".
2. Published by Alexander Strahan (1833–1918) to which Anthony Trollope and Charles Reade, among others contributed. From December 1865 to November 1866 it serialized Reade's controversial novel of sexual jealousy *Griffith Gaunt*.

To Mrs Harriet Collins, 8 July [1866]

MS: PM

9, Melcombe Place | N.W. | Sunday July 8

My dear Mother,[1]

I send you the play by book-post. Don't let anybody see it – for there may be changes made in it yet.

Yesterday, I sent you The Reader – and on Friday next, I propose being with you at Southborough. I would have come earlier in the week – but Mrs Sartoris[2] has asked me to some private theatricals in which Katie appears, on Wednesday and Thursday evenings. I have accepted for Thursday – being engaged on Wednesday – and I know you will like me to bring you a report of your daughter-in-law's appearance on the private stage.

I will send Ben with the cards to inquire after the public servant.

As for Mrs Gray,[3] I want her address. She has been "[letting] me off" at some people who have a job for her, and who have asked me, through a mutual friend where she lives. Send me the information by return of post.

I think you in the back drawing-room and Mrs Gray in the [erased word] front drawing-room would make a very nice subject for a farce. I'll propose it to Buckstone,[4] if you will go. I met Henry Gray,[5] the other day. He has a picture-dealer's shop in Old Cavendish St. "Gray and Jones, Picture-dealers, and Photographic Miniature Painters" – Such is the inscription! His eyes were rayless – his cheeks were haggard – his beard was mangy – and he chuckled feebly when I congratulated him on being a married man.

Send me the title of that book of [Mr] Aidé's[6] that you want. Careful dieting, and refusal of all invitations have checked the gout – with a little assistance from Potash of course.

I shall stay with you, I hope, from Friday next to the following Friday. Saturday the 21st is the day at present fixed on for going to the sea-side and getting a week's boating.

Count the cheap claret again, please. I want to know how many bottles are left and tell me if I can bring anything down besides the book. Glad to hear the Whitlows are fine. Ever yours aftly | W.C

Notes

1. Envelope, postmarked: "LONDON – W | 7 | JY 9 | 66".
2. Née Adelaide Kemble (?1816-1879: *DNB*), soprano, younger daughter of Charles Kemble. Married to Edward John Sartoris; see Dickens, *Letters*, VII, 185, n.1.
3. Probably a reference to WC's mother's sister Catherine who married John Westcott Gray. See Clarke, p. 222, n.42, and Donald Whitton, *Grays of Salisbury*, (San Francisco, 1976).
4. John Baldwin Buckstone (1802--1879: *DNB*), comedian and dramatist.
5. i.e., WC's cousin.
6. [Charles] Hamilton Aidé (1826–1906: *DNB*), novelist, poet, composer.

To Mrs Harriet Collins, 24 July [1866]
MS: PM

9, Melcombe Place | Dorset Square N.W. | July 24

My dear Mother,[1]

We got back last night, after a great success. It ended in our going where we ought to have thought of going in the first instance – to [the: erased] Ryde. Pigott and I belong to this yacht club – and we introduced Benham – as a visitor. Slept at lodgings provided by the club – breakfasted and dined excellently at the club – had a boat provided by the club – and, in short, found everything we wanted ready and waiting for us, weather included. Saturday, Sunday and Monday, all three fine days, with a steady breeze and a smooth sea! – My luck seems, as they say, "on the turn".

Today [seems: erased] is overcast and threatening in London. I hope your lawn party won't be damped and the Honorable Mrs Cropper disarranged, by any untimely fall of water from that sky which bends over Mrs Cropper's head and which is, or ought to be, the occasional object of Mrs Cropper's devout contemplation.

I have no settled plan beyond going for a day or two to Gadshill next Saturday. Tell me how you are, and whether you have, or have <u>not</u>, decided to ask Jane, so that I may make my arrangements accordingly for [erased word] going to see you again.

I send you a Saturday Review, which Pigott brought for railway reading on his journey down. Nobody at the Hampstead party, but one guest besides myself. We were very cosy and cordial at one end of a long table laid for many visitors.

Ever affly yours | W.C

Note

1. Envelope postmarked: "LONDON. N.W. | X | JY 24 | 66".

To Nina Lehmann, 26 October 1866
MS: Princeton

Milan. Oct 26th 1866

My dear Padrona,

Are you angry with me for leaving your charming letter so long unanswered? You well might be – and yet it is not my fault. I have been living in a whirlwind, and have only dropped out of the vortex in this place. In plainer English, the first quarter of an hour which I have had at my own disposal since you wrote to me, is a quarter of an hour tonight, in this very damp and very [erased word] dreary town. Last night my travelling-companion (Pigott) and I, went to a public ball here. We entered by a long dark passage – passed through a hall ornamented with a large stock of fenders, grates and other ironmongery for sale on either side – found ourselves in a [erasure] spacious room lit by three oil lamps, with two dis-reputable females smoking cigars, ten or a dozen depressed men – about four hundred empty chairs in a circle – one couple polking in that circle – and nothing else, on my sacred word of honour, nothing else going on! Tonight, I am wiser. I stay at the hotel, and write to the Padrona.

Let us go back to England.

How came I to be so dreadfully occupied when your letter reached [erasure] me? Surely, I need not tell you, who know me so well, the particular circumstance in which my troubles took their rise. Of course, I caught a Cold. Very good. I had four different visits to pay in the country, and they had to be put off till I was better. I also had a play ("The Frozen Deep") accepted at the Olympic Theatre, and to be produced at Christmas. I also had my engagement with Pigott to go to Rome on a certain day. Very good again. It turned out, as soon as I was better, that all my four visits must be paid together in ten days – in consequence of the infernal cold seizing on me by the nose, teeth, face, throat, and chest, in succession, and keeping me at home till the time for going to Italy was perilously near at hand. To make matters worse, the play with which the Olympic season opened, proved a failure, and "The Frozen Deep" was wanted in October instead of at Christmas. I paid a visit in the country – and came back to London, and read the play to the actors. I paid another visit, and came back, and heard the actors read their parts to me. I paid another visit, and came back to a first rehearsal. I paid a last [erased word] visit, and came back to see the stage "effects" tried – and went away again to say goodbye to Mama Collins at Tunbridge Wells – and came back again to "sketch" the play bill and hear the manager's last words – and went away again to Folkestone and Boulogne – and stopped in Paris a day to discuss the production of my other play "Armadale" on the French stage, with my good friend Régnier, of the Theatre Français – and went away again through Switzerland and over the Splügen with Pigott, whose time is limited, and whose travelling must not be of the dawdling and desultory kind – and [erased passage] so it happens that tomorrow night, if all goes well, I shall be at Bologna, while "The Frozen Deep" is being performed for the first time in London, and the respectable British Public is hissing, or applauding me, as the case may be. In the midst of all this, where is the time, but between ten and eleven tonight at the Albergho Reale in Milan. Have I justified myself? Hein?

Well, and what next? I don't exactly know. We were to have gone and stayed with Thomas Trollope in his new villa at Florence. But [erasure] a woman has got in the way. A charming person of the sex was governess to [erasure] the daughter of Thomas Trollope, widower – and Thomas Trollope is going to marry her tomorrow at Paris[1] – and so, there is an end of the Florence scheme. I don't complain – I am all for Love myself – and this sort of thing speaks volumes for women, for surely a man at a mature age, with a growing daughter, does not marry again without knowing what he is about and without remembrances of Mrs Number One, which surround as with a halo Mrs Number Two? But this is mere speculation. Let me get back to facts. We shall go all the same to Rome, I think – and when we leave Rome towards the end of next month, and take the Steamer for Marseilles, I will write again, and say my last word about a visit to Pau. If I can come (though it may be only for a few days), depend upon it, I will – for I long sorely to see you again. It will all depend on my letters from London and Paris next month – and as soon as those letters are received, you shall hear from me once more.

In the meantime, need I say how glad I am to hear such good news of you? You know how glad I am. But are you learning to take care of yourself for the future? Don't say "Stuff!" Don't go to the piano (especially as I am not within hearing), and forget the words of wisdom. Cultivate your appetite – and your appetite will reward you. Purchase becoming (and warm) things for the neck and chest. Rise superior to the devilish delusion which makes women think that their feet cannot possibly look pretty in thick boots. I have studied the subject – and I say they <u>can</u>. Men understand these things. Mr Worth of Paris dresses the fine French ladies who wear the "Falballá", and regulates the fashions of Europe. He is about to start "comforters" and hob-nail boots for the approaching winter. In two months time it will be indecent for a woman to show her neck at night, – and if you don't make a frightful noise at every step you take on the pavement, you abrogate your position as woman, wife and mother, in the eyes of all Europe. Is this exaggerated? No! a thousand times no! It is horrible – but it is the truth.

Has Fred returned to you? If he has, give him my love, and ask him to bring you to Rome in the middle of next month. Oh dear! dear! how pleasant it would be if we could all meet in the Forum! But we shan't. Kiss Miss Lehmann for me – and give my love to the boys. The lamp is going out, and I must start early tomorrow morning, and there is nothing for it but to repeat that everlasting business of unbuttoning and going to bed. Goodbye for the present.

Yours affly, | W.C.

Note

1. Thomas Adolphus Trollope (1810–1892: *DNB*), novelist and elder brother of Anthony, married his second wife Frances Eleanor née Ternan (?1834–1913), novelist, who was governess to his twelve-year-old daughter, Bice (Beatrice) in Paris in 1866.

To Mrs Harriet Collins, 6 January 1867
MS: Private Possession

9, Melcombe Place [6 January 1867][1]

Summary:
WC likes "the cold & snow – now there is a thaw ... Smith and Elder made me <u>no</u> offer for the copyrights. The market has, I suppose, been overstocked with my books. What am I to do next, you will ask. I am going to open communications with the penny journals (the proprietors of which applied to me a year or two since) – and we shall see what an entirely new public has to say to me.

In the meantime I am going to add to 'The Rogue's Life' – make a two volume novel of it – and astonish the [idiotic] British Reader with a lively book from the first page to the last. If 'The Woman in White' – with which

I shall start the other experiment – takes with the penny public, I will write a new book for them. I have got the idea of the new book and my friend Benham, who is legally connected with the proprietors of some of these journals is coming this week to settle the thing with me ... I am full of ideas for books and plays. The Smith Elder mess has fired me – Smith, mind, writes most kindly, lamenting the 'slow sale', and the impossibility of his making any offer which I should think it worth while to accept. I have got my name and my brains – and I will make a new start, with a new public!"

Note

1. Mrs Harriet Collins at "Mr Anderson's, Southborough".

To Mrs Harriet Collins, 8 January 1867
MS: Private Possession

8, Melcombe Place | Jany 8 1867

Summary:
WC notes that Charles Ward, Pigott "& the Doctor to dinner for his birthday". He is sorry she doesn't like his photos. "NB. I have a splendid idea for boiling down the Lighthouse, The Frozen Deep, and the Red Vial into <u>One Novel</u>. If the penny journals take to the Woman in White, the penny journals shall have the new Novel. It will be just the thing for them.

Did I tell you that the dramatic version of the book [<u>Armadale</u>] by an American lady has been a great success in New York? I am going to start on the 3rd act of Regnier's version and mine – and to finish (after doing Act 4 here) in Paris under Regnier's eye – if all goes well ...

You mustn't revile [Smith & Elder]. I suspect old Low of 'flooding the market' with my books – and <u>then</u> selling them to [Smith & Elder]. It is not <u>their</u> fault that the sale is 'slow'. All they have done is to risk their money most liberally on me – and I am afraid not to be gainers by it.

We shall see one of these days, what the books will do in another form, and at another price."

To Mrs Harriet Collins, 26 February 1867
MS: PM

Hotel du Helder | Paris | Feby 26th 1867

My dear Mother,

I have got half an hour to spare before I go to my friend Regnier for the usual day's work on the play – and I employ the half hour in reporting my safe arrival in Paris to you.

The day of my journey was simply perfect, as far as weather went – and weather goes a long way, with me. A calm sea – a brilliant sun – and (to my surprise) only a moderately-filled steamer. I found two nice little rooms (sitting room and bedroom), and a hearty welcome, waiting for me here. The rheumatism plagued me a little on the journey – but four and twenty hours in the dry air of Paris relieved me of it entirely, and I am in every way, the better for the change.

The play promises to do great things. The first act, in French, has been read to one or two good judges privately. They are quite astonished at the originality of it – and they predict a great success, if we can go on as we have begun. We can go on – I venture to think – better than we have begun. But we must work for it. The second act must be in great part re-written – in order to adapt itself to the last two acts of the play. The third will only want a few corrections. The fourth is just begun – and the fifth we are now engaged in putting together. I shall take the 5th act – that is to say, the sketch of it – back with me, and write it in London[.] But the rest must be done here, while I can be in daily communication with my collaborateur. I doubt whether I shall get back in time for George Russell's marriage – but we shall see what can be done in the next three or four days. Everything that can be sacrificed to the play, must be sacrificed to it. A great chance is open to me – and I must make the best possible use of it. Regnier talks already of our dramatising The Woman In White next. Successful play-writing means making a fortune here – and there is no really great French writer now in our way.

The Carnival is supposed to be going on in Paris. On the Saturday night of my arrival, the Boulevards were hardly passable, for the crowds – and five public masked balls were all going on together! Last night, I was at the first representation of a new opera. You never saw a theatre so full in your [erasure] life – and the intense interest of the whole audience in the new musical and dramatic event was something quite electrifying. It turned out to be but a poor work after all. I was more pleased with the enthusiasm which the people showed for art – simply for art's sake – than with anything else that I saw or heard in the theatre.

My half hour is wearing away – and I must soon close my letter. Write here on the 1st, 2nd, or 3rd of March – and I am sure to get your letter. I saw Charley the night before I left – and found a very decided change in him for the better. The diet here would soon cure him. I have breakfasted this [three erased words] morning on eggs and black butter, and pigs' feet a la Sainte Mémèhould! Digestion perfect. St Mémèhould lived to extreme old age on nothing but pigs' trotters.

Mind you write, and let me hear how you are.

Yours ever afty | W.C

To Mrs Harriet Collins, 11 March [1867]
MS: PM

9, Melcombe Place | N.W. | Monday March 11[1]

My dear Mother,[2]

I am back again in London, safe and sound. The sudden change in the weather – from mild heat to bone-searching cold – was frightful at Paris. Everybody felt it – in everybody's weak place. I got the rheumatism of course and had a smartish attack which hurried me back to London – in case of a lay-up. However, the weather softened a little at the end of last week and as events [erased word] proved, I physicked myself in the right way. The attack has threatened and has gone off again.

All that I went to Paris to do, I have done. We have put together a complete outline of our fifth act (the great difficulty) – and have made a new second act, also in outline. These, I have come back to write for the stage – and when that is done, my troubles (so far as the play is concerned) are at an end. Regnier will do all that must be done to put the play on the stage.

I had a very pleasant time in Paris, before the rheumatism. Was presented to some of the great French authors, and honoured with some very pretty compliments – saw some excellent acting – received every imaginable kindness from my good friend Regnier – and in short made "a great success" of the trip.

I have got you two pairs of boots. One pair for your dinner-parties. One for walking in. I tried them on. You can have the heels shaved down, if you like – it was impossible to get them without high heels. But in other respects, I think they will do. And observe, they are cheap![3] Both pairs cost together only 22 shillings.

I heard from Charley at Paris – who wrote alarmed by a false report of my being laid up with gout. I hope he will soon be able to go and see you.

Send me a line to say how you are – and whether you have had the Athenaeum regularly.

Yours ever aftly | W.C

Shall I send you the boots by rail – in a small parcel?

Notes

1. Alongside the address WC writes "I enclose a newspaper criticism on the performance of 'Armadale' at New York." The criticism is no longer with the holograph letter.
2. Envelope, postmarked: "LONDON – N.W. | X | MR 11 | 67".
3. "Cheap" is underlined three times – each underlining being shorter than the other.

To Mrs Harriet Collins, 11 May 1867
MS: PM

9, Melcombe Place | N.W. | May 11th 1867

My dear Mother,

I have been too busy to write before today – between my negociation with <u>All The Year Round,</u> and my readings [erasure] in the Club Library of works that I must consult for my new book. They leave <u>me</u> to ask my terms at All The Year Round – for doing half the Christmas Number, and for giving them the periodical right of publishing my new book. I have sent in my terms (basing my demand on what Smith & Elder gave me) for doing half the Christmas Number. Forty eight of my written pages will fill half the Christmas number – and these, at the Smith & Elder rate, are worth £400. I have not yet heard from Wills. He only got my proposal yesterday. The other matter of what I am to ask for the serial publication of my story is not yet settled. But it is not to begin, before next November – and whereas "No Name" ran to 45 numbers – this book is only to run to 26.[1] So, at any rate, I am taking it easy this time. You shall hear again as soon as the terms for both works are settled at All The Year Round.

As for the play – I am going to post it to Paris and have done with it, <u>this</u> day!

Charley and I have tossed for the pictures, and Frith is coming today to value Charley's half. Charley won the toss and chose first (to my astonishment!) the <u>upright</u> Sorrento – (with the chestnut tree) – leaving the <u>sea</u>-Sorrento (afterwards repainted large for Gibbons)[2] to fall to <u>me</u>. We then went on alternating. Charley chose next, the small park-[paling] landscape, with the shadows on the road (near Hendon I think). <u>I</u> followed, and took the Roman boy's Heads! Charley followed [with: erased] and took the green pool & weeds. I took next the Devonshire stream. Charley took the (upright) Bembridge Sands. I took the trees at Pond St. Charley took the copy from De Hoog.[3] I took the portrait of my Grand Mother, and there it ended. I am quite content, and so is he. You must certainly come to town – and see my Sorrento in its new, and beautiful, frame!

I am afraid you have been suffering dreadfully from the heat – and the Pitts gone away, just when you ought to have been staying there, and sitting in their cool garden! For myself, copious perspiration, and invincible unwillingness to walk, have been the principle symptoms. As soon as I can finish the bargaining for my book &c – and my reading of the necessary works – I will be back at Southborough. In the mean time, write – only a few lines – to tell me how you are. I [shall: erased] send the Athenaeum.

Yours ever aftly | W.C

Notes

1. i.e., *The Moonstone*, serialized in *All The Year Round* from 4 January to 8 August 1868.
2. See *Memoirs of the Life of William Collins*, II, 190–1.
3. *Ibid.*, I, 264.

To W.H. Wills, 13 May 1867
MS: PM

9, Melcombe Place | Dorset Square. N.W. | May 13th 1867

My dear Wills,
    The point you mention had escaped me. I at once admit that there is no difference – so far as you are concerned – between the absolute sale of my work in MS to a publisher, and the absolute sale to "All The Year Round".
    I might mention, at the same time, that it is to be said, on my side, that the sale remains – in your case as in the publisher's – an absolute sale, so far as I am concerned.
    But I feel that an arrangement which publicly associates my name with Dickens's and which privately associates me with him in the production of a work of fiction, is an arrangement which appeals to me on no ordinary grounds, and which I cannot consent to regulate by any ordinary considerations.
    I accept unreservedly the pecuniary point of view as you put it – and I will write my half of the forthcoming Christmas Number for Three hundred pounds.[1]

very truly yours | Wilkie Collins

P.S. | The other question, about the Serial story is not so easily settled. I ought to have remembered – when I suggested consulting the "No Name" precedent – that the literary commodity purchased of me then was my time, and, not the right of periodically publishing my book. Your accountant's figures – quite right as far as they go – don't represent a third of the sum that I actually received for "No Name". Dickens' cheques, in payment of my share of the profits [necessarily] [erased word] do not appear – and the fact that my salary and my profits were going on – not only while the book was being published in your journal – but also while I was thinking it out, and writing it for press – are [erasure] facts unregistered by the accountant, because the accountant knows nothing about them. I will try [once more] to send you a statement of the figures from my banking book – and of the time from my old diaries. But I am not quite sure that I can undertake the responsibility of asking terms, because my estimate this time cannot be based on actual facts and figures – and the Virginity of a new book is as difficult a thing to sell – (with or without benefit of clergy) as the Virginity of a new Girl!

Note

1. In pencil, not WC's, above "hundred" is written "No Thoroughfare".

To Mrs Harriet Collins, 30 May 1867
MS: PM

9, Melcombe Place | N.W. | Thursday. May 30th 1867

My dear Mother,

What do you say to my coming to see you at Southborough on Tuesday 4th June? Tell me if this will do – and also if anything more is wanted besides pens and brandy.

Charley has, I suppose, written to tell you [of: erased] that Dickens has added to – or rather doubled – Katie's marriage portion. This certainly comes at the right time – is liberal and just – and suggests that Charley's luck (if you believe in luck as I do) is at last on the turn.

I shall have the first weekly number of my new book to read to you when I am at Southborough. Yesterday, I dined with the Lehmanns. She is not very well – the detestable weather, varying between cold and debilitating heat, is evidently too much for her. She sends you her love. The house is doubled in size – and most beautifully decorated.

I have no engagement after Monday [erasure] next till the Wednesday week June 12th – when I have accepted an invitation from the E.M. Wards to dinner. Richmond[1] – whom I saw the other night – sends you his love, and says his daughters want very much to see you again.

Yours ever affly | W.C

I sent you the Cornhill the other day.

Note

1. George Richmond (1809–1896: *DNB*), well-known portrait painter, had accompanied William Collins in Rome on his return from Naples in 1838 and gave Wilkie some background of the visit for the biography of his father. See W.W. Collins: *Memoirs of the Life of William Collins RA*, 1848, II, 130–2.

To Mrs Harriet Collins, 1 July [1867]
MS: PM

9, Melcombe Place | Dorset Square | N.W. | Monday July 1st

My dear Mother,[1]
    I am safe back tonight, from Gadshill. You will be glad to hear that Dickens is delighted with my new story. He thinks the old man excellent – and he predicts that this will be the most successful book I have ever written. The grand point of the story – about three parts of the way to the end, took him – when I told it roughly, viva voce – as completely by surprise as if he had been an ordinary novel reader. You may imagine, from this, what the effect will be on the General reader. I certainly never expected to [erased word] astonish Dickens with [two erased words] an effect in a novel – which is carefully prepared for, and which is yet invisible till it comes.[2]
    There was no company at Gadshill. We were very merry – and it was a very pleasant time.
    Next week, I must go to Farley Hill – having found another letter here to remind me from Mrs E. Sunday [erasure] next, there is a dinner at Lehmanns. Landseer, Millais, Charley, Katie, &c. ... [Lehmann gives] me, I am sorry to say, a poor account of his wife.
    Write when you have time, and tell me how you are. I have put off the publication of my story till the new year, I hope, if somebody can be found to write a short story to fill up the time. This would get me half through my work, before the public see it.
    There is a chance of my getting a large sum from America,[3] this time – from a new paper, which wants to publish my new book.

Yours ever affl | W.C

Notes

1. Envelope, postmarked: "LONDON–N.W | 7 | JY 2 | 67".
2. Dickens in a letter to Wills, 26 July 186[8] reversed his favourable opinion of *The Moonstone*. Dickens wrote to Wills [13 June 1867] "I have read the first three numbers of Wilkie's story this morning and have gone minutely through the plot of the rest to the last line ... It is prepared with extraordinary care, and has every chance of being a hit. It is in many respects much better than anything he has done" (cited in Hutton, pp. 146–7).
3. i.e., from Harper Brothers, however "all the precautions that [they] could take failed to prevent the simultaneous appearance of four separate editions" (Robinson, p. 218).

To Mrs Harriet Collins, 18 July [1867]
MS: PM

9, Melcombe Place | N.W. | July 18th

My dear Mother,[1]
    I am in a whirl of work. A difficult part of the story to manage. A bargain with America for the advance-proofs (£750!) – making with "All The Year Round" £1600 for the periodical use of the story only. Another bargain with America still to settle for a short original story. A new place of residence still to find – I think it will be Cornwall Terrace.
    These things keep me in town this week – and next week, I am to get a little sailing with Pigott. But, after that, I shall get to see you, I hope, and, in the meantime, Charley proposes going to you on Monday next, he tells me. He dines with me on Saturday next.
    Send me a line to say how you are. London is topsy-turvy with excitement about illustrious foreigners.

Ever yours aftly | W.C

Note

1. Envelope, postmarked: "CHARING CROSS | 7 | JY 19 | 67".

To Mrs Harriet Collins, 27 July [1867]
MS: PM

9, Melcombe Place | N.W. | Saturday July 27

My dear Mother,[1]
Many thanks for the cases: [erased word] you shall have back the canvas & cord. The Cornwall Terrace plan has broken down. Somebody else was after the house – and I suspect that Somebody "bid the highest figure".

There is another chance at Gloucester Place, Portman Square. Pending this negociation, I am going today to sail, off Ryde with Pigott & C. Ward – to return next Tuesday. On the Saturday, after that, I go to Mrs Elliot and Lady Devonshire[2] if possible – and, after that, I hope to the Dowager Duchess of Southborough – [Anderson] Palace – whose eldest son (having to leave his present residence in ten days, and not having found another yet) appears likely to end as an outcast in the streets.

Charley was here yesterday to take away his pictures. I hear that he, and Katie are going to see you Thursday next – to stay till the 12th. About the end [erased word] of their visit will, according to my calculation, be [erased word] the beginning of mine. So you will have a succession of visitors. I enclose a letter just received from H. Bullar. John's case seems serious.[3]

You shall hear of course, the moment my habitation is settled, if it ever is. In the meantime, go on addressing me here.

Ever yours affly | W.C

Notes

1. Envelope, postmarked: "LONDON–W | 7 | JY 27 | 67".
2. Lady Devonshire, probably the widow of William George Spencer Cavendish, 6th Duke of Devonshire (1790–1858: *DNB*), friend of Dickens and other writers.
3. Letter from Henry Bullar dated "July 25. 1867" from Switzerland also at PM. concerns the poor health of his father John Bullar (1806–1867), a Southampton barrister.

To Mrs Harriet Collins, [3 August 1867]
MS: PM

90, Gloucester Place | Portman Square W. | Saturday

My dear Mother,[1]

I am delighted to hear this good news about Charley. His luck is on the turn, and the ball is at his foot at last. Horray!

On Tuesday next I am to complete the purchase of the house at the lawyers in Gray's Inn. Later in the week, I shall probably be at Gadshill again – for a second consultation about the Christmas Number. If I can get on to you [after: erased] afterwards – across country – I will. It depends on how things get on here. I am gradually settling down – but the work people are slow, and my pictures and books – and my bath and my drains – are still to be arranged. No bad smells – only alterations and improvements which it is as well to make once for all, before I am [erased word] settled.

How do you bear the heat? Your back room helps you I hope.

Ever aftly yours | W.C

You shall hear again as soon as I have heard from Dickens.

Note

1. Envelope, postmarked: "LONDON–W | [7] | AU 4 | 67".

To Mrs Harriet Collins, 1 September [1867]
MS: PM

90, Gloucester Place | Portman Square W. | Monday Sept 1st

Summary:
He is going to Dickens (to work on the Christmas Number) on Tuesday next – and from him (at last!) he is coming on across country to her. Either Thursday or Friday next will be the day. He will write again from Gadshill. He is "beginning to settle down. In another ten days, most of the workers will be out of the house. The pictures are hung." He has "had the frames re-gilt and they look beautiful. The prints and drawings must wait till" he gets back from Southborough. Address him up to Tuesday morning in London. After Tuesday, at Gadshill. He hears Charley and Katie are there. Asks how she has borne the heat. He is "melting at this moment".

Note

1. Envelope, postmarked: "LONDON W | 7 | SP 1 | 67". In the left-hand margin of the first leaf of the letter WC writes "I sent you the Cornhill yesterday. The Athenaeum has been, [in the] confusion forgotten."

To Mrs Harriet Collins, 4 September 1867
MS: PM

Gad's Hill Place, | Higham by Rochester, Kent | 1 Wednesday Sept 4

Summary:
Has got her letter. He will be in London tomorrow to get some books which he wants to consult for a coming part of the Christmas Number. He will leave so as to get to town before twelve – and will then go (later on the same day), from London to her. She is to expect him "tomorrow (Thursday) by

the train which leaves Charing Cross at 4.5. and gets to T. Wells at 5.34 … in good time for dinner with her at $\frac{1}{2}$ past 6, tomorrow".

Note

1. WC uses Dickens' Gothic printed stationery. Envelope, postmarked "ROCHESTER | 6 | SP 4 | 67".

To Frederick Lehmann, 10 September 1867
MS: Princeton

Southborough | Tuesday, September 10th

My dear Fred,

Have you made up your mind that I am a Humbug? Naturally, you have.

Weeks since, you write me a kind letter from Rothsay – giving me delightful accounts of the Padrona, and asking me to join you. And that letter remains unanswered to the present date!

Disgraceful!

What is the cause of this ungrateful silence?

The cause is, 90 Gloucester Place | Portman Square. W.

=

When your letter reached me, I had an old house to leave – a new house to find – that new house to bargain for, and take, lawyers and surveyors to consult – British Workmen to employ – and, through it all, to keep my own literary business going [erased word] without so much as a day's stoppage. Is there no excuse in this? Ach Gott! Ya – voll! Si – [gewiss]!

Here then is a letter of apology which – if Mamie Dickens's information is correct – ought to meet you on your return to Woodlands. My best love and congratulations to the Padrona. The same from Mama Collins – with whom I am staying to get a little quiet for working in. I return on Thursday next. Come and see me on my new perch. The dining-room is habitable – and the drawing-rooms are getting on.

Ever yours, | Wilkie Collins

To Mrs Harriet Collins, 12 September 1867
MS: PM

90, Gloucester Place, | Portman Square. W. | Sept 12th 1867

My dear Mother,

I am safe back again among the British Workmen. The Statement now is that they will be done in a week. Ha! ha! Never mind. A certain necessary place has got the most lovely new pan you ever saw. It's quite a luxury to look into it.

I have left your note at Fortnum's. Am just back from dining at the Club with Dickens. We have created some sweet things, for the forthcoming number. Dickens most kindly offers to see Chapman himself about my copyrights on Monday next – (if Chapman is in town) – you shall hear the result.

I have written to Smith & Elder to say that I will give evidence if needful against the ruffian who has taken my name and my books in vain. We must stop him – or Heaven only knows what he [erased word] may do next in the character of my self-appointed agent.

I am at the end of my news. A kitten who has drifted into the house from some unknown mother is galloping over my back and shoulders, which makes writing difficult – and it is time to go to bed.

Hart – sends his love. He will soon be at Southborough.

Write soon.

Ever your aftly | W C

To Mrs Harriet Collins, 25 September 1867
MS: PM

90, Gloucester Place, | Portman Square. W. | 1 25th Sept 1867

My dear Mother,

I was just thinking of writing to you, when your letter came this morning, and gave me some news of you.

I have been staying with the Lehmanns at Highgate – out of the way of the hammering here. They were very kind – gave me a delightful room to write in – and surrounded me with luxuries and comforts. Last night, I came back – and found that the top story of the house was done at last. The end of the week, I am told, will see the end of the workman all over the house. I take your gloomy view – and don't believe it.

My servants are models of human excellence. They work hard – never grumble – submit to everything – . I am going to give them a new gown apiece, in recognition of their extraordinary merit.

Smith (the great railway bookseller) is in treaty for my copyrights in combination with Chapman & Hall. If we come to terms, [the: erased] having Smith interested in my books, will insure the pushing of them [erasure] at every railway station in England.

We are getting on with the Christmas Number – more than half done. Dickens is greatly [harassed] about fin<u>al</u>ly deciding on the American tour. On Monday next, he must definitely decide – Yes, or No.

An American newspaper proprietor has asked me to propose terms for writing a short story for him. I have told him that <u>he</u> must propose the terms to <u>me</u>.

I will keep those books I proposed sending to you – at your disposal. Charley will hardly get into his new house, I should think, on Michaelmas Day.

You did quite right to move the bed into the back-room. My writing-room will be the front bedroom next time, I should think, now the grocer has broken out into building at the back. [erased word] Watch the house in front – and let me know when the hammering is over there – so that I may pick my time for coming to see you again. Also, don't imagine that I am harassed. I am like old Mrs Dickinson – I possess a "sublime composure". Nothing upsets <u>me</u>. Ever afty yours | W.C

Note

1. At the top of his printed paper, WC writes "The Athenaeum only costs 3^d. I sometimes d<u>o</u> read it. Nothing will induce me to save 3^d a week. It's an idiosyncrasy of mine. In a few days, I shall send you some more brandy."

To Mrs Harriet Collins, 1 October [1867]
MS: PM

90, Gloucester Place | Portman Sqr | Tuesday Oct 1

My dear Mother,[1]
I have just ordered Justerini & Brooks[2] to send you, by S.E. Rail tomorrow morning 6 Bottles of Brandy.

I have no small cases – and I dare but send you a whole dozen of <u>my</u> brandy – for you would be horrified at the quantity. Justerini's Brandy is excellent – quite as good as mine and liked better by many people.

Don't turn up your eyes about the expense – it is the expense of six bottles instead of twelve. So it is a saving.

Charley will be with you on Wednesday. He will no doubt tell you what <u>he</u> thinks about the will. I saw him yesterday. While he was with me, enter the Revd Alexander Geddes from Lincolnshire (!!!!). The Revd gentleman thinks of adding to his Income by Literature, and came to ask my advice. He described himself as rather a pretty hand with the pen – but as not exactly knowing what to write about!

Yours ever aftly | W C

Note

1. Envelope, postmarked, "LONDON–W | [ ] | OC 2 | 67".
2. Justerini and Brooks were wine merchants WC used (see Clarke, Appendix C, pp. 228–9).

To Mrs Harriet Collins, 11 October 1867
MS: PM

90, Gloucester Place, | Portman Square. W. | October 11th 1867.

My dear Mother,

I am going to Gadshill this afternoon, with Dickens, to finish the Christmas number. Yesterday I dined, and slept, at Lehmann's. I don't [know] whether Charley & Katie are still at Gadshill.

What I have room for, I will "warehouse" with pleasure. I have an airtight cupboard (which locks) in the Yard – and this is almost the only really empty place in the house. I should think the cupboard will hold all you & Charley want to send here. Let me hear before the [things] come: of course, your [book]-folios shall be kept <u>in-doors</u>. Works of art I have plenty of room for.

Next week, I hope I shall be back at work on my Serial Story. Keep me informed when the hammering is over – so that I may see you as soon as I can. I shall probably bring C. Ward with me next time, for a few days. He is copying my Serial Story, to send in America – and he can get two days holiday, and work under my inspection. You can easily get a bedroom for him next door, I suppose?

I have given [erasure] Margaret Ward a new silk dress – and have got in exchange for it, your portrait by Mrs Carpenter. They are, nearly profile – still like you after all these years! [Corsy] (who had it as a gift from his

Grandmother) wanted to give it to me for nothing – but I insisted on the dress. The portrait will hang in my study. I wonder whether you remember it?[2]

Write soon | Every aftly yours | W C

Brandy and peppermint for the Gripes?

Note

1. "When [Holman] Hunt saw her portrait by her sister, Margaret Carpenter, showing her in all her girl-like beauty, 'the portrait explained the riddle'" i.e. why S. T. Coleridge "had singled her out at an evening party and had talked with her" (Clarke, p. 56).

To Mrs W.P. Frith, 11 October 1867
MS: National Art Library, Victoria and Albert Museum, London

90, Gloucester Place, | Portman Square. W. | October 11th 1867

My dear Mrs Frith,
     I accept your kind invitation for Friday the 18th at 7 with the greatest pleasure. The address at the head of this letter is the last new spot in which I have pitched my tent. This time I have been obliged to "buy a lease" – so there is some reasonable prospect (unless my new lease ruins me in alterations and repairs) of my being settled at last!
     With kindest remembrances to all.

Believe me | Most truly yours, | Wilkie Collins

To Mrs Harriet Collins, 26 October 1867
MS: PM

90, Gloucester Place, | Portman Square. W. |[1] October 26th 1867

My dear Mother,
     I have sent your letter to Charley. He will be as sorry as I am to hear that the change to Bentham Hill has done you no good this time. I shall be anxious to hear how you are when you have got back – and when you can receive me.

Dinners, public and private, to Dickens on his departure, are filling my engagement book. On the 31st, (the only day he has) he dines here to warm the house. On November 2nd, I must go to the public dinner to him, of which I am a steward. On the 5th – Beard gives him a farewell dinner. On the 8th, I have promised (at Dickens's request) to go with him [erased word] to Liverpool, and see him off on the morning of the 9th – Saturday.

Suppose I [erased word] go to you on Monday November 11th? The knocking will surely be over, and the new servant found, by that time? Or I could be with you, for a day and a half, before that time – arriving on Wednesday 6th, and returning on Thursday night (7th), to be ready for the journey to Liverpool on Friday morning (8th) – and then going back again to you, for a week at least, on Monday 11th. After this last date, I am free. Tell me what you think about it. I have got back again to work on my book – and I hope I shall have some more to read to you when we meet. If I am not utterly mistaken, the last new story of mine will be a "hit". You will not be sorry to hear that (on consideration) I have taken the clergyman out of the story[2] – he is <u>Mr</u> Godfrey Ablewhite now, instead of the Reverend. And his line in life is – to manage and advise <u>Ladies' Charities</u>. He is the inevitable gentleman who sits at the Ladies' Committees, and helps them through the business – and I don't think he has been done in fiction before.

[erased word] Write a few lines soon | every yours afly | W.C

Notes

1. Above the printed address, WC writes: "Your portrait is hung in my study – and looks very well. It <u>is</u> the portrait in the white dress – but cut short off – as to the dress – at the bosom."
2. *The Moonstone.*

To Harper Brothers, 12 November 1867
MS: Princeton: Text, Coleman

90, Gloucester Place, | Portman Square. W. | London. |
November 12th 1867

Dear Sirs,

I send you above,[1] a proof of the title. It has only just been decided on, and it has not yet been advertised in England. So far as I know, your advertisement of the title will appear simultaneously with the advertisements here.

The first weekly part of the story will be published in "All The Year Round", <u>on Wednesday January 1st 1868</u>. We shall therefore appear on both sides of the Atlantic on New Year's Day.

I send you (under another cover) by this mail – Tuesday November 12th – a first portion of the first half of the MS copy of the story. This instalment leaves England 50 clear days before the first weekly part is published in England. The quantity of MS now sent comprises at least seven weekly parts of the story. The remainder, the first half of the complete MS copy shall follow as rapidly as possible. It proceeds more slowly than I had anticipated, from these causes. My own MS, for the proof here is so altered and interlined as to be very difficult to read – and the literary necessities of this story force me to correct and re-correct the first half, [with a: erased] special view to what is to come in the second. If I am a few days later than the 30 days advance with what is to come, I hope you will take into consideration that I have been a few days earlier with what is already sent.

With regard to the printed proofs; I hope to begin sending them to you in a week's time, or less. The alterations which you will find, here and there, between the proofs and the MS – though important in a literary point of view – are not likely to [embarrass] the illustrator.[2] They are alterations in the form only. The substance of the book (as presenting subjects for illustration) will remain the same in MS as in print.

Mr Charles Dickens (who left for America by the steamer of the 9th Nov^r) will call on you, while he is in New York – and will kindly say for me anything I may have omitted to say here.

Please acknowledge the receipt of the first portion of MS copy, and the receipt of this letter.

Faithfully yours | Wilkie Collins

To | Messrs Harper & Brothers

Notes

1. Attached to the letter is a proof of the title: "THE MOONSTONE, | a New Serial Story | by | WILKIE COLLINS".
2. i.e., William Samuel Lyon Jewett: see WC to Harper Brothers, 30 January 1868.

To Mrs Harriet Collins, 6 December 1867

MS: Private Possession

[90, Gloucester Place | December 6 [1867]]

Summary:

"If I had time, I would run down to Southborough and kill the grocer! Your account of the [hammering] horrifies me. It is impossible you can be well, with such an agravation going on next door. Will you try that hotel at Hastings, which you and I went to? If you will, say the word, and ... I will pack up and go with you.

The play is done. Webster[1] and Fechter[2] are coming here on Monday to make the final corrections with me. On Tuesday the 10th I am to read it to the actors. On the 26th it must be performed in public. How we shall get through the stage preparations in 15 days – the play being in 5 acts and 15 scenes – I don't know. But as Doctor Johnson said – "Sir! what must be done, will be done!"

WC must get on with Moonstone – but "One thing I have determined to do, which is to dine with you on Christmas Day. Hart is going to the [Aldernans]. Ask the [Aldernans] to ask us also – and let us be jolly."

Tells his mother that the Christmas number of All the Year Round will be sent to her.

"I have let my stables for £40 a year. So there is my rent covered to a very payable figure. The next thing is to pay the Xmas bills for doing up the house. Some of the people will wait. In the spring I shall have plenty of money.

I must now correct 'The Moonstone' and The Play, to go to New York by tomorrow's mail. Dickens will get up the play in New York, and bring it out on the same night when it is brought out here. This will get us some money for America. In London we have 10 per cent ... The theatre holds two hundred ... That is £20 a night between us. £60 a week each.

The 'Armadale' play is also being finished in Paris. So the [deuce] is in it, if the stage doesn't bring me in some money now! ...

My doctor has just been ... He is astonished at the manner in which I sustain my work – and attributes it to these large airy rooms, and to this dry soil."

Notes

1. Benjamin Webster (1797–1882: *DNB*), actor, manager of the Theatre Royal Adelphi, who played the part of Joey Ladle in *No Thoroughfare*.
2. Charles Albert Fechter (1824–1879), Anglo-French actor, friend of WC, Dickens and others (see Gasson).

To Mrs Harriet Collins, 12 December 1867

MS: Private Possession

[All the Year Round Office | Thursday December 12 1867]

Summary:
WC writes that he must postpone his visit. However he is determined to come at Christmas in spite of "innumerable worries of work". He is bringing a deed for her to sign.

"When you talked about making your will ... I sent a copy of Mrs Davis's will to my lawyers. They have discovered a clause in it, which, if nothing is done to set it right, leaves Charley or me – if we die <u>before you</u> – without any interest in the money which we can leave by will. To obviate this – and to save you the trouble and ceremony of making a regular will, my lawyers have drawn a deed for you to sign ... the deed binds us all three to do two things 1st Charley and I resign our reversionary interest in Aunt Davis's money, to <u>you</u> – 2^{ndly}. You secure to yourself the yearly income from the five thousand pounds, during your life and after your life you absolutely leave the five thousand pounds in equal half shares to Charley and to me. The practical result of this (to take Charley's case) is – that if Charley died before you, he could leave his half share to his wife. As things stand he could not do this ... I cannot guarantee the repayment of what is not yet worked out of my loan here – supposing I died tomorrow. ...

The play is rehearsing – such work!

If you receive a circular from the Bank of England, asking if you have sanctioned the issue of a <u>power of attorney</u>, <u>you need take no notice of it</u>. It is only a part of the Deed business – a mere formality."

To Mrs Harriet Collins, 20 December 1867

MS: Private Possession

[90, Gloucester Place | December 20 1867]

Summary:
WC promises to come on Christmas Day. "The delays and difficulties of this dramatic work have been dreadful. I have had to write a new 5th Act – which has been completed <u>today</u> – and the play must be performed on Wednesday next with a Sunday and Christmas Day between!

Your much-battered son has hardly got a minute he can call his own. But the writing of the play is at last complete."

To Mrs Harriet Collins, 30 December 1867
MS: Private Possession

[90, Gloucester Place | December 30, 1867]

Summary:
WC is returning to her on Thursday, January 2. "The play is bringing money. It is a real success – we shall all be rich." He is bringing papers for her to sign.

To Mrs Harriet Collins, 1 January 1868
MS: Private Possession

[90, Gloucester Place] | January 1, 1868

Summary:
WC is coming on Friday, not on Thursday. "I will bring Nepenthe and some of my brandy on Friday." He hopes that her pains will get better.

To Frederick and Nina Lehmann, 4 January 1868
MS: Princeton

90, Gloucester Place, | Portman Square. W. | 4th Jany 1868

The Collins–Lehmann Correspondence No. 3. Lock Fred up – or he will be taking places![1]
   Stop! Stop! Stop!
   Don't, for God's sake, go to the Pantomime at the Royal Alfred Theatre, before Saturday. I want to take you there. I hear it is a good Pantomime – it is also close by. Dinner on Saturday punctually at five,[2] instead of half past 4.
   The Surrey business has broken down – as I guess.[3] A note from The inimitable Reade informing me that he encloses a letter from the Manager which "is without a parallel in his (Reade's) experience". Of course, there is no letter enclosed!!! But I infer that we are treated by this atrocious manager with the utmost contempt. Oh Heavens! Have we lived to be rejected by a [transpositive] Theatre? But, no matter, we gain half an hour, for dinner time on Saturday – and we have only a little distance to go to the Theatre – and we shall do as well in Marylebone as in Surrey – if I am

only in time to stop you and Fred from seeing <u>that</u> Pantomime also – without <u>me</u>![4]

Yours affly, | W.C

P.S. The Royal Alfred Theatre is in Church Street, Portman Market. A gorgeous building. Opened by his Royal Highness Prince Alfred in person. There!

Notes

1. This sentence is written above the printed address.
2. "iv" of "five" underlined twice.
3. "u" of "guess" underlined twice.
4. "me" singly underlined: "e" also doubly underlined.

To Mrs Harriet Collins, 17 January 1868
MS: Private Possession

[90, Gloucester Place | January 17 1868]

Summary:
WC writes that it is a great relief to hear she had made the move "and established yourself under Mrs Wells's care!

The play goes on wonderfully. Every night the theatre is crammed. This speculation on the public taste is paying, and promises long to pay me, from fifty to fifty-five pounds a week. So make yourself easy about my money matters." WC is nearly half-way through *The Moonstone*.

To William Holman Hunt, 18 January [1868]
MS: Huntington

90, Gloucester Place, | Portman Square. W. | Saturday Jany 18 | $\frac{1}{2}$ p 2

My dear Hunt,
   My dear Mother is I am afraid sinking. A telegram calls me away to her instantly.
   You will understand, and feel for me.

Yours aff[l] | Wilkie Collins

To William Tindell,[1] 19 January 1868
MS: Glasgow

Bentham Hill Cottage | near Tunbridge Wells | Sunday Jany 19th

My dear Tindell,

I have been summoned away from London by the serious illness of my mother. If she is no worse, between this and then, I hope to get to London on Wednesday night, and to see Mr Boucicault.[2] In that case, I will call on you about the assignment of copyright for Australia, on Wednesday at 5 – or soon after.

Yours ever | Wilkie Collins

Notes

1. WC's solicitor and friend from the 1860s until 1877.
2. Dion Lardner Boucicault (1822–1890: *DNB*), prolific dramatist.

To E.M. Ward, 21 January 1868
MS: Texas: Coleman

Bentham Hill Cottage | Near Tunbridge Wells | 21 January 1868

My dear Ned,

You will all be grieved, I know, at the miserable news which I have to tell you. My dear old mother is dying. She is perfectly conscious – perfectly clear in her mind. But the internal neuralgia pain which she has suffered so long, has broken her down – and at her great age, there is now no hope. Charley is with me here. All that <u>can</u> be done to soothe her last moments is done. The end may be deferred for a few days yet – but it is now only a question of time. I can write no more.

Give my love to all.

Yours affectionately, | Wilkie Collins.

To William Holman Hunt, 28 January 1868

MS: Huntington

Bentham Hill Cottage | near Tunbridge Wells | Jany 28th 1868

My dear Hunt,

On Saturday last, I persuaded my poor mother to see another doctor – my friend Frank Beard. He has relieved the most alarming symptoms – and he leaves her out of <u>immediate</u> danger. But at her age, and in her state of weakness, there is no knowing from day to day, what may happen. She sends you her kindest love, and often talks of you. I remain here till Charley comes next week to take my place – He is far from well himself. My mother has the best of good and kind [nurses]. We are obliged to keep her quiet – and to deny admittance to her room to everybody.

I am (luckily) obliged to work – in other words obliged to resist the suspense and distress of this anxious time. All the leisure I can spare from my mother, must be devoted to my book.[1] Hence this short letter – and the time that has passed before I could thank you for your kind and brotherly words.[2]

Affectionately yours | Wilkie Collins

Notes

1. i.e., *The Moonstone*.
2. The letter from "I am (luckily)" to "brotherly words" is marked in the margin of the letter with a single vertical line.

To Harper Brothers, 30 January 1868

MS: Princeton: Text, Parrish[1] and Coleman.

Bentham Hill Cottage, near | Tunbridge Wells, England | January 30th 1868

Dear Sirs,

Your kind letter has reached me at a time of painful domestic anxiety. The dangerous illness of my mother has called me to her cottage in the country – and I am working at my story, as I best can, in the intervals of my attendance at her bedside. Mr Dickens had already written to tell me of the liberal manner in which you had met my proposal. And now your letter comes, telling me of an additional concession to my convenience, at a time when your consideration for me speaks with especial friendliness, and when I assure you I feel encouraged in no ordinary degree by the kindness of my American publishers.

You will receive with this a corrected revise of the twelfth weekly part of The Moonstone, and a portion of the thirteenth weekly part. The completion of the thirteenth weekly part will follow, I hope, by Tuesday's mail. But for the inevitable delay in transmitting the manuscript and receiving the proofs by post, caused by my absence from London, you would have received the whole weekly part by the mail of February 1st. I will arrange to send slips (for the convenience of your artist) by every mail, so long as my mother's critical condition obliges me to remain here. And I will be careful – as I have hitherto been careful – to forward the duplicates regularly, in case of accidents by the post. After the next two or three weekly portions, I shall hope to be able to send you, beforehand, a list of subjects for the artist, referring to a part of the story which is already settled in detail, and in relation to which he may feel secure against any after-alterations when I am writing for press.

The two numbers of the Weekly have reached me safely. The illustrations to the first number are very picturesque – the three Indians and the boy being especially good, as I think. In the second number, there is the mistake (as we should call it in England) of presenting "Gabriel Betteredge" in livery. As head-servant, he would wear plain black clothes – and would look, with his white cravat and grey hair, like an old clergyman.[2] I only mention this for future illustrations – and because I see the dramatic effect of the story (in the first number) conveyed with such real intelligence by the artist[3] that I want to see him taking the right direction, even in the smallest technical details.

You may rely on my sparing no effort to study your convenience, after the readiness that you have shown to consider mine. I am very glad to hear that you like the story, so far. There are some effects to come, which – unless I am altogether mistaken – have never been tried in fiction before.

Believe me | Dear Sirs | With sincere esteem & regard
Truly yours | Wilkie Collins

Messrs Harper & Brothers

Notes

1. Letter laid into First American Edition of *The Moonstone* (1868).
2. In the 11 January 1868 issue of *Harper's Weekly*, Gabriel Betteredge wears a dark short waistcoat, knee-pants, hose, and a long white coat.
3. i.e., William Samuel Lyon Jewett who worked for *Harper's* from 1859 to 1876.

To William Tindell, 21 February 1868
MS: Glasgow

90, Gloucester Place, | Portman Square. W. | Feby 21st 68.

My dear Tindell,
Thank you for the draft licence. I am still miserably weak and ill. I can only move from one room to another on the same floor. Could you manage to meet Fechter here, say between six and seven on any evening next week. I am quite helpless, and can only move in the matter in this way,

Yours truly, | Wilkie Collins.

To Harper Brothers, 22 February 1868
MS: Texas: Coleman

90, Gloucester Place, | Portman Square W. | London | Saturday | 22 February 1868

Dear Sirs,
You will, I hope, receive with this a carefully-corrected proof (for the artist) of weekly portion 15 of The Moonstone. Receiving this – you will receive, so far as I can now calculate, one full half of the book.
This weekly part, and the lst, have been partly dictated, partly written by me, in intervals of severe pain from a rheumatic attack – which has tortured my eyes this time as well as the rest of my body. I am now getting better – with little to contend against but the weakness caused by the suffering – and by the action of the remedies employed. Rather better accounts of my mother have, I am glad to say, cheered me on my sick bed. Assuming that I have had my share for the present of the afflictions of human life – I shall hope to get on faster into the second half of The Moonstone than with the first. "Miss Clack's" narrative will be finished in one or two more weekly parts. And "Franklin Blake's narrative" will follow it. In this part of the story, I hope to be able to send the artist some subjects beforehand.
I send with part 15, duplicate of revised part 14 – and a [duplicate] of the corrected slip in part 13. You now have all my latest corrections – and the American and the English publications of The Moonstone are literally the same.

Depend – barring accidents – on my steadily doing my best to increase the present advance [i.e. sheets]. I have declined all new proposals made to me here – I am to work uninterrupted at <u>The Moonstone</u> until it is done.

Believe me, Dear Sirs, | Faithfully yours, | Wilkie Collins

To William Holman Hunt, [22 February 1868]
MS: Huntington

90, Gloucester Place, | Portman Square. W. | Saturday

My dear Hunt

I was very sorry to miss seeing you again last night. The gout has come – to keep the rheumatism company – and I sleep badly – and the doctor says I must keep quiet an hour or two before going to bed. If you ever take your walk this way, after light fails for painting, do look in and tell the servant that you are to come up. Between 6 & 8 is my good time.

Accounts of my mother still tell me that she is keeping her hold on life and suffering less than she did.

Yours affly | W. Collins

To William Holman Hunt, 19 March 1868
MS: Huntington

90, Gloucester Place, | Portman Square. W. |[1] March 19th 1868

My dear Hunt,

One line to tell you that my dear mother died at 3 this morning.

I am still too ill to have any hope of joining poor Charley in following her[2] to the grave.

Yours affly | Wilkie Collins

Notes

1. Written on black-edged printed mourning paper.
2. Wilkie "escaped the ordeal of her funeral" (Peters, p. 292).

To William Holman Hunt, 21 March 1868
MS: Huntington

90, Gloucester Place, | Portman Square. W. |[1] March 21ˢᵗ 1868

My dear Hunt,

Thank you for another proof of your affection which is very welcome to me in this grief.

I have sent your note on to Charley. I am sure it will be a comfort to him to see the face of a dear old friend whom my mother loved, and whom we love, on the day of the funeral.[1] He will write you word of the day and hour – which I don't yet know – and I can tell you about trains &c. You will represent me.

Yours ever afftly | W.C

Note

1. The letter is written on black-edged printed mourning paper.

To Nina Lehmann, May 1868
MS: Present whereabouts unknown. TL/copy: Texas. Text Coleman

[90, Gloucester Place, | Portman Square. W.] | Friday

Dearest Padrona,

Your note, and your charming flowers, and your nice eggs, came like three angels, after the thunderstorm had torn my wretched shattered nerves to pieces. Thank you a thousand times! I am having a hard fight of it to finish my book[1] in my exhausted state. I shall have done I hope next month – and then I shall be at your entire disposal. Come when you like – only mind it is before 4. I am carried out to be aired at 4.

Yours ever, | WC

Note

1. The serialization of *The Moonstone*, in *All the Year Round*, 4 January to 8 August 1868. Published by Tinsley in book form, 1–14 July 1868.

To William Tinsley,[1] 11 July 1868
MS: PM

90, Gloucester Place, | Portman Square. W. |[2] Saturday 11th July 1868

Dear Sir,

Many thanks for the Subscription List of "The Moonstone".

Both you and I might have good reason to feel discouraged, if this List indicated anything more important than the timidity of the Libraries – and possibly the poverty of the Libraries as well. As things are, we have only to wait a few weeks – until the book has had time to get talked about. I don't attach much importance to the Reviews – except as advertisements which are inserted for nothing. But the impression I produce on the general public of readers is the lever that will move anything – provided the impression be favourable. If this book does what my other books have done, in the way of stimulating the first circle of readers among whom it falls – that circle will widen to a certainty. It all depends on this. If [Mr: erased] Mudie is right in believing 500 to be a sufficient supply – then ((judging from past experience) three fourths of my readers have deserted me! I, for one, won't believe this – and I am glad to find, from the close of your letter, that you have not lost confidence in the book either. It is (in the opinion of more than one good judge) the best book I have written. I believe it myself to have a much stronger element of "popularity" in it than anything I have written since "The Woman in White". That book, Mr Mudie,[3] and the Librarians took in driblets – just as the public forced them. And this book, let us hope, will be another example of that sort of legitimate sale which springs from a genuine demand.

I have also to thank you for sending me my "author's copies" – which came here safely yesterday.

Faithfully Yours | Wilkie Collins

W.Tinsley Esqre

P.S. The "No Name" figures were 1st Edition. Four thousand copies, all sold.

2nd Edition, Five hundred copies. This proved to be over-printing. The 500 copies being on hand, and diminished, instead of adding to, the profits.

Notes

1. William Tinsley (1831–1902), publisher: see Gasson.
2. WC uses black-edged printed mourning paper.
3. Charles Edward Mudie (1818–1890), founder of Mudie's Lending Library.

To Charles Benham, 19 July 1868
MS: Glasgow

Woodlands | ¹ Sunday July 19ᵗʰ 1868

My dear Benham,

I got your letter here last night.

This time, it does certainly appear to me that the misunderstanding began in your room at Essex St. When we were speaking of the security which I could give to your client, and afterwards when I was signing the necessary papers, you never informed me that you contemplated putting a distringas on £5000 of stock, as additional security for a loan of £800! When the brokers discovered the "Distringas", it seems to me that it was the duty of my bankers to inform me of it.

However, as this is now arranged, it is useless to dwell on it any longer – except with a view to the future. Half the £5000 (odd) belongs to my brother – and he wishes to reinvest it. If you had maintained the "distringas" – or if you were to put it on again – would he be able to reinvest without asking your leave or the leave of your client? If he is not at perfect liberty to do what he likes with his own (in consequence of my having borrowed money, of your client) pray tell me so – and I will pay the £800 back at once. The loss of 3 or 4 months of interest is of no great importance.

As for myself again, I suppose I am not at liberty to reinvest my half of the £5000, under any circumstances whatever. [erased word] Am I at liberty to sell out £800 to repay your client – or any part of that sum, supposing I can't make it up? And when I pay the money back do I receive back the paper which I [received erased] signed, making over to your client my share in this little inheritance?

I write these questions, instead of going to Essex St. as I proposed, and putting them viva voce – because your letter renders the interview which I contemplated unnecessary. Also because I want tomorrow afternoon for a consultation with Mr Fechter, on the subject of a play founded on "The Moonstone". I shall probably be detained in town until Wednesday by this dramatic matter – so there will be plenty of time for you to send me a line to say how I stand – and how my brother is or is not affected by my position towards your client.

I go abroad on the 1ˢᵗ August – and I want to go, leaving my poor mother's affairs, my brother's affairs, [word erased] and my affairs, settled. In the present high state of the Funds – the repayment of the £800 may be commercially to my advantage. For the sacrifice of a few months of interest-money may be less than the sacrifice of selling out next winter when the funds may have dropped again.

Yours ever, | W.C.

Note

1. Address written above erased printed address.

To Charles Ward, 28 July 1868
MS: PM

90, Gloucester Place, | Portman Square. W. |[1] 28th July 1868

My dear Ward,

I have got your kind letter of the 25th telling me of the safe receipt of Jane's cheque, and also the safe receipt from Charley of the Power for Mrs Davis's money. So far, so good.

But, as to the <u>two</u> Powers which <u>followed</u> the Power for Mrs Davis's money – and which <u>I</u> received, the next day after executing Mrs Davis's Power – here is Charley, hesitating to sign and "wanting to know the reason why". I signed – knowing that the Powers come from Coutts's – without looking at them. But Charley wants preliminary explanations which I am quite unable to give. I have no choice but to follow you in your holiday – most unwillingly – with a new worry connected with this endless business.[2] I enclose Charley's letter – in the hope that y<u>ou</u> may be able to quiet his mind in three lines – or that you can instruct Mr Shannon to do so in a note which it would take you two minutes to write.

Our places are taken in the Antwerp Steamer for Sunday next. But it is doubtful if Lehmann can go. I shall hear tomorrow.

My foot has been bad again – and is mending again. I hardly know what I shall do – except that I <u>must</u> get away – if Lehmann fails me. The child of the partner who was to have taken his place is dangerously ill.

Anyway, I am here till Saturday.

Yours ever | W.C

I will send a photo to Jane – <u>of course</u>!

Notes

1. WC uses black-edged printed mourning paper. Above the printed address WC writes: "P.S. I have, of course, written to Charley that our banks can neither sell out nor buy in, without a written order authorizing it from ourselves."
2. For details of WC's Mother's will, see Clarke, pp. 116–17.

To Charles Ward, 18 August 1868
MS: PM

St Moritz | Tuesday, August 18th 1868

My dear Ward,

As I calculate it, this letter will probably meet you on your return to the Strand. Will you, as soon as you conveniently can, go to Gloucester Place, and open my letters? They are all put together in a drawer of my study table (by the window in the back drawing-room) – the drawer on your left hand as you sit down at the end of the table at which you used to write for me when we had copying to do. Any letters which require answers, you will kindly [erasure] answer perhaps, in three lines – just saying that I am in Switzerland and am expected back in September. There may be cheques in some of the letters, and possibly a remittance (which ought to be at once acknowledged) of £250 from America. Will you take care of these pecuniary documents for me, in your desk, until I get back? and if there is a letter from Fechter, will you forward it – also if there is anything else in my correspondence which I ought to know, will you write me word – at Baden? address: Mr Wilkie Collins | Poste Restante | Baden- Baden | Germany. | I expect to be at Baden on the 25th of this month, and to stay till the 26th or 27th – not later probably than the 27th. You will calculate if there is time for you to write to me under these circumstances. If I don't find a letter from you at the Poste Restante, I will assume that there is not time – and will write again telling you what my plans are for returning, either in the first or second week in September – I have not yet settled which.

This place has done great things for me. Exquisite scenery, and mountain air blowing over glaciers and through pine woods. I don't meddle with the baths and waters – I take the air alone – and it [erasure] costs me a guinea a day for the privilege of breathing it, in an "apartment" of three rooms only. The people here make hay while the sun shines – we are a helpless crowd of foreigners at St. Moritz, completely at the mercy of the Swiss inhabitants.

Lehmann and his eldest boy are living in a house close to mine. We leave this together on Saturday next the 22nd, and travel to Baden (probably) in company. There Lehmann leaves me, and rushes home as fast as the trains can take him – which is considerably faster than I can travel.

I hope you are all the better for your holiday. My love to Jane and the Girls.

Yours ever, | W C

To Charles Benham, 25 September 1868
MS: Glasgow

90, Gloucester Place, | Portman Square. W. |[1] 25th September 1868

My dear Benham,

By all means let your office do what is necessary with the inland revenue. I had thought that we were at the end of our troubles – but this administration business is an exception to all other mortal affairs – it never comes to an end.

You are quite right to turn the screw on Tinsley. We ought to know whether he has, or has not, done with the book.

I want to find out what "Mrs Gelverton's" grievance is in "a nutshell" – with a view to making it the starting point in a play (this between ourselves). Can you tell me, in what point her marriage, was "null and void"? If a letter will do, I need not bother you by coming to Essex Street – or if you can come here and dine at $\frac{1}{2}$ p 5 on Monday next – it will be better still. If not, I can come to you on Monday next at 3. At 4, I take my Bath, at 5, I get out – amidst thunder and lightning. At $\frac{1}{2}$ p 5, I am ordered to dine – with thunder in my stomach & lightning in my head.

Ever yours | W.C.

Note

1. WC uses black-edged printed mourning paper. Above the printed address, WC writes: "One Line in answer, will be enough."

To Charles Benham, 25 September 1868
MS: Glasgow

90, Gloucester Place, | Portman Square . | 25th Sept 1868

My dear Benham,

Here is an entirely new official monster, terrifying me with mysterious formulas. Can we set him at defiance? or (better still) can we cheat the revenue? Will you do what is best? or will you tell me how to do it? I am sorry to trouble you – but I don't know whether this last "officer" ought to be pitched into the waste paper basket or not.

I have begun the electric baths. Rating the pores of my skin at only 7 million – I have had 7 million currents of electricity running through me for 45 minutes. The result is great cheerfulness and great disinclination to pay inland revenue. | W.C.

Plate 9 Martha Rudd.

Plate 10 Wilkie Collins with Martha Rudd.

Plate 11 The cover of *The Bookman*, June 1912.

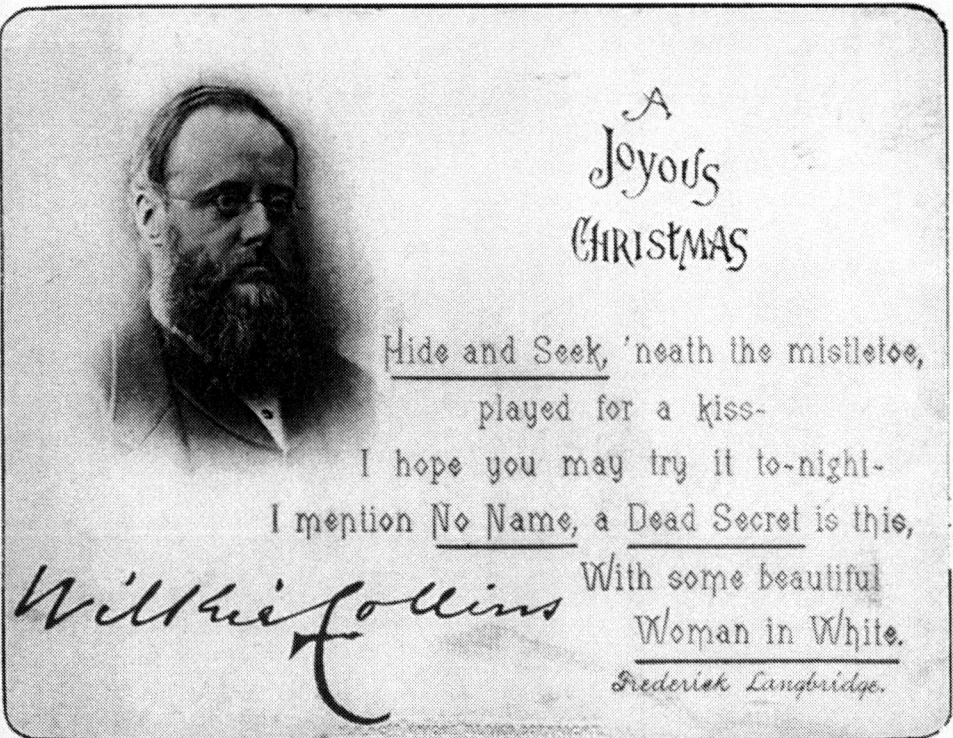

Plate 12 A Christmas card featuring titles by Wilkie Collins, actual size.

Plate 13 F.W. Waddy's caricature of Collins, 1872.

52, WIMPOLE STREET,
W.

Sept 21

I am

They are driving me

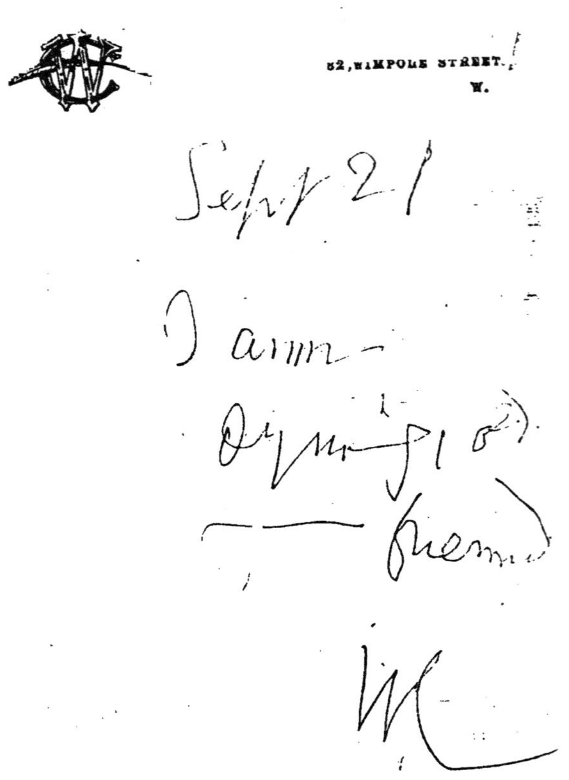

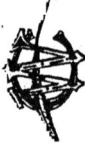

Plate 14 “I am dying old friend.”

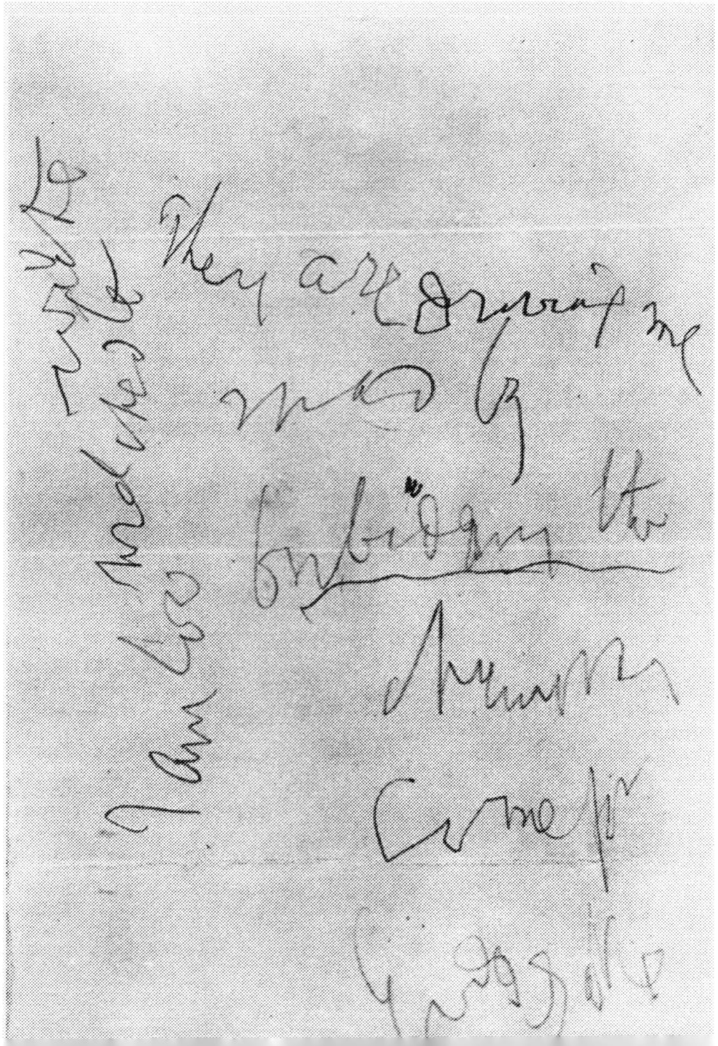

Plate 15 “I am too muddled to write. They are driving me mad by forbidding the [Hypodermic] Come for God’s sake.”

The last letters Wilkie Collins wrote to his doctor.

Part VI
Martha and the American Triumph
1869–February 1874

Introduction

There is no mention in the 1869 letters of Martha Rudd, whom he had clearly been seeing following their meeting in Great Yarmouth. She probably moved to London in 1868. He confesses to Mrs Benzon that the "doctor [is] trying to break me of the habit of drinking laudanum" [26 February 1869]. Wilkie has problems with a tenant – his "pious bitch" [22 March 1869]. An enigmatic note is struck when Wilkie writes to Fred Lehmann "thus far, the money anxieties are not added to the other anxieties which are attacking me" [24 April 1869]. Problems with Fechter and health worries are referred to, but not Martha's first pregnancy.

The remainder of the year is largely devoted to the writing of *Man and Wife*. For the first six weeks of 1870 he is "confined to [his] room, blinded for the time being ... For the present [he is] quite helpless" [25 January 1870]. Wilkie finishes *Man and Wife* on the 9 June 1870. The next day he tells Tindell, his solicitor, that he "fell asleep from sheer fatigue – and was awakened to hear the news of Dickens's death". Exhausted and deeply involved with proofs "the day of Dickens's Funeral was a lost day to me" [16 June 1870]. There are problems with Ellis, the publishers, over the publicity for his novel. In spite of a brief, summer yachting expedition, early September finds Wilkie "out of sorts again" and he tells Charles Ward "I work with infernal pains on the inside" [2 September 1870].

Preoccupied with copyright, the dramatization of his works and other literary matters, he yet has time to comment occasionally on the progress of the Franco-Prussian war. In one despairing comment on the war ([August 7, 1870]), he even foreshadows nuclear weapons and the stalemate of the Cold War: "What is to be said of the progress of humanity? ... I begin to believe in only one civilising influence – the discovery one of these days of a destructive agent so terrible that War shall mean *annihilation* and men's fears shall force them to keep the peace."

He floats to George Smith the possibility of a popular edition of his works and begins *Poor Miss Finch*. Periodic attacks of rheumatic gout, and the birth of Martha's second daughter, Constance Harriet, account for changes in his will and a codicil including Caroline and Martha. The dramatization of *Man and Wife*, *The Woman in White*, problems with copyright and piracy, the opening at the Olympic on 9 October 1871 of *The Woman in White*, are just a few of the topics of his letters.

By February 1872 Wilkie is talking of a proposed visit to North America. There is a reference to his elder daughter, Harriet, in a letter to his solicitor Tindell [18 June 1872]. Involvement with a new novel *The New Magdalen*, is interrupted. He writes to Tindell from Ramsgate, where he is with Caroline, that he is "suffering tortures of the damned with another attack of gout in the eye" [27 September 1872].

Hard at work writing a new serial story and getting his play *Man and Wife* at the Prince of Wales, Wilkie proposes to go to America to read. *The New Magdalen* runs in *Temple Bar* from January to December 1873, *Man and Wife* opens at the Prince of Wales on 22 February 1873, and *The New Magdalen* has its opening night at the Olympic on 19 May 1873. His new novel, *The Dead Alive*, is published in December 1873. In the midst of this literary activity Wilkie writes of "the calamity that has fallen on me". On 9 April, 1873, his brother Charles dies, seemingly from a "cancerous tumour in the stomach" [10 April 1873].

Three days before he sails for America on the Steamship *Algeria* [14 September 1873] he signs details of his new will which includes provision for both the family of Martha Rudd (who became "Mrs Dawson" when in his company; Wilkie becoming "William Dawson, barrister at law") and Caroline. After his first weeks in America, 26 distinguished personalities attend a dinner at the New York Union Club in his honour. "Thriving in health and in public (as reader)" [21 November 1873], he reveals his concern for Martha to Tindell and seeks his help. Christmas, 1873, is spent with his publisher, Rose, in Toronto and he begins a correspondence with Schlesinger, which is to continue until his death.

New Year, 1874, finds Wilkie at Buffalo, moving along the shores of Lake Erie, through Ohio to Chicago. After his readings there he returns to New York and Boston. He finally leaves for home on 7 March 1874. The Steamship *Parthia* lands at Liverpool on 18 March 1874. His visit is to affect the rest of his life, leaving him with tremendous feelings of affection for North America and with friends with whom he is to continue to correspond. As he comments to Fred Lehmann, their "enthusiasm and kindness are really and truly beyond description" [2 January 1874].

To Mrs Elizabeth Benzon,[1] 26 February 1869
MS: Private Possession

90, Gloucester Place, | Portman Square. W. |[2] February 26th 1869

Dear Mrs Benzon,

One line (written most unwillingly) to ask you to forgive me if I am absent tomorrow night. My doctor is trying to break me of the habit of drinking laudanum. I am stabbed every night at ten with a sharp-pointed syringe which injects morphia under my skin – and gets me a night's rest without any of the drawbacks of taking opium internally. If I only persevere with this, I am told I shall be able, before long, gradually to diminish the quantity of morphia and the number of the nightly stabbings – and so emancipate myself from opium altogether. I am ashamed to bore you with these trumpery details – but still I mention them to show that I have really no choice but to ask you to accept my excuses for tomorrow night.

I hope you were not the worse for the concert. As for me, Herr Schumann's music, Madame Schumann's playing, and the atmosphere of St. James's Hall, are three such afflictions as I never desire to feel again. I think of sending a card to [erasure] Ezards: – "Mr Collins's compliments, and he would be glad to know how the poor piano is?"

Believe me | dear Mrs Benzon | Vy truly yours | Wilkie Collins

Notes

1. Elizabeth (Lehmann) sister of Frederick and Rudolf Lehmann, wife of Edmund Ernst Leopold Schlesinger Benzon (d. 14 September 1873), steel manufacturer and patron of the arts.
2. WC uses black-edged water-marked printed mourning paper.

To Nina Lehmann, 11 March 1869
MS: Princeton: Coleman

90, Gloucester Place, | Portman Square. W. | 11 March 1869

Dearest Padrona,

I, too, am losing my senses. I protest I don't remember whether I was, or was not, the favoured object of those two invitations. Of course, I shall be delighted to dine with you on Sunday week – the 21st, and I will put on my silk stockings, and a new dress shirt, in honour of Saturday – if the rheumatism will only let me put anything on besides a mustard poultice. I am all over pain to-day – obliged to shift the pen from my right hand to my left to get a dip of ink. Fechter[1] is improving. My troubles are "much the same" – nothing settled yet. Keep Easter Monday open – if you can – for the first night.[2] If no new misfortunes overtake us, we hope to produce the piece on that evening.

Yours affectionately, | WC

[PS]
My beautiful flower – the sickly man (how appropriate!) is as beautiful as ever. I water him carefully, every day.

Notes

1. Charles Albert Fechter (1824–1879), Anglo-French actor.
2. Of WC's play *Black and White*.

To James Payn,[1] 21 March 1869
MS: Texas: Coleman

90, Gloucester Place, | Portman Square. W. | Sunday 21 March 1869

Summary:
Would have called to talk the American matter over with him, but he too is on the sick list. He suggests he write and make his proposal to "Messrs Harper and Brothers, Publishers, New York, USA". Offers them – if his "forthcoming book begins as a weekly serial – advance sheets of each periodical part, posted from England, week by week, six weeks in advance of the weekly date of publication here". Asks him to say he has introduced him. "Say that you are introduced to them by me, and – inquire what they will give." He says they are again hard at work "rehearsing [Black and White] at the Adelphi". He believes he caught his "cold in the deadly draughts on the stage in the daytime". He hopes they will appear on Easter Monday.

Note

1. James Payn (1830–1898: *DNB*), journalist, novelist, friend of Dickens, Charles Reade, Wilkie Collins, and others. Edited *Chamber's Journal* and *The Cornhill*, worked on *Household Words*.

To Charles Ward, 22 March [1869]
MS: PM

90, Gloucester Place, | Portman Square. W. |[1] Monday March 22nd

My dear Ward,

I am confined to the house by a severe cold in the chest.

Is the Jones fund[2] (may "the Lord" soon take her!) paid into <u>my</u> account regularly? I think we arranged to save trouble, that it should be so. Will you look at the "order"-book, and see?

If it only rests with <u>me</u> to decide the matter, pay this pious bitch the two quarters (Lady day and Midsummer 1869) together – so that we may be the longer rid of her. Telling her, at the same time, that it must be distinctly understood that this is not to be drawn into a precedent – and that the next quarterly payment will on no account be [erasure] remitted, before Michaelmas next.

I enclose a cheque for £25,,–,, out of which take the Jones money, and expenses of P.O. orders. Can you bring on your way home, or send me the balance, any time before, or <u>on</u>, the 25th. I want the balance for servants' wages &c &c. I am glad to see you are well enough to be at the Strand again. It is doubtful still when <u>I</u> can get out.

Yours ever | W.C

Let me have a line to say you have got this safely – and also to tell me whether [erased word] (by the help of the Lord) Mrs Jones's dividends are now regularly paid to my account only. I don't want to pay Mrs Jones (and the Lord) out of my own pocket.

Notes

1. WC uses black-edged mourning paper. Above the Gothic printed address WC writes: "P.S. If you think it rash to advance Mrs Jones's dividend – then only pay her the quarter. Say I am abroad – or in Abraham's bosom – and, in the absence of instructions from m<u>e</u>, you are compelled to pay as usual. I leave this to y<u>our</u> discretion. W.C."
2. By the terms of WC's father's will "small legacies were left (in a codicil added just before his death)" in 1847 to the four sisters of WC's mother. "There was an annuity to a cousin, Mrs Elizabeth Jones, of the interest on a sum of £700, a provision which was to become a recurrent irritation to Wilkie" (Peters, p. 73).

To Frederick Lehmann, 24 April 1869

MS: Princeton: Coleman.

90, Gloucester Place | Portman Square | Saturday | 24 April [1869]

My dear Fred,

Thank you, from the bottom of my heart, for your kind letter. No man – whatever his disappointments may be[1] – can consider himself [erasure] other than a fortunate man, when he has got such a friend as you are.

But, for the present, my head is "well above water". I have few debts unpaid – I have three hundred pounds or so at my bankers – and a thousand pounds in Indian & Russian railways, which I can sell out (if the worst comes to the worst) at a gain instead of a loss. I may also, in a few months, sell another edition of The Moonstone (cheap edition) – and get two or three hundred pounds in that way. So, thus far, the money anxieties are not added to the other anxieties which are attacking me. If my health gives way, and my prospects darken as the year goes on – you shall be the first man who knows it. Till then, thank you most sincerely once more.

I am coming to take pot-luck on Monday next at 7 – if you and the Padrona have still arranged to dine alone on that day. Don't trouble to write – unless there is an alteration. I am refusing all invitations on the plea of being "out of town". It is necessary to "lay the keel" of something new – after this disaster – and I am trying to keep myself as quiet as I can.

Yours ever, | W.C

I shall pay the Arts. Damn the Arts!

Note

1. WC's troubles could have been a combination of (i) financial losses from the short run of his play *Black and White*; (ii) his financial relations with Fechter, the leading actor in *Black and White*; (iii) his relationship with Caroline Graves, who had recently left him; and (iv) the pregnancy of Martha Rudd (see analysis in Clarke, pp. 119–20).

To John Forster, 15 May 1869

MS: Yale

90, Gloucester Place, | Portman Square. W. | 15th May 1869

My dear Forster,

My heartiest congratulations on the completion of "Landor",[1] and my best thanks for the copy of the book which you have so kindly sent to me. I shall read it with no common interest and attention – first as coming from y<u>ou</u>; secondly as saying, what no one else could have said so well, in vindication of Landor's claims to a great place in English literature. You taught me to understand "Eliot"[2] – and you will find me willing to learn (if I can) to understand "Landor".

Ever affly Yours | Wilkie Collins

Notes

1. WC's marked copy of Forster's *Walter Savage Landor: A Biography*, published by Chapman and Hall, 2 vols, 1869, lot 27 at the sale of WC's library, 20 January 1890.
2. Both George Henry Lewes and WC were friends of Edward Pigott. WC visited Lewes and George Eliot in October 1859 when they lived at Holly Lodge, Wandsworth. WC joined them in musical evenings in 1862 when they lived at 16 Blandford Square. Otherwise there was little contact between them.

To Joseph Charles Parkinson,[1] 17 July 1869
MS: Private Possession

Woodlands | Southwood Lane | Highgate | N |
Saturday 17th July 1869

My Dear Parkinson,

Here – at last – are some of my questions on the matter of physical education.

I have been waiting to get to a point in my proposed story,[2] at which my inquiries would naturally suggest themselves, and would grow out of the necessities of my work.

1. What is the average length of time occupied in training for a boatrace? Also, for running races, and leaping races?

2. In these two latter cases – the running and the leaping – does the University student in Athletics come into contact with a low order of man acting as trainer or instructor? In this matter of rowing, I understand him to be trained and instructed by his equals in the university. Is this the case with other athletic accomplishments? In other words, does physical education, in any of its branches, lead to degrading social associations, by necessitating a low order of professional instructor?

3. If I suppose a young man of three or four and twenty to have trained for the university boat race – to have also trained (later in the same year) for [erasure] athletic sports – and to be in course of training (for the third time) for the next year's anniversary boat-race – would such excess of training be amply sufficient to account for his breaking down, and dying, under the effects of the third in this series of trainings? Again, would this

be an exaggerated case to take? and would a smaller number of trainings be sufficient to justify the break-down?

4. Can you furnish me with any slang expressions of the Muscular School (like the "three belts of muscle", for instance) which would be likely to be spoken, at a country house, in a mixed assembly of Ladies and Gentlemen?

=

These are, for the present, all the questions I need trouble you with. Answer them entirely at your convenience. I am staying here with some friends – where we can talk things over, and make far more progress than we could make by corresponding.

If any more questions turn up between this and then, I shall send them without standing on ceremony – and I thank you beforehand for helping me to illustrations of character which are especially needful to such a design as I have in view.

Yours ever | Wilkie Collins

J.C. Parkinson Esqre
I am writing, within hearing of that form of cultivation of the national stupidity called Croquet – and I hope (but am by no means sure) that I have made myself intelligible.

Notes

1. Joseph Charles Parkinson (1833–1908: *DNB*), journalist, civil servant, social reformer. Contributed to the *Daily News*, *All the Year Round*, *Temple Bar*, among other periodicals. Married in 1867 the daughter of George Elliot – the industrialist. Friend of W.P. Frith, Edmund Yates, and others: advocate for Poor Law Reform.
2. WC was writing *Man and Wife*, "affectionately dedicated" to Fred and Nina Lehmann.

To Joseph Charles Parkinson, 21 July 1869
MS: Private Possession

Woodlands | Southwood Lane | Highgate | N | July 21st 1869

My Dear Parkinson,

A thousand thanks for your assistance – so speedily rendered, and so valuable to me in every way. I am putting my story together (this time) in the dramatic form first – and I shall forthwith incorporate your information with my "scenario" of the third act – and set to work on my return to town. It will exactly fit what I have done thus far, to make my man one of the "showy" sort. When I have done the third act, I shall ask you to look at the piece – and make your remarks and corrections on the blank page. <u>All</u>

details are acceptable – I can put anything into the people's mouths that is necessary – having a whole stage full of characters grouped for that purpose in the third act, and having also (as I hope) fixed the public attention by a strong story developed in the two first acts.

Don't forget that any day after the 27th which will suit y<u>ou</u> will do for m<u>e</u>. And so, thank you again,

Yours ever | W.C

To Joseph Charles Parkinson, 15 September [1869]
MS: Private Possession

90, Gloucester Place, | Portman Square. W. | September 15th

My dear Parkinson,

The h<u>um</u>an statement complicates matters. I don't feel so sure. But here go the titles as they occur to me.

1. Studies From The Life.
2. From The Life.
3. Ourselves.
4. You and I.

(N.B. These two last (3 & 4) mean everything under the sun. Number 4, strikes me as best.)

5. Light Reading.
6. Persons and Places.

No. 6. doesn't seem bad. And your own title "This and That" – is – as I think a good one.

Let me hear if this note helps to decide you. If not, I'll try again.

Yours ever | W.C

P.S.

On looking at your letter again, I find y<u>our</u> title is "Here and There". Add "This and That" to <u>my</u> contributions. "Here and There" is quite as good.[1]

Note

1. Above his "P.S." on the blank integral leaf WC writes: "Keep the titles you don't use. They <u>may</u> come in useful for you or for me. – Excuse incoherence | I have | done work." He settled on *Man and Wife*.

To Frederick Lehmann, 25 October 1869
MS: Princeton

90, Gloucester Place, | Portman Square. W. |[1] October 25th 1869

My dear Fred,

The Stoughton Bitters arrived this morning from Liverpool. At the same time appeared a parcel of country sausages from Beard. I sent him back a bottle of the Bitters with instructions to drink your health in brandy bitters and to meditate on the immeasurable virtues of intoxicating liquors for the rest of the day. On my part, I suspended an immortal work of fiction, by going down-stairs, and tasting a second bottle, properly combined with Gin. Result delicious! Thank you a thousand times! The first thing you must do on your return to England, is to come here, and taste Gin and Bitters. May it be soon!

Have I any news? Very little. I sit here all day, attacking English Institutions – battering down the marriage laws of Scotland and Ireland and reviling athletic sports – in short writing an <u>un</u>popular book,[2] which may possibly make a hit from the mere oddity of a modern writer running full tilt against the popular sentiment, instead of clinging to it. The publishers are delighted with what I have done – especially my American Publishers, who sent an instalment of £500,,–,,– the other day, on receipt of only the first weekly Part. I call <u>that</u> something like enthusiasm. Produce me the English publisher who treats his author in this way.

I am to meet the Padrona at Procter's on Thursday. And I did meet her at Payn's last week – looking very well, and beautifully dressed. But two [erased word] events occurred worth mentioning. The Padrona – assisting the [erased word] force of a few sensible remarks by appropriate gesticulation, knocked over her tumbler of Champagne, and flooded the table. Shortly afterwards <u>I</u> assisted a few sensible remarks on my part, by appropriate gesticulation, and [erased word] knocked over <u>my</u> tumbler, and flooded the table. <u>And</u> Mrs Payn, seeing her cloth [erased word] ruined, kept her temper like an angel, and smiled upon me while rivulets of Champagne were flowing over <u>my</u> dress trousers and <u>her</u> Morocco [erased word] leather chair. Excellent woman!

Reade has been here, and has carried off my book about the French Police (Mémoires tirées des Archives,[3] &c &c). He begged me to go and see him at Oxford. I said – "Very well! Write and say when." Need I add that he has <u>not</u> written?

I had a friend to dinner at the [indecipherable word] Athenaeum the other day. Our remonstrance has produced its effect. I declined to order <u>anything</u>, after our experience. "A dinner at so much a head. If it isn't good I shall personally submit myself for examination before the Committee, and shall produce specimens of the dishes, reserved by myself." The result was a very good dinner. When you come back, let us try the same plan. Nothing like throwing the whole responsibility on the cook.

I had a day at Gadshill, a little while since. Only the family. Very harmonious and pleasant – except Dickens's bath, which dripped behind the head of my bed all night. Apropos of Gadshill, your cutting from the New York Times, has been followed by a copy of the paper and a letter from Bigelow.[4] I don't think Dickens has heard of it – and I shan't say anything about it, for it might vex him, and can do no good. Why they should rake up that old letter now, is more than I can understand. But then a people who can spell Forster's name without the "r", are evidently capable of anything.

Fechter has refused – what appears to everybody, but himself to be an excellent offer from America. He seems determined to go "on his own book" in December next – and will find the managers whom he has refused his enemies when he gets there. I am afraid he has made a mistake.

Charley and Katey are back in town. Charley dined here yesterday – no Saturday. He is very fairly well.

Mrs John Wood had made the St James Theatre a perfect fairy palace – and is playing old English Comedy – with American actors.[5] Scenery and dresses marvellously good. A great success. The other great success I am going to see on Wednesday – monkeys, who [erasure] are real circus riders – jump through hoops, dance on the horse's back, and bow to the audience voluntarily when they are applauded. We shall see them in Shakespeare next – and why not? They can't be worse than the human actors, and they might be better.

Where will you be, when this reaches you? I am told you have got to San Francisco. That will do. Come back – leave well alone – and come back. I will describe Japan to you – and take you to see the manufacturers afterwards, at the Baker Street Bazaar. Goodbye for the moment.

Yours, my dear Fred, ever, [WC]

Notes

1. Above the Gothic printed address, WC writes: "I send this to Naylor & Co. 'to be forwarded'. Let me hear from you, when you know your plans. I am glad Bigelow was serviceable – he is a very fine fellow. As for my health, I am getting along pretty slick, Sir! A third of my book just done. Have seen nothing of Forster. Shall see him, if we last till November 21st at dear old Procter's birthday celebration. Reade & Charley send loves."
2. *Man and Wife.*
3. WC's six-volume copy of J. Peuchet's *Mémoires tirées des archives de la police ...* (Paris, 1838) lot 209 in the 20 January 1890, Puttick and Simpson sale of his library.
4. John Bigelow (1817–1911), owner of the New York *Evening Post* (1848–61), journalist and activist for the Union cause. A signed copy of John Bigelow's autobiography of *Ben Franklin* (1868), was in WC's library at his death.
5. Mrs John Wood took over the St James' Theatre on 16 October 1869. Her revival of *She Stoops to Conquer* ran for over 100 performances. She left in 1871 for the USA.

To Belinfante Brothers,[1] 10 November 1869
MS: Present whereabouts unknown. Corrected proofs, PM

90, Gloucester Place, Portman Square, W. | London |
November 10 1869

To Messrs Belinfante Brothers
GENTLEMEN, -
I beg to acknowledge the receipt of your letter informing me that you are desirous of translating into the Dutch language, and of publishing in a Dutch magazine, a novel of my writing, which is about to appear in England in *Cassell's Magazine*.

Before I enter on this question I must venture to set you right on a trifling matter of detail, as to which you are completely mistaken.

Your letter is addressed to me as "*Madame* Wilkie Collins". I avow it with sincere regret; but the interests of truth are sacred. The trumpet of Fame, gentlemen, has played the wrong tune in your ears. I am not the charming person whom you suppose me to be. I wear trousers; I have a vote for Parliament; I possess a beard; in two dreadful words, I am – a Man.

This little error set to right, let us return to business.

I observe with profound surprise and regret that your request for permission to publish my book in Holland, in your magazine, is not accompanied by the slightest hint of any intention on your part of paying for that privilege. All that you offer me is a copy of the magazine. What am I to do with a copy of the magazine? I don't understand Dutch. All that I can do is to look at your magazine, and mourn over my own neglected education.

Permit me to suggest that you might acknowledge the receipt of the right to translate "Man and Wife" in a much better way than by giving me the magazine. It is quite a new idea – you might give me some money.

Why not, gentlemen, if you publish my book? Do your translators write for nothing? Do your printers work for nothing? Do your paper-makers give you paper for nothing? Do you yourselves publish for the honour and glory of Literature, without making a single farthing by it? If all this happens to be the case, don't read another word of my letter. It is written under a totally erroneous impression, by a man who is incapable of understanding the Dutch nation.

But if all of you do make something by the publication of my book, then I have the honour of reminding you that I am the man who sets you all going, and that the first and foremost person to be paid in this matter is the person who puts the employment into your hands, and the remuneration into your pockets. I take up the pen – and, behold, profitable industry animates your dormant establishment. And what do I get? oh! fie! fie! a copy of the magazine!

You may – and probably will – tell me that the profits are miserably small. Gentlemen, make your minds easy. My boundless love of justice knows no limit, either upward or downward. However small the profits are, let us be as cheerful as we can under the circumstances; and, in the name of justice, let us share what there is. I once extracted twenty-five pounds from some colonial publishers who had pirated a book of mine, and I have never made any money by literature which was so precious to me as that. Call the profits, if you like, a shilling a week, and give me the indescribable satisfaction of seeing, for thirty or forty weeks to come, this entry in my banker's book: By Messrs Belinfante Brothers' Sense of Justice – six-pence.

Does this eagerness of mine to share the profits shock you? Are you amazed to find that the honour of being translated into Dutch is not enough to satisfy me? Gentlemen, I can't see the honour. The injustice done to me gets in the way and closes the prospect.

If, therefore, you want my permission to publish "Man and Wife", you have it on this condition – that you and I share between us the profits of the publication.

But here a little bird whispers in my ear, "*Madame* Wilkie Collins, there is no treaty of international copyright between England and Holland. You are quite helpless, my poor dear! Messrs Bellinfante Brothers can take your book, whether you like it or not, and are not bound by law to pay you a single farthing for it."

Am I to adopt *this* view of the question between us? What! you can not deny that I ought, as a matter of decent fair-dealing, to have a share in any profits realized by the publication of my own book – and yet you decline to give me what is morally my right, because a law doesn't happen to have been made which forces you to do it! Perish the thought! My boundless love of justice has been already alluded to. It absolutely declines to admit that a firm of respectable Dutch publishers is capable of being influenced in its commercial transactions by other than strictly honourable considerations. Here is the dignity of man involved in a trumpery question of money. Gentlemen, if we respect the question of money, let us, for Heaven's sake, pay at least a similar tribute to the dignity of man.

Besides, I have experience to justify me in taking my present view of the matter. My friend, Baron von Tauchnitz, of Leipzig, reprints my books for continental circulation. He is not obliged by law to pay me a farthing for doing so; but he invariably does pay me nevertheless. His own sense of honour is law enough, in this particular, for Baron von Tauchnitz. Is their own sense of honour not law enough also, in this particular, for Messrs Belinfante Brothers?

The answer to that serious question, gentlemen, rests entirely with yourselves. Be so kind as to let me have it at your earliest convenience; and, believe me, faithfully yours, | Wilkie Collins

Note

1. WCs' letter and the subsequent correspondence were published in *Harper's Magazine* in New York. WC's English spelling of words such as "honour" appeared in *Harper's* as "honor". His letter to the Dutch publishers, Messrs Belinfante Brothers, was in reply to a request from them for his permission to publish his novel *Man and Wife* in their magazine. They offered him a copy of the magazine. In their first reply to his letter of November 10, they argued that in contrast to Tauchnitz, who published books, they published novels in their magazine, whose profits were small, and that they had been polite in seeking his permission. After subsequent correspondence, the firm of Belinfante Brothers gave in, though WC hardly benefited in monetary terms.

To Belinfante Brothers, 18 November 1869

MS: Texas: Coleman. Proof, PM. Published Robinson, pp. 233–5; D. Flower, *The Book Collector's Quarterly*, VII (July–September 1952), pp. 25–7.[1]

> 90, Gloucester Place | Portman Square. W. |
> London, November 18 1869

Gentlemen:

The grave error that I have committed is the error of assuming you to be more just and more enlightened men than you are.

Your answer to my letter tells me what I was previously unwilling to believe – that you have persisted so long in publishing books by authors of all nations, without paying for them, that any protest against that proceeding on my part, which appeals to your sense of a moral distinction between right and wrong, appeals to something that no longer exists.

What am I to say to men who acknowledge that they and the people whom they employ, all derive profit from publishing my book; and who, owning this, not only repudiate the bare idea of being under any pecuniary obligations toward me as the writer of the book, but shamelessly assert their own act of spoliation to be a right – because no law happens to exist which prohibits that act as a wrong? There is nothing to be said to persons who are willing to occupy such a position as this. What is to prevent men who trade on such principles as these, from picking my pocket if they see their way to making a profit out of my handkerchief?

There is absolutely nothing to prevent their picking my pocket, and, what is more, indignantly informing me that it is their right – unless by some lucky chance, English handkerchiefs are better cared for than English literature, and are protected in Holland by law.

Suppose international copyright to be one of these days, established between England and Holland, what would become of you and your right then? You would have no alternative left but to curse the cruel fate which made you Dutchmen, and retire from business.

Returning before I close these lines to your answer to my letter, I have to add, that I have not in the least mistaken the nature of your application to me on the subject of the illustrations. It is the most indecent application I ever heard of in my life. You ask me to help you to pay honestly for obtaining the illustrations to my story – telling me, in the same breath, that you claim a right to take the story itself without paying for it. And this to me, as the author of the story! Do you expect me to notice such an application as that? It would be accepting an insult to notice it.

For the rest – whether you do or do not, take my book from me – I persist, in the interest of public morality, in asserting my right to regard as my own property the produce of my own brains and my own labour, any accidental neglect in formally protecting the same in any country notwithstanding. I declare any publisher who takes my book from me with a view to selling it in any form for his own benefit – without my permission and without giving me a share in his profits – to be guilty of theft, and to be morally, if not legally, an outlaw and a pest among honest men. And I send the correspondence between us to an English newspaper of wide circulation[2] by way of openly recording this protest, and openly exposing the principles on which Dutch publishers trade. In this way my views on the subject of fair-dealing with foreign authors may possibly reach the ears of those other persons of larcenous literary habits, who are ready, as you kindly inform me, to steal my story without the preliminary notice of their intention which you yourselves were personally compelled to give me by the honourable conduct, in this affair, of my English publishers.

Your obedient servant, | Wilkie Collins

Notes

1. Our text is from proof copy at PM: the letter not in WC's hand but signed by him.
2. *The Echo.*

To the editor of *The Echo*, 18 November 1869

MS: Texas: Coleman. Published D. Flower, *The Book Collector's Quarterly*, VII (July–September 1952), pp. 28–9.

[90, Gloucester Place, | Portman Square. W.] | 18 November 1869

Dear Sirs,

I enclose Messrs Belinfante's answer (of which I have had a copy made) – together with a copy of my rejoinder (sent by today's post), which, so far as I am concerned, closes the correspondence. These letters are numbered 3 and 4. Numbers 1 and 2 are already in your hands. There really does seem to be need of exposing such entirely shameless disregard of the commonest principles of honour and fair-dealing as these men show. I have laid the lash on their thick hides pretty smartly – and I shall send the printed correspondence (when it is published) to America – and try what I can do through my French and German publishers, to have the matter taken up by the journals in those countries.

Faithfully yours, | WC

P.S.
You will see that it is impossible for <u>me</u> to [enter] on the question of the [cheques] with Belinfante Brothers. But – if you think these men to be depended on to pay (which I don't) by all means write to them to say that I have left the decisions about the [cheques] entirely in your hands.

To James Payn, 30 November 1869

MS: Texas: Coleman

90, Gloucester Place, | Portman Square. W. | 30 November [1869]

My dear Payn,

Postscript to the article. Belinfante Brothers give in! "Of their own free will" they offer me a share in the profits of the Dutch <u>Man and Wife</u> if there are any. If you have <u>not</u> written the article, don't trouble about it <u>now</u>. If you have – add this information as a clincher. In today's or tomorrow's <u>Echo</u>, I publicly rehabilitate the Dutchmen. My share may or may not be worth five shillings purchase. But they concede the principle.[1]

Yours ever, | WC

P.S.
I am sorry to hear from Webster that his verdict is adverse.[2]

Notes

1. Belinfante Brothers paid WC "one hundred guilders, £8.6.8d" (Peters p. 325).
2. i.e., *The Substitute*, a drama by Payn eventually performed in 1876.

To Charles Reade, 30 November [1869]

MS: Taylor Collection, Princeton University

90, Gloucester Place, | Portman Square, W. | [1] 30th Nov. (Tuesday)

My dear Reade,

The horrible weather kept me at home yesterday – and today I must go in another direction. If you can find your proofs, leave them out for me like a good fellow – and I will call at the first opportunity.

I have conquered the Dutchmen! They offer me – of their own free will – a share in the profits, if any. So the principle is conceded. If you and I could get our brethren to fight without being paid for it – and to agree together – we should have international copy right all over the world. But (except Dickens) who will take the trouble?

Of course, I publish the result as an act of justice in today's or tomorrow's Echo.

Yours ever | WC

If <u>you</u> would like <u>my</u> proofs – of course they are at your service and at Mrs Seymours,[2] any time after this week. But I think you like the weekly instalments. Two weekly parts are published in advance, in this month's[3] (December) <u>Part</u>.

Notes

1. Above the address Collins writes: "Very sorry to miss you on Sunday. At home till five – after today – if you are coming my way." In Reade's hand there's the observation: "Wilkie Collins an artist of the pen. There are terribly few of these among writers."
2. Mrs Laura Alison Seymour (?1820–1879), actress and Charles Reade's companion for over 20 years.
3. WC doubly underlines "months".

To Charles Reade, [November 1869]

MS: Princeton[1]

Considerations for R[2]

=

I start from the December number – and I say the interest in the character is so strong, the collision of human passions is so admirably and so subtly struck out, that the public will have no more of new trades' Unions, and their outrages. They will skip pages 3, 4, 5 in the November number – they will resent the return to the subject in the December number. I don't suggest alterations of these. I only say, what I say, as a warning for the future. Keep to the Cutlers, and keep the Cutlers mixed up with Henry & Coventry – Grace and Jael – and you are safe.

Now – as to the brick-makers. I have [had: erased] read the report. They are even worse than the cutlers. But, [you: erased] as an artist and a just man, you don't take the worst case for illustration. You take the medium case, which may apply generally to all trades' unions.

If I had this story to finish – I should make the industrialist's difficulty in setting up the buildings for working Henry's invention arise from his knowledge of what brick-makers will certainly do – I should make him put this forcibly in dialogue to Henry – and I should make Henry feel, <u>exactly what the reader will feel</u>,[3] immeasurable disgust at this repetition of tyranny, outrage, and murder. "What! am I to go through it all again with the brick makers? <u>More</u> conspiracies, explosions, mutilations and deaths?" – "That's the prospect, Mr Little." – "Am I to give up my inventions, and are you to give up your profits?" – "No – we are to look out for a ready-made article in the shape of an empty building which will suit us – and give the brick-makers the go-bye in that way."

The building is [ground], as is your plot – and these are the brick-makers just touched, and disunified – and the story running on again – with the setting-up of the saw-grinding machinery, and all [the] incidents which follow. With this additional advantage that Henry does not [do] over again with the brick-makers, what he has already done with the cutlers.

=

As to other points: – First,

[Hurry] the story (if possible) to Henry's proposal to Grace to marry him and go away with him, and to Grace's refusal. You want that strong point, and that definite result, after keeping the suspended interest so long vibrating backwards and forwards between Grace's two lovers.

Second,

I doubt a <u>second</u>[4] blowing-up with Gunpowder. Can the necessary results be arrived at in no other way? Can it not be done by a pre-arranged escape of gas, for instance? Or by some other explosive, or destructive agent?

=

<u>Query</u>.[5] The scenes in the ruined church are so admirable, and so original, that I want the church to play an important part in the story. Would it be possible to make Mr Raby repair and re-consecrate it <u>for public worship</u>? Then to make the marriage of Grace and Coventry take place in it. And then to have the[6] marriage invalidated by some informality in the consecration, or in the registration for marriages, of the newly-restored church?

I don't know whether such an event as this would be legally possible – or whether if it <u>could</u> be possible – you could harmonise my idea, with your notion of the uncertificated clergyman? But it seems to <u>me</u> a good point to make the old church in which Henry has worked and suffered for Grace, the retributive agent in defeating Coventry, and uniting Henry to the woman whom he loves.

The f<u>irst</u> marriage celebrated in the church might be the marriage of Coventry and Grace – and so all difficulty about the marriages of other couples might be avoided.

Or, perhaps, you already mean to end the story with the marriage of Henry and Grace in the restored old church? Anyhow, I, as reader, certify the church to be "an interesting character".

Notes

1. In Reade's "Letterbook", Robert H. Taylor Collection. Reade notes on his letter: "I was so fortunate as to please him at last" (cited Peters, p. 282). Cf. WC to Reade, 29 May 1871.
2. Reade's *Put Yourself in His Place*, serialised in *Cornhill*, March 1869–July 1870 and was illustrated by Robert Barnes. Smith Elder published the novel in 3 vols, between 16–31 May 1870. Reade's serial opens with a Horatian tag: "I will frame a work of fiction upon notorious fact." His inspiration came from the persecution of non-members by the Sheffield trade unions in 1867. The plot centres around Henry Little – disowned by his landowning family because of his mother's marriage – who refuses to join the Edge Tool Forgers' Union. Reade appears to have followed WC's recommendations: Henry's forge is gunpowdered; he falls in love with Grace Carden; his Amazonian servant Jael Dence saves him from a further assassination attempt (this time by bow and arrow); Henry leaves for America following further death threats; Coventry, the villain, "simulates" Henry's death and diverts his letters home; Henry returns to find Grace married to Coventry. In the finale the Hillsborough dam bursts: Henry heroically saves Grace and Coventry who is crippled – "below the waist, an inert mass"; their marriage is revealed as invalid – the officiating clergyman is an imposter; Henry wins Grace; Jael marries an aristocrat (cf. Sutherland, pp. 515–16).
3. WC doubly underlines "exactly what the reader will feel".
4. WC doubly underlines "con" of "second".
5. WC doubly underlines "uer" of "Query".
6. WC marginally marks from "part in the story ... takes place in it. And then to have the". In his margin he writes: "This, so far, is no doubt already in your place – Mr Raby having alluded to [erased word] restoring the desecrated building."

To P.S. Conant,[1] 1 January 1870
MS: PM

90, Gloucester Place, | Portman Square. W. | London January 1st 1870

Dear Sir

Accept my thanks for your letter. I am sorry – writing in haste on the last occasion – that I failed to clearly express, what I intended to express, that you were entirely at liberty (if you thought it right) to publish the corres-pondence – adding to it, in justice to Messrs Belinfante, a statement of the manner in which the matter in dispute between us has been arranged.

Since I wrote to you, I have heard again from Holland – and I am enabled to make the necessary statement more complete than it might otherwise have been.

Messrs Belinfante, not only agree, of their own free will, to give me a share in any profits realised by the Dutch translation of my novel – but they also declare to me their intention of treating any other English writers whose works they translate, with the same just regard to the moral right which they have shown in my case. Add to this, that a second (piratical) Dutch translation of "Man and Wife" has been started in Holland – and that I am now helping my ex-enemies (in the capacity of their partner) to distance competition by sending them advance-sheets – and you have the curious termination to their affair complete!

The pecuniary results of the transaction will no doubt be trifling enough – depending as they do on the circulation of my book in such a small and thinly populated country as Holland. But it appears to me, to be something[2] to have obtained a recognition of the principle of international copyright, in a country which has hitherto set that principle at defiance. All legal protection to property springs, in the first instance, from authoritative recognition of moral right. Five thousand years ago (in a previous state of existence), I grew my own flax, I [indecipherable word] it into linen, I made the linen into a shirt. My next door neighbour not being able to do this, and wanting something of his next door neighbour, took my shirt away from me, and bartered it for what he wanted. When I told him, he was a thief, he answered "Your shirt is not protected by law – therefore you have no right to complain of my taking it." All the wise men of the time agreed with him – and reproved me for showing temper in the matter.

Five thousand years later (in another state of existence) precisely the same thing happened to me with a book that I had made. But, on this occasion, the person who had taken my book ended in admitting that I was right. "Here", I said to myself, "is progress. If I make my own shirt, in this enlightened age, the law declares the man who takes it from me to be a thief. Surely the law will end in declaring the same thing, all over the world, of the man who takes my book – especially when it finds the man himself ashamed of having taken it!"

This little apologue is – I submit – a fair statement of the case for American readers.

Very truly yours | Wilkie Collins

P.S. Conant Esqre | Editor Harper's Weekly

Notes

1. P.S. Conant, Editor, *Harper's Weekly*.
2. WC doubly underlines "ethi" of "something".

To William Tindell, 25 January 1870
MS: Glasgow

90, Gloucester Place, | Portman Square. W. |[1] January 25. 1870

Summary:
His brother will take the letter to Dickens to sign.[2] The gout has got him in the eye, and he is confined to his room blinded. For the present he is "quite helpless".

Notes

1. With the exception of the closure "W.C." the letter is not in WC's hand.
2. "In January 1870 Dickens wrote a formal letter, requested by [WC] for legal reasons, establishing his copyright to everything by him published in *Household Words* and *All the Year Round*" (Gasson).

To William Tindell, 12 May 1870
MS: Glasgow

90, Gloucester Place, | Portman Square. W. | Friday 12th May 1870

Summary:
Cannot see him tomorrow. Wishes to ask some questions of Savill & Edwards about paper, binding and type and of Mr Ellis about bad debts and payments. He also wishes to know how much the edition will bring in. On advertising the question is whether they had better not risk an edition of 1500 copies. He asks for answers and then will be able to decide on Monday.

To William Tindell, 16 May 1870
MS: Glasgow

90, Gloucester Place, | Portman Square. W. |[1] Monday 16th May 1870

Summary:
He thinks the percentage perfectly fair. But paying him when the librarians pay, means paying him something some years hence. He finds that Mudie

"is heavily in debt to some of the publishers". Mr Edwards "is not a great publisher". Mudie "is <u>not</u> in debt to him, and therefore not in his power". The position is "disheartening, degrading, bitterly helpless". He doesn't "know <u>when</u> the libraries generally will pay". Something must be done. He suggest two proceedings. 1st to ascertain from Mr E. when the librarians pay – at what date. 2nd to see if Savill & Edwards "will start with <u>500 copies</u> only". He puts forward his own estimate of profit at £102. He adds: "I could surely sell 500 copies. And £100 gained is better than £100 lost by a higher venture".

Note

1. Above the Gothic printed address, WC writes "Private", underlined twice and "I can't get to you tomorrow (<u>Tuesday</u>) – having French friends coming to dine here at six."

To Harper & Brothers, 28 May 1870
MS: PM

90, Gloucester Place | Portman Square | London. |
Saturday May 28th 1870

Dear Sirs,

I have received your kind letter.

"Man and Wife" will be completed in the 37th Weekly Part – published July 27th. The republication here, will be one month in advance of the conclusion of the story in its periodical form. The novel will be published, in three volumes, on the 27th of next June.

As to the dramatic version (the greater part of which I have completed) I find (since I wrote to you) that the denouement of the book, cannot properly be followed in the play. After considering the question carefully, I feel that I must invent an entirely new conclusion for the drama. There is no fear of the theatrical banditti being able to do this – and I am also informed (by Mr Dion Boucicault) that there is no fear of any appearance of an unauthorised version during your <u>hot</u> season, when theatrical speculation in the United States is at a standstill. Under these circumstances, the production of the play may possibly be deferred. In accepting therefore your kind proposal to give the dramatic version a notice in the "Weekly" – which I do most gladly – I venture to suggest that nothing more should be said about time. It will be sufficient, I think, to announce that a dramatic version of the novel is being written by me for performance in the United States as well as in England – that the play will be in four acts; the three first acts closely following the book, and the fourth act containing a new conclusion to the story invented by the author, with a view to stage necessities and effects – and lastly that I have already appointed an agent to represent me in the United States, who will communicate on the subject with American managers in due time. This latter notification will spare me many letters – and will be considered an additional favour by me on that account.

I have also to thank you for your proposal, relating to the writing of some short stories in your magazine. For the present, I must rest. When the novel and the play are both done, I propose going to Switzerland to idle in the mountain air. If you will allow me, therefore, I will defer answering this part of your letter definitely until later in the year, when I shall know better than I know now what my plans are likely to be for future work.

With this, you will receive additional proofs of Parts 34 and 35. The greater part of 36 is at press, but it is so covered with corrections that I wait to send you a Revise by the mail of Saturday June 4<u>th</u>. The 36th Part is published on the 20th of July – which still leaves an advance of six weeks.

I am very glad to hear that you think well of the story. It has cost me – especially the latter part of it – no slight effort of thought, and has laid on me no common stress of work.

Very truly yours | Wilkie Collins

Messrs Harper & Brothers

To Charles Reade, 29 May 1870
MS: Mrs Juliet Noel (née Reade)

[90, Gloucester Place, | Portman Square. W.] |
Thursday May 29 (In bed)

My dear Reade,

I tried to get to you last night – but I had no idea where you were, and could not find out – until you bowed from a Private Box. And <u>then</u> I could not get upstairs in time to meet you.

My verdict is that the immense difficulties of dramatizing the story have been met and conquered in a most masterly way – and that the play contains some of the most interesting and the most original scenes that I have beheld for many a long year past. The acting decidedly good. Neville – Grotait – the work-men (those silent as well as those speaking) all excellent. Of the ladies, Miss Erskine best – judged by last night's ordeal. She was well <u>in</u> her part, and has unquestionable ability. Miss Young – personally (to me) much the more interesting woman of the two, appeared to be over-weighted. But I <u>thought</u> she was terribly frightened – and I wait to see her again. At present, she strikes me as a charming actress in sentimental comedy – called upon a little too suddenly to rise to the expression of strong emotion in strong drama.

Now as to making the piece popular – in other words as to cutting out. Here are my views (right or wrong) Act I

Shifty Dick, on his entrance, doesn't express himself to those who have not read the story. Who is he? Why does he come on, disguised as a Frenchman? I should take the scene out, and bring him in later – after he has been talked about so that the <u>audience may recognize him when he appears.</u>

Act II

The old church. Admirable scene. <u>Less</u> forging – it is excellently done – but you destroy the effect of making the knife, by the previous hammering & beating. <u>No ghosts – no marriage vision</u> – the people don't understand it. Don't let Neville speak when the door is taken off its hinges – he <u>prevents the audience from seeing the door disappear</u> – Let him look at the door – say "Did I hear something <u>outside</u>?" and wait, looking at the door. <u>Then</u> the people will look at the door – and that admirable scene will be heightened. N.B. Mr Ashley must not wear a chimney pot hat on a country excursion – don't let him try to look as if he had been snowed on. "Suppose" the snow, unless you can be <u>sure</u> of having it well done.

Act IV

Don't let Shifty Dick stand waiting to be caught. Out with his marriage speech – don't let him appear until Neville has come on, and Ashley has taunted him. Then let Shifty Dick be brought on to be identified by living evidence as well as photographic evidence – in his clergyman's clothes – supposed to have been arrested as he was leaving the vestry to join the wedding party. "Is this Shifty Dick?" – "Yes!" – Hooray! and on with the handcuffs.

Act III

I find myself with less vivid recollections of this act than of the others. An excellent scene with Grotait and the fulminating box is before me vividly – and the blown-up mill I remember. But no more. Are there bits that might come out here? I suspect there are.

1

<u>Mr</u> Cheatham must be made to <u>speak up.</u> Down with that damned "Prompter's Box" advertisement over the door – and up with the old church, and the fight, in its place.

Advertise more largely in Times and Daily Telegraph and Standard.

I see no advertisement in the Echo – an immense circulation. Rectify this.

A big Poster of the old church on all the prominent boardings.

2

All these things I would have called and <u>said</u> – but my miserable book <u>won't</u> get finished. I must stay at home and work. So I send Mrs Graves with this. Between 3 and 4, if you are this way, you will find me. After 4 I go out – and then dine at Highgate. Lehmann has come back.

Once more I congratulate you on this piece. All depends now on judicious cutting and judicious management. If there is anything I can do, command me.

Yrs ever | WC

Notes

1. WC puts a line across his page in his letter written "after the opening night of" Reade's *"Free Labour*, the dramatic adaptation of *Put Yourself in His Place*, staged at the Adelphi" (Clareson, p. 118).
2. WC puts a line across his page.

To William Tindell, 10 June [1870]
MS: Glasgow

90, Gloucester Place, | Portman Square. W. | 10th June

Summary:
"I finished 'Man and Wife' yesterday – fell asleep from sheer fatigue – and was awakened to hear the news of Dickens's death."

To William Tindell, 16 June 1870
MS: Glasgow

90, Gloucester Place, | Portman Square. W. | 16th June 1870 | 5.30 p.m.

Summary:
The day of Dickens's Funeral was a "lost day" to him. He is backward with the proof for the book. Savill & Edwards don't print as correctly from printed copy, as Petter & Galpin's did from MSS. At present, he has got no part of Vol. 3 in proof and has the greater part of Vol. 2 still to "read". The last two weekly parts of the story are not yet corrected at press at Petter & Galpin's. What happens to his copyright if they cannot get ready by the 27th? Would it not be well to bind up a set of proofs – and enter that at Stationers' Hall? Forgive an incoherent letter – he is so "fagged".

To Frederick Lehmann, 20 June 1870
MS: Princeton

90, Gloucester Place | Portman Square | Monday 20 June

My dear Fred,

My telegram will have told you that I have unluckily accepted a dinner-engagement for tomorrow evening. I shall be obliged to leave early, and return to the proofs of <u>Man</u> <u>and</u> <u>Wife</u>. It is published next Monday. I have dedicated it to you and the Padrona – and you shall have an early copy.

I am so utterly worn out, with all I have gone through – and Beard is so utterly worn out too – that we propose going to Antwerp on Thursday next – simply for the voyage – and returning by Sunday's boat. If anything stops this arrangement, I will ask for the hospitality of Woodlands[1] <u>this</u> <u>week</u>. If we go – <u>then</u> I will ask for it next week. I long to see you and the Padrona again – but it has been impossible to manage it, while the printers were waiting for me.

Love to all at Woodlands. I will write again.

Yours ever, | WC

I am so weak, I can hardly write even a note.

Note

1. The Lehmanns' home.

To Frederick Lehmann, 22 June 1870
MS: Princeton

90, Gloucester Place | Portman Square | Wednesday | 22nd June

My dear Fred,

Antwerp is put off till next week. Are you at Woodlands or in town? If you are at Woodlands, send me a telegram to say if I can be taken in. I am quite worn out and want a little rest badly. Tell the Padrona, with my love, that I dedicate Sunday to Woodlands at any rate. The question is, whether I [can: erased] may stay a day or two <u>before</u> Sunday or <u>after</u>. Whichever is most convenient to <u>you</u> will do for <u>me</u>.

Yours ever, | WC

To William Tindell, 26 June [1870]
MS: Glasgow

Woodlands | Southwood Lane | Highgate | N.W. | [1] Sunday June 26th

My dear Tindell,

I shall be in town on Tuesday, and I will call in Essex Street to add the name of a new executor to my will, (in the place of Henry Bullar)[2] – and to hear any news you may then have relating to the sale – thus far – of "Man and Wife".

In the meantime, Mr Ellis is damaging the chances of the book by keeping its publication as profound a secret as he can. There was <u>no</u> advertisement in the Saturday Review for June 18th – I looked for it in vain. Also nothing in the Times and nothing in the Telegraph. How are the people to know that the book is ready? I am sorry to keep on bothering about this – but pray send word to Mr Ellis, on receipt of these lines to attend a little better to the advertising. He is losing the whole advantage of my name and position with novel-readers, by the manner in which he is neglecting the advertising, at the very time when the book stands in the utmost need of it. It is really serious. Pray stir him to do something at once.

Yours truly, | Wilkie Collins.

I will call on you at 3 o'clock on Tuesday. If that won't do, send a line to Gloucester Place to say what hour will do up to 5 p.m. on Tuesday.

Notes

1. Written on embossed printed paper from the home of his friends the Lehmanns to whom he dedicated *Man and Wife*.
2. WC's old friend the barrister who died in 1870.

To Charles Ward, 30 June [1870]
MS: PM

Woodlands | Southwood Lane | Highgate | N | 30th June

My dear Ward,

The first Edition (of a thousand copies) is all sold – and the orders for the second edition (of 500) are coming in rapidly. So the book is beginning well at any rate. It looks, at present, as if we should beat "<u>The Moonstone</u>".

(In haste) | Ever yours | W.C

To Dr Emil Lehmann,[1] 7 August 1870
MS: Princeton

90, Gloucester Place | Portman Square | London | Aug[th] 1870

Wise Doctor Lehmann,

Yesterday – Saturday – I sent you, by book-post, the three monthly parts of Cassell's Magazine for August.

Reports of disturbances of postal regularity at Hamburg, in consequence of this horrible war, made me hesitate at sending you the magazine this time. I find however, from your brother Frederick, that these reports are without foundation – and, on my return to London, I hasten to forward the magazine as usual. The publishers contrived to keep the final chapters of "Man and Wife" for publication in the September monthly part. So I shall have to send you three more copies of next month's issue – and then it will be done.

I am, like the rest of my countrymen, heartily on the German side in the War.[2] But what is to be said of the progress of humanity? Here are the nations still ready to slaughter each other, at the command of one miserable wretch whose interest it is to set them fighting! Is this the nineteenth century? or the ninth? Are we before the time of Christ or after? I begin to believe in only one civilising influence – the discovery one of these days, of a destructive agent so terrible that War shall mean <u>annihilation</u>, and men's fears shall force them to keep the peace.

Yours very truly, | Wilkie Collins

Please let me hear when you have received the number of the magazine.

Notes

1. Emil Lehmann (1829–1898), brother of Frederick, translator.
2. The Franco-Prussian War.

To Charles Ward, 2 September [1870]
MS: PM

90, Gloucester Place, | Portman Square. W. | Friday Sept. 2nd

Summary:
Is out of sorts again. "Dyspepsia and gout", he suspects. He must wait to see Beard before going away. Could he tell the hotel manager that his

"departure from London is post-poned for a few days" and he will give him three days' notice of arrival at the Granville Hotel. It is "damp and detestable in London". He works with "infernal pains in the inside ... not diarrhoea, but neuralgia", the "symptoms my poor mother used to complain of". He goes to Woodlands if well enough on Saturday & Sunday.

To Hunter Rose & Co.,[1] 10 September 1870
MS: Princeton

90, Gloucester Place, | Portman Square. W. | London |
Saturday Sept 10th 1870

Summary:
Thanks them for copies of the Canadian Edition of "Man and Wife" and for the Certificate of copyright. They have made a "thoroughly readable Volume" ... "printed in excellent type". Hopes the sale is proceeding to his satisfaction. "Here, bookselling is beginning to suffer, through all-absorbing interest excited by the War."

Note

1. WC's Canadian publishers in Toronto: see Gasson.

To George Smith, 28 March 1871
MS: NLS

90, Gloucester Place, Portman Square, W. | 28th March 1871

Summary:
WC agrees to Smith reprinting of *The Woman in White* and to cheap editions of *The Moonstone* and *Man and Wife*. They may be able to double the circulating literary sale at least. "'The Moonstone' reached two thousand in the three volume form – and 'Man and Wife' bade fair to beat it, when the war got between me and my readers." It will help if they can have a new binding. He adds: "The real hero of 'The Moonstone', for instance, is a yellow diamond of great size. If the Diamond could appear on the cover – without serious increase of the binding expenses – it would help to make the book visible on the stalls."

To François Joseph Régnier,[1] 7 June 1871

MS: University of Illinois, Urbana

90, Gloucester Place, | Portman Square. W. | 7th June 1871

My dear Regnier,

While the full measure of calamity has fallen on unhappy France, I have had my little Trumpery share of trouble. Another attack of rheumatic gout has confined me to my bed – blinded one of my eyes, for a time – and caused me great suffering. I am now getting better again – and my first thought is anxiety about you and your family. Send me a line to reassure me about you and Madame Regnier and your children. Say where you have been, and how you have all got through the trials that have fallen on your unfortunate country. I direct this letter to your house in the Chausse [d'Auton] – not knowing where else to address you. The last news I had of you was the news of your retirement from the stage.

I purposely say nothing about the state of things in Paris. It is beyond all words. I don't despair of France. I wait, in silence.

Write as soon as you can – and let me hear what your plans are for this future. I own I was sorry – when I heard that you had really left the stage, in the prime of your rare powers. But it is done. And you know best.

Give my affectionate remembrances to the members of your family and believe me, my dear friend,

Affectionately yours, | Wilkie Collins

Note

1. François Joseph Régnier (1807–1885), leading French comedian at the Théatre Français: WC's dedicatee of *The Law and the Lady* (1875): see Gasson.

To William Tindell, 8 August 1871

MS: Glasgow

90, Gloucester Place, | Portman Square. W. | 8th Augt 1871

Summary:

Rearranges visit. "[C]annot find the Codicil appointing Lehmann exor". The only codicil he can find relates to a "sum in ready money to be left to C[aroline] and M[artha][1] on my death" – and is "incorporated in my last executed Will".

Note

1. i.e., Caroline Graves and Martha Rudd.

To Hunter Rose & Co., 12 August 1871

MS: Princeton

90, Gloucester Place, | Portman Square. W. | London |
August 12th 1871

Dear Sirs,

I beg to thank you for your letter, and for the extracts from the Canadian newspaper relating to copyright in the colony. I have read the extracts with great interest.

I return the two forms filled in, signed, and witnessed. I also send to you, on the next leaf, the analysis of the story.

Having had the pleasure of personally seeing Mr Hunter and learning the address, I have been enabled to send the advance proofs of "Poor Miss Finch" direct to Mr Desbarats.[1] I hope to continue the transmission of proofs regularly every week.

Believe me, Dear Sirs, | Faithfully yours, | Wilkie Collins Messrs Hunter, Rose & Co.

Analysis of the story called: – "Poor Miss Finch".

The object of the story is to show the modifying effect of the circumstances on the calamities that afflict human life.

The calamity selected for illustration is Blindness. The person afflicted is a young girl.

She is first presented to the reader as having been blind from infancy. She is afterwards operated on, and recovers her sight for a time. The interval past, her sight fails her again, and her blindness is renewed for life.

The incidents of the story are so managed as to make the happiest days of the girl's life – <u>not</u> the days when she enjoys the brief restoration of her sight – but the after-days when the operation has failed, and the blindness has permanently returned. The story leaves her, at its end – by a perfectly natural succession of circumstances – happier, under the return of her calamity, than she had been at the earlier period of her life when her sight was restored for a time.

Note

1. One of Hunter Rose & Co.'s employees.

To George Smith, 17 October 1871
MS: NYPL (Berg)

90, Gloucester Place, | Portman Square W. | 17 October 1871

Summary:
Concerns details of negotiations with Galpin of Cassell, Petter and Galpin for publication of his "novels in penny illustrated Parts – beginning with 'The Woman In White'". Places detailed proposal before Smith.

To Frederick Lehmann, 18 October 1871
MS: Texas: Coleman

90, Gloucester Place, | Portman Square. W. | 18 October 1871

Summary:
"My best thanks for another tin of those heavenly biscuits. Life (in spite of applications by every post for free admissions to the Olympic Theatre[1]) now becomes once more endurable being associated with Boston Crackers."

Note

1. For the dramatic version of *The Woman In White*, which opened 9 October 1871 and ran for 19 weeks.

To Charles Reade, 20 October 1871
MS: Mrs Juliet Noel (née Reade)

90, Gloucester Place, | Portman Square. W. | 20th Oct 1871

Summary:
The "business", the dramatization of <u>The Woman in White</u> "promises famously". "Receipts of the first week £475 – which gives a good profit to those interested at starting. This week's returns, steadily larger every day than last week's." Assures Reade that a private box awaits him, especially early in the week. WC reminds Reade:
"A new stock of <u>Moselle</u> is at this moment being put into the cellar. Come and draw a cork between 3 & 4, as soon as you get to town – or at 7.30, when there is dinner.

The two Carolines send you their love, and join in asking you not to forget No. 90. I am all in arrears with 'Poor Miss F.' – in consequence of these dramatic doings. You don't say a word about your play. Another reason for tasting the Moselle. I want to hear about it."

To George Smith, 23 October 1871
MS: NYPL (Berg)

90, Gloucester Place, | Portman Square. W. |[1] 23rd Oct: 1871

My dear Smith,

I beg to thank you for a cheque for £40 – for a new issue of 4000 copies of "The Woman In White" now about to be put to press.

Let me also say that I am much obliged to you for the advice which you kindly [gave] me as to the pirated editions in parts, and for the friendly manner in which you leave the decision in my hands. I must take a day or two to consider; but my present feeling is – reluctance to go with the speculation at all unless I see a fair prospect of y<u>our</u> benefitting by it too.

I ought to say that I stipulated with Messrs Cassell, when they first negotiated with me for the issue in parts, to have the sole right of deciding whether The Woman In White should be followed by the other books. The objection on their side to this, was – that they proposed to spend a large sum of money, at the outset, in advertising and canvassing, with a view to a return on the <u>other</u> books as well as "The Woman In White". They suggested a margin of profit to be agreed to on both sides as representing [success] – and on this, if I remember rightly, the negotiation broke down.

My own impression is that a <u>very few</u> years more will see a revolution in the publishing trade for which most of the publishers are unprepared – and that I shall do wisely to leave my interests entirely in your hands, as things are. I don't believe in the gigantic monopolies, which cripple <u>free</u> trade, lasting much longer. The Mudie monopoly and the W.H. Smith monopoly are anomalies in a commercial country.

Vy truly yours | Wilkie Collins

George Smith Eqr
P.S.
Of course you shall hear how I finally decide. I am a good deal [pressured] just now with other proposals for the book-issue of "Poor Miss Finch".

Note

1. Above the Gothic printed address WC writes: "<u>Private</u>".

To George Smith, 7 November 1871
MS: NYPL (Berg)

90, Gloucester Place, | Portman Square. W. | 7th November 1871

Summary:
Thanks him for cheque for £33.6.8 – being Royalty on a new issue of 2000 copies of "Hide and Seek" and 2000 copies of "The Dead Secret". Delighted he had a pleasant evening at the Olympic and that he thinks so well of the Play. "Man and Wife" is to come out next (as the conclusion of the "run" of "Caste")[1] at The Prince of Wales's Theatre – probably next spring. "Pleasant to find the books doing better. How the people get at them, and the chaos of rubbish" he sees on the "Railway Book Stalls is a mystery to me". He supposes "Natural Selection" has something to do with it.

Note

1. T.W. Robertson's *Caste*.

To William Tindell, 28 December 1871
MS: Glasgow

90, Gloucester Place, | Portman Square. W | 128th Decr 1871

Summary:
Instructs Tindell to serve the tenants of his "stables with a notice to quit". Asks for marriage licence information for the writing of *Poor Miss Finch*.

To William Tindell, 30 January 1872
MS: Glasgow

90, Gloucester Place, | Portman Square. W. | 30th Janry 1872 | 3:45. P.M.

My dear Tindell,
    Up to this time, the rent for the stables has not reached me – though Mr Binder told Miss Graves, he would send it yesterday – Monday.
    There are a carriage and a horse or horses in the stables. So distrain away! But, better let the "officers" apply here first to know if the money has been received between this and then. Do you send notice of the distraint, beforehand? I suppose so.

As to the copyright – how do I know how long I am going to live? I can only state the 42 years from publication as the duration of my copyrights – if I am called on (as I am) to state when my copyrights expire. You don't tell me whether I am right or wrong in doing this. And what else to do I don't know. Oh the English Law!

Yours ever | W C

To C.S. Carter,[1] 27 February 1872
MS: Private Possession

90, Gloucester Place, | Portman Square. W. | London |
February 27th 1872

Dear Sir,

Pray accept my apologies for this late answer to your kind letter. I have been away from London – and I have had no earlier opportunity of writing to you than this.

There is no hope of my being able to make my appearance in The United States during the present year. The year 1871 has been a year of severe hard work for me. Engagements which I had hoped to separate by sufficient intervals of time, claimed fulfilment one close as another. "Poor Miss Finch" – the Christmas Story "Miss or Mrs?" – and my dramatic version of "The Woman In White" (played at the Olympic Theatre here), have all come within the compass of one year's work. The result is that I must have a long rest. I am thoroughly exhausted for the present. But there is this good sign for the future – that I have, thus far, escaped without any renewed attack of rheumatic gout.

I have to add, on the hopeful side of the question, that I am refusing all the proposals made to me for writing a new novel – and that I am determined during the whole of the present year, to undertake only such literary work as will not fatigue me. All that rest and freedom from literary responsibility can do to fit me physically for a visit to America – they <u>shall</u> do. My pen may not remain altogether idle – for my pen represents, in my case, the habit of a life. But I am positively resolved not to saddle myself with the heavy strain of another <u>long</u> story, for a year to come at least.

I have now written enough to show you, I hope, that I am seriously bent on doing all that I can to train myself successfully for a visit to The United States. Personally, I am heartily sorry to miss the opportunity which your letter offers to me. But there is no help for it. I must be stronger than I am now before I take the serious responsibility of meeting my American readers in public.

With kindest regards, | Believe me My dear Sir |
Vy truly yours | Wilkie Collins

C.S. Carter Esqre

Note

1. C.S. Carter, American magazine editor.

To William Tindell, 10 May 1872
MS: Glasgow

90, Gloucester Place, | Portman Square. W. | 10th May 1872

My dear Tindell
  Case. 6/8
  1. "Miss or Mrs" published Decr 13th 1871 in "The Graphic" Newspaper.
  2. Reprinted – 13th June 1872 – in book-form by Tauchnitz of Leipzig for Continental Circulation only – but introduced into this Country, by purchasers returning from their travels.
  3. Copyright, and sole right of republication conceded to me by the Proprietors of The Graphic.
  4. No use made by me of these concessions, so far as England is concerned – at the date of June 13th 1872. Separate publication in book form put off here, until I can write (and add) another story to "Miss or Mrs" – and so make two volumes instead of one.
  5. Does Tauchnitz's Reprint, jeopardise my copyright? or does the prior publication here in the newspaper assert it sufficiently?
  6. If my copyright be not endangered, do you see any other objections to Tauchnitz reprinting the story in book-form at Leipzig before I reprint in London?

=

Vining[1] gives up the Tour. You will have the agreements to burn in a few days – the performances under his direction not having even produced money enough to pay for the drawing of the agreements!!! Pleasant – isn't it?

Yours ever | W C

I have been a mass of gout – still ailing. Not able to go to Paris.

Note

1. George J. Vining (1824–1875), actor-manager, took *The Woman in White* on an unsuccessful provincial tour: see Gasson.

To William Tindell, 18 June [1872]
MS: Glasgow

90, Gloucester Place, | Portman Square. W. | 18th June

My dear Tindell,
Have y<u>ou</u> got the agreement with Miss Aytoun for my Stables? I have let them to another "Miss" – through Mr Binder.
Mr B. offers to prepare the agreement for a guinea but I think it safer (having a woman to deal with) to stick to your agreement. Can you get me two copies made – leaving blanks for the lady's name and address, for Mr Binder to fill up?
I have looked vainly for the agreement among my papers.

Yours, drenched in perspiration, with gout in every toe, | W.C

I have been in great trouble. My poor little eldest child has broken her leg. All going on well <u>now</u>.

To George Smith, 24 September 1872
MS: NYPL (Berg)

90, Gloucester Place, | Portman Square. W. |[1] September 24 th 1872

My dear Smith,
Here I am – Getting better in the brisk sea air (though it <u>is</u> raining hard today).
I can use my good eye for a few hours now – and I hasten at once to write to you about "Poor Miss Finch".
The present idiotic system of publication in 3 Vols (there is no other word for it) has left me no honourable alternative but to place the first one volume edition in the hands of the publisher of the three volume edition of "Miss Finch" – Mr George Bentley.
Mr Bentley purchased of me the right of issuing an edition of the book – a large one, in these wretched times – relying of course on the Libraries to

take <u>his</u> issue of the story, in place of Cassell's issue in the shape of the volume of their Magazine in which the story appeared periodically. Mudie stood by us. But the Railway Circulating Library kept their subscribers waiting until Cassell's miscellaneous Volume came out – and then bought four hundred copies of it, and served my story out to their customers in th<u>a</u>t form. The subscribers submitted – and the result is that Mr Bentley has not made a halfpenny by his bargain. [heavily erased words] Four hundred copies more sold of the book would have nearly exhausted the edition.

They are now on hand, and Mr Bentley refuses to let me return to him any of the purchase money. Under these circumstances, I felt bound to offer him the chance of making something out of the ne<u>x</u>t edition – reserving for <u>our</u> uniform series, the right of issuing the two shilling Edition, after allowing Mr Bentley a term for the sale of the 6/- Edition in one volume which he now proposes to publish.

In this way, the 2/- "Miss Finch" will I hope follow the 2/- "Moonstone" and "Man and Wife". I was very sorry to break our series even for a time only and in one form only – but I felt that something was due (after what had happened) from me to Mr Bentley.

This explanation is of course <u>for your eye only</u>. I hope you will feel as I do in the matter. <u>Commercial</u>ly, it is of course impossible to blame the Railway Library Company. They buy in the cheapest market. The public (of Subscribers) has no remedy and <u>I</u> have no remedy.

Excuse this long letter. I wanted to make my position quite plain to you.

Yours truly | Wilkie Collins

George Smith Eqre

Note

1. Above the printed address WC writes "Private" (doubly underlined) and "14 Nelson Crescent | Ramsgate".

To William Tindell, 27 September [1872]
MS: Glasgow

14, Nelson Crescent | Ramsgate | Sept 27th

My dear Tindell,

At last, I send you my new tenant's agreement for the Stables – to be stamped as you suggest.

I have been suffering the tortures of the damned with another attack of gout in the eye. A week here has done wonders for me – I can use my pen again as you see.

I shall stay here some weeks more to get strong again. How are you? Is your holiday over? or is there a chance of seeing you at Ramsgate? I am comfortably established here with my womankind.

Send me a line

Yours ever | W.C

To Harper & Brothers, 1 November 1872
MS: PM

90, Gloucester Place | Portman Square | London | November 1st 1872

Dear Sir,

In sending you the Duplicate of the Fourth Monthly Part of "The New Magdalen" I must also send you – what may, or may n<u>o</u>t, prove to be a welcome piece of news. I find that I cannot possibly finish the Story, so as to do it any sort of justice, in Six Monthly Parts. With severe compression I hope and believe I can complete it in Eight[1] monthly Parts, (8). Two Parts you have already published in your old volume. Six more Parts (as I calculate) will just run to the end of your new Volume.

Here, the first chapters of the story have produced such a strongly favourable impression that the proprietor of "Temple Bar" is not only willing, but glad, to widen my limits. But I cannot tell what the reception of my work has been, so far, in the United States. Your present political excitement is unfavourable to literature – and the story may (commercially-speaking) not be worth lengthening on the present terms. In this event, I hasten to say that I am quite ready to consider myself – <u>as to terms</u> – bound by my undertaking to occupy no more than six monthly parts. As to the other question of sp<u>ace</u> I regret that I should have unintentionally misled you, <u>as</u> well as myself. But, enclosed with this, you have the Fourth Monthly Part, and I am now barely half way through the story. I cannot spoil it, and I cannot finish it (without spoiling it) in two more monthly parts. There is the case, frankly stated. I heartily wish I could have been more accurate in my estimate. But (alas!) a work of fiction is not a work of machinery.

Believe me dear Sirs | Always Faithfully yours | Wilkie Collins

Messrs Harper & Brothers.

Note

1. WC underlines "Eight" once and the letters "igh" twice.

To John Forster, 16 November 1872
MS: Princeton, Parrish.[1]

90, Gloucester Place, | Portman Square. W. | 16th Novr 1872

My dear Forster

For three days past I have been trying – and vainly trying – to get to Palace Gate House, and to thank you as heartily (as I thank you now) for the new volume of the Life. I am devouring you at night (the only time when I have any "leisure hours" at my disposal) – and I am more interested than any words of mine can tell in your admirable narrative – to my mind, the most masterly biographical story you have ever told. More of this when I <u>do</u> contrive to see you. In the meantime, I congratulate you with all my heart.

Ramsgate cured me. I was there five weeks – and felt better and better every day.

How are <u>you</u>? I have heard a report (which I hope and trust is as false as most reports) that you are suffering again. Pray send me a line to say what the truth is; and whether you are settled in London for the present.

I know you will be glad to hear that my story ("The New Magdalen") is, so far, a great success. Will you wait till it is done? Or shall I send you the proofs, when the number I am now writing is in type – say in a week's time?

Pray give my Kindest regards to Mrs Forster and believe me

Ever affectionately yours | Wilkie Collins

Note

1. Laid into first volume of *The New Magdalen* (1873): Parrish, pp. 89–90. The first volume of Forster's *Life of Dickens* was published in 1872. WC's annotated copy sold at 20 January 1890 Puttick and Simpson auction of his books (lot 63).

To Emanuel Oscar Menachem Deutsch,[1] 20 November 1872
MS: British Library

90, Gloucester Place, | Portman Square. W. | 20th Nov 1872

My dear Deutsch,

Here is a petition, from a bewildered literary brother. My poor father paid (I think) £90 a year for my education. I learnt Latin & Greek – and nothing else, because nothing else was taught, in my time. To this day, I don't know my English Grammar – and, what I lament much more, I don't know German.

A German lady (personally a stranger to me) has resolved to translate my next book. She has found the publisher, and she sends me a specimen of his abilities – and I can't read a word of it!

Will you kindly look it over, when you have ten minutes to spare – and tell me if it is [a] fairly good work? The lady has translated as her specimens the first two or three chapters of "Poor Miss Finch". I will send you the English with the German – if you will do me this kindness, and if you will tell me where to direct to you, at your private address?

Believe me | Vy truly yours | Wilkie Collins

I ought to add that I have decided on no longer employing the German translator who has hitherto taken my books in hand. So if this lady can only do fairly well, it will be a relief to me to settle the matter at once. Don't trouble to read more than two or three pages.

Note

1. Emanuel Oscar Menahem Deutsch (1829–1873: *DNB*): Rabbinic and Talmud scholar employed by the British Museum.

To Marie Effie Bancroft,[1] 28 November 1872
MS: Present whereabouts unknown. Text: *The Bancrofts: Recollections of Sixty Years. Marie and Squire Bancroft* (1909), p. 396.

[90, Gloucester Place, Portman Square, W.] | 28 November, 1872

My Dear Mrs Bancroft,

I am sincerely sensible of the kindness which has prompted the compliment you pay me. Bancroft's note tells me nothing about your health – so I gladly assume that the Brighton air is proving itself to be the best of all doctors. It either kills or cures. In my case, it kills. I can neither eat, drink, sleep nor walk at Brighton. Cold perspirations envelope me from head to foot, and Death whispers to me: "Wilkie! get out of this, or much as I should regret it, just as you are beginning to write for the most popular theatre in London, I shall be obliged to gather you in the flower of your youth!"

Believe me, dear Mrs Bancroft, | Always truly yours, | Wilkie Collins

Note

1. Marie Effie, Lady Bancroft, née Wilton (1839–1921: *DNB*), wife of Sir Squire Bancroft (1841–1926), joint actor-managers of the Prince of Wales Theatre: see Gasson.

To Harper & Brothers, 30 November 1872
MS: PM

90, Gloucester Place | Portman Square | London |
Saturday Novr 30th 1872

Dear Sir,

A line to thank you for your kind letter of the 15th which has just reached me. It is needless to say that I am very much pleased to hear of the popularity of the Story, and that I am very sensible of the liberal construction on your side, of the terms of our agreement. The pecuniary arrangement between us shall be kept strictly secret.

I will speak to Mr Bentley on the subject of the republication, and I may answer for him that he, like me, will readily do his best to meet your views. It is not possible for me to say whether the Story will stretch into the June Monthly Part. The Fifth Monthly Part (February), of which I send herewith a duplicate, is a long "Part" owing to the literary necessities of this part of the story. But the remaining "Parts" – now that I have reached my turning-point in the work will be shorter than Number Five. And if I <u>can</u> run to 9 numbers (without damaging the effect of the story) I will.

The Pirated Edition of 'Poor Miss Finch' has reached me. How much longer will the great American nation lag behind Europe in the march of literary civilisation? <u>Turkey</u> concedes international copyright – and The United States refuses it! What an anomaly!!!

Very truly yours | Wilkie Collins

Messrs Harper & Brothers

To George Smith, 5 December 1872
MS: NYPL (Berg)

90, Gloucester Place | Portman Square | W | 5th Decr 1872

My dear Smith,

I think your idea about "Man and Wife" is an admirable one. B<u>ut</u> I am sorely unwilling to drop down at once to that miserable 2/- price, which leaves us such a small margin of profit. Could we not "split the difference" and try 3/6 – with a <u>pictorial cover by all means</u> – the more striking the better.

3/6 might justify a little extra advertising – besides the advertisement of the performance. But it is even a question (with <u>me</u>) whether 3/6 is enough. I may certainly, without undue arrogance, consider myself to be a rather better novelist, with a rather wider reputation than Mrs Henry Wood.[1] I happen to know that she averages a thousand a year profit to herself by the sale of her novels [erasure] – <u>all</u> in six shillings a volume. I mention this, in support of my notion that it is undesirable to lower my price in the case of <u>Man and Wife</u> and The <u>Moonstone</u>. It appears – where a writer is really popular with readers – to be simply a question of making the book known by means of one or two reliable travellers working in combination with the retail booksellers in town and country. Let me hear what you think about this question of price. The performance of the piece will advertise us – and "The New Magdalen" will help. This last story is liked so much here and in America that the publishers (who pay me by <u>quantity</u>) are urging me to lengthen the story! There could not be a better time for a new edition. The one consideration is – <u>price</u>.

Yours ever | W.C

Excuse blots and haste! I am <u>so</u> hard at work

Note

1. WC may well be thinking of Mrs Henry Wood's (1814–1887) best-seller, *East Lynne* (1861) "By 1876 Bentley had printed 65,000 copies", and she received an unusually high price from Bentley for the copyright (Sutherland p. 678).

To George Smith, 11 December 1872
MS: NLS

90, Gloucester Place, | Portman Square. W. | 11th Dec 1872

My dear Smith,

I abandon the 3/6 proposal – in deference to your opinion.

But I am too thoroughly discouraged by the pecuniary results of the sale at 2/- to feel disposed to try it again. Let us stop at the 5/- price. If the dramatic "Man and Wife" succeeds, and causes any demand for the book, it will be easy to print a few hundred copies from the plates.

Sooner or later, I shall find some new way of getting at the public. In the meantime, the fatal mistake of lowering the price of "The Woman In

White"[1] seems to **me** to be a warning "not to do it again" – <u>unless</u> there is an infinitely better market for us than the market we have now.

I will inquire about the working of Mrs Wood's copyrights. My information as to her profits rests on excellent authority. It would be an infinite relief to me to discover that I am mistaken in my estimate of that estimable lady's income! When I first heard of it it struck me speechless – and I have been partially paralysed ever since.

Yours always truly | W.C

Note

1. *The Woman in White*, published in 3 vols by Sampson Low. Smith regretted that he missed the opportunity to publish the successful novel. He subsequently published one-volume editions of the novel.

To George Smith, 12 December 1872
MS: NLS

90, Gloucester Place, Portman Square. W. | 12th Decr 1872

My dear Smith,

I have been making inquiries, in various quarters, about the sales of 5/- and 6/- volumes of novels. It is [indecipherable word] to trouble you with the general length. I will cite one case only – which seems to suggest that we might do something yet with the 5/- "Man and Wife".

<u>A Novel by a Lady</u> – who is, as to the public, quite an unknown writer – has been lately republished at <u>six shillings</u>. The sale, up to the present time, has been <u>four thousand copies</u>.

Inquiring as to <u>how</u> this sale has been obtained informs me that the book has been "worked" by two "travellers", taking it to the retail booksellers all over England, and making certain allowances to encourage those booksellers to speculate in the work.

I am not allowed to mention names – but I am absolutely certain of my facts.

Unknown writer. 4000 copies.

(I think this was the edition we printed – was it not?)

W.C. 2400

Yours ever | W.C

To Harper & Brothers, 28 December 1872
MS: PM

90, Gloucester Place | Portman Square | London |
Saturday | December 28th 1872

Messrs Harper & Brothers: –
Dear Sir,

I send to you (under another cover) by this mail the Sixth Monthly Part of "The new Magdalen" – being the number for March 1873.

Since I last wrote, I have spoken to Mr Bentley, on the subject of the republication here, in book-form – that is to say, in two Volumes [post] 8vo, for distribution among the Circulating Libraries. Mr Bentley's opinion is, that if we do not publish "The New Magdalen" <u>at least</u> five or six weeks in advance of its completion in the Magazine, we shall probably suffer a loss of several hundred pounds. In plainer words, the "Libraries" will cut out the Magazine Pages – bind them up – and issue them as the book. In deference to your wishes, we deferred the republication of "Poor Miss Finch" – making the date of issue a fortnight later than we had arranged. Result: – a large library Company kept the public waiting till the Magazine Volume, in which the story originally appeared, was published, and bought 400 copies of <u>that</u>, at 5/6 a copy, instead of 400 copies of [<u>our</u>] edition (selling at 18/- a copy). The loss here, again, is easily calculated.

The only remedy for this state of things is – of course – to publish the book-issue of the story at a cheaper rate, and address a larger number of customers. But the <u>machinery</u> for this sort of sale is not in working order, in England, as yet – and publishers are afraid to try the change.

Under these circumstances – with y<u>our</u> interests pointing one way, and <u>my</u> interests pointing the other – Mr Bentley and I have thought of a compromise.

What do you say to publishing the <u>last</u> monthly part of the story (in your Magazine), <u>one month in advance</u> of our periodical publications here? In other words, to publishing the last Part, and the last Part <u>but one together</u>?[1] Add the ten or eleven days, consumed in the Voyage across the Atlantic to the advance thus obtained, and your conclusion in Harper's Magazine, will appear simultaneously with our book-publication here – enabling you to make your own arrangements for y<u>our</u> re-issue in book-form (which, however, must not be <u>in advance</u> of the English re-issue, or my copyright may be damaged).

Will you consider this proposal, and let me hear what you think? Your object – as I understand it – is to prevent my b<u>ook</u> – publication from reaching New York before yo<u>ur</u> <u>period</u>ical publication is completed. The plan I propose would exactly meet this view, so far as I can see.

If there are objections which I have overlooked, I can only say that I shall be glad to give my best attention to any suggestions on your part, which may enable us to meet the difficulty in which the absurd English system of publication now places on us.

Believe me, Dear Sir, | Faithfully yours | Wilkie Collins

P.S. | It may be desirable to remember, in this connection, [the] dramatic version of the story must appear in the U.S. in advance of the novel – or the <u>theatrical</u> pirates will [pinch it].²

Notes

1. WC underlines twice "eth" of "together".
2. Bentley published *The New Magdalen*, in 2 vols, 17 May 1873. The stage version was first produced on 19 May 1873 at the Olympic Theatre and published by WC in a single volume in 1873.

To John Hollingshead,¹ 25 February 1873
MS: Huntington

90, Gloucester Place, | Portman Square, W. | 25ᵗʰ February 18[7]3

My dear Hollingshead,

My best thanks for your kind note, and for your friendly support.

Yes! I read the trial – with the conviction that the current state of the law is a disgrace to the nation as well as an infamous wrong inflicted on the writer. Whatever I <u>can</u> do to help to set the matter right, I <u>will</u> do – and I feel personally indebted to Mr Toole for bringing the questions to a trial. The obstacle against us lies in the barbarous indifference of the House of Commons where the interests of Literature and Art are concerned. The remedy rests with the Commons. If Disraeli's books were dramatic enough to be stolen for the stage I should recommend (quite seriously) an immediate adaptation of one of them, without asking his leave. If <u>he</u> could be made to move in this matter, something might be done. I am to see Tindell on the subject on Thursday. My "Poor Miss Finch" has been dramatised (without asking my permission) by some obscure idiot in the country.

I have been asked to dramatise it, and I have refused, because my experience in the matter tells me that the book is eminently <u>unfit</u> for stage performances. What I dare not do with my own work, another man (unknown in Literature) is perfectly free to do, against my will, and (if he can get his rubbish played) to the prejudice of my novel and my reputation. This is surely "a case in point".

I shall look anxiously at the result of the new trial. Nothing can be done until we are <u>sure</u> of the present state of the law.

Yours ever | W.C.

You know the case of Mrs Henry Wood's "East Lynne"? <u>I believe</u>, she has never received sixpence of the money which the piece has made.

Note

1. John Hollingshead (1827–1904), theatrical manager and journalist, on 21 December 1868 opened the newly built Gaiety Theatre in the Strand. "A theatre and restaurant were now first combined in London in one building" and there were "many innovations, including the system of 'No fees', and inaugurated continual Wednesday and Saturday matinees" (*DNB*).

To William Holman Hunt, 11 March [1873]
MS: Huntington

90, Gloucester Place, | Portman Square. W. | 11th March

My dear Holman,

I was very sorry to miss you [erased word] the other night, and [erased word] I am vexed at not having been able to propose an evening before this for your visit with Mr Fergusson.[1] But a recent decision in a Court of Law has declared that anybody may dramatise any of my novels or of any other man's novels, without the leave of the author. Two plays on "Man and Wife" are all ready to compete with <u>my</u> play in the country theatres – and I am obliged to make arrangements with the Bancrofts to meet this competition <u>instantly</u> – or I shall get nothing by "Man and Wife", <u>as performed in the country theatres.</u>

Add to this that I am obliged to dramatise the novel I am now writing,[2] <u>against time</u> – and bring it out [erased word] forthwith in London – or the thieves will take <u>that</u> from me also. The result is that I must ask your indulgence and Mr Fergusson's – for I really don't know when I have an hour to myself in this whirl of work and worry. I only sustain it by going to bed – when I <u>am</u> at home – at nine o'clock to rest my brains.

Yours aff^{ly} | W.C

You shall hear the moment I am at leisure.

Notes

1. Unidentified.
2. Probably *The New Magdalen* serialized in *Temple Bar*, January–December 1872, published in two volumes by Bentley, 20 May 1873 and opened at the Olympic Theatre 19 May 1873.

To W.P. Frith, 10 April 1873

MS: National Art Library, Victoria and Albert Museum, London.

90, Gloucester Place, | Portman Square. W. | 10th April 1873

My dear Frith

I cannot let such an old and dear friend as you are see the first announcement of the calamity that has fallen on me in the newspapers. After only a few days' illness, my brother died last night at half past eight o'clock. He was without pain and without consciousness. The medical theory of the death is cancerous tumour in the stomach. I know that you and yours will feel for me. With my love.

Yours affly, | Wilkie Collins.

To George Smith, 10 April 1873

MS: NYPL (Berg)

90, Gloucester Place, | Portman Square. W. | 10th April 1873

My dear Smith,

I am sure you will be sorry to hear the sad news which this letter must contain. My brother's sufferings are at an end. After a few days only of serious illness, he died last night – without pain and without consciousness.

If you can spare room for a paragraph in the Pall Mall Gazette, I send you the bare particulars of his career on the next leaf.

Yours truly | Wilkie Collins

George Smith Esq
Charles Allston Collins

=

Died April 9th 1873, aged 45. Disease, internal tumour.

Contributor to "All The Year Round" and to other Periodical Journals. Author of "A Cruise Upon Wheels", "The Eye-Witness", "The Bar-Sinister", and other works.

Was the second son of the late William Collins R.A. Began life as a painter, and exhibited pictures at the Royal Academy. Married the youngest daughter of the late Charles Dickens – who survives him.

To William Holman Hunt, 11 May 1873
MS: Huntington

90, Gloucester Place, | Portman Square, W. |[1] 11th May 1873

My dear Holman,

Thank you most heartily for your kind letter. The drawing shall take its place among my dearest pleasures. But let me, I beg of you hold it at your disposal when you return to England – for you too were his brother, if love makes brotherhood. In any case, I will leave it on record, in writing, that the drawing is to go to Cyril Benoni Hunt, when "life's idle business" has ended for me.

Yours always aff^{tly} | Wilkie Collins

To | Holman Hunt Esqre

Note

1. WC uses Gothic printed black-edged mourning paper.

To William Tindell, 18 July 1873
MS: Glasgow

90, Gloucester Place | Saturday July 18th 1873

My dear Tindell,

My place is taken in the Algeria for New York to sail on September 13th.

My will must be executed, and there is the insurance of Mrs Dawson's furniture[1] at 55 Marylebone Road.

Shall these things be settled before your holiday or after?

I am away to Paris tomorrow. Return at the end of the month. Yours to command in August. Will write you my address in Paris.

In haste | Ever yours | W C

Note

1. Mrs Dawson is Martha Rudd. WC became William Dawson, barrister at law, when with Martha.

To William Tindell, 21 July 1873

MS: Glasgow

Hotel des Bains | Boulogne Sur Mer | 21st July 1873

Summary:
"I go to Paris tomorrow." Further instructions regarding WC's American tour.

To William Tindell, 4 September 1873

MS: Glasgow

90, Gloucester Place, | Portman Square. W. | 4th September 1873

My dear Tindell,
   A short clause in the Will.
   A portrait in chalk of my brother Charles – taken immediately after his death by Holman Hunt, and presented to me, is to be returned to Hunt at my death. If Hunt is not living at the time, then the portrait is to go to Hunt's son (and only child) Cyril.

Yours ever | W.C.

To William Tindell, 12 September 1873

MS: Glasgow

90, Gloucester Place, | Portman Square. W. | 12th Sept 1873

My dear Tindell,
   I signed the Will yesterday. It appears to me to be exactly what I wished for – viz: – Half what I leave behind me to C E Graves and her daughter – and half to Martha Rudd and my two children. On the deaths of Mrs Graves and her daughter, (if they die first) then half to go to Martha Rudd and my

two children, [erased word] as surviving legatees. The other eventualities it is needless to mention here.

My man-servant (Edward [Grosvissier]) has not succeeded in getting a place – so I am obliged to give him a written character before I leave. He tells me that people require <u>verification of handwriting</u> in these cases – so I refer to "my Solicitors". He can speak to my writing and satisfy enquirers that the "character" is genuine.

My address at New York (City) will be Westminster Hotel. When I am away my letters will be forwarded.

I know you will, like a good fellow, give personal as well as professional advice to those whom I leave to the care of old friends like you – if they need it. Help them here and at Marylebone Road,[1] when they want help. and oblige your friend,

Wilkie Collins

I leave a sealed letter, in my strong box in the study – to assist my exors in case of need. If you think it better to have the box at your office, write to Caroline, and she will bring it to [erased word] Essex Street in a cab. I will write from New York if all goes well.

Note

1. Martha Dawson (née Rudd) was living at 55, Marylebone Road with her two daughters.

To Unknown Recipient, 14 September 1873
MS: Present whereabouts unknown. TL/copy. Text, Coleman

Steamship Algeria | Queenstown Harbour | 14 September 1873

We sail for New York at 4 P.M. I am quite well. Love to you all. Goodbye. | Wilkie Collins

To William A. Seaver,[1] 16 November 1873
MS: Princeton[2]

Westminster Hotel | 16th Nov 1873

Summary:
Thanks him for his message.

1. Colonel William A. Seaver (d. 1883), New York *Raconteur*. Conducted from 1868 the "Editor's Drawer" of *Harper's Magazine*.
2. With the letter is a menu of "Mr William A. Seaver's Breakfast to Mr Wilkie Collins. Union Club [New York], October 22d, 1873", also a diners list of 24 names including William Cullen Bryant, the Austrian and Spanish ministers, the governor of Connecticut, a justice and the Harper Brothers.

To William Tindell, 21 November 1873
MS: Glasgow

The Westminster Hotel | New York City | United States America | 21st November 1873[1]

My dear Tindell,

A line in a great hurry to ask you to advise and help Martha[2] – if she should want it – in making some new arrangements at 55 Marylebone Road. The landlord & landlady are perfectly respectable people – but Martha might want a little assistance. She will write to you, if she does want advice.

I am thriving in health and in public (as reader). If my health could stand constant reading I should make a little fortune. But I am obliged to be careful. My reception wonderful everywhere.

I had only five minutes to spare – and they are gone. I have been writing for seven hours. Goodbye and God bless you!

Yours ever | Wilkie Collins.

You remember the name at 55? <u>Mr and Mrs Dawson</u>.

Notes

1. Above the written address WC writes "Private" which he doubly underlines.
2. Martha Rudd (1845–1919).

To Sebastian Schlesinger,[1] 25 December 1873
MS: Harvard

Toronto | Canada | December 25th 1873[2]

My dear Schlesinger (let us drop "Mistering" each other!), here is a line to report favourably of the Canadian trip, so far. At Montreal a hard frost and a distinguished audience – slippery walking in the Streets – and horrid stenches in the hotel. On Tuesday we – that is to say Mr Redpath, Ward, and I – started for Toronto. Fifteen mortal hours of railway travelling. We pulled through it, with a compartment to ourselves, a faithful and attentive nigger to wait on us, dry champagne, and a cold turkey. Here the hotel is a good one, and my Canadian publishers (Hunter Rose & Co), who live in [erased word] Toronto, are taking the greatest care of us. We dine with them today (Christmas Day). Tomorrow I read here. Every seat in the hall is sold already. Unhappily, the hall is not a very large one. Such is life. My next duty is a severe one – Niagara. The lake here makes me feel rheumatic. What will the waterfall do? Besides I don't like waterfalls – they are noisy. I prefer mountains – and other silent works of Nature.

I miss those pleasant evenings at Marlborough Street sadly. Dinner is served here on the American plan, in (say) forty soup dishes, all round you, with a servant at the back of your chair to see that you eat out of every one of them.

After Niagara, I resume reading <u>at Buffalo</u>. Tifft House is the address there until this day week – Thursday, January 1st.[2] After that, we invade the Western States, and our address shall be forwarded.

Ward becomes more and more indispensable to my existence every day. He sends his kindest regards – and I add my best thanks for all your kindness to

Yours ever | Wilkie Collins

My letters received from [erasure] your office, this morning, quite safely.

Notes

1. Sebastian Benzon Schlesinger, Boston employee of Ernst Benzon of Naylor Vickers, to whom WC dedicated *The Haunted Hotel* (1879). Executor of WC's will.
2. Envelope, addressed to: "Sebastian Schlesinger Esqre | Messrs Naylor & Co | Boston | Mass: | U.S. America" and signed "Wilkie Collins".
3. WC numbers his new leaf "2" which he encloses in a half circle.

To [Joseph W. Harper, Jr],[1] 2 January 1874
MS: PM

Buffalo | N.Y. | 2nd January 1874

My dear Mr Harper,

I don't expect you to believe me – but I declare it is true that I have grace enough left to feel ashamed at myself, when I look at the date of <u>your</u> letter and when I write the date of <u>mine</u>.

When you kindly sent me the new editions of "Basil" and "The Dead Secret", I was involved in the double difficulty of breaking off all connection with the agents who had managed my "readings" up to that time, and of making a fresh start under new auspices. This little "coup d'état" accomplished I was hurried away to New England – and thence to Canada. I have no more to say for myself except that I trust to your indulgence to excuse me this time – and I have only to add that "I won't do it again."

I have "read" my way by Montreal and Toronto very successfully to this place. From Buffalo, my tour takes me to the Western States – perhaps as far as Salt Lake City itself. If all goes well, I hope to be back in New York at the beginning of March – and I have planned to return to England during the last fortnight in that month.

This is all I know at present. My address until further notice is | care of | Naylor & Co | Boston | Mass; – | who will forward all my letters.

Wherever I go, I meet with the same kindness and the same enthusiasm. I really want words to express my grateful sense of my reception in America! It is not only more than I have deserved – it is more than any man could have deserved. I have never met with such a cordial and such a generous people as the people of the United States. Let me add that I thrive on this kindness. I keep wonderfully well.

With kindest remembrances to my good friends in Franklin Square, and to my other friends in New York when you see them.

Always truly yours | Wilkie Collins

P.S. My best thanks for the "Plate" (my portrait) which you have so kindly sent me.

Note

1. Joseph W. Harper, Jr (d. 1896), took over the running of the family publishing house on the death of his father Joseph Wesley Harper (1801–1870).

To Hunter Rose & Co., 2 January 1874

MS: Private Possession

Tifft House | Buffalo | 2nd January 1874

Dear Mr Rose,

You have I hope received my telegram, acknowledging the receipt of your letter, and further confessing that I could not answer the copyright questions within the limits of a telegram.

I object though, as an English writer to any other than a voluntary arrangement on my part with a Canadian publisher. In any other commercial transaction what would be said to "rigid rules and a specific fee" – binding the buyers and sellers of a commodity? I recognise no difference between the purchase and sale of a book and the purchase and sale of any other marketable commodity. I claim as an English citizen, my English copyright in an English colony – subject to the authority to the Queen of England.

To this, the Canadian publisher – as I understand him – answers thus: "If I do not secure to myself the right of publishing your book in Canada, an American pirate will sell it in Canada, and thus injure my business."

My answer to this is – Prohibit by law the sale of English reprints by American booksellers in Canada, and you place the Canadian publisher and the English publisher on the same level. If the Canadian Legislature really means to do equal justice to Canadian publishers and to English writers – here and here only is the way. Am I asking for an impossibility? We perform that impossibility in England. We prohibit the introduction of the Tauchnitz reprints of English works, in England. Baron Tauchnitz is perfectly satisfied with this arrangement, and English writers and publishers are perfectly satisfied with it. Why cannot the same sensible plan be followed in Canada? There may be difficulties in carrying it out. But the business of a Legislature is to encounter and conquer difficulties.

These are my views, briefly and hastily stated. I think nothing of the money difficulty. Make no other than a Canadian publication of English books possible in Canada, and the English books must be published at the market price, or not published at all.

Truly yours, Wilkie Collins

=

P.S.

Reverting to personal matters, my Godson and I have to thank you for more than your kindness and Mrs Rose's kindness to us in Toronto. Your friendly consideration followed us to Niagara – Saw us through the Custom House under the auspices of good Mr Smeaton – and showed us the Falls under the best possible guidance. No words can tell how these wonderful Falls astonished and impressed me. It is well worth the voyage from England to see Niagara alone. Pray give our kindest remembrances to Mr[s] Rose. We are really gratefully sensible of all that you and she did to make our visit to Toronto one of the most agreeable visits in our travelling experience.

We stay here until Tuesday next. I read on Tuesday evening. After that date, my address will be, c/o Naylor & Co | Boston Mass: – who will forward all letters.

The Draft reached me quite safely. Many thanks.

To [Frederick Lehmann], 2 January 1874

MS: Present whereabouts unknown. Extract published, R.C. Lehmann, *Memoirs of Half a Century* (1908), pp. 65–6; Robinson, pp. 269–71.

[Tifft House | Buffalo | 2nd January 1874]

[Dear Fred]

I hear you have called like a good fellow at Gloucester Place, and have heard something of me from time to time. No matter where I go, my reception in America is always the same. The prominent people in each place visit me, drive me out, dine me, and do all that they can to make me feel among friends. The enthusiasm and the kindness are really and truly beyond description. I should be the most ungrateful man living if I had any other than the highest opinion of the American people. I find them to be the most enthusiastic, the most cordial, and the most sincere people I have ever met with in my life. When an American says, "Come and see me", he means it. This is wonderful to an Englishman.

Before I had been a week in the country I noted three national peculiarities which had never been mentioned to me by visitors to the States.

I. No American hums or whistles a tune either at home or in the street.

II. Not one American in 500 has a dog.

III. Not one American in 1,000 carries a walking stick.

I who hum perpetually, who love dogs, who cannot live without a walking stick, am greatly distressed at finding my dear Americans deficient in the three social virtues just enumerated.

My readings have succeeded by surprising the audiences. The story surprises them in the first place, being something the like of which they have not heard before. And my way of reading surprises them in the second place, because I don't flourish a paper knife and stamp about the platform, and thump the reading desk. I persist in keeping myself in the background and the story in front. The audience begins at each reading with silent astonishment, and ends with a great burst of applause.

As to the money, if I could read often enough I should bring back a little fortune in spite of the panic. The hard times have been against me of course, but while others have suffered badly I have always drawn audiences. Here, for example, they give me a fee for reading on Tuesday evening next – it amounts to between £70 and £80 (English). If I could read five times a week, at this rate (which is my customary rate), here is £350 a week, which is not bad pay for an hour and three-quarters reading each night. But I cannot read five times a week without knocking myself up, and this I won't do. And then I have been mismanaged and cheated by my agents – have had to change them and start afresh with a new man. The result has been loss of time and loss of money. But I am <u>investing</u> in spite of it, and (barring accidents) I am a fair way to make far more than I have made yet before the last fortnight in March, when I propose to sail for home. I am going "Out West" from this, and I <u>may</u> get as far as the Mormons. My new agent, a first rate-man, is ahead making engagements, and I am here (thanks to the kindness of Sebastian Schlesinger) with my godson Frank as secretary and companion ...

The nigger waiters (I like them better than the American waiters) are ringing the dinner bell. I must go and feed off a variety of badly cooked meats and vegetables ranged round me in (say) forty [soup] dishes. Otherwise I am comfortable here; I have got the Russian Grand Duke's bedroom, and a parlour in which I can shake hands with my visitors, and a box at the theatre, and the freedom of the club.

[Yours ever | Wilkie Collins]

To Frank Archer,[1] 6 January 1874

MS: Present whereabouts unknown. Text: Frank Archer, *An Actor's Notebooks*, (1912), pp. 156–7.

Buffalo, | New York State. | 6 January 1874

My Dear Archer,

I have got both your kind letters (dated Dec. 6 and Dec. 16). I entirely agree with you about the Charing Cross Theatre: but a letter from Miss Cavendish – as I understand it – informs me that she has actually taken the theatre, on her own responsibility. Under these circumstances, there is nothing to be done but to "make the best of it". I have written to Miss Cavendish on the subject. For the rest I can only thank you for your advice, and say that I sincerely hope you will give the experiment the advantage of your assistance by playing Julian Gray. The one thing needful in the interests of the piece is to prevent any possible impression from getting abroad that the revival is a failure. It would be well, with this object in view, to advertise that the theatre cannot possibly be obtained for longer than a limited period.

My "readings" are getting on famously. The one drawback is that I cannot read often enough to make a large sum of money, without the risk of injuring my health. Everywhere there is the same anxiety to hear and see me, but I cannot endure the double fatigue of railway travelling and reading on the same day. Thus three or four days a week are lost days (in the matter of money), but gained days (in the matter of health), and I have suffered enough to make health my first consideration. As to my personal reception in "the States", it has really and truly overwhelmed me. Go where I may, I find myself among friends. From this place I go to Chicago (stopping at certain smaller towns on the way). From Chicago, I go "West" – perhaps as far as the Mormons. This will be my last tour. I propose giving farewell readings early in March, in Boston and New York, and sailing for home during the last fortnight in March. I shall be very glad to hear how this venturesome Charing Cross experiment promises to turn out, if you have time to tell me. My address is, etc., etc. With all good wishes

Yours truly, | Wilkie Collins

Note

1. Frank Bishop Archer (?1845–1917), actor, who played Julian Gray in the original production of *The New Magdalen* at the Olympic in 1873: see Gasson.

To George Bentley, 9 January 1874
MS: NYPL (Berg)

Sandusky | Ohio | 9th January 1874

Summary:
Thanks Bentley for arranging publication of de Leon's[1] article. Is "careful not to fatigue" himself "by 'reading' too often. The result is that I can lose money – but I gain health. I am still wonderfully well. The snow is falling and the Lake is close to my windows – and yet I am writing to you without rheumatism!" Harpers "publishing a very good Library Edition of my books".

Note

1. Edwin De Leon's "The Southern States Since the War", appeared in *Fraser's Magazine*, 90 (August 1874), 153–63; (September 1874), 346–66; (November 1874), 620–37.

To Mr and Mrs John Bigelow,[1] 17 January 1874
MS: NYPL (Bigelow family papers)

Sherman House, | Cor. Clark & Randolph Sts. |
... Geo. W. Pearson, Superintendent. | Chicago, 17th January 1874

Summary:
"Don't tell anybody but the truth is I am not sorry to leave Chicago. The dull sameness of the great blocks of iron and brick overwhelm me. The

whole city seems to be saying 'see how rich I am after the fire and what a tremendous business I do!' and everybody I meet uses the same form of greeting. 'Two years ago, Mr Collins, this place was a heap of ruins – are you not astonished when you see it now?' I am not a bit astonished. It is a mere question of raising money – the rebuilding follows as a matter of course."

Note

1. John Bigelow (1817–1911: *DAB*), journalist and diplomat.

To William Tindell, 27 January 1874

MS: Glasgow

St James's Hotel | Boston | Mass: | January 27th 1874[1]

My dear Tindell,

I hope to sail for England towards the latter half of March.

In the meantime, I must ask you to have an eye to my interests in the matter of "The New Magdalen" (the drama).

I find that Miss Cavendish's Stage Manager has written to Mr Archer ("Julian Gray")[2] to ask him to play in a revival of the piece – at the <u>Holborn Ampitheatre</u>, of all the places in the world! This preposterous project has fallen through, in consequence of Mr Archer's wise refusal to perform, without my direct authority. <u>Nobody</u> has any right to authorise the performance of the piece in London – <u>but myself</u>.[3] Miss Cavendish has a year's lease of the piece in <u>the Country only</u>[4] – London being [erased word] expressly excepted by myself – the owner of the copyrights. I have requested Mr Archer to let you know if any similar liberties are taken with the play in my absence – and I hereby give you my authority to stop any [erased word] representations in London of the New Magdalen which are not authorised by me.

Very truly yours | Wilkie Collins

W[m] F. Tindell Esq

P.S. I am very well – only suffering a little in some places, so far as audiences are concerned, by the "panic".[5] The mischief is far from being at an end yet.

The landlord has left the house at 55 Marylebone Road – and has taken another. He offers me the option of buying the lease – which I cannot and will not do. I have written to say this – and it is understood that he takes no further steps until I return. If by any chance he should let the house before I get back, Martha has by agreement a right to a quarter's notice to quit. If she is at all bothered I have told her to apply to you – but I do not anticipate this – as the landlord is a very civil respectable man. I had hoped we were settled – but there is no such luck for me. (N.B. <u>You remember our name</u> – Mr and Mrs "Dawson").

Notes

1. Above the Hotel address WC writes: "<u>Private</u>".
2. Frank Archer (d. 1917, aged 72), played Julian Gray in the original production of *The New Magdalen* produced at the Olympic Theatre by Ada Cavendish (Mrs Frank Marshall) (1839–1895), actress-manageress.
3. "mys" of "myself" underlined twice.
4. "on" of "only" underlined three times.
5. i.e., the financial conditions.

Part VII
Domesticity
March 1874–1879

Introduction

Wilkie returns to Martha and his children and to Caroline and her daughter in Gloucester Place on 19 March 1874, and a continuation of his intense literary activity. The writing of *The Law and the Lady*, negotiations with George Bentley, George Smith and Andrew Chatto (of Chatto and Windus) over the rights of his novels, also preoccupy him. On 19 November 1874, he forms an agreement with Chatto and Windus who are to publish his subsequent novels. On Christmas Day 1874, there is a "Christmas Box in the shape of a big boy" [29 December 1874], a son William Charles Dawson, his and Martha's third child.

The Law and the Lady is published, not without its share of problems, in *The Graphic* from September 1874 to March 1875. Wilkie's son is added to his will on 24 March 1875. In a letter to Oliver Wendell Holmes, Wilkie writes "All through the last cruel winter I have been on the invalid list and my pen and I have been both 'out of gear' together" [17 May 1875]. He begins in February writing to Kate Field, one of many actresses he corresponds with. Attempting to combat the "devil whose name is Rheumatic Gout [which is] in full possession of me" [7 June 1875], he spends time on *Miss Gwilt*, the dramatic adaptation of *Armadale*, which finally opened at the Alexandra Theatre, Liverpool [9 December 1875].

"I am going abroad for a month ... to lay in a stock of health (if I can) for the coming winter" he writes to Bentley [8 October 1875], prior to leaving for a brief Low Countries expedition in October. By December he is hard at work "keeping in advance of the printers" who "chain him to his desk" [30 December 1875] writing *The Two Destinies*. This is published in Bentley's *Temple Bar*, January to August, 1876. Feeling his age – he was 52 on 8 January, 1876 – Wilkie writes to Charles Reade: "another old friend gone – in Forster" [2 February 1876]. For most of the remaining months he is "forbidden dinners, theatres" and, building up "arrears of work", is beset by recurring eye troubles. He can write to Lehmann: "Work, walk. Visit to my morganatic family – such is life" [26 April 1876]. Forced to miss the successful 15 April Globe production of *Miss Gwilt*, he is back at work by the early summer. He goes to Paris in September and October and then continues his intense labours on a new novel and dramatic adaptations.

For the first half of 1877 he suffers from severe rheumatism. The dramatic version of *The Moonstone* opens on 17 September 1877, and has a poor run. Wilkie contributes to journals, such as *Barnes International Review* and *The*

Belgravia Annual. Accompanied by Caroline, October to December, he visits Munich, Venice, Florence and Paris. Writing to "Padrona" (Nina Lehmann) he observes that "all sorts of impediments – literary and personal ... keep [him] in England" [28 December].

The year 1878 consists of "hard work and poor health" with Wilkie leading "the life of a hermit" [20 December 1878]. *The Fallen Leaves* takes up much of his time, as does *The Haunted Hotel*, for which he drew upon his recent Venetian trip. He has time to write lengthy letters, for instance to William Winter, on his literary tastes and on acting and actresses [5 August 1878]. Harriet, Caroline's daughter, marries Henry Powell Bartley, Wilkie's new solicitor, on 12 March 1878. Wilkie spends August and September in Ramsgate with Caroline. He acts as a reader for Bentley and is at pains to deny rumours that he is responsible for the completion of Charles Dickens' *Edwin Drood* [18 December 1878].

Wilkie avoids the funeral of his old friend, E.M. Ward, in January 1879. Bentley republishes, on 6 March 1879, the novella *A Rogue's Life*. In July Chatto publishes a three-volume edition of *The Fallen Leaves*. "Cruising about the English Channel" [27 July 1879], with Ramsgate as his base, he returns to London to work on short stories and a new novel, *Jezebel's Daughter*, which he negotiates for syndicated publishing by Tillotsons of Bolton.

To William Tindell, 3 March 1874
MS: Glasgow

New York City, U.S.A. | 3rd March 1874

My dear Tindell

Your letter of Feby 11th received. I am here for two days to say goodbye – and I propose sailing for England on March 7th from Boston by the Cunard Steamer <u>Parthia</u>.

All news, when we meet, I write in a tearing hurry – with the room full of people.

In case I am drowned, I send you particulars (enclosed) of Insurances on my Life in Boston. Policies in safe keeping with an old friend (partner of Lehmann), and a merchant in Boston. [Receipt] for Policies sent to Charles Ward. Whole amount of Insurance 2000.[1]

"Vive la Republique"!

Ever yours | Wilkie Collins

Insurances on the Life of | Wilkie Collins | effected in Boston U.S. America
1. February 6th – Policy for $5000 (1000 sterling) in the Manhattan Life Insurance Company (No 37019)
     Annual Premium $227.00
2. February 12th – Policy for $5000 (1000 sterling) in The New England Mutual Insurance Company (No 53, 404)
     Annual Premium $235.00

First year's Premiums paid. Second year's Premiums due February 6th and February 12th 1875, at the offices in Boston (U.S.)

Policies deposited with Sebastian B. Schlesinger Esq, firm of Naylor & Co. 6 Oliver Street. Boston. U.S.

Mr Schlesinger's receipt for the Policies has been posted to Charles Ward. Coutts & Co.

Note

1. "000" underlined twice, the rest of the sum once.

To Henry Wadsworth Longfellow,[1] 6 March 1874
MS: Harvard

Boston | 6th March 1874

Summary:
Very much regrets he is unable "to get to Cambridge and to take your hand at parting". Hopes to return to America and then visit Longfellow and his family.

Note

1. Henry Wadsworth Longfellow (1807–1882), poet. His home at Cambridge, Mass., "became a shrine for Americans and a point of visit for distinguished foreigners". He had three daughters and two sons (see *The Oxford Companion to American Literature*, sixth edition, eds, James D. Hart, Phillip W. Leininger, 1995, p. 388).

To George W. Childs,[1] 16 March 1874
MS: Private Possession

Steam Ship Parthia | At Sea. March 16th 1874

My dear Mr Childs,

Incessant interruptions on shore have allowed me no earlier opportunity of writing to tell you of my return to England. [erasures] I had hoped to remain a few weeks longer in the United States – and to pay you my promised visit [erased word] during this month. But letters from home have obliged me to hasten my departure – and to leave America at the beginning, instead of at the end of March – as I had planned to do.

Need I say that I reckon among my chief disappointments the loss of the pleasant days I had hoped to pass under your roof? But I had no other choice than to get back, and attend to some business which was all going wrong in my absence.[2]

I can only trust to your indulgence to forgive me and to make my apologies to Mrs Childs. More than this, I venture to hope that my visit is still only put off until a later date than we had calculated on. If all goes well with me, I shall return to my good American friends at the first opportunity that I can find. I leave you with a grateful heart – with recollections of American kindness and hospitality which will be, as long as I live, among the happiest recollections to which I can look back.

Let me once again thank you, and thank Mrs Childs, for happy hours at Philadelphia – and let me earnestly hope for more of those hours in the time to come.

With kindest remembrances to Mrs Childs, and with sincere esteem and regard,

always truly yours, | Wilkie Collins

If you should be in London, before I cross the Atlantic again, don't forget my address:
90, Gloucester Place, | Portman Square.

Notes

1. George W. Childs (1829–1894: *DAB*), Philadelphia publisher.
2. Martha's landlord was selling the house she lived in and wanting her to move.

To Mrs W.P. Frith, 21 March 1874
MS: National Art Library, Victoria and Albert Museum, London

90, Gloucester Place, | Portman Square. W. | 21st March 1874

Dear Mrs Frith,

I shall be delighted to dine with you at 7.30 on Thursday April 2nd – as you kindly propose. We were lost in a fog on the voyage back – but the captain's seamanship brought us safely through our difficulties. The rolling of the boat is still in my head – and I feel like a foreigner in my native climate.

With best love to Frith, | Yours ever, | Wilkie Collins

Note

1. He had returned from Boston on the Cunard liner Parthia and docked in Liverpool three days earlier on March 18th. He was already beginning to suffer from the English damp climate.

To Mrs W.P. Frith, 2 April 1874
MS: National Art Library, Victoria and Albert Museum, London

90, Gloucester Place, | Portman Square. W. | April 2nd 1874

Dear Mrs Frith,

I am obliged, I regret to say, to ask you to forgive my absence this evening. I came back from America with a new stock of health – as I supposed. But my native climate has already made me so "bilious" that I can hardly see. My eyes are yellow, and my head aches and the doctor positively forbids dinner today and prescribes fasting and physic for the next four and twenty hours. I am very, very sorry to miss the pleasant meeting with you and Frith tonight.

Pray accept my excuses and believe me, | Truly yours, | W.C.

To George Bentley, 16 May 1874
MS: NYPL (Berg)

90, Gloucester Place, | Portman Square. W. | 16th May 1874

Dear Mr Bentley,
I will write to Mr Smith next week. The copyright of the book is entirely mine. Your account of the sale of "East Lynne" amazes me.[1]
I hope you are going on well. I have got the gout [flying] about me – and keeping me nervous and unfit for work.
With many thanks for your letter.

Vy truly yours | W.C

The Moonstone has been published in one 5/- Volume. Sale, so far as I know, a little over 3000 copies so far. And this book has been translated into all the European languages!!

Note

1. "By 1876 Bentley had printed 65,000 copies of " *East Lynne* (Sutherland, p. 678).

To William Tindell, 14 June 1874
MS: Glasgow

90, Gloucester Place | W. | 14th June 1874

Summary:
Concerns agreements for the new book for *The Graphic*.[1] Wants to know where to find "the Trial of Madeleine Smith at Glasgow for poisoning a young Frenchman". WC wants "that Trial, and any other <u>Criminal</u> trials

which show the course of procedure under the Scottish Law in cases of murder".

Note

1. *"The Law and the Lady, Graphic,* 26 September 1874 to 13 March 1875. Its plot focuses on an assumed murder by poison and attacks the Scottish verdict of "not proven", in a murder case.

To William Tindell, 15 June 1874
MS: Glasgow

90, Gloucester Place | W | 15th June 1874

My dear Tindell,

I enclose the heads of agreement with the Proprietors of <u>The Graphic</u>.

Am I right in supposing that if a man marries a woman under an assumed name, the marriage is nevertheless a lawful one, if the woman has acted in good faith believing it to be the man's own name, and if the witnesses present are also innocent of all knowledge of the fraud?[1]

A line to confirm me in this.

Yours ever Wilkie Collins

Note

1. In *The Law and the Lady,* Eustace Macallan conceals his real identity. He marries Valeria under an assumed name.

To George Bentley, 27 October 1874
MS: NYPL (Berg)

90, Gloucester Place, | Portman Square. W. | 27th Oct: 1874

Dear Mr Bentley,

I have waited to trouble you on another matter of business – until I could hear that you were still improving in health. I gladly heard, the other day, from Mr Munnings,[1] that you had appeared again in New Burlington Street for a few hours.

I have had a proposal made to me to pay me a sum of money for seven years' lease of <u>all</u> my copyrights.[2] The proposal contemplates a further expenditure to purchase back my copyrights in the possession of Messrs

Smith and Elder – if they can be obtained on sufficiently favourable terms. This accomplished, the publication of a complete new edition of all my novels is the object proposed.

I have anxiously considered this offer. It is, in a pecuniary sense, an indisputably advantageous offer, judged by comparison with the profits which I am now making. It relieves me of anxiety, and it offers the advantage to the books themselves of being all published by one firm, with a pecuniary interest of unusual importance in the speculation. Under these circumstances, and, in my position, I feel that I have but one choice. I have accepted the proposal.

It is needless to say that I personally regret removing "Poor Miss Finch" and "The New Magdalen" from your friendly care. But I have long felt uneasy at the division of my books between the publishing houses; and I am under the impression that they will do better by themselves in one series, than they do now in "Standard Libraries", and in close competition with other books. Whether I am right or wrong in this – as a matter of business I have no wise alternative but to thank you heartily for your friendly interest in my books, and to try the experiment.

My present plan – if it is convenient to you – is to transfer the two novels on the 1ˢᵗ of February next. The Stereo plates, and stock on hand at the time, to be taken at a valuation.

Will you kindly let me know if this arrangement will suit you, as soon as you can conveniently let me have a line? Believe me | Always truly yours | Wilkie Collins

To | George Bentley Esq[3]

Notes

1. Bentley's office manager.
2. Andrew Chatto offered WC £2000 "for the exclusive right to publish Wilkie's earlier novels in Great Britain, Ireland and the English Colonies except Canada ... He persuaded Bentley to relinquish his rights." Smith however refused to give up the rights he had on *No Name*, *After Dark* and *Armadale*. These titles " were not published by Chatto & Windus until 1890 ... All Wilkie's subsequent novels appeared with the Chatto & Windus imprint" (Peters, p. 369).
3. In his margin WC writes: "'The Frozen Deep' will wait, of course, until the Circulating Library Edition has had its full and fair chance."

To Chatto & Windus, 19 November 1874

MS: Chatto and Windus Archives (University of Reading). Weedon, pp. 179–80.

[90, Gloucester Place, | Portman Square. W. | 19th Novr 1874]

Summary:
Agreement: States that copyright of the following 13 works should be granted to Chatto and Windus for the period of seven years from 31 March 1875. WC receives £2000. Chatto agree to republish all works within twelve months from 31 March 1875 and not to publish the novels for less than 2/-. Stereos, eight steel plates for six of the volumes and some wood cuts were bought from Smith and Elder for £650 (estimated by George Bell of Bell and Sons). The novels are: *Antonina; Basil; Hide and Seek; The Dead Secret; The Queen of Hearts; The Woman in White; The Moonstone; Man and Wife; Poor Miss Finch; Miss or Mrs?; The New Magdalen; The Frozen Deep; My Miscellanies.*

To William Tindell, 29 December 1874

MS: Glasgow

90, Gloucester Place, | Portman Square. W. | 29th Decr 1874

My dear Tindell,
   Is there any news for us yet, in the matter of Smith & Elder and the sale of the Stock in hand? Or are the filthy "Christmas festivities" still an insurmountable obstacle to any proceeding that is not directly connected with the filling of fat bellies, and the exchange of vapid good wishes?

Yours ever | W C

P.S. I have had a Christmas Box, in the shape of a big boy.[1] We must add him, in a codicil (I suppose?) to the new Will – merely stating that he is to have his share with the two girls. If you will kindly make a draft of the document, I will see to filling up the dates and names.

Note

1. William Charles Collins (1876–1913) son of Wilkie and Martha, born Christmas Day 1874.

To Mrs [John] Bigelow, 31 December 1874
MS: NYPL (Bigelow family papers)

[90, Gloucester Place, | Portman Square. W. | 31st Decr 1874]

Summary:

"In your country, I felt five and twenty years old. In my country I (not infrequently) feel five and ninety.

I cannot even tell you about Forster's health, having seen nothing of him, and heard nothing of him, for months past. Did I tell you how he once distinguished himself on landing at Boulogne-sur-mer ... ? ... Dickens and I went to the Port to 'clear' Forster (in the custom-house phrase) ... He could neither speak nor understand French at that time – whatever he may be able to do now. In due time, he landed, walking in his most majestic manner between the custom house lines of rope ... he was ... accosted by a very small French military official, in these customary terms: – 'Avez vous rien a declarer, Monsieur?' Forster paused, smiled his sweetest smile, bowed his grandest bow, and answered in his most mellifluous tones: – 'Bon jour!' ... he was instantly seized, and Dickens had to become answerable for him. To see F.'s astonishment and the little Frenchman's indignation – is to have lived to some advantage and to make the most of life."

To William Tindell, 29 January 1875
MS: Glasgow

90, Gloucester Place | Friday Jany 29/75

My dear Tindell,

Since I wrote to you, I have seen today's "Graphic". The "castrated" passage is restored[1] in a note at the end of this week's instalment of the story! in deference to information received from Mr W.C. "through his legal advisers"!!

With this, and the assurance for the future we may be satisfied. We have made these blackguards behave like gentlemen at last – thanks to "Benham & Tindell". Yours ever W C

Note

1. "is restored" doubly underlined.

To Kate Field,[1] 25 February 1875

MS: Boston Public Library. Published: L. Whiting, *Kate Field: A Record*, (Boston, 1899), pp. 345–6.

90, Gloucester Place, | Portman Square, W. | London | Sept. 25, 1875.

Dear Miss Field, – I have just got back, and have held court of justice on my servants. They all declared that no such lady as Miss Kate Field ever appeared at this house, or did me the honour of leaving her card; and they all remember perfectly that I expressly instructed them to show Miss Field upstairs into my study on the day when I expected to have the pleasure of receiving her. The only explanations of this <u>contretemps</u> are two in number. 1, That the servants have all three lied. 2, That you called at the <u>wrong</u> Gloucester Place. There are <u>two</u> Gloucester Places in London; the oldest and first named I live in. It is close to <u>Portman Square</u> (underlined on this address). The other Gloucester Place lies out Bayswater way, close to Westbourne Terrace; and is known as Gloucester Place, Hyde Park. The Editor of the Louisville "Courier Journal", when he was last in England, went to the wrong Gloucester Place (being invited to lunch with me). I asked a "party" to meet him, and while we were waiting vainly for him here, he was waiting vainly at the other Gloucester Place for <u>us</u>. I am so sorry and so ashamed at what has happened that I take kindly in the theory that <u>you</u> have followed the lead of the editor. In any case, pray accept my excuses, and pray give me another chance when we are next in London together.

You deserve to succeed in these days of mean intriguing and puffery. Your resolutions and self-respect are doubly admirable. Whatever I can do to help you shall be gladly done. If you go to Edinburgh, I know the Manager of the new theatre and winter garden there, – Mr Wybert Reeve[2] (my Count Fosco in America), – and a letter to him is heartily at your service. As for me, I am better, but not yet well. In a week or so, I think of going to Germany for a month. Letters will be forwarded from this address.

Yours truly, | Wilkie Collins

Note

1. Mary Katherine Keemle Field (1838–1896), American actress, journalist, advocate of women's rights, with whom "Trollope developed a long-standing romantic attachment" (N.J. Hall, ed., *The Letters of Anthony Trollope*, I, 126, n.7).
2. Wybert Reeve (1831–1906), actor and friend of WC: see Gasson.

To Edmund Yates,[1] 20 March 1875

MS : "Proof" PM. Published: *The World*, 24 March 1875, p. 21; J. Bourne Taylor, ed.: *The Law and the Lady* (Oxford: 1992), pp. 416–18.

90, Gloucester Place, | Portman Square, W. |
London, March 20th 1875

Sir,

In your last week's number you naturally express some surprise, after reading a paragraph in the Graphic reflecting in disparaging and discourteous terms on a story which I published periodically in the columns of that newspaper. Wherever I go, I find that persons who take any interest in literary matters share your view. Letters have even reached me from perfect strangers, asking (to use the picturesque language of one of my correspondents) "What the newspaper means by running down its own author?" Will you permit me to explain the mystery in your columns by means of a brief narrative of facts? It may be possible to amuse some of your readers who are my readers also, if I inform them of the curious difficulties which a writer has sometimes to contend with when addressing himself to the public.

At the express request of the proprietors of the Graphic I consented to permit them to publish a new work of mine, called The Law and the Lady, periodically, in their newspaper. The negotiations were conducted by their literary editor. Speaking as a mouthpiece of his proprietors, this gentleman's main anxiety in respect to my forthcoming work appeared to be, that it should "give no offence to the family circle" – the sensitiveness of this same "circle" being estimated, in the present case and in the interest of the proprietors, by the editor who was then dealing with me. As a means of quieting his fears, I informed him that I was about to write, this time (autobiographically) in the character of a young lady, and that I hoped I might be sanctioned, under those circumstances, as a perfectly harmless person by that British Domestic Inquisition, otherwise known as the family circle. On the editor's departure, considering what had passed between us – and not forgetting Swift's immortal aphorism, which declares that a nice man is a man of nasty ideas – I thought it wise to insert a clause in my agreement forbidding the alteration of any portion of my story by anybody employed in the interests of the Domestic Inquisition at the Graphic office, without first obtaining my consent and approbation. The agreement, thus guarded, was signed on both sides, and the The Law and the Lady made its appearance periodically in the columns of the Graphic newspaper.

Towards the latter portion of the story, I had occasion to describe an attempt made by one of the male personages in the story to kiss one of the female personages – an incident, permit me to add, which, being of frequent occurrence in "the family circle", was therefore an especially fit incident for the pages of the Graphic. The little scene was described (autobiographically) by the heroine of the story in these words: "He caught my hand in his and devoured it with kisses. His lips burnt me like fire. He twisted himself suddenly in his chair, and wound his arm around my waist. In the terror and indignation of the moment, vainly struggling with him, I cried out for help." That is all. The story is now in circulation at the libraries (in book form), and is accessible to anyone who wishes to make sure that I have correctly transferred the language used in the novel to your columns.

To my indescribable amazement, I found this passage, on its publication in the Graphic, clumsily altered, abridged and mutilated (without a word of warning to me), so as to make certain allusions which followed in the next number simply ridiculous. I at once wrote (with some natural indignation) to complain of this scandalous breach of courtesy, which was also a plain breach of the agreement. In reply, I received a letter from the editor, informing me that he had placed a nasty interpretation of his own on the perfectly innocent passage which I have just quoted, and that he and "the Directors" and other "members of the establishment" – all simmering together in a moral miasma of their own dirty raising – actually interpreted what I had written as describing "an attempted violation of the heroine of the story". I have kept the letter, and I beg to assure you that I quote the writer's language word for word.

It was impossible for me, after that, to communicate directly with the person with whom I had unfortunately connected myself for the time being. In other words, it was useless to appeal to their sense of what was due to Literature, or due to a writer who had for more than twenty years held an honourable place in the public estimation. I appealed (through my lawyers) to the agreement. The omitted passages were restored, under protest, in the next number of the newspaper; and the consequent explosion of spite, which you have justly described as "a gross violation of the rules by which literary courtesy and good feeling are governed", follows as a natural explosion of the editor's insolence and the editor's hostile feelings towards myself. It is quite needless for me to defend the perfectly innocent passage which has been so indecently misinterpreted. It has been reprinted in America, in Australia, and in Canada; it has been translated into the French, German, Italian, Russian and Dutch languages, and not a word of objection has reached me in any form. In no country but England does a writer meet with obstacles at once so contemptible and so irritating as the sort of obstacle as I have described. Your excellent article is, in this sense, a service rendered to Literature, as well as a service rendered to me. – Accept my sincere thanks, and believe me faithfully yours, WILKIE COLLINS.

Note

1. Edmund Hodgson Yates (1831–1894: *DNB*), novelist, journalist, dramatist, editor, who founded, in July 1874, *The World: A Journal for Men and Women*. On 17 March 1875 his editorial supported WC in his dispute with *The Graphic*.

To William Tindell, 24 March 1875
MS: Glasgow

90, Gloucester Place, | Portman Square. W. | 24th March 1875

My dear Tindell,

Here is the cheque enclosed.

Please tell the clerk to return the statement receipted – and all will be well.

Don't forget my codicil, relating to my son – William Charles – born 25th December 1874 at 10 Taunton Place, Park Road, Regents Park, London – whom I acknowledge to be my child, and who is to share with his sisters in all benefits devisable under my Will.

See said Will, as relating to the other two children.

Yours ever | Wilkie Collins.

To William Tindell, 27 April 1875
MS: Glasgow

90, Gloucester Place, | Portman Square. W. | 27th April 1875

Summary:
WC returns approved Draft and arranges meeting with Tindell. "'Keates' is a nickname for Caroline (Mrs Graves) ... Is the fellow's brain softening? Of course no notice has been taken of his letter."[1]

Note

1. i.e., Joseph Clow (d. 1927), whom Caroline married 29 October 1868 (see Clarke, p. 130).

To Moy Thomas,[1] 7 May 1875

MS: Texas: Coleman

90, Gloucester Place | Portman Square West | 7 May 1875

My dear Sir,

I am still ailing, and I am ordered to leave town by my doctor. But if I can possibly manage it, I will be with you on Monday.

The strongest case to put is probably the case of Mrs Wood's <u>East Lynne</u>.[2] If I am rightly informed the novel was dramatised without asking her permission, and against her will – and not a sixpence of the large profits produced by the piece has ever found its way into Mrs Wood's pocket. I am not personally acquainted with the lady – but I should think if this "association" applied to her to state her own case in writing (so that no mistakes may be made) she would willingly [apprise] us.

<u>My</u> case is unluckily – in one respect – a weak one. I complain, in the abstract, of the gross injustice of the present state of the law – but I cannot also complain (<u>in Great Britain</u>) of any personal injury. I have dramatised my own books in the face of existing piracies. If I were asked the question I should be obliged to acknowledge that the piracies have been (financially) failures, and that my own dramatic adaptations have, in every case, yielded me a good return in money. The obvious retort to this is – then – "what have <u>you</u> to complain of?"

Mrs Wood's case – <u>if I am right in my facts</u> – is an unanswerable case of the cruellest injustice.

Believe me, | Very truly yours, | Wilkie Collins

Notes

1. William Moy Thomas (1828–1910), drama critic of the *Daily News*, 1868–1901.
2. Mrs Henry Wood (1814–1887: *DNB*), novelist. After *East Lynne* was published in the *New Monthly Magazine* and in book-form in England, it was republished in New York in a 75-cent paperback version, without Mrs Wood's permission. Dramatic adaptations were performed throughout the United States and in 1930, the novel was filmed.

To Oliver Wendell Holmes,[1] 17 May 1875

MS: Library of Congress: Text, Coleman

90, Gloucester Place, | Portman Square. W. | London | 17th May 1875

My dear Doctor Holmes,

That you possess all the social virtues, I know by pleasant experience. May I hope, for my own sake, that you also possess a certain reserve fund of indulgence for the social failings – and especially for that particular failing which produces a bad correspondent? Seriously, I have but one excuse for my otherwise unpardonable neglect in acknowledging your kind letter and the volume which accompanied it. All through the last cruel winter I have been on the invalid list, and my pen and I have been both "out of gear" together. I sincerely hope that you have been, all this time, setting me an example of health, spirits, and literary activity. In any case, I am indebted to y<u>ou</u> for some of the happiest hours I have spent during this (to me) dreary year. Your last Poems have been – <u>in</u> bed and <u>out</u> of bed – my always welcome companions. I know them well enough to have my special favourites. "The Organ Blower" delights me by its delicate irony and its true and charming feeling. "At the Pantomime" – where the sudden revulsion of feeling is so finely touched – is, as I think, another masterpiece. Of the "War Songs" all have the "ring" of true poetry in them. "Never or Now" is the finest thing of the kind I have read since Campbell[2] laid down his pen for ever. Again, in quite another way the delightful "Class Meeting" Poems have the same masterly hold over the feelings of the reader – simple, pathetic, unaffected and finely true. I am not a little proud to find the "Toast" with which you honoured me at that memorable dinner, included among your Poems.[3] I may say for myself honestly that the kindness which has thus distinguished me has not been thrown away on an ungrateful man – and I may add that the little which I have here ventured to say on the subject of your Songs of Many Seasons is said truly with my whole heart.

There is no Art-news to tell you – even if I had left myself room to write at greater length. Except that "Salvini"[4] in Othello has stirred the London waters, we are otherwise stagnant on this side of the Atlantic. For myself, I am still looking forward to my return to the States, and to a renewal of our too brief intercourse at Boston – and still unable to fix a date for my departure. The one thing I know is, that, when the opportunity comes, I shall not be slow in seizing it. Meanwhile with sincere regards,

believe me, | my dear Doctor Holmes | Always truly yours, |
Wilkie Collins

My kindest remembrances to Mr Longfellow when you see him.

Notes

1. Oliver Wendell Holmes (1809–1894: *DAB*), poet, physician, humourist. WC met various American literati, including Bryant, Clemens, Holmes, Longfellow, and Whittier, at a 22 October 1873 breakfast party in his honour. During the party Holmes read the following toast:

   A Toast to Wilkie Collins
   The painter's and the poet's fame
   Shed their twinned lustre round his name,
   To gild our story-teller's art,
   Where each in turn must play his part.

What scenes from Wilkie's pencil sprung,
The minstrel saw but left unsung!
What shapes the pen of Collins drew,
No painter clad in living hue!

But on our artist's shadowy screen
A stranger miracle is seen
Than priest unveils or pilgrim seeks
The poem breathes, the picture speaks!

And so his double name comes true,
They christened better than they knew,
And Art proclaims him twice her son,
Painter and poet, both in one!

2. Thomas Campbell (1777–1844), Scottish poet.
3. *The Poems of Oliver Wendell Holmes* (Boston, 1875). A presentation copy of Holmes' *Songs of Many Seasons 1862–1874*, (Boston 1875), was in WC's library when he died.
4. Tomasso Salvini (1829–1916), Italian actor, performed Othello at Drury Lane in April 1875, creating a sensation.

To William A. Seaver, 7 June 1875

MS: Princeton

90, Gloucester Place, | Portman Square. W. | London. | 7th June 1875

My dear Seaver,

The sight of your handwriting did me good – even when the devil whose name is Rheumatic Gout was in full possession of me. I have been long in thanking you for your letter, and for that excellently-timed and friendly little article which you enclosed. But I have also been long in getting to be "my own man again" – and with that excuse I throw myself confidently on the indulgence of my friend and comrade over many a good bottle of wine, in that happy time of my life which I passed at New York.

If I could have my own way, I should start from Liverpool by the Steamer which will bring you this letter – call at your office in Broadway – and say "Seaver, come and dine at the Brunswick." But I have involved myself somehow in certain dramatic experiments to be tried on the British public this year – and in England I must stay, whether I like it or not, until I am "damned" or "ovated" as the case may be.

But only let me get over this year – and then a sea-voyage I must have – and to New York it shall be – and what is more, before the Centennial Celebrations if possible. We have been literally drenched in Exhibitions in the Old World. My feet ache, and my head whirls, and my stomach sickens, when I think of <u>another</u> exhibition and more Arts and Sciences and industrial triumphs and improvements of the mind and international courtesies and all the rest of it. But this is <u>morbid</u> sentiment – this is an unhealthy view – let me hasten to withdraw it – and let me look forward to meeting next year, unless you come to England in the meantime.[1]

I have got some dry Champagne and some decent cigars and a hearty welcome thrown into the bargain. N.B. Travel by <u>Cunard</u> – he takes soundings in a fog, and is not in such a damned hurry that he has no time to think of the lives of his passengers.

Goodbye for the present, my dear Seaver – give my love to my friends in New York – and believe me

Always truly yours | W.C

Note

1. WC draws a hand and an index finger before the paragraph.

To George Bentley, 12 September 1875
MS: NYPL (Berg)

Lowestoft | 12th Sept 1875

Dear Mr Bentley,

Your kind letter has followed me to this place. I am wandering about the Eastern Coast, on the way back to health. But the weather is against me so far – and I feel the damp of my native shores in my back and shoulders. However, I have ceased to be one of our friend Beard's patients – and I must not complain. In ten days I propose to return to London. If the rheumatism goes back with me, I am afraid I shall not be fit for the Welsh mountains – I shall be obliged to try Harrogate. I gladly infer from your letter that you and the asthma have parted company in Wales.

Many thanks for your proposal. A short story, beginning and ending in one monthly number of the Magazine, is I am afraid out of the question. I have got an idea of another new story (of the fanciful kind with a touch of the supernatural in it) – but it would occupy four or five numbers at least. When I get to work on the new experiment,[1] – I will gladly report proposals to you, before I say a word about it in any other quarters of the periodical world. The sooner I take up my pen again, the better for me, now.[2]

Vy truly Yours | Wilkie Collins

P.S.

Wherever I may go, my letters will follow me from Gloucester Place. to |

George Bentley Esqre

Excuse this smeared page. Even my writing paper feels the sea-damp.

Notes

1. Probably a reference to *The Two Destinies* serialized in Bentley's *Temple Bar* between January and September 1876.
2. WC underlines "now" twice.

To George Bentley, 8 October 1875
MS: NYPL (Berg)

> 90, Gloucester Place, | Portman Square. W. | 8th Oct: 1875

Summary:
WC is "going abroad ... to lay in a stock of health (if I can) for the coming winter".

To Nina Lehmann, 26 October 1875
MS: Texas: Coleman

> Hotel de Flandre | Brusselles | 26 October 1875

Dearest Padrona,

The address must plead my apology. I need not say how sorry I am to have missed the dinner with you and the Sebastian S's. But the sea is between us – I may waft my regrets and wishes, but I may <u>not</u> waft myself.

I have been here for a fortnight building up my shattered constitution, and writing the first monthly part of a new story which is to appear in <u>Temple Bar</u> for the next four or five months, dating from New Year's Day 1876. I hope I shall have some proofs for you before that time.

To-day, having finished my number, I go to have another look at Rubens, and the Cathedral, at Antwerp – then to the Netherlands with my Dutch publishers at the Hague – then back here – and then to England early in next month. I will not fail to report myself in Berkeley Square.

I am delighted to hear of Fred's safe arrival. Give him my love and good wishes when you write.

Ever yours, | Wilkie Collins

I hope the Sebastians will be in London when I return.

To William Tindell, 12 November 1875
MS: Glasgow

90, Gloucester Place | 12th Novr 1875

My dear Tindell,

We are just back from Brussells and Antwerp – much the better for the change. I wish you had been with us. You would have returned a new man.

A friend of Poles[1] (to whom, of course, he has behaved in the most infamous manner) is raising a small subscription to bury him. I respect the friend's practical Christianity and give two pounds – but I privately think the money would have been more appropriately bestowed on a living object of charity, <u>not</u> an irreclaimable scoundrel. His friends have been written to – and his papers are in a lawyer's hands.

Yours ever | W.C.

I am hard at work again.

Note

1. Stefan Poles managed WC's theatrical affairs while he was in America.

To William Tindell, 16 December 1875
MS: Glasgow

90, Gloucester Place, | Portman Square. W. | 16th Decr 1875

Summary:
Requests Tindell's services as power of attorney to: invest his Australian agent Biers of the Office of Crown, Lands and Survey, Melbourne "with the sole authority to represent him in respect of all" new productions of his dramas, and "new stories, reprinted and published" in Australia and New Zealand; supply his Italian agent with powers of attorney – if Tindell sees no objection. Asks Tindell to obtain a copy of the "International Copyright Treaty between England and Italy".

To Mrs Laura Seymour,[1] 30 December 1875
MS: Mrs Juliet Noel (née Reade)

[90, Gloucester Place, | Portman Square. W. | 30th Decr 1875]

My dear Mrs Seymour,

I had hoped to be able to call today and thank you for the delicious prawn. But the horrid necessity of "keeping in advance of the printer's" chains me to my desk – so my gratitude must exhale itself on paper. When I say that I don't go to bed without a bit of the prawn to keep me company, you will understand that your present is appreciated as it ought to be.

In a little while I hope to have some proofs for you to read. Meanwhile, Caroline sends you some German cake which has just arrived from Berlin – and begs you to accept. I had asked her to go and see how Reade was (not being able to go myself) – and so she was unfortunately out when you called.

My love to Reade

Yrs affly | WC

We had great luck with the Dramatic "Armadale" at Liverpool. The audience received the piece with open arms. It never was in jeopardy for a moment.[2]

Notes

1. Mrs Laura Alison Seymour (?1820–1879), actress and Charles Reade's companion for over 20 years.
2. First performed at the Alexandra Theatre, Liverpool, 9 December 1875: see Gasson.

To Jane Ward, 10 January 1876
MS: Private Possession

90, Gloucester Place, | Portman Square. W. | 10th January 1876

My dear Jane,

Thank you heartily for that very kind and very pretty token of your remembrance of me on my birthday. I keep it in my study, and look at it while I am at work, and try (quite ineffectually) to forget that time has turned me into an elderly gentleman of fifty two!

Yours affly | Wilkie Collins

To Hunter Rose & Co., 24 January 1876

MS: Princeton

90, Gloucester Place, | Portman Square. W. | London January 24th 1876

Summary:
Sends "brief analysis of <u>The Two Destinies</u>:
The book tells the story of two lovers, who are separated at an early period in their lives. They meet again, after a lapse of years, under circumstances which prevent them from recognising each other, and which appear to oppose an insurmountable barrier to their union. Events occur which lead unexpectedly to a recognition on either side. The obstacles to their marriage are removed, and they become, what their 'Destinies' have fore ordained them, from the first, to be – Man and Wife."

To Nina Lehmann, 25 January 1876

MS: Princeton: Text, Coleman.

90, Gloucester Place | Portman Square W | 25 January 1876

Dearest Padrona
　　I am never "out of town" to <u>you</u>. On Saturday, February 5th, then with the greatest pleasure.
　　This is every way a sad day – I am just writing a line to Boucicault – and this was dear Charley's birthday.[1]

Yours affectionately, | WC

Note

1. Charles Collins died three years before of stomach cancer.

To Charles Reade, 2 February 1876

MS: Mrs Juliet Noel (née Reade)

[90, Gloucester Place, | Portman Square.W. | 2 February 1876]

Summary:
　　"Another old friend gone – in Forster![1] He was angry with me because I did not 'consult him' before I went to America! I am glad to think now I was never angry with <u>him</u>."

Note

1. John Forster died 1 February 1876.

To George Bentley, 15 March 1876
MS: NYPL (Berg)

90, Gloucester Place, | Portman Square.W. | March 15. 1876.

Dear Mr Bentley

I am again laid up with Rheumatic Gout in the eye. So far the attack is not so serious as on former occasions, but there is enough pain to make dictation to an amanuensis not very easy. The result is that the May Number of the "Two Destinies", will be in any case a short one, and I may have to ask you for an extra (or seventh) month so as to spare my head, by concluding the Story in three short Monthly Parts instead of (as I had proposed) two long ones.

In a day or two, I will send the copy already completed for the May Number to New Burlington Street, and I will try what I can do to lengthen it a little by dictation.

I hope you are keeping well in this boisterous weather.

Believe me very truly your[s] | Wilkie Collins[1]

George Bentley esq^re

Note

1. The signature is the only part of the letter in WC's hand: the rest probably that of "Carrie" [Elizabeth Harriet Graves] who acted as his secretary.

To Charles Reade, 21 March 1876
MS: Mrs Juliet Noel (née Reade)

[90, Gloucester Place, | Portman Square. W. | 21st March 1876]

My dear Reade,

Just a word (by means of Miss Graves's pen) to thank you heartily for your friendly and consoling letter.[1] You know what a very high value I set on your opinion in questions of Art, and you will not be surprised to hear that you have encouraged me just at a time when I wanted such encouragement as only a brother writer can give.

I am beginning to hope that I have passed through the worst and [fiercest] ordeal of the pain, and that the disease will be content this time with attacking one eye only. In the inevitable absence of poor Beard still laid up,

I am looked after by Mr Critchett,[2] who is not only a great occulist, but also the kindest and pleasantest of men.

Thank Mrs Seymour for her kind words, and with my love to you both,

Always yours,- | Wilkie Collins[3]

Notes

1. Reade wrote to WC, 19 March 1876: "In this story, in Temple Bar, as far as I have read it, there is a pace of language, and a vein of sweet tenderness running through the whole, which reveal maturing genius."
2. George Critchett, MD, (1817–1882), WC's eye surgeon.
3. Clareson writes "This is the only letter in the entire group [of WC's letters to Charles Reade and Laura Seymour] in the hand of his amanuensis, Mrs Graves's daughter" (p. 117).

To Andrew Chatto,[1] 11 April 1876
MS: Princeton

90, Gloucester Place, | Portman Square. W. | 11th April 1876

Summary:
Owing to "gout in the eye" WC has fallen behind with "The Two Destinies".

Note

1. Andrew Chatto (d. 1913, aged 73), took over the publishing firm founded by John Camden Hotten (1832–1873) in 1855. Chatto & Windus issued its first catalogue in July 1874 and in 1876 bought *Belgravia*. Chatto published WC's *The Law and the Lady* in 1875 and thereafter became his main publishers (see Gasson).

To George Bentley, 14 April 1876
MS: NYPL (Berg)

90, Gloucester Place, | Portman Square. W. | Good Friday 1876

Summary:
Forced to "devote all" his energy to rehearsals of his "new play".[1]

Note

1. *Miss Gwilt* opened at the Globe Theatre on 15 April 1876. It was a resounding success.

To Mrs Laura Seymour, 19 April 1876
MS: Mrs Juliet Noel (née Reade)

[90, Gloucester Place, | Portman Square. W. | 19th April 1876]

[My dear Mrs Seymour,]
[You are] the trump of trumps – and the best and truest of friends [for praising "Miss Gwilt"].

I have but one excuse for not having sent you the best places in the theatre – I was <u>afraid</u> to ask any of my friends to go to the first night. Though I had but one eye to look through, on the few last occasions when I could go to rehearsal, I saw that the scenery was so backward and (excepting the first act) so bad, and the people connected with this theatre[1] (for the most part) such a set of incapable idiots and blackguards – that I fully anticipated a failure on the first night – and I own I did not like the idea of inviting my friends to hear me hissed! The kindness of the audience, as things really were (I believe they caught it mesmerically from <u>you</u>) has really left me deeply grateful. Never before have I been so indebted to my good and dear public.

At 8 o'Clock the scenes were not all ready! At 9 o'clock the scoundrels of carpenters were lying about <u>drunk</u> – and their chief utterly lost his head. No more of it! I have not been able to prevail upon myself to go near the theatre since.

[Yrs affly | WC]

Note

1. i.e., The Globe theatre.

To Kate Field, 22 April 1876
MS: Boston Public Library. Published, L. Whiting, *Kate Field: A Record*, (Boston, 1899), p. 346.

90, Gloucester Place, | Portman Square. W. | April 22, 1876

Dear Miss Field, – I was very sorry to miss you, but I sleep badly since my illness, and cannot get up in the morning. The doctor allows me to get out for a walk (with a patch over my eye), but he has not yet allowed me to see my own play, and he forbids me to see your "matinée". The lights and the atmosphere are the things he objects to, and I am afraid he is right. The pain I have suffered has seriously weakened me. I can only wish you success most sincerely, and hope for another chance of making one of your audience.

I am glad you liked the piece and the acting. You must have been looking at the wrong "compartment" when Cecil drew the curtains and opened the windows. It is (of course) the first thing he does on entering the "drawing-room". The play cannot end unless he does it, for the matron and the policeman in plain clothes (who bring the curtain down) enter by the window. The rest of your questions I hope to answer <u>viva voce</u>, but I <u>am</u> surprised at your never having met in real life with a woman who fell in love with a man utterly unworthy of her. Oh, Miss Keemle, Miss Keemle, have you still to discover one of the brightest virtues of the sex?

Yours always truly, | Wilkie Collins

To Frederick Lehmann, 26 April 1876
MS: Princeton

90, Gloucester Place, | Portman Square. W. | 26th April 1876

My dear Fred,

Tell me about Sebastian. He kindly called here when Critchett had forbidden me to see anyone – and he left word that he was "going away". If I had known it was S. I would have disobeyed orders. He has not "gone away" to Boston U.S. I hope. Where can I find him – or rather when does he return to London?

I am slowly mending – able to use my good eye, and still obliged to take care of the other. Add arrears of work on any story that must be made up, and a play for Bancroft that is in progress – and you will not be surprised at my failing to call in Berkeley Square. I am still forbidden Dinners, Theatres, and all assemblies in which part of the pleasure consists of breathing vitiated air and swallowing superfluous particles of flesh given off by our fellow creatures and ourselves in the act of respiration. Work, walk. Visit to my morganatic family – such is life to yours affly, | W.C.

My love of loves to the Padrona.

To George Maclean Rose, 3 May 1876
MS: Princeton

90, Gloucester Place, | Portman Square. W. | London | 3rd May 1876

Dear Mr Rose,

I am indeed grieved to hear so sad an account of Mr Hunter.[1] Change of air and scene are – as I should think – the very remedies for such a case as his. But if y<u>ou</u> cannot prevail upon him, <u>I</u> have but little chance of succeeeding, I fear. Pray assure him of my sympathy and of my best wishes for his complete restoration to health.

I only wish I could take that pleasant voyage to Canada this summer. I have too pleasant a recollection of the days I spent with you and Mr Hunter, not to wish to see Toronto again. But I have engagements to produce new plays in London which will not allow me to leave England until the fine season is over. I have some hope – if all goes well – of returning to the "States" perhaps in 1877 – and of then seeing you once more.

In the meantime, believe me always truly yours | Wilkie Collins

P.S. I am getting on well towards recovery. Nothing wrong with the gouty eye now but weakness. I shall send more "Two Destinies" soon.

Note

1. Hunter (d. 1877), George Maclean Rose's partner.

To George Bentley, 31 May 1876
MS: NYPL (Berg)

90, Gloucester Place, | Portman Square. W. |[1] 31st May 1876

My dear Mr Bentley,

I beg to thank you for a Cheque for the June number.

It is a matter of regret to me that I should have (unintentionally) misled you on the subject of the length of the "Destinies". The story is a very difficult one to manage – and I am now considering how I can turn it so as to be able to finish it in August. It is mainly a question of my being able to write a long number – instead of the short numbers with which my illness has hitherto forced me to be content since May last. At the very worst, I cannot possibly be later than September – but I repeat I hope to finish in August.

There is another point about which I am not quite comfortable. When you kindly met my views on the subject of terms, we both supposed that we were dealing with a short story. May I venture to suggest – as [an old] friend – that the June number should be considered as terminating our agreement, so far as the extra terms are concerned, and will you let me send you the concluding numbers of the story at the average paper-remuneration of the "Bar"? I am sure I may trust to our long friendship to excuse my making this proposal frankly – as an act of plain justice towards you.

Believe me | Always truly yours | Wilkie Collins

George Bentley Eq

Note

1. Above the Gothic printed address WC writes: "Private", which he doubly underlines.

To William Winter,[1] 18 June 1877
MS: Folger

90, Gloucester Place, | Portman Square. W. | 18th June 1877

My dear Sir,
You need no introduction to me – though I am glad to hear from my friends Whitelaw Reid[2] and Boucicault. I was one of your readers in America, and was sorry that I missed the opportunity – which you now kindly offer to me – of becoming personally acquainted with you.

Until within the last few weeks, I have been confined to my room by rheumatic gout. The malady has now descended from my eyes to my knees. Getting in and out of a carriage and taking a chair or leaving a chair are still such serious difficulties to me that I must ask you to forgive me, for the present, if I fail to follow my letter personally. But, when you are passing near this street, pray take the opportunity (if you can spare me a few minutes) of letting me see you here. I am always at home until half past two in the afternoon. Soon after that time, I am taking to certain electric baths, which I hope are helping me to get well. Choose your own day, and think only of your own convenience – and, meanwhile, believe me,

Faithfully yours | Wilkie Collins

William Winter Eqre

Notes

1. William Winter (1836–1917), dramatic critic of *the New York Tribune*: see Gasson.
2. Whitelaw Reid (1837–1912), Cincinnati journalist and editor from 1872 of the *New York Tribune*.

To Fanny Davenport,[1] 28 July 1877

MS: Present whereabouts unknown. TL/copy. Text, Coleman

90, Gloucester Place, | Portman Square. W. | 28th July 1877

My dear Miss Davenport,

I am indeed sorry to hear that you are obliged to hurry your departure – but I see the necessity, and deplore it.

The best likeness of me is unfortunately not on card-board. I enclose it, as a temporary offering, until I can send something more durable. Thank you most sincerely, for the charming photographs which have accompanied your kind letter. The make-up in Posthumia[2] is really marvellous – quite as true to nature, and quite as effective in a dramatic point of view as the make- up of the French actress.

I must ask you to let me send the piece[3] after you. The printers have not got more than half way through it – and the manuscript is in their hands. You shall have the proofs. If I address to the Fifth Avenue Theatre, N.Y. I suppose my letter will reach you.

Whatever I can do, shall be done, rely on it, when you return to us. In the meantime, I will keep The Moonstone piece free, so far as America is concerned, until you have kindly sent me a line to say whether the principal part is "a part of Miss Davenport" – or not. We begin here on the 1st or 8th of September next.

My rheumatism keeps me terribly dependent on the weather. But I will try hard to get to you on Monday just to say goodbye, and then to run away again, a few minutes before six. If the damp cripples me as it crippled me today – then I must put up with my disappointment, and heartily wish you and your fellow travellers, the most peaceful and prosperous of all possible voyages (in this letter).

Yours most truly, | Wilkie Collins

Notes

1. Fanny Davenport (1850–1898: *DAB*), American actress.
2. Unidentified.
3. The dramatic version of *The Moonstone* opened on 17 September 1877 at the Olympic and ran to poor houses for a month.

To Carlotta Leclerq,[1] 1 August 1877
MS: Texas: Coleman

90, Gloucester Place, | Portman Square. W. | 1 August 1877

My dear Mrs Nelson,

Let me first assure you that I am not guilty of the rudeness of leaving your earlier letter unanswered. I never received it. And I only heard of your marriage through "The [indecipherable word]". My congratulations are late – but they are still sincere. I know you will understand this.

As to Black and White, the whole piece was written by me. Fechter suggested the subject and helped me with the scenario – and therefore thought it right that his name should appear with mine on the original playbills. Strictly speaking, the right (so far as Great Britain and Ireland are concerned) rests with me as the writer of the piece. I have never allowed it to be published, or to be placed on the list at the Dramatic Author's Society.

But, where you are concerned, I will gladly assume that a small share in the piece is all that I need claim, in the matter of fees only. I allow no piece of mine to be performed in the country, except on payment of five pounds a night. Halve that – and you are welcome to Black and White (and to my name), for two pounds, ten shillings a night. If this arrangement suits you, you have only to write and say so – and to ask Mr Nelson to sign the letter also (in case of my executors interfering in the matter!) – and there is the business settled.

I have been so wretchedly ill that the reference to my executors is not quite so good a joke as it might once have been. Rheumatic gout again – first in my eyes – now in my knees. When my new Moonstone piece is produced in September next at the Olympic, I go to try what the mountain air of Switzerland or the Tyrol will do for me – and I may be obliged to winter out of England. I will write to you again before I go – if you will kindly send me a general address "at headquarters", from which letters can be forwarded wherever you may be.

In the meantime, with all good wishes, and with my compliments to Mr Nelson,

Believe me, | Always [but] yours, | Wilkie Collins

There is a little story of mine published in The Summer (Extra) number of All the Year Round called "Percy and the Prophet"[2] which may amuse you on a long railway journey, and which has dramatic capabilities. I have not got a copy left – or, I would have sent one (Price 6d!). You will find it at all railway stations.

Notes

1. Carlotta Leclerq (Mrs John Nelson) (c.1838–1893), who played Miss Milburn in *Black and White*.
2. 2 July 1877.

To Nina Lehmann, 28 December 1877
MS: Princeton

90, Gloucester Place | London. | W. | 28th December 1877

Dearest Padrona,

I guess I shall be just in time to wish you and Fred, and the sons and the daughter, all possible health and happiness in the year to come. If I could have offered you my good wishes at your villa, need I say how much better I should have been pleased? But there are all sorts of impediments – literary and personal – which keep me in England at the most hateful of all English seasons (to <u>me</u>), the season of Cant and Christmas.

Good natured friends tell me that I look twenty years younger after my travels. I am certainly much stronger than I was – and I hope to fight through the winter. The fog and rain met me at Paris, and prepared me for the horrors of London.

I am charmed to hear that the Cannes climate has done you so much good. Thirty years ago, I remember it as a delightfully snug, small, cheap place – with t<u>wo</u> English people only established in it, Lord Brougham, and another Britisher whose name I forget. It is plain that I should not know Cannes again if I saw it now. Brougham – beginning with a B[1] – reminds me of "Samuel Brohl & [Co]".[2] I am going to begin the book tonight in bed. Thank you for remembering to send it. But for Christmas-time, I should have read it long ago. I have returned to heaps of unanswered letters, bills, payments to pensioners, stupid and hideous Christmas cards, visits to pay – and every other social nuisance that gets in the way of a rational enjoyment of life. As to modern French novels <u>in general</u>, I read them by dozens on my travels – and my report of them all is briefly this: – Dull and Dirty. The "Nabob" by Daudet (of whom I once hoped better things) proved to be such realistic rubbish, that I rushed out (it was at Dijon) to get something "to take the taste out of my mouth", as the children say. Prosper Merimée's delicious "Columba"[3] appeared providentially in a shop window – I instantly secured it, read it for the second time, and recovered my opinion of French Literature. You know the book of course? If not, I must sent it to you instantly!

There is no news. Everybody is eating and drinking and exchanging conventional compliments of the season. You are well out of it all. Give my love to Fred, and thank him for his kind letter – and write again and tell me that you are getting immense reserves of health, and announce when y<u>ou</u> too are likely to be recaptured by the great London net. Goodbye dear Padrona.

Yours affly | W.C

Notes

1. "B" underlined twice.
2. Cherbuliez, *Samuel Brohl and Partner*: one of Vizetelly's Popular French Novels series, first published Paris, 1877.
3. A copy of the French writer Prosper Merimée's (1803–1870) *Théatre* was in WC's library: Puttick and Simpson *Catalogue*, 20 January 1890, item 179.

To Unknown Recipient, 4 January 1878

MS: Princeton

90, Gloucester Place | London. W. | 4th January 1878

Dear Sir,

I have been travelling abroad for the last three months – and the first letter to which you refer has not reached me. I now send with pleasure the information you ask in your second letter of December 17th, last.

My father and Mother are both dead. My father was born in London on the 18th September 1788. As <u>William Collins R.</u>A his name is well known in Great Britain, and among picture-collectors in America. He was a Royal Academician of the English Academy of Arts – and he is celebrated as a painter of the Coast Scenery and the cottage life of England.

My mother was born in the near neighbourhood of the Cathedral town of Salisbury (England). Her father was an officer in the army – and her maiden name was Miss Harriet Geddes.

I was born in London on the 8th of January 1824. I was christened "Wilkie" after the name of the famous Scottish Painter, David Wilkie, who was my father's dear and intimate friend.

=

With this contribution to your collection,

I remain, Dear Sir, | Faithfully yours | Wilkie Collins

To Andrew Chatto, 7 January 1878
MS: Princeton

90, Gloucester Place, | Portman Square. W. |[1] 7th Jany 1878

Dear Mr Chatto,

Inquiries have been addressed to me on the subject of publishing my next work of fiction in a Magazine. And I write to you confidentially, before I reply that I am free to negotiate.

I have an idea – if I can carry it out – of dividing my next novel into three Parts,[2] or Books, each sufficiently complete in itself for separate publication. Each Part would occupy from one hundred to one hundred and thirty pages (100 to 130) of my customary MSS, as I now calculate – and [word erased] my MS page may be taken as representing roughly a printed page of "Belgravia".[3] I should propose to be guided by the public reception of the first Part in the matter of continuing the work in the same form through the two other Parts – and I should not be ready to publish the first monthly instalment of the first Part or Book before June or July next. I should, as usual, reserve the copyright, and the right of deciding in what form the reprint should be issued on the completion of the first part of the story periodically.

Will you kindly let me know whether you wish to arrange with me for the right of periodically publishing the first "Part", or not.

In the event of the work assuming larger proportions than I now contemplate, [or if the state of my health obliges me to defer writing the work,][4] I should propose to give my publisher due notice, and to substitute some other (and shorter) complete story – so that the magazine might still have me as a contributor, and at the same time be perfectly free to consult its own convenience in the matter of [re-opening] the original negotiation on a larger scale.

Believe me | Dear Mr Chatto | Very truly yours | Wilkie Collins

To Andrew Chatto Esq

Notes

1. Above the Gothic printed address, WC writes "Private" which he underlines twice.
2. The letters "ar" are underlined twice.
3. WC's "The Haunted Hotel" seralized in *Belgravia Magazine*, June–November 1878. On 1 January 1879 *The Fallen Leaves* began in *The World*.
4. Written in the margin.

To Andrew Chatto, 12 January 1878
MS: Princeton

90, Gloucester Place, | Portman Square. W. |[1] 12th Jany 1878

Dear Mr Chatto,

I have decided, on reflection, to defer arranging for the periodical publication of my contemplated novel. The question of issuing the story as a monthly serial requires longer consideration than I am able to give to it just now.

As to a shorter story, complete in itself, I have an idea of writing one of about the same length as "My Lady's Money" (which occupies 110 of my MSS pages), with a view to republishing the two together in two volumes (Circulating Library Form) about next Christmas time. Would it help you in making an arrangement with me for "Belgravia" if you had the rights of republishing the new story[2] and "My Lady's Money" for the Libraries?

Will you kindly consider this idea, at your convenience, and let me know what you think of it?

Very truly Yours | Wilkie Collins

Andrew Chatto Esq

Notes

1. Above the Gothic printed address, WC writes "Private" which he underlines twice.
2. "My Lady's Money: an Episode in the Life of a Young Lady" appeared with "The Haunted Hotel" in book-form in two vols, published by Chatto & Windus in October 1878.

To James Payn,[1] 13 February 1878
MS: Texas: Coleman

90, Gloucester Place, | Portman Square. W. |[2] 13th Feby 1878

My dear Payn

Few words to thank you for your friendly letter – and to report that I am (say) half alive. While I was away last year in France and Italy, I was 25 years old. Towards the end of '77, being obliged to return to my native damps and changes, I became, by rheumatic "reckoning", 95. And what is the moral of this? The moral is – not to pass another winter in England. As to making calls – we can't either of us do it, and thank God we both know it and are as old friends and as true friends as ever. Keep the publishing business active – or the water will drown it!

My kindest regards to Mrs Payn

Always yours truly, | W C

Note

1. James Payn (1830–1898; *DNB*), novelist: see Gasson.
2. WC changes his printed stationery. The print no longer uses Gothic lower case but bold upper case throughout with the "WC" monogram at the top left of the paper.

To William Winter, 5 August 1878

MS: Stanford. Published with variants in J.T. Bender, *Six Letters of Wilkie Collins*: W. Winter, *Old Friends* (1909), pp. 206–8.

90, Gloucester Place, | Portman Square. W. |[1]
London August 5^t 1878

My dear Mr Winter,

Your kind and friendly letter found me in a darkened room, suffering again from one of my attacks of rheumatic gout in the eye. I am only now well enough to use my eyes and my pen once more – and I hasten to ask you to forgive me for a delay in writing to you which has been forced upon me, in the most literal sense of the word.

Let me get away from the disagreeable subject of myself and my illnesses – and beg you to accept my most sincere thanks for the gift of your last volume of poems. My first renewal of the pleasure of reading is associated with your pages. I ought to warn you that I am an incorrigible heretic in the matter of modern poetry, of the sort that is now popular. I positively decline to let the poet preach to me or puzzle me. He is to express passions and sentiment in language which is essentially intelligible as well as spiritually noble and musical – or I will have nothing to do with him. You will now not be surprised to hear that I delight in Byron and Scott – and, more extraordinary still, that I am a frequent reader even of Crabbe![2] Having made my confession, I am sure you will believe I speak sincerely, when I thank you for some hours of real pleasure, derived from your volume. Both in feeling and expression I find your poetry (to use a phrase which I don't much like, but which expresses exactly what I mean to say) "thoroughly sympathetic". "The Ideal", "A Dirge", and "Rosemary" are three among my chief favourites. I thank you again for them – and for all the rest.[3]

I have been too completely out of the world to have any news to tell you. As to literature, we are in a sadly stagnant state in London. And as to "the

British Theatre" the less (with one or two rare exceptions) said about it the better. Writing of the theatre, however, I am reminded that my "New Magdalen" Ada Cavendish sails on the 24th to try her fortune in the United States. She has, I think, more of the sacred fire in her than any other living English actress of "Drama" – and she has the two excellent qualities of being always eager to improve and always ready to take advice in her Art. I am really interested in her well-doing, and I am especially anxious to hear what y<u>ou</u> think of her. In the "Magdalen" and also in "Miss Gwilt" (a piece altered, from "Armadale", by Régnier (of the Théatre Français) – and by myself), she has done things which electrified our English audiences. If you should be sufficiently interested in her to give her a word of advice in the art, she will be grateful, and I shall be grateful too.

I am "bestowing my tediousness" on you without mercy – and my paper warns me that the time has come to say for the present Goodbye. Let me come to an end by expressing a hope that you will give me another opportunity of proving myself a better correspondent. In the mean time, with all good wishes, believe me Ever yours Wilkie Collins

Notes

1. Above the printed address, WC writes: "When you see Mr Jefferson pray remember me kindly to him."
2. An eight-volume Crabbe was in WC's Library at his death.
3. A copy of Winter's *Thistledown: a Book of Lyrics* (1878) and other works by Winter were in WC's library at his death.

To William Seaver, 6 August 1878
MS: Princeton

90, Gloucester Place, | Portman Square. W. | [1]
London 6th Aug[t] 1878

My dear Seaver,

The nerves sufficiently – to be – damned – and – blasted – rheumatic gout, has [erased word] hit me in one of my eyes again. I am only now able to use my other sound eye without damaging its inflamed neighbour. The illness sees me just after I had called on Miss [Eytinge], and had a most pleasant talk with her. From that time to this, to my great regret, I have not been well enough to see her again – and next week I am to be exiled to the seaside by my doctor's order. Forgive me for boring you with these troubles – I only want you to know that I am never wilfully neglectful of any friend of mine.

And now, there goes sailing to long suffering America, a<u>noth</u>er English actress – but this time a true artist. My nice little "New Magdalen", Ada Cavendish, leaves us for New York on the 24th of this month. See her in the "Magdalen" and in "Miss Gwilt" (my "Armadale" transformed for the stage) – and if you <u>can</u> do her a kindness, don't forget that it is another kindness shown to <u>me</u>.

Goodbye, my dear friend, for the present.

Yours ever | Wilkie Collins

Note

1. Above the printed address WC writes: "My last morsel of note-paper – until the Stationers send some more!"

To Andrew Chatto, 31 August 1878
MS: Princeton

[4, Nelson Crescent, Ramsgate] Augt 31st 1878

Dear Mr Chatto,

The cheque followed me to Ramsgate, the day after I received your kind note. On the next page you will find the formal acknowledgements.

If you see Bret Harte again,[1] pray give him my kindest remembrances – I am very sorry to miss seeing him during his present short visit to London.

As soon as I begin the International Review story I am to hear from the London Editor when they propose to publish. You shall know the date without fail.[2] The last breezy days have soaked me in salt water – and the wind seems to have blown my brains out of my head.

But I hope to make a beginning next week.

Very truly yours, | W.C.

I enclose the Revise of the October number – to go to the printers, please, with some new corrections for press.

Proofs of the last number received this morning. Sunday 1st September.

Notes

1. Francis Brett Harte (1836–1902), distinguished American author and US consul at Crefeld, Rhenish Prussia (1878), and Glasgow (1880–1885). Harte was among the guests at the Lotus Club, New York dinner in WC's honour, 27 September 1873.
2. WC has erased a line. *The International Review* published "A Shocking Story" in November 1878.

To Sebastian Schlesinger, 12 November 1878
MS: Harvard

> 90, Gloucester Place, | Portman Square. W. | London |
> 12th November 1878

My dear Sebastian Schlesinger,

If today's Steamer to Boston gets along nicely, it will bring you a little box, with two volumes of a new book of mine – and if you will look at the 1st Volume, on the Dedication page, you will see that I have taken the liberty of inscribing the book to you and Mrs Sebastian[1] – to whom I beg to send my kindest remembrances.

Tell me if you get the book safely and if you both forgive me, I have been long wanting to send you some little token of my remembrance of those happy days in [Marlborough] Street – and I only waited until I had done something especially successful. Here – and in Germany and Russia – "The Haunted Hotel" has been one of the most popular stories I have ever written – so I took my opportunity in case I might write something worse next time – or cheat my dear American insurance offices by dying too soon – or Lord knows what else.

I have been trying to get nice and healthy by cruising at sea. The yacht was too small – otherwise I should have brought my books to Boston myself.

With best wishes to both of you

> Yours ever | Wilkie Collins

Note

1. WC inscribed *The Haunted Hotel* to "Mr & Mrs Sebastian Schlesinger, in Remembrance of Much Kindness and of Many Happy Days".

To George Bentley, 14 December 1878
MS: NYPL (Berg)

> 90, Gloucester Place, | Portman Square. W. |[1]
> 14th Decr. 1878

Dear Mr Bentley,

I was indeed sorry to hear that I had missed seeing you when I got back to the house yesterday evening.

Let me thank you for the kind manner in which you have settled the matter of the "Marmaduke" story[2] (the formal acknowledgement is on the next leaf) – and for the addition which you have been so good as to make to my library. It seems to me to be an excellent idea – carried out (so far as externals are concerned in the first place) with thorough good taste, and I don't doubt equally well managed in relation to the literary substance inside. I am already deep in the "Penal Servitude"[3] – a book I had long wished to read – and I am delighted with it. The writer (whoever he may be) is not only a born observer – he has also the rare merit of being able to make other people really see what he has seen himself.

If you are likely to be in New Burlington Street, on Tuesday next, I will take my chance of shaking hands with you, between two and three o'Clock. Don't trouble to write again – unless Wednesday will do better than Tuesday.

Vy truly yours | Wilkie Collins

Notes

1. Above the printed address WC writes: "One word about reserving the right of translation. My German publisher tells me that 'All rights reserved' reserves nothing in <u>his</u> country. The phrase must be 'The Right of Translation is Reserved' – because that is the <u>only</u> right you and I have in Germany!!!"
2. "The Mystery of Marmaduke" published in *The Spirit of the Times*, 28 December 1878.
3. In 1877 Bentley published *Five Years' Penal Servitude, by One Who Has Endured It*.

To the Editor of *Harper's Bazaar*, 18 December 1878
MS: Houghton, Harvard

90, Gloucester Place, | Portman Square. W. |
[1] London. | 18th December 1878

In the "Sayings and Doings" column of <u>Harper</u>'s <u>Bazaar</u>, for the 14th of December there is a paragraph which states that I am the author of a completion of "Edwin Drood", recently published, in the French language in Paris.[2]

I shall be obliged if the Editor will publicly contradict this report – so far as I am concerned in it – at the earliest opportunity. I never even heard of the work falsely attributed to me, until I saw the allusion to it in the <u>Bazaar</u>.

The writer of the paragraph in question, accounting for the publication of the spurious "Edwin Drood" in French, further adds that "British copyright law does not prevail in Paris" – thus associating me, by implication, with a meanly-planned evasion of the law of my own country, in relation to the unfinished work of one of my oldest and dearest friends!

It may not be amiss to inform the contributor to "Sayings and Doings" – who must surely have been thinking of the United States while he wrote – that there is an International Copyright Treaty between England and France, and that the rights of literary property (duly asserted under the Treaty)[3] are strictly respected in Paris.

Wilkie Collins

Notes

1. Above the printed address, WC writes: "To The Editor of Harper's Bazaar".
2. See Peters, pp. 364–5.
3. WC underlines the first letter of "Treaty" twice.

To Nina Lehmann, 20 December 1878
MS: Princeton

90, Gloucester Place, | Portman Square. W. | London |
20th Decr 1878

I have but one excuse, dearest Padrona, for not having long since thanked you for your kind letter – the old excuse of hard work and poor health. But I hold up my head still – and lead the life of a hermit – and (may I confess it?) enjoy the life. Your Wilkie is getting old – there is no mistake about that!

And how do you like Paris! And how does my dear "blonde Mees" Nina finish her education? She must remain like herself mind – she must not be made into a French <u>ingénue</u>. With this important message, take my love and give a bit of it to N.

Do you sometimes lie awake, and want a little something to read you to sleep again? I send you by book-post two little stories which they have bribed me to write in America – and which have been of course republished here. Don't trouble to send them back. Tear them up when you have done with them.

Later I shall have more proofs (of the love story which is coming out in Th<u>e</u> World)[1] to send to you – perhaps to bring it I can make a holiday, six weeks or so hence.

We have had lights <u>all day long</u> in London – and the fog has got into my head – and I must go and walk it <u>out</u> again – and get an appetite for the glorious [paté] which the good Fred has sent to me.

Will you write again, I w<u>on</u>der, to your affectionate <u>W.C</u>?

Note

1. *The Fallen Leaves – The First Series*, published in *The World*, 1878 to 1879, and *The Canadian Monthly*, February 1879 to March 1880.

To Leslie Ward,[1] 20 January 1879
MS: Texas: Coleman

> 90, Gloucester Place, | Portman Square. W. |
> 20th Jany 1879

Dear Leslie Ward,

No ordinary engagement would prevent me from paying the last tribute of affection to my dear lost friend. Illness alone makes it impossible for me to join those who will follow him to the grave tomorrow. I am suffering from rheumatism – and, in the present state of the weather, the doctor's advice obliges me to give up the hope of being with you.

I first knew your father when I was a boy – forty years since – and it is no figure of speech, it is only the sad truth, to say that I do indeed share in your grief, and feel the inexpressible loss that you have suffered as, in some degree at least, my loss too. I do not venture to intrude so soon on your mother's sorrow, after the dreadful calamity that has fallen on your household. I only ask you to assure her of my heartfelt sympathy, when it is possible for her to think of old friends.

> Believe me, | Always most truly yours, | Wilkie Collins

Note

1. Sir Leslie Ward (1851–1922: *DNB*), cartoonist, second son of E.M. Ward. The latter committed suicide in January 1879.

To George Bentley, 5 March 1879
MS: NYPL (Berg)

> 90, Gloucester Place, | Portman Square. W. |
> 5th March 1879

Dear Mr Bentley,

I hope to send the Rogue corrected for Press to the printers this week – with a few prefatory lines,[1] relating to the original publication of the Story.

As well as I can remember – the enclosed Draft – represents the arrangement which we made in that never-to-be-forgotten sanctuary of literature which I first entered more than a quarter of a century since![2] Will you kindly look the Dft over, and, if it satisfies you, let me have it back again to be fair copied in duplicate?

> Vy truly yours | Wilkie Collins

George Bentley Eqre
Excepting the portion which relates to the half profits, the Dft is merely a
copy of the customary formal document which I have used for some years
past.

Notes

1. In "Introductory Words", dated "March 6th 1879", to *A Rogue's Life*, published 7 April 1879
   by Bentley, WC writes: "The critical reader may possibly notice a tone of almost boisterous
   gaiety in certain parts of these imaginary Confessions ... I can only plead, in defence, that
   the story offers the faithful reflection of a very happy time in my past life. It was written
   at Paris, when I had Charles Dickens for a near neighbour and a daily companion, and
   when my leisure hours were joyously passed with many other friends, all associated with
   literature and art" (pp. [iii]–iv).
2. Bentley published WC's first novel *Antonina: or the Fall of Rome* (1850).

To George Bentley, 10 March 1879
MS: NYPL (Berg)

> 90, Gloucester Place, | Portman Square. W. |
> 10th March 1879

Summary:
Accepts Bentley's financial proposal. Has read "with interest" William
Howitt's (1792–1879: *DNB*) letter. "Literary men are – God Knows why!
such a divided body in England that I never personally knew Howitt"
even when he lived and worked in England.

To Georgina Hogarth, 18 March 1879
MS: University of Illinois, Urbana.

> 90, Gloucester Place, | Portman Square. W. |
> 18th March 1879

My dear Georgina
    My opinion is decidedly against publishing either of the two letters.
    The letter relating to Bentley, refers to a matter afterwards arranged
amicably – and, as you remember, the late Richard Bentley was Dickens's
guest at Gadshill. The injury being forgiven – it is most undesirable to
return to it now.
    The second letter would lead, I think, to a very false idea of Dickens's
character in the reader's mind. The references to Scott, Bulwer, and Marryat

would be misunderstood as expressions of overweening self-esteem – and the present Chapman would not like the tone in which the partners are referred to. I vote for suppressing this letter too.[1]

Can I help you with the brief biographical narrative preceding the first "epoch" (or collection) of the letters – briefly describing his social and domestic positions – his residences, his work, his old and new friends within the interval embraced in his earlier letters? If Yes – you have only to say so. It is most important that the public should be placed, in some degree, in the position of persons who knew him, at the time when he wrote the letters.

I am obliged to worry you with <u>my</u> affairs. I am bringing an action in Paris against the man who has written (or translated) a conclusion to Edwin Drood, and put my name to the published French book, with Dickens's. It is an outrage offered to Dickens's reputation to associate his great name with rubbish which is utterly unworthy of it – setting my own injury out of the question. The formal declaration which I enclose may be wanted at the trial. If you feel the slightest hesitation about signing it, tear it up and say nothing about it. If not, you will be doing me a kindness, if you let me have it back signed at your earliest convenience. I ought perhaps to add that the only object of the action is to force the man to declare by public advertisement that I have never written a conclusion to 'Edwin Drood', and to make the publishers take my name off the title of the book.[2]

always yours affly | W.C

Notes

1. Georgina Hogarth was preparing an edition of Dickens' letters: See Peters, p. 348 and Dickens, *Letters*, I, ix–x.
2. An 1879 French forgery of the conclusion to *Drood* attributed to WC and Charles Dickens Junior incensed WC. They took legal advice to stop publication.

To Frederick Chapman,[1] 28 March 1879
MS: British Library

[90, Gloucester Place, | Portman Square. W.]
28th March [1879]

My dear Sir

Miss Hogarth agrees with me that the book which I send to you with this Note ought to be seen by your firm.

The person responsible for this fraudulent use made of Dickens's name and of mine is one Bernard Derosne[2] – employed as a translator. I have never written a line of this work attributed to me, and I am bringing an action against Derosne in Paris which will be probably decided in two or three days time.

The [indecipherable word: lawyer] (and friend) who is managing the matter for me in Paris has recently compared the French Book with "Edwin Drood" – and finds that there is not even a pretence of translating Dickens's uncompleted Story. His <u>Name</u> also has been used to sell a book which contains nothing of his writing.

I should add that M. Dentu (The publisher) has undertaken to remove my name from the title page and Cover of "Le Crime de Jasper".

Faithfully yours | Wilkie Collins

To | Frederic Chapman, Esq

Notes

1. Frederick Chapman (1823–1895), publisher who ran Chapman and Hall, Dickens' principal publisher, who from 1870 controlled all Dickens' copyrights (Sutherland, p. 116).
2. C. Bernard Derosne, translator of *Man and Wife* (Paris, 1872), and *The New Magdalen* (Paris, 1873).

To George Bentley, 13 May 1879
MS: NYPL (Berg)

90, Gloucester Place, | Portman Square. W. |[1]
13th May 1879

Summary:

Sends more proofs and makes publication arrangements: "you will see that the treatment which shows the girl (from physical causes) to be the innocent victim of a degradation which is her misfortune and not her fault, is continued. Her life with 'Amelius' will be left a pure life at the end of the present division of the story."[2]

Notes

1. Above the printed address WC writes "Private" which he underlines twice.
2. *The Fallen Leaves: First Series* published in three vols by Chatto & Windus, 1–16 July 1879; serialized in *The World*, 1 January–23 July 1879; and in *The Canadian Monthly*, February 1879–March 1880.

To George Bentley, 27 July 1879
MS: NYPL (Berg)

Ramsgate | [1] 27th July 1879

Dear Mr Bentley

I think I told you that I was advising Miss Hogarth and Miss Dickens, in the business of editing Dickens's Letters. They ask me to help them to decide the question of price. The book will be in two volumes demy oct: and each volume will contain 456 pages. – Thirty shillings or Two pounds – which is the wisest selling price to decide on? Do you think I am right or wrong in supposing that the lower price (£1..10..–) is the safest price to ask in these times?

I am ashamed to trouble you on a subject in which the interest of other persons are concerned. But you have great experience in this matter[2] – and my ignorance only asks for (literally) one line of reply, as a favour to <u>me</u>.

Vy truly yours | Wilkie Collins

I am cruising about the English Channel. Letters addressed to 90 Gloucester Place, as usual, will always follow me.
To | George Bentley Eqre

Notes

1. Above the town WC writes "<u>Private</u>".
2. Published in three volumes by Chapman & Hall, 1880–82. Volume 3 cost 14 shillings; the first two volumes 8 shillings each.

To Georgina Hogarth, 23 October 1879
MS: University of Illinois, Urbana.

90, Gloucester Place, | Portman Square. W. |
Thursday Oct 23/79

My dear Georgina,

I <u>must</u> make one minutes' use of my sound eye to thank you with all my heart for the beautiful and welcome gift that reached me yesterday. A more charming token of remembrance could not have been offered to me.

In spite of the damp foggy weather, I don't fall back – the sight is only slightly affected – and the pain is trifling. I have every hope of escaping one of my long illnesses this time.

Pray remember that I am still entirely at your service. Don't sanction s<u>mall</u> advertisements. <u>One</u> "across columns" in the weekly newspaper, (one big one) is worth a dozen little ones – and costs less.

Yours always affectionately dear Georgina | W.C

To Georgina Hogarth, 28 November 1879

MS: University of Illinois, Urbana.

90, Gloucester Place, | Portman Square. W. |
28th Novr 1879

My dear Georgina,

It is difficult to estimate what the Continental Reprint is really worth to Tauchnitz (I don't even know how many of his Volumes it will fill) that I should advise putting the [questions: erased] matter thus to [young] Tauchnitz:

"We publish the book at our own risk and cost in England and have therefore had no dealing with publishers which can at all guide us in asking terms. We know that we are treating with friends as well as publishers in sending our book to your father and to yourself – and we therefore venture to ask you, who can estimate the value of the continental reprint better than we can, to afford us the benefit of your experience, and to tell us frankly what terms you think you are justified in offering."

You are dealing with Gentlemen – and I think something of this sort will produce a reply that may be satisfactory on both sides.[1]

When you next write, I hope and trust to hear that Mamie's[2] health is improving. I think of <u>my</u> poor dear Mother's death bed and know but too well how long-continued [sorrow] and suspense affect the body as well as the mind.

With love to you both, your ever affty | W.C

"Freiherr von | Tauchnitz" | is the title on | Tauchnitz Junior's cards.

Notes

1. Tauchnitz published Dickens' *Letters, Edited by His Sister-in-Law and His Eldest Daughter*, in 3 vols, February 1880 (see Todd and Bowden, item 1868, p. 299).
2. i.e., Mary Dickens (1838–1896).

Part VIII
Illness, Work and Family
1880–1885

Introduction

March and April 1880 were spent at Ramsgate cruising, writing and enjoying his family. Already Wilkie is into another serial novel. Letters to American friends such as Louise Chandler Moulton, William Seaver, Sebastian Schlesinger, and others are the order of the day. In the first of many revealing letters to his French collaborator and translator, Robert du Pontavice de Heussey, he asks for "some trustworthy person" to handle his French literary affairs [2 April 1881]. "Tortured" for weeks "with rheumatic gout" [20 June 1881] Wilkie is confined to his sofa: he is heavily sedated with "Calomel and Colchicum" [27 July 1881].

Preparing a collection of his short stories, he writes letters to William Winter in New York on the reception of *The Black Robe* which was published on 13 April 1881, and other literary and personal matters [3 September 1881]. Recuperating in Ramsgate in September, he produces a memoir of Charles Albert Fechter, and in the autumn of 1881 refers to himself as "the Corsican brothers of human infirmity". Wilkie tells the scholar William Ralston Shedden-Ralston that he doesn't "remember whether Dante's hell includes among its tortures Gout in the Eyes" [20 October 1881]. He produces his annual Christmas story for Chatto, "How I Married Him" and for *Belgravia Annual* "Your Money or Your Life".

With the exception of a brief Ramsgate respite, Wilkie is hard at work on *Heart and Science*. He is "<u>quite mad</u> over [his] new book" [11 July 1882]. Working seven hours a day, he is exhausted in the evening. Letters to Chatto concern details of proof-correcting and part division: the anti-vivisectionist, Frances Power Cobbe, is drawn upon for background information for the novel, which is serialized in *The Belgravia Magazine* [August 1882–June 1883] and published by Chatto in book form in April, 1883.

Plagued by gout in the eye, he labours to finish *Heart and Science* and begins a new novel, *I Say No*, serialized in *Harper's*, 22 December 1883–12 July 1884. In the spring and early summer of 1883 he also works on a play *Rank and Riches* which opens disastrously at the Adelphi on 9 June 1883. He is "at work till 3 PM. Then I eat and drink" [3 December 1883] on his new novel. He writes to Nina Lehmann that his "novels are to be translated into the <u>Bengali language</u> and read by the native inhabitants of India!!!!" [29 November 1883].

The writing of *I Say No* does not prevent Wilkie from writing a series of lengthy letters to the Carolina poet, Paul Hayne, on a diversity of literary subjects. He also gives Charles Kent advice on doses of specially prepared laudanum. An autumn North Sea yachting trip provides him with ideas for another novel which he works on intensely. *The Evil Genius* preoccupies Wilkie for the next year and is published in newspaper format from 11 December 1885 to 30 April 1886.

Suffering from attacks of gout in the eye and angina, Wilkie struggles to complete *The Evil Genius*. He writes "Mrs Zant and the Ghost" and contemplates a novel with an American setting. The death on 28 August 1885 of his beloved Scotch terrier Tommy leaves him even more bereft. June, October and November 1885 are spent in Ramsgate with his growing family. Letters to William Winter, to Sebastian Schlesinger, and to his translator, de Heussey, take on a reminiscent hue: a 14 August 1885 letter to de Heussey reflects at some length on Dickens' strengths and weaknesses.

To Louise Chandler Moulton,[1] 22 June 1880

MS: Library of Congress

90, Gloucester Place, | Portman Square. W. |
22nd June 1880

Dear Mrs Moulton,

I have read your Kind letter with sincere pleasure. The expression of your sympathy is one of those encouragements which I very highly prize.

The Second Series will be written – if all goes well with me – when our English system of publication sanctions the issue of the first cheap edition of "The Fallen Leaves". That is to say, the first Edition which really appeals to the people. I know "the General reader", by experience, as my best friend and ally when I have certain cliques and classes in this country arrayed against me – and, when I "return to the charge", I shall write with redoubled resolution, if I feel that I have the Great Public with me – as I had them (for example) in the case of "The New Magdalen".

The married life – in the second part – will be essentially a happy life, in itself. But the outer influence of the world which surrounds the husband and wife – the world whose unchristian prejudices they have set at defiance – will slowly undermine their happiness, and will, I fear, make the close of the story a sad one.

With renewed thanks | Wilkie Collins

Note

1. Louise Chandler Moulton (1835–1908), American poet and journalist: literary correspondent of the *New York Tribune*, 1870–76.

To Andrew Chatto, 23 September 1880

MS: Princeton

90, Gloucester Place, | Portman Square. W. |
23rd Sept 1880

My dear Mr Chatto,

Pray accept my best thanks for the new "Jezebel's Daughter" – bound so tastefully in my favourite colour. As you kindly encourage me to look back towards similar editions of Jezebel's predecessors, I may say that I have not yet received "The Haunted Hotel" and "The Two Destinies" – in the same

form as "Jezebel" and "The Fallen Leaves" – which last story you kindly
sent me on its publication in one volume form, (cloth).

I should have called in Piccadilly to say this – but I am hard at work again,
and likely to be soon leaving town.

                    Always truly Yours | Wilkie Collins

To William Seaver, 26 October 1880
MS: Yale

                    90, Gloucester Place, | Portman Square. W. | London |
                              26th October 1880

My dear Seaver

The sight of your handwriting is the one cheerful circumstance in my
present existence. You left the vilest weather behind you when you wisely
returned to the happy country which has its Garfield and its Handcock,[1]
and which even contrives to keep the Irish quiet.

While you have "settled down into steady laziness", I have settled down
into rheumatism, agravated by printers. If I had only finished my new
story, I should follow you across the American Channel. But I have not
finished. So here I stay, and (well or ill) stick to my work.

I well remember that pleasant lunch[2] – celebrated over again in the N.Y.
Times. But as to my share in the conversation – that has slipped away from
me into oblivion. You see I talked perpetually for six months in the U.S. –
and very nearly succeeded in catching the "American accent".

Goodbye, old friend, for the present. Be idle and happy – and accept Mrs
Graves's Kindest remembrances, and mine. At existing dates this is all you
can do for me. Yours affly | Wilkie Collins

Notes

1. James A. Garfield (1831–1881: *DAB*), 20th American president who defeated the Democratic
   candidate Winfield Scott Hancock (1824–1886: *DAB*) in the 1880 presidential election.
2. A reference to the 22 October 1873 banquet in WC's honour organized by Seaver at the
   Union Club in New York.

To Kate Field, 14 December 1880

MS: Boston Public Library. Published: L. Whiting, *Kate Field: A Record*, (Boston, 1899), pp. 404–5.

90, Gloucester Place, | Portman Square. W. | Dec. 14, 1880.

Dear Miss Field,

I am suffering from my native winter climate, and I am writing a serial story (with printers and publishers waiting here, there, and everywhere, New York included, for their weekly instalments). Add to this, correspondence and "taking care of one's health", and you will, I hope, excuse me for not having more speedily answered your letter.

If you are not in a hurry – a very serious "if", in these days – I will gladly search my archives for such few letters of poor dear Fechter as autograph-collectors have left to me. And if there is anything I can tell you besides, you shall be welcome to some of the least melancholy recollections associated with my old friend.[1] But if the book must be published immediately, I fear I must wait for a new edition. The strain of this last story is heavy on me. But I hope to be free from my "Black Robe" in six weeks' time.

Very truly yours, | Wilkie Collins.

I have received a letter from Mr Osgood on the same subject. I write to acknowledge it, and I venture to refer them to you for the things called "particulars".

Note

1. Charles Albert Fechter (1824–1879), Anglo-French actor and close friend of WC and Dickens. He left England for America in 1869, where he died ten years later neglected and embittered. See Gasson.

To George Maclean Rose, 27 January 1881

MS: Princeton

90, Gloucester Place, | Portman Square. W. | London |
27th January 1881

Dear Mr Rose,

Pray accept my thanks for your kind letter and for a B/ E for £20 ,, ,, in payment of one half of the purchase money agreed on for the Canadian right of publishing "The Black Robe".[1]

The story will be completed periodically in the 26th weekly Part – published here, on March 26th next. A "syndicate" of country newspapers subscribe to buy the periodical right for G[t] Britain. They are, I think, ten in number –[2] and they all publish of course on the same weekly date. The "Sheffield Independent" undertakes the payment of my fees – and one local London paper of great circulation, called "The South London Press" is among the subscribers. I set my own terms – and I have every right of republication in my own hands.

Frank Leslie's paper reprints in the U.S. They are a few days <u>behind</u> the weekly publication here. At present, I don't know whether we shall republish in London a week before the close of the periodical publication or not. But if it will help you against the pirates, I see no objection to y<u>our</u> print appearing on the 19th March instead of the 26th – When I send you the remaining weekly parts to the end, I should be able, I hope, to write more definitely as to our date of republication.

The thaw has come at last. I lament it. The harder the frost, the better I am. I ought to be with you in Canada.

Lord B. is the greatest imposter of modern times. In politics a glib tongue and no scruples will do wonders. But literature under false pretences, betrays the pretender. I sincerely believe that man to be the very worst novelist that has ever appeared in print.[3]

Yours always Wilkie Collins

I begin the last weekly part tomorrow. It is a great success with periodical readers here.

Notes

1. *The Black Robe* was serialized in the *Canadian Monthly*, November 1880–June 1881.
2. Following "–" WC places an "x" and in his margin writes: "x my utmost limit in the agreement is t<u>welve</u>".
3. Peters observes that WC "was incensed at the £10,000 paid for *Endymion*, Disraeli's last novel" (p. 397).

To Kate Field, January 1881
MS: Boston Public Library. Published: L. Whiting, *Kate Field: A Record*, (Boston, 1899), p. 403.

90, Gloucester Place, | Portman Square. W. |
January, 1881.

Dear Miss Field,

If you are in the U.S.A. and if you ever see Frank Leslie's "Illustrated Newspaper", you will find a serial story in it which may suggest indulgence to an overworked man. If you know nothing of "Heart and Science", I go down on both my knees and beg your pardon. I am in sober earnest, so weary after finishing my story that a sinking of the soul (and body) comes over me at the sight of a pen. As to writing letters while I am at work, "that way madness lies". Is there any fatigue in this weary world which is equal to the fatigue that comes of daily working of the brains for hours together? George Sand thought all other fatigues unimportant by comparison – and I agree with George S.

Let me thank you for "Fechter".[1] The illustrations (excepting the photographed head of him in "Hamlet") are so utterly unlike, and I should not have known what man they were meant for; and his old doctor here (Carr Beard), to whom I showed the book, agreed with me. This is my only objection. I think your part of the volume eminently readable – and done in an excellent spirit. Here and there, poor dear F., or somebody else, has misled you about his importance in Paris, but that is no fault of yours. And I repeat my congratulations and my thanks.

"Boz" rhymes (in sound) to "was".

Oh, good lord! referring to your letter I find <u>no address</u>. "Hotel Victoria", – that, I swear, is all. Oh, woman, lovely woman! What is a man to do, who remembers Victoria Hotels in his own country, in your country, at Naples, at Rome, and on the continent generally? Will Osgood[2] forward? Here [goes] at Osgood. Farewell.

Yours ever, | Wilkie Collins.

Notes

1. WC's "Recollections of Charles Fechter", were published in Kate Field, *Charles Albert Fechter* (Boston, 1882, pp. 154–73).
2. James Ripley Osgood (1836–1892), American publisher.

To Sebastian Schlesinger, 17 February 1881
MS: Princeton

90, Gloucester Place | London. W. | 17th February 1881

My dear Schlesinger,

Both your kind letters are received. I shut my eyes and see myself again, ascending the steps of that nice house, under protection of the consular pole, and hear your voice in the innermost regions when the door is opened, calling to me to come in. You have the rare merit, in a man, of bringing yourself personally before your correspondent, by writing as you talk. The women are masters in this art – but the men are few who can write their letters naturally.

But the main object of these few lines is to send you the autograph for Miss Blaine.[1] Her celebrated father it is needless to say I know by reputation. Miss Blaine must not have a common autograph. I have copied a few lines, on the next leaf, from "The Moonstone" – and signed them. Tear it off please, and send it to the lady with my compliments as a little contribution to her book. "George Eliot's" autograph is very difficult to find. She had some strange objection to writing it. But I don't despair of finding a letter or at least a signature – if you give me time to inquire. The one or two little notes I received from her, in past years, have long since been taken away by collectors.[2]

This is not a letter – it is only an excuse – an upside-down excuse, as I see by the printed address at the bottom instead of the top of the page. I will behave better next time.

Yours always truly W.C

Notes

1. Possibly the daughter of James Gillespie Blaine (1830–1893: *DAB*), distinguished American statesman.
2. No letters from George Eliot to WC are in G.S. Haight's *The George Eliot Letters* (9 vols, 1954–1955, 1978).

To Robert du Pontavice de Heussey,[1] 2 April 1881
MS: Princeton

90, Gloucester Place, | Portman Square. W. |
London | 2nd April 1881

Summary:

"I am afraid I must trouble you – as I have, for the present, no agent in Paris – to refer me to some trustworthy person with whom I can communicate on the subject of registering the story, in its book-form, so as to protect the right of translation. This has hitherto always been done for me – and I am not quite sure whether one copy, or two copies, are required to complete the registration by French law."

Note

1. Robert du Pontavice de Heussey (1850-1893), "Breton author ... a cousin and biographer (1893) of Villiers de l'Isle-Adam ... [who] gives evidence of having spent considerable time himself in England" (J.P. Couch, *George Eliot in France* [1967], p. 109). He translated WC's work into French and represented his interests in Paris and elsewhere. His *Medeliene, pièce en 4 acts ... d'après Wilkie Collins* was published in Paris in 1887.

To George Maclean Rose, 7 April 1881
MS: Princeton

90, Gloucester Place, | Portman Square. W. |
London | 7th April 1881

Summary:
Thanks for payment "for the Canadian Edition of" *The Black Robe*: "The French Government has acted most wisely ... in getting rid of the Jesuit enemies of the Republic.

We are all shivering here in a bitter East wind that has been blowing for weeks." Doesn't "blame the American people – it is the Government which is answerable for the shameful theft of the literary property of foreigners which degrades America in the eyes of Europe."

To Charles Kent,[1] 20 June 1881
MS: Princeton

90, Gloucester Place, | Portman Square. W. |
20th June 1881

My dear Kent,

All that I can do for you by writing to my friends at the Club (sadly reduced in number by deaths) I will gladly do. Under happier circumstances, I should have personally looked after your interests. But adverse Fate has tortured me with rheumatic gout for weeks past – and my recovery is so slow (or rather my weakness is so great) that I can only crawl up and down the sunny side of the way for half an hour, and return to the sofa with legs that tremble as if I was ninety years old!

With sincerest wishes for your "triumphant entry"[2] on Monday next,

Always truly yours | Wilkie Collins

Note

1. Charles Kent (1832–1902), edited *The Sun* (1853–71) and the *Weekly Register* (1874–81), worked on *Household Words*, friend of Bulwer Lytton and Dickens. Kent noted that WC's "eyes were literally enormous bags of blood!" (Robinson, p. 163). Cf. Dickens, *Letters*, V, 280, n.5.
2. Probably to the Athenaeum Club.

To Nina Lehmann, 22 June 1881
MS: Princeton: Text, Coleman.

90, Gloucester Place, | Portman Square. W. | 22 June 1881

Two words, dearest Padrona, to thank you for those kind pencil lines on your card. The inflammatory and painful part of this last gouty visitation is at an end. Weakness is now the obstacle to be got over – my knees tremble on the stairs, and my back aches after half an hour's walking – no, tottering – on the sunny side of the street. I am told to "drive out" – but I won't. An "airing in a carriage" is (to me) such a depressing proceeding that I am ready to burst out crying when I only think of it. I will get stronger on my wretched old legs – and report myself in Berkeley Square[1] as soon as I have ceased to be a human wet-blanket.

Yours affectionately, | WC

Note

1. The address of the Lehmann London residence.

To Charles Kent, 27 July 1881
MS: Texas: Coleman

90, Gloucester Place, | Portman Square. W. | 27 July 1881

Charles Kent, Esq. | 1. Campden Grove | Kensington W.

My Dear Kent,
    Only a line to convey to you my thanks and my excuses. Calomel and colchicum[1] so completely "floored me" on the day when you kindly called that I was too pitiable and speechless an object to be presented to the view of my friends. I am now getting better again (after my relapse) but so weak that even the writing of this little note is an effort.[2]

Yours truly | Wilkie Collins

Notes

1. Calomel, a highly toxic drug, used for local infections, syphilis, and constipation; colchicum was used in the treatment of gout.
2. WC's "handwriting shows obvious fatigue and possible pain in its lack of definitive strokes" (Coleman, p. 258).

To William Winter, 3 September 1881
MS: Princeton. Published, W. Winter, *Old Friends* (1909), pp. 218–19.

90, Gloucester Place, | Portman Square. W. | London, |
September 3rd, 1881.

My Dear Winter:

If you have long since dismissed me from memory, you have only treated an inexcusably bad correspondent as he deserves. When I was at school, – perpetually getting punished as "a bad boy", – the master used to turn me to good moral account, as a means of making his model scholars ashamed of their occasional lapses into misconduct: "If it had been Collins I should not have felt shocked and surprised. Nobody expects anything of him. But You!!" – etc., etc.

In the hope that you, by this time, "expect nothing of Collins" I venture to appeal to your indulgence. In the intervals of rheumatic gout I still write stories – and I send to you, by registered book-post, my latest effort, called "The Black Robe", in the belief that you will "give me another chance", and honour me by accepting the work. It is thought, on the European side of the Atlantic, in Roman Catholic countries as well as in Protestant England, to be the best thing I have written for some time. And it is memorable to me as having produced a freely offered gift of forty pounds from one of the pirates who have seized it on the American side!!!

I write with your new editions, – so kindly sent to me, – in the nearest book-case. In the Poems I rejoice to see my special favourites included in the new publication – "The Ideal", "Rosemary" and the exquisitely tender verses which enshrine the memory of "Ada Clare".

I have heard of you from Miss Cavendish. May I hope to hear of you next – from yourself?

Always truly yours, | Wilkie Collins

To Mrs John Bigelow, 6 September 1881
MS: NYPL (Bigelow family papers)

90, Gloucester Place, | Portman Square. W. |
[September 6th, 1881]

Summary:
WC's idea concerning the disposal of flowers "is that they were 'cremated' in the kitchen fire – a form of burial I should like to receive for myself, when

I fall in pieces like the flowers, but the expense is too great. One has to be taken to Germany. British liberty does not include the burning of British bodies yet.

I am well on the way to recovery ... <u>Both</u> my eyes see again as well as ever. But they are so weak, after what they have gone through, that I am forbidden to use them except for a few hours by daylight. So when evening comes, I sit and think – and smoke when I am tired of thinking – and wish I was on my way again to my dear United States, when I can neither smoke nor think any longer – and then my dear old dog[1] comes, looks at me, wags his tail, and groans. This means in <u>his</u> language 'Now, Wilkie, it's time to go to bed.' So the evening closes."

WC is "going to the seaside – as soon as the present unmercifully cold and rainy weather will let" him.

Note

1. Tommy, WC's Scotch terrier, features in his short story "My Lady's Money" of 1878, in which he acts as detective, and helps to unravel the mystery (Clarke, pp. 178–9).

To Charles Kent, 21 September 1881
MS: Fales Collection, NYU

Ramsgate | 21st September 1881

My dear Kent

(Let us drop "Mistering each other) – and let me report myself to be winning back the lost strength, not very quickly, but steadily as I hope and believe. My eyes are still weak enough to want an umbrella over them when I swallow my sea-air in the balcony here. Time however will put this defect right. As for the "dolce far niente" [happy doing nothing] I am too lazy even to write my letters – and I begin to believe myself to have been an author in some former state of existence.

Lord Lytton kindly brought the "Brutus" play to me while I was in town. And, in spite of my weak eyes, I read with delight and admiration that masterly work. As dramatic poetry it is, to my mind, far in advance of "The Lady of Lyons" and "Richelieu" – and as an acting play there is such true power in the characters and the "situations" that I could <u>see</u> the scenes on the stage while I was reading them. And this masterpiece remains unacted![1] If you want to know why, look at the theatrical advertisements in the newspaper – and don't forget that the theatres are in a state of unexampled prosperity.

Ever yours | Wilkie Collins

My plans for staying here are still unsettled. All letters forwarded from Gloucester Place.

To | Charles Kent Eqr

Note

1. Bulwer-Lytton's unpublished tragedy *Brutus*, (1847), was produced as *The Household Gods*, produced by Wilson Barrett at the Princess's Theatre, in 1885. See The Earl of Lytton, *The Life of Edward Bulwer First Lord Lytton*, (1913), II, 96. Bulwer's *The Lady of Lyons* was performed in 1838, his *Richelieu*, in 1839. WC appeared with Dickens and others in a Royal Command performance of Bulwer's *Many Sides to a Character* in May 1851 (see *ibid.*, II, 139–40).

To Unknown Recipient, Autumn 1881

MS: Present whereabouts unknown. Extract Robinson.

[Ramsgate]

We are the Corsican Brothers[1] of human infirmity. For three months the gout has again tortured my eyes – and here I am recovering within two miles of you! Are you well enough to get here by railway (if walking is still bad for you) and take your luncheon, on any day you like, from 2 to 2.30? I could then answer your questions in the pleasanter way – besides sparing my eyes letter-writing at length, in the interests of some light work which I am just able to do after four months of utter literary eclipse. Why don't I go to you at Broadstairs? It is the most dreadful place in the world to me now. The ghosts of my brother, Dickens, Augustus Egg, and of two other dearly-loved friends – who all lived with me at Broadstairs – now haunt the place. Two years ago I tried to go to Broadstairs. At the first view of "The Fort House" the old and dear associations completely overwhelmed me and I turned back to Ramsgate.

Note

1. Don Boucicault's *The Corsican Brothers*, (1852), was a highly successful drama.

To William Ralston Shedden-Ralston,[1] 20 October 1881
MS: Armstrong Browning Library, Baylor University

90, Gloucester Place, | Portman Square. W. |
20th October 1881

Dear Mr Ralston,

I don't remember whether Dante's Hell includes among its tortures Gout in the Eyes. If the Divine Poet has not anticipated me, I may claim without presumption to have invented an infernal circle of my own, and to have suffered in it lately for more than three months. My sight is saved – and I am steadily on the way to recovery. But to my sincere regret, I am not yet quite strong enough to take my place at your table on Saturday next. It is really a disappointment to me to miss the opportunity of meeting Mr Tourgèneff, and of thanking him for the happy hours that I owe to his masterly and delightful pen. Do you remember kindly giving me your translation of one of his most subtly and delicately treated stories? Incautiously opening the book, with a hard day's work before me, I scattered "the materials of our craft" to the winds, and spent the day with "Lisa".[2]

Be my good friend still – and accept my thanks and my excuses.

Ever yours | Wilkie Collins

To | W.R.S. Ralston Esqe

Notes

1. William Ralston Shedden-Ralston (1828–1889: *DNB*), Russian scholar, assistant Department of Printed Books, British Museum, 1853–75.
2. Ralston's translation of "Lisa" published in 1869.

To Unknown Recipient, 3 December 1881
MS: Private Possession

90, Gloucester Place, | Portman Square. W. | London |
3rd December 1881

Every night when I take my feet out of my slippers – every morning when I put my feet in again – I shall turn in a south easterly direction (towards John Street Adelphi) and include in my other devotional practices the adoration of Lucy. I possess already a fur cap and a fur great coat. Never, until now, has my existence been completed by fur slippers. I kiss the hands that have perfected my winter wardrobe – and will not trust myself to say more.

W.C.

To A.P. Watt,[1] 5 December 1881
MS: Private Possession

[90, Gloucester Place. | Portman Square. W.] |
Monday 5th Dec.1881

Summary:
Wishes to consult "on the subject of the periodical publication of a serial story, which I contemplate writing in the course of next year". Suffering "from rheumatic gout" and may not be "able to keep an appointment if the weather is against me".

Note

1. Alexander Pollock Watt (1834–1914), literary agent to whom WC turned increasingly for advice.

To Mrs John Bigelow, 2 January 1882
MS: NYPL (Bigelow family papers)

90, Gloucester Place, | Portman Square. W. |
[2nd January 1882]

Summary:
"I too have my agreeable associations with Baltimore. I well remember the lovely women, the pleasant City, the successful public reading of my story ... Comparing the two cities (Boston & Washington) – may I confess it with all humility, in a whisper? – I greatly preferred Boston. The prodigious streets and 'avenues' at Washington depressed me indescribably and I never could get over the idea that the enormous cupola of the Capital was slowly squeezing the weak and attenuated building underneath, into the earth, from which it had feebly risen.

I am better than I was when you cheered my wretchedness in the character of my good angel bearing flowers. But the merciless gout still hangs about me."

To Charles Kent, 8 January 1882
MS: Princeton

> 90, Gloucester Place, | Portman Square. W. |
> 8th January 1882

My dear Kent,

Some flowers on my table remind me that this is my birthday – and that I cannot find a better occasion for offering to you my best wishes for the New Year.

I began the year badly – with a threatening of gout, and terrifying appearances in one of my eyes. But the doctor and I have made a good fight of it this time – and I hope I am safe.

Condemned to the nastiest drink (not actually physic) that I know of – weak brandy and water – I am filled with morbid longings to destroy myself and my character by getting drunk on the excellent port in the solemn coffee-room at the Athenaeum. You shall receive the "due notice" if this longing overpowers my better sense.

In the meantime, when you pass this way again, come upstairs. If I am hard at work, we can at least shake hands – produce a few whiffs of tobacco smoke – and adjourn to a leisure hour at the first opportunity. You understand what literary work is. I say no more.

> Ever yours, | Wilkie Collins

To A.P. Watt, 8 February 1882
MS: Private Possession

> [90, Gloucester Place, | Portman Square. W.] | [8 Feb 1882]

[Dear Watt]

Mr Chatto called here yesterday – and told me that you are still being worried by some of the curious savages with whom you are unfortunately in negotiation on my behalf. For your sake, as well as for mine, this must be stopped. Please direct your clerk to copy the enclosed letter, and send it to Mr Bartlett[1] – and send other copies to those other people in the north. They are wasting our time – and we shall do wisely to open negotiations with other periodicals or newspapers.

Dear Sir,

I hear with surprise that your negotiations for the periodical sale of my next novel are delayed by certain proprietors who wish to see the MS – to know what the characters are, and what the title is to be – before they can decide to purchase the right of publishing the work in their newspaper columns.

In twenty years' experience, this extraordinary form of distrust approaches me for the first time.

The late Mr Charles Dickens neither read, nor wished to read, a line of "The Woman in White" before we signed our agreement for the appearance of the work in "All the Year Round". Neither did he know the title until after the work had been advertised as "a new story". The same confidence in me was testified by Messrs Cassell & Co. when I published "the Two Destinies" in "Temple Bar" – by Chatto and Windus, when I published "The Haunted Hotel" in "Belgravia"- and by Messrs Leader & Son of "The Sheffield Independent", who purchased the periodical right of my last work "The Black Robe". Every one of these gentlemen remembered that my works were circulated by hundreds of thousands wherever the English language was read, and were translated into all the languages of Europe. They understood that a man with this reputation and this responsibility was to be implicitly trusted as a writer. If the proprietors with whom you are now in treaty do not see that they are bound to do me this same justice, I beg that you will at once close the negotiations. In justice to former publishers and proprietors, and in justice to myself, I refuse to communicate a line of my MS. – or mention my title, until I think it right to do so. My forthcoming novel will deal with English life, and the period will be the present time. I may say this – but I will say no more.

[Yours W Collins]

Note

1. Sir Ellis A. Bartlett (1849–1902: *DNB*), owner of the metropolitan Tory weekly *England* which serialized *Heart and Science* (22 July 1882 to 17 February 1883, omitting 6 January 1883: information from Dr Graham Law).

To William Winter, 10 February 1882
MS: Princeton. W. Winter, *Old Friends* (1909), pp. 209–11.

90, Gloucester Place, Portman Square, | London, | February 10, 1882.

My Dear Winter:

You were indeed happily inspired when you sent me that generous and sympathetic article in "The Tribune". Still tormented by the gout, I forgot my troubles when I opened the newspaper, and felt the encouragement that I most highly value – I mean the encouragement that is offered to me by a brother-writer.

If what I hear of this last larcenous appropriation of my poor "Magdalen" be true, what an effort it must have been to <u>you</u> to give your attention, even for a few hours only, to dramatic work so immeasurably beneath your notice! How did you compensate your intelligence for this outrage offered to it by this latest "adapter" of ideas that do not belong to him? Did you disinfect your mind by reading, or writing, – or did you go to bed, and secure the sweet oblivion of sleep?

I wonder whether I ever told you of an entirely new view taken of "Magdalen" by the last of the great French actresses – Aimée Desclée.[1] After seeing the piece in London she was eager to play, on her return to Paris – <u>Grace Roseberry</u>! "Develop the character a little more , in the last act," she said to me; "I will see that the play is thoroughly well translated into French – and I will make <u>Grace</u>, and not <u>Mercy Merrick</u>, the chief woman in the piece. Grace's dramatic position is magnificent: I feel it, to my fingers' ends. Wait and see!" She died poor soul, a few months afterward, and <u>Grace Roseberry</u> will, I fear, never be properly acted <u>now</u>. Don't forget me, my dear Winter – and let me hear from you sometimes. I set no common value on your friendship and your good opinion.

Ever yours, | Wilkie Collins.

P.S. I address you as Mr on this envelope. Our curiously common mock-title of Esquire is declared by Fenimore Cooper[2] to be a species of insult, and even a violation of the Constitution of the United States, when attached to the name of an American citizen. Is that great Master (shamefully undervalued by Americans of the present day!) right or wrong about Esq.? N.B. I have just been reading "The Deerslayer" for the <u>fifth</u> time.

Notes

1. Aimée-Olympe Desclée (1836–1874), French actress.
2. A 32 vol. *Novels* of J. Fenimore Cooper was in WC's library at his death.

To William Seaver, 3 May 1882

MS: Princeton

90, Gloucester Place, | Portman Square. W. | London | 3rd May 1882

My dear Seaver,

You are a man of multiform capacities. Having already contemplated you from many points of view, I now approach you as – a fountain of information.[1]

MR GEORGE DOLBY, who acted as manager and confidential agent for Charles Dickens during the novelist's last tour in America, proposes to publish all the letters Dickens wrote him on business.[2] It is said that these epistles describe American audiences in the same vein of caustic pleasantry that pervades "Martin Chuzzlewit".[3]

This announcement has appeared in all sorts of newspapers here – and in the U.S. The publications of the letters in England has been forbidden by Miss Hogarth (sole surviving Executor of Charles Dickens) – supported by the laws which make her the proprietor of the copy right of the letters. The request – as we are informed in other newspaper reports – is that the book is to be published in America. And it has been further rumoured that Messrs Harper are to be the publishers. I have written to Harper's London agents, and have heard from them in return. They have no information on the subject. Now, oh Fountain, can you spout?

(1) Is the book to be published in the U.S.?

(2) Are Messrs Harper [word erased] to be the publishers?

We know that we can do nothing to prevent the American publication. But – if reprints or piracies make their appearance in England the hammer of the law is in hand – and down it comes! But we don't want to be on the look-out for Nothing. And we should be glad to hear if the letters are likely to be published on the other side.

In any case, here is a chance of hearing how you git along. After another fight with the gout I am "alive and Kicking". By Kicking I mean preparing a new serial story which (if all goes well with me) you will see, on your side towards the end of July next.

Always, my good friend. | Yours truly | Wilkie Collins

Notes

1. WC has a double underlining between this paragraph and the printed announcement pasted on to the letter.
2. Dolby's *Charles Dickens as I Knew Him*, published 1885.
3. WC places double underlining following the printed announcement.

To James Payn, 22 June 1882
MS: Texas: Coleman

90, Gloucester Place, | Portman Square. W. | London | 22 June 1882

My dear Payn,

I was indeed sorry to miss seeing you when you kindly called here. Gout, calomel, and colchicum do succeed (when I am hard at work) in putting my tail down afterward – and my way of acknowledging that humiliating circumstance is, going asleep! If you ever come my way again take the servant by the throat (if it is the man) and round the waist if it is the plump parlour-maid or the small girl – and, for God's sake, step up and wake me. I got out for a walk yesterday for the first time – with a patch over my bad eye. Why does everybody, when they see you with a patch on, look as if you had personally insulted them? Be assured, Barttelot[1] is going to ask the question in Parliament.

Ever yours, | WC

Note

1. Colonel Sir Walter Barttelot of Sussex (1820–1893), Member of Parliament 1860–1893, sponsored many bills in the Commons, 1867–1889 (*DNB*).

To Frances Power Cobbe,[1] 23 June 1882

MS: Huntington. Published, F. Power Cobbe, *Life of Frances Power Cobbe as Told by Herself* (1904), pp. 558–9; *Heart and Science*, ed., S. Farmer (1996), p. 370.

90, Gloucester Place, | Portman Square. W. | London | 23[d] June 1882

Dear Madam,

I most sincerely thank you for your kind letter and for the pamphlets which preceded it. The "Address" seems to me to possess this very rare merit of forcible statement combined with a moderation of judgement which sets a valuable example, not only to our enemies, but to – some of – our friends. As to the "Portrait", I feel such a strong personal interest in it that I must not venture in criticism. You have given me exactly what I most wanted for the purpose that I have in view – and you have spared me time and trouble in the best and kindest of ways. If I require further help, you shall see that I am gratefully sensible of the help that has been already given.

I am writing to a very large public both at home and abroad – and it is quite needless (when I am writing to you) to dwell on the importance of producing the right impression by means which keep clear of terrifying and revolting the ordinary reader. I shall leave the detestable cruelties of the laboratory to be merely inferred – and, in tracing the moral influence of those cruelties on the nature of the man who practices them, and the result as to his social relations with the persons about him, I shall be careful to present him to the reader as a man not originally wicked and cruel, and to show the efforts made by his better instincts to resist the inevitable hardening of the heart, the fatal stupefying of all the fine sensibilities, produced by the deliberately merciless occupations of his life. If I can succeed in making him, in some degree, an object of compassion, as well as of horror, my experience of readers of fiction tells me that the right effect will be produced by the right means.

Believe me, truly yours | Wilkie Collins

To | Mrs Frances Power Cobbe

Note

1. Frances Power Cobbe (1822-1904: *DAB*), philanthropist, feminist, leading anti-vivisectionist, writer.

To Frederick Lehmann, 5 July 1882

MS: Princeton: published, Coleman; *Heart and Science*, ed., S. Farmer (1996), p. 371.

90, Gloucester Place, | Portman Square. W. | 5 July 1882

My dear Fred,

My absence from Berkeley Square will have told you my gouty story – and my silence (when I ought long since to have thanked you for your most kind letter) only means that I am too weary of myself to write about myself. It has been a milder attack this time – and I am going to leave off my patch.

When you write to the Padrona – give her my best love – and tell her to be as happy in Scotland as the happiest woman living. When she comes back to London, she will completely fulfil my aspirations, if she will let me know of it.

I have nothing else to say. My life is in my new book. Some critic said "The Woman In White" was "written in blood and vitriol". This book[1] is being written in blood and dynamite.

Yours ever affly | WC

Note

1. *Heart and Science*: for publication details see Gasson.

To James Payn, 5 July 1882

MS: Private Possession: published, H.N. Pym, *A Tour Round my Book-Shelves* (1891), 50–1.

90, Gloucester Place. | Portman Square. W. | 5th July 1882

My Dear Payn,

Thank you most sincerely for "Vice-Versâ."[1]

If everybody who reads the book likes it as well as I do, there ought to be such a sale as will encourge the author to set to work again instantly. Quaint humour and excellent observation of character, combined with a very rare fertility of invention, seem to me to be the main, and (in these days) the remarkable literary merits of the new writer. The schoolmaster, the German teacher, and the little girl are my favourites; and the one fault I have to find with one of these characters is, that there is nothing like enough of him – I mean the German teacher. He is not only amusing – he is sketched with such fine knowledge of human nature, on more than one side of it, that he is really interesting, and even pathetic. Being myself (as poor Thackeray used to say) "an old fiddler", I should not have had the heart to dismiss him so speedily – as he is now dismissed – from the story. If the writer's next book is written without a fantastic supernatural notion as part of its groundwork, I shall anticipate a better book even than "Vice-Versâ".

There is some monotony in the development of that queer transformation – so far as the father is concerned – due, as I think, to the limited range (thus far) of the author's imagination. His hold on truth is already certain, but his wing is weak when he soars into the regions of grotesque fancy. In the meantime, there cannot be a doubt of it – he has a career before him.

Ever yours, | Wilkie Collins

Note

1. F. Anstey's *Vice Versa, or A Lesson to Fathers* was published in 1882.

To Elizabeth Harriet Bartley, 11 July [1882]

MS: Princeton

[Ramsgate] | 11th July [1882]

My dearest Carrie,

A word to thank you for your nice letter and for this list – which is the very thing I wanted – could not be better.

Come – the sooner the better – and bring <u>all</u> the children. Good heavens! Don't I like Dah[1] and the quiet little curlyhead? I wish I was a baby again – with nothing to do but suck and sleep.

Don't tell anybody – I <u>am quite mad</u> over my new book. [It] is [as if] at the present [I am] writing half a dozen books, with four or five hundred characters – and full of immoral situations.

Ever yours affly, | W.C

Note

1. Doris Edith Bartley, "Dah", Harriet's eldest daughter, born 1879. See Clarke pp. 169 and 224.

To A.P. Watt, 26 August 1882
MS: Private Possession

[90, Gloucester Place, | Portman Square. W.] | 26th Augst 1882

Summary

A "vile press error" in *Heart and Science* revises needs correcting. Hopes he is "looking at sand and sea, instead of streets and omnibuses".

To Robert du Pontavice de Heussey, 3 November 1882
MS: Princeton

90, Gloucester Place, | Portman Square. W. | 3rd Novr 1882

My dear Collaborateur,

This is my first opportunity of writing to you. I have been at the seaside, sailing and fishing, in the intervals of work.

Your silence was attributed by me to the sad cause which you mention – and for that reason, I hesitated to write, on my side. To my mind, there is no other calamity so cruel and so hard to endure as domestic calamity. Pain and poverty are bad enough – but courage can face them. But where is the man to be found, who is not conquered by anxiety and distress <u>at home</u>? I hope it is needless for me to say that you have my truest sympathy – little enough to offer, but all that I have to give.

To turn to a less painful subject.

I am now publishing – in periodicals – a new story called "<u>Heart and Science</u>". Here and in America it has produced a very strong impression – and is considered (rightly as I think) a great advance on "The Black Robe". Abroad, three Italian newspapers will publish the translation – and, in Germany, two publishers have been "bidding against each other" for the German translation. I have also had a proposal from Paris – to which I have replied that I am not now at liberty to [erasure] negotiate. In character and humour, I have never, as I believe, done anything like it before. I mention this, because it is a question – after you have waited so long, and have been encountered by such unexpected obstacles – whether it might not be advisable to let "Heart and Science" precede "The Black Robe", on the chance that it may produce better terms for y<u>ou</u> under those circumstances. I will of course send to you cuttings from one of the newspapers here which publishes the work – so that you may judge for yourself.

On the other hand, after what has happened – I hesitate to ask you to take the responsibility of publishing this new book. The loss of the <u>periodical</u> publication is a serious loss to you[1] – and is also the failure of an excellent advertisement for the novel in book-form. Shall I try, through my agent here, to dispose of the French right of translation – stipulating that you shall be the translator[?] If I can manage in this way to secure a French newspaper for the <u>feuilleton</u> – this might be an additional reason for postponing "<u>The Black Robe</u>". If "<u>Heart and Science</u>" succeeds in the newspaper, the proprietors might be ready and willing to let "The Black Robe" follow. Will you consider this? In the meantime, – if you don't agree with me – I enclose the letter of introduction to Hachette.

Ever yours | W.C

P.S. It has just struck me, that Hachette might treat for the right of newspaper publication. Or that you might at least try to make this right a part of your negotiation.

Note

1. WC double underlines the word "you".

To Frances Power Cobbe, 21 November 1882
MS: Huntington

> 90, Gloucester Place, | Portman Square. W. |
> 21st November 1882

Dear Miss Cobbe

Pray forgive this scandalously late acknowledgement of your very kind letter and of this terrible book which accompanied it. I have been leading the life of a hermit – away from my friends and my correspondents – devoted wholly to my Story. The last chapters are only now in view – and I am beginning to feel the continued [indecipherable word] and excitement severely. When the day's work and the hour of exercise that follow are over, I am fit for nothing but my armchair and my cigar – having just life enough left in me to feel the pleasure and the encouragement which I [see] in your letter.

> Believe me | Most truly yours | Wilkie Collins

I must not do more than allude indirectly to the detestable cruelties revealed in "Bernard's Martyrs".[1] Half of <u>my</u> audience, at least, – if I told them a tenth part of what <u>you</u> know – would close the book.

Don't believe in that delusion which declares tall men to be good natured because they are tall – it is nothing but one of the results of our inveterate [insular] adorations of size and strength. I did my best to attack similar prejudice about fat people in the character of "Count Fosco".

Note

1. *Bernard's Martyrs: a comment on Claude Bernard's Leçons de physiologie opératoire*, published by the Anti-Vivisection Society, Westminster (1879) and also the subject of a 1888 pamphlet by Frances Power Cobbe attacking Bernard's experiments on living animals.

To Ada Cavendish, 29 December 1882
MS: Princeton

> 90, Gloucester Place, | Portman Square. W. |
> 29th Decr 1882

My dear Ada

<u>Nobody</u> has seen me – except Beard. For months, I have been shut up over my work – and now it is done, I am so completely exhausted that it is

an effort to me even to write these lines. I am not strong enough to travel – there is nothing for it but rest and peace.

Yours aftly | with all good wishes | WC

To Unknown Recipient, 1 January 1883
MS: Private Possession

90, Gloucester Place, | Portman Square. W. | London |
1ˢᵗ January 1883

Dear Madam,

Hardly a week passes, in my experience, without bringing me a letter which, in substance, resembles your letter. Under these circumstances, I hope you will not think me wanting in sympathy if I assure you that I have no time to look over any specimens of your work.

But I can at least be of some service to you if I can relieve your mind of the delusion (prevalent among so many writers who are beginning their career) that the influence of "powerful friends" can smooth the way which leads to literary success. No publisher is foolish enough to risk his money in publishing a work because it is recommended to him by other persons – no matter who those persons may be. The manuscript must make its way on its own merits. If it has merit, there is not a respectable publisher in London who will not be ready and glad, to open his purse and his publishing house to this author. I had no friends to introduce me – no influence of any sort to [erased word] smooth the way for me – when I sent my first manuscript to the publishers. It was the work of an obscure young man, left to plead for itself – and it was accepted, paid for, and published solely on its own merits. There is my experience – at your service. If you possess the abilities – and the capacity for taking pains in the exercise of those abilities – which make a writer of fiction, the way to success is clear before you. In the other case, no influence and no recommendations can help you.

Having spoken plainly – which, in such a case as this, is equivalent to speaking kindly – I have only to add the sincere expression of my sympathy with you, under the hardest to endure of all anxieties – domestic anxieties.

Believe me, sincerely yours | Wilkie Collins

To William Winter, 14 January 1883
MS: Princeton

90, Gloucester Place, | Portman Square. W. |[1] London |
14th January 1883

My dear Winter

Am I still in time to send you my hearty good wishes for 1883? In time or not, I send them. Accompanied by apologies? No: not to a brother in the art – I can count on h<u>is</u> indulgence surely? – long as I have been in writing.

But let me stand aside and let those two charming sprays that you sent to me take the front place. "Charming" is a wretched commonplace word – but it expresses in some degree the feeling of pleasure with which I welcome true enthusiasm in writing (as well as in feeling), in days when the tone of a clown in a circus is too frequently the tone in which personal experiences and opinions are set up in printers' types. Besides you are one of the few poets (between ourselves) who can write prose. And there is another agreeable surprise – for which I have to thank you.

The gout (to answer your friendly inquiry about my health) keeps away wonderfully, so far. And this in spite of my [word erased] "vital power" (as the doctor calls it) having been severely tested by my last story. When a man is "old enough to know better", he generally commits some of his most flagrant indiscretions. This new book ("Heart and Science") so mercilessly excited me that I went on writing week after week without a day's interval of rest. Rest was impossible. I made a desperate effort, – rushed to the sea, went sailing and [erased word] fishing, and was writing my book all the time, <u>in my head</u> (as the children say). The one wise course to take was to go back to my desk, and empty my head – and then rest. My nerves are too much shaken for travelling. An armchair and a cigar – and a hundred and fiftieth reading of the [word erased] glorious Walter Scott (King, Emperor, President, and God Almighty of [erased word] novelists) – there is the regimen that is doing me good! All the other novel-writers I can read while I am at work myself. If I only look at the "Antiquary" or "Old Mortality",[2] I am crushed by the sense of my own littleness, and there is no work possible for me on that day.

Don't forget that I am to send you the new book – when it <u>is</u> a book, and has got my latest corrections. The story has been published periodically in a monthly magazine here, as well as in several weekly newspapers. The magazine doesn't gobble it all up until June next. The newspapers will have swallowed the last morsel on the 27th of this month. In this dilemma, we "split the difference", and publish in book-form in April next.

You knew Anthony Trollope[3] of course. His immeasurable energies had a bewildering effect on my invalid constitution. To me, he was an incarnated gale of wind. He blew off my hat; he turned my umbrella inside out. Joking apart, as good and staunch a friend as ever lived – and, to my mind, a great loss to novel-readers. Call his standard as a workman what you will, he was always equal to it. Never in any marked degree either above or below his own level. In that respect alone, a remarkable writer, surely? If he had lived five years longer, he would have written fifteen more thoroughly readable works of fiction. A loss – a serious loss – I say again.

Goodbye for the present. Ever yours Wilkie Collins

Notes

1. Above the printed monogram, WC writes: "My love to Seaver. I last heard of him with a sense of blank terror, as having reprinted a dinner invitation!!! Don't let him sink into an invalid!" In his margin WC writes: "When you see Mr Lawrence Barrett, remember me Kindly to him. I wish I had seen more of him. Let me hear (when you have nothing to do) how you 'git along'. "Lawrence Barret (1838–1891), American actor and producer who took over Irving's Lyceum in 1884 while Irving toured America.
2. Four lots of Scott are found in Puttick and Simpson's 20 January 1890 sale of WC's Library: "Waverly Novels ... 'Illustrated edition' ... 48 vols ... 1859" (lot 86); "Prose Works ... 28 vols ... 1834" (lot 87); "Poetical Works ... 12 vols ... 1833" (lot 88); "Life by Lockhart ... 10 vols ... 1848" (lot 89).
3. Trollope died 6 December 1882.

To William J. Bok,[1] 17 February 1883
MS: Fales Collection, NYU

90, Gloucester Place, | Portman Square. W. |
17th February 1883

Summary:
Sends New York journalist photographic portrait of himself "by my good friend Sarony (of Union Square N.Y.)[2] – true works of Art, sold at moderate prices". Is "still a prisoner in my room – so weakened by the terrible remedies employed that I cannot write for long together".

Notes

1. New York journalist.
2. Napoleon Sarony (1821–1896), dedicatee of *Heart and Science*.

To Nina Lehmann, 25 February 1883
MS: Texas: Coleman

90, Gloucester Place, | Portman Square. W. |
25th February 1883

Dearest Padrona,

The sight of your handwriting was delightful – and the sight of you will
be better still. Anybody who says there is no such thing as luck – lies. Last
year, I was too ill to get to you at all. This year, I am only not well enough
to get out to dinner at nights. But I might come to lunch – when you have
no company – if you will choose from one day and hour, and make travel
allowances for Wilkie's infirmities. For six months – while I was writing
furiously, without cessation, one part sane and three parts mad – I had no
gout. I finished my story[1] – discovered one day that I was half dead with
fatigue – and the next day that the gout was in my right eye.

No more of that! I am nearly well – and I pull off my black patch indoors.
But I am forbidden night air – like old Rogers.[2] But <u>he</u> was only eighty – I
am a hundred.

With love to you particularly – and to everybody else generally – your
always affectionately,

WC

Weak brandy and water – and <u>no</u> wholesome joints.

Notes

1. *Heart and Science.*
2. Samuel Rogers (1763–1855 *DNB*), "a rich banker, a poor poet, a wicked wit, and a delightful
   entertainer" (W.T. Shore, *Charles Dickens and his Friends* [1909], p. 53).

To Nina Lehmann, 1 March 1883
MS: Texas: Coleman

Thursday | 1 March 1883

Yes, dearest Padrona, I shall be delighted to lunch at 1:30 – on Tuesday next.
How long is it since I last set ungouty eyes on you? I only remember that
you looked ten years younger. How many years younger are you going to
look next time? Yesterday, being out for a little walk, and wearing a <u>paletot</u>
<u>with a hood</u> for travelling – I heard a woman remark as I went by to another

woman, "To think of a man wearing such a coat as that – at <u>his</u> time of life!" The question that arises is – shall I dye my beard?

It was very nice and kind of Ernie[1] – and how unlike the average young Englishman of today! – to remember me in <u>that</u> way.

Yours my dear, | Affectionately, | WC

Note

1. One of the Lehmann children.

To Roma Le Thière,[1] 10 March 1883
MS: Fales Collection, NYU

90, Gloucester Place, | Portman Square. W. |
10th March 1883

Dear Miss Le Thière,

You have suffered – as I know by bitter experience – the one irreparable loss that death can inflict on us. Fifteen years have passed since my Mother died – and, when I think of her, I still know what the heartache means. Let me add my poor tribute of sympathy – as one more among the many friends who feel for you.

Always yours most truly | Wilkie Collins

Note

1. Probably Roma Guillon Le Thière, actress (see C.E. Pascoe, *The Dramatic List*, 1880, p. 250).

To Christian Carl Bernhard Tauchnitz,[1] 26 March 1883
Extract in Kurt Otto, *Der Verlag Bernhard Tauchnitz 1837–1912* (Leipzig, 1912), 78.

90, Gloucester Place, Portman Square, W., | London, March 26th, 1883.

My vocation in life is to find words for thoughts. <u>Your</u> kindness is, really and truly, too much for my resources – I call on my stock of words, and I find it exhausted. When you come to my age, and have in the course of nature lost some good and true friends, you will value as I do the friends who are still left. I say no more.

Note

1. Baron Tauchnitz (1816–1895), publisher, dedicatee of *Miss or Mrs? And Other Stories in Outline* (1873). See Gasson.

To Andrew Chatto, 14 April 1883
MS: Princeton

90, Gloucester Place, | Portman Square. W. |
14th April 1883

My dear Chatto,

My best thanks for the presentation copies of Heart and Science.

When Solomon said there was nothing new under the sun, he was without a prophetic sense of your [erased word] inexhaustible resources in the matter of designs for binding. Both in colour and ornament, our "new dress", is such a striking object[1] that the binder will help us in calling special attention to the new book. For your sake and for mine I feel an anxiety about the success of this novel, which I have not felt about any other work of mine for years past.[2]

Ever yours | Wilkie Collins

Andrew Chatto Esq

Notes

1. "Light blue smooth cloth, the front cover blocked in brown at the top with a band of ivy, beneath a rule, and, in the centre, with an owl, ivy, and a heart, and, at the bottom, above a rule, a band of ivy; the back cover blocked in brown with a publisher's monogram; the spine blocked in brown and lettered in gold beneath a rule and a band of ivy" with "white and green floral end papers" (Parrish, p. 116).
2. For reviews of *Heart and Science*, initially well-received, see *Heart and Science*, ed. S. Farmer, pp. 329–38.

To William Winter, 27 April 1883
MS: Princeton

90, Gloucester Place, | Portman Square. W. |[1]
Friday 27th April 1883

My dear Winter

The mail of Tuesday last took to The Tribune office (in three separate packets by registered book-post and sent to you) the first Edition of the revised "<u>Heart and Science</u>". I addressed the three volumes to the office, in case of their being stopped at your Custom House, as three separate works – hoping that some official person might be at the "Tribune" – disposal capable of "clearing", my importunate little gift. Our post office authorities here tell terrible tales of duty being visited on – unless we write "valued at not more than one dollar" on the address. And even then – if it is more than <u>one</u> Volume [erased word] (say a novel in three Volumes) the [word erased] official British Intellect doubts. If "Heart and Science" never reaches you – or if it is torn to pieces (which Proctor – astronomer and lecturer[2] – declares happened to some books of his) we will try the Tauchnitz Edition next, bound in one Volume.

What you kindly say of <u>The Dead Secret</u> has greatly pleased and encouraged me. I cried so myself over that passage [erased word] in writing it, that I was obliged to make a fair copy of [erased words] the page, when I was able to compose myself.

The slip, containing Mr Bellews' "recollections"[3] reminds me of days that can never come again – and raises the ghosts of many a beloved relative and friend associated with my happy early life. Submission – there is nothing for it but dogged submission to the "all-wise and beneficent Providence" who created all living beings [erased word] to die – and to eat each other, while they live.[4]

Instead of resting, I am now in all the turmoil of negociating for the production of a [erased letter] new play of mine – (did I mention it to you?) – which has been kept waiting for an actress. Miss Lingard[5] has taken us all by storm here; she is just the artist I want. I saw her the other night in the very worst adaptation of Young Dumas' Dame aux Camélias that could possibly be produced. She was badly supported – and the death-act was allowed to be far too long. But, in the third act – from the time when the father comes in to expect her to break her heart by giving up his son, to the end – I have seen nothing since [Aimee] Desclée in "Frou-frou"[6] so true, so passionate, so various, and so finely disciplined in the matter of Art. I am resolved to keep my piece waiting till I can give her a thoroughly good "cast". Then, you shall hear more – and I hope you will also read the piece in MS, and give me your critical opinion.

I am obliged to break off. Here is the copyist come for "instructions".

Ever yours my dear friend, | W.C

P.S. I have taken the liberty of giving a young Frenchman a letter of introduction to you. He is on an official mission connected with "studs" [erased word] and horse-breeding. If you will only tell him what [actors] to see in his evenings – you will be kind to him and to me. As to the horses, I have given him another letter to Buck.[7]

Notes

1. WC uses printed paper with his monogram, above which he writes: "London" and "All those short stories have still to be collected. It will be done one day – and they shall be yours. I dare not publish my plays – theatrical thieves would steal them – I mean in England and in remote places – with bankrupt managers for receivers of stolen goods."
2. R.A. Proctor (1837–1888: *DNB*), astronomer and author.
3. Probably a reference to John Bellew (1823–1874), author, preacher, and orator, who made an unsuccessful American reading tour in 1871 "quarreled with the theater managers, and lost his health". He returned "home sick and penniless to die" (Davis, p. 280).
4. Cf. Andrew Treverton in *The Dead Secret*: "My business in this world is to eat, drink, sleep, and die. Everything else is superfluidity – and I have done with it" (Chatto and Windus, [1861], 66).
5. Australian actress who played the leading role in the disastrous production of *Rank and Riches* at the Adelphi, 9 June 1883.
6. Ludovic Halevy's and Henri Meilhac's *Frou-Frou* (1869) was a highly successful comedy.
7. i.e., Edward Buck, editor of the *Boston Transcript*.

To William Winter, 3 July 1883
MS: Princeton

90, Gloucester Place, | Portman Square. W. | London |
3rd July 1883

My dear Winter,

A MS copy of my Play ("Rank and Riches")[1] was sent by Saturday's mail (3d June) to E.A. Buck "Shirt of the Times" office.

At this season you are doubtless as seldom as possible in "the Metropolis". I only tell you where the piece is – and leave it to your kindness to look it over for my sake, – [two erased words] and to tell me what you think of it, when you have an hour or two to spare. We (I mean by "we" my dear good actors as well as myself) have been brutally treated. The "clique" ("pickers and stealers" from the French – actors' art of engagements through the production of my piece – critics whom I had <u>not</u> invited to supper) [arms twisted] by a pit and Gallery – as incapable of understanding the piece as if it had been written in Hebrew. I was fool enough to trust an "Adelphi audience" – and I have paid the penalty. With one or two generous [erased word] exceptions, the newspapers were more brutish and more insolent than the audience.

I am mainly sorry for poor Miss Lingard. Knowing how seriously my success and her interests were bound together, I read the piece three times, to audiences of "experts" – and not one of them had the faintest forewarning of what really happened. I said myself, "<u>My</u> doubt is whether the ignorant part of the audience can follow this story." Nobody shared my doubt. And the first Act (both Tableaux included) justified their confidence – on trial. So far – all went well. In the second act the jeering and hooting began – checked by the admirable acting of Sugden and Alexander[2] in the Scene between the "Duke and Cecil" – only to break out again into <u>yells of laughter</u> over the great situation of the 3rd Act – (Like the rest of the piece, mind most admirably played!) I leave you[3] to look at that situation, and to say if my work is not worthy of another trial. It is only fair to add that strangers <u>to me</u>, who were present on the first night, have expressed their sympathy and indignation.

For the present – good bye | W.C

I hope you have received "Heart and Science". The success of the book here has been extraordinary. "Benjulia" has matched "Fosco". While the dramatic critics declare that I have written Vilest rubbish – the literary critics congratulate me on the production of a masterpiece!

Notes

1. Manuscripts of *Rank and Riches* are now at the Phillips Exeter Academy in New Hampshire.
2. Charles Sugden, (b. 1850), see C. E. Pascoe, *The Dramatic List* (1880), p. 321. Sir George Alexander (1858–1918), distinguished actor-manager.
3. Doubly underlined.

To Charles Reade, 17 July 1883
MS: Mrs Juliet Noel (née Reade)

90, Gloucester Place, | Portman Square. W. |
17th July 1883]

My dear Reade,

In clearing out a drawer filled with old letters, my hair has stood on end at the discovery of a letter of mine (addressed to <u>you</u>) – shuffled up with the other papers. It was a reply to a kind letter of yours telling me of your illness and asking me if I could recommend any good modern novels that you might find worth reading. How I could have missed my own letter with the others the devil, who must have possessed me, only knows. But what must <u>you</u> have thought of your old friend? I can only remember that you are the kindest of men, and that you will excuse the frail fellow creature who signs himself yours always truly | Wilkie Collins

You have lost nothing by the loss of the letter. It only acknowledged <u>my</u> inability to read any <u>new</u> novels – and referred you facetiously to the <u>old</u> novels that you know already.

To Edward Pigott, 1 August 1883
MS: Huntington

90, Gloucester Place, | Portman Square. W. | 1st Augt 1883

My dear Ted,

Thank you most sincerely for your friendly care for my interests. The letter you propose to write cannot possibly be improved. Well, indeed, did Pope say "the life of a writer is a warfare on earth."

I was indeed sorry to hear that I had missed seeing you. The thunder in the air yesterday had its usual effect on my nerves. I slept a stunned sleep in my chair – went to bed, and <u>slept again</u>!!!

Yours always aftly
WC

A capital little vessel – and a glorious time of it at sea, excepting the Saturday. Two [reefs] in the mainsail, and the top mast on deck, and <u>such</u> a sea off the Foreland!

To Frederick Lehmann, 21 October 1883
MS: Princeton: text, Coleman

90, Gloucester Place, | Portman Square. W. |
Sunday 21st Oct: 1883

My dear Fred,

Thank you heartily for your friendly letter and for the partridges. I am so much better now that I get out (in the character of Robert Macaire) with a patch over my eye. Give my love of loves to the Padrona, and ask her to let me have one line to say on what afternoon this week (at 4 o'Clock or thereabouts) she is disengaged, and will let me call and see her. I am allowed to use the sound eye – and, of course, I am at work again all the morning – living in a new world of my own.

Yours affectionately, | WC

To Nina Lehmann, 25 October 1883
MS: Princeton

Thursday 25th Oct:

Dearest Padrona,

Whatever you ask me to do, is done as a matter of course. I will lunch with you all – tomorrow at 1:30 – with the greatest pleasure.

N.B. Please order up a handy stick out of the hall, for your own use at lunch – (in this way) – namely, to rap me over the knuckles if you find me raising to my guilty and gouty lips any other liquor than weak brandy and water.

Always your affly, | W.C

To A.P. Watt, 11 November 1883
MS: Private Possession

[90, Gloucester Place, | Portman Square. W.] |
11th November 1883

Summary:
Title for Christmas Story "She Loves and Lies".[1] "You see I am taking to queer titles in my old age." Posted Harper proofs. "Many thanks for Trollope's story of his life.[2] The early part of it is very interesting – but when he comes to his own opinions on his own books —— let that dash express my sentiments."

Notes

1. "She Loves and Lies", *The Spirit of the Times*, 22 December 1883.
2. Anthony Trollope, *An Autobiography*, 2 vols, published October 1883 by Blackwood.

To Nina Lehmann, 29 November 1883
MS: Princeton

[90, Gloucester Place, | Portman Square. W. |] 29th Nov 1883

Dearest Padrona,

When did I ever say No – to you?[1] I am hard, hard, hard at work – and I shall enjoy the Saturday half holiday that you offer to me as I enjoy few pleasures now-a-days!

Your ever affly | W.C

A boasting postscript – which y<u>ou</u> will understand. Only think! My novels are to be translated into the Bengali language and read by the native inhabitants of India!!!!

Note

1. "ou" of "you" doubly underlined.

To Charles Kent, 3 December 1883
MS: Princeton

90, Gloucester Place | W. | 3rd Decr 1883

Summary:

"When is the Wheel of Fortune going to turn the right way for you? Shall we trust to 'the law of chances' – and go to Monte Carlo? Y<u>ou</u> to go inside (with my money in your pocket as well as yours) and break the bank – while I wait round the corner?" WC will give further guidance when Kent calls on him.

To Sebastian Schlesinger, 29 December 1883
MS: Harvard

90, Gloucester Place, | Portman Square. W. | London |
29th December 1883

Here is another year coming to an end, dear Sebastian – and here is your infirm old friend still keeping alive, in deference to the interests of his

Insurers in the United States. There is every temptation to die. We have not seen the sun for three weeks, in London – the plague of Christmas Cards is on the increase – my dear old four-legged friend and companion ("Tommy") has refused to eat his breakfast this morning – and Mr Bradlaugh[1] has issued his one hundred and fiftieth assertion of his right to ignore God and to take his seat in Parliament. Oh, what a miserable world to live in!

But there are moments of compensation. There is the moment in which I beg you to give my love to Mrs Sebastian – and there is the other moment in which I wish for your happiness and hers, in the year to come, with all my heart and soul and strength.

On this side of the Atlantic there is such an utter and unendurable dearth of news that we all screamed with delight when we heard (from your side) that General Grant had fallen on the "side-walk" and hurt his leg. Not in the least from any want of sympathy and admiration for the General – but merely because we found something to read about in the English newspapers, which had actually happened. We don't know what the German Prince-Imperial talked about with the Pope – or what Gladstone is going to do, in February next, with the British Constitution – or whether Henry Irving has or has not fascinated the American public. Until last night, we were not certainly informed that Tennyson was to be made a Lord.[2] Now (Heaven be praised) the rise of T. is a fact which we cherish side by side with the other fact of the fall of G. I am one of the literary men who think T. is right in accepting a peerage – not as a distinction conferred on himself, but as a recognition of Literature which has its use and its value in such a country as England. Since the baronetcy conferred on Walter Scott – who ought to have been created a Prince if he had only written "The [erasure] Antiquary" and "Ivanhoe" – no purely literary man has been ennobled in this country. Bulwer Lytton and Macaulay were politicians as well as writers. For these reasons, I take off my old felt hat, and salute Lord Tennyson.

By-the-bye, I have [erased word] gained my little distinction, since you last heard of me. My novels are so popular among the native races of India (who can read English) that they are to be translated into the Bengali language for the native inhabitants who want to read me. The Series is to begin with "The Woman in White". There seems to be some promise, in this, of the stories being still alive when the story-teller is dead.

Here is the end of the paper – and there is my novel now in progress (with the queer title of "I Say No") waiting to be continued.

I have just room left to ask for a nice long letter telling me about you [erasure] and yours – and to subscribe myself your affectionate friend | Wilkie Collins

Notes

1. Charles Bradlaugh (1833–1891: *DNB*), was elected M.P. "for Northampton in 1880 but was denied his seat when, as an atheist, he demanded to be allowed an affirmation rather than the customary parliamentary oath. Although he was re-elected three times, the case was prolonged until 1886, when he was finally seated after being allowed to take the oath" (*The Collected Letters of George Gissing*, ed. P.F. Mattheisen, A.C. Young, P. Coustillas (Athens, Ohio, 9 vols, 1990–1997), 11, 16, n.3. *Gissing Letters*, II, 16, n.3). Bradlaugh and WC met at a dinner at the Lotus Club, New York, on 27 September 1874, when WC was guest of honour (Peters, p. 357).
2. Following the underlined "Lord" WC places an "X" with points around it. In the margin of the letter he places the same symbol and underlines twice the letters "No" of "Note" and writes:

> Note: Looking at the address of this letter, it has just occurred to me to ask whether I am right in ennobling you (like myself) by the title of "Esqre". If you are an American Citizen, Q I have made a dreadful mistake.: You are "Mr". Or are you – "Herr German-Consul? Oh, do tell me!"

According to Sue Lonoff, Schlesinger was "a German resident in Boston ... a diplomat (seventeen years as German consul)" (Smith and Terry, p. 46).

To Mabel W. Wotton, 14 January 1884
MS: Fales Collection, NYU

90, Gloucester Place, | Portman Square. W. |
14th January 1884

Summary:
WC informs unidentified correspondent he is "working hard at 'I Say No'[1] ... It is all so real and true to me ... I believe the characters are living people." He addresses one of his servants by the name of the heroine "Emily".

Note

1. Serialized in the *Glasgow Weekly Herald*, 15 December 1883–12 July 1884, and other newspapers: see Gasson.

To A.P. Watt, 30 January 1884
MS: Private Possession

[90, Gloucester Place, | Portman Square. W. | 30 Jan 1884]

Summary:
"I return the Trollope Autobiography – thinking you might wish perhaps to lend it to other friends. I am not worthy of the book – for I could not read

it through. The first part I thought very interesting – but when he sits in judgement on his own novels and on other people's novels he tells me what I don't want to know and I bid him goodbye half way through the journey!"

To Charles Kent, 7 March 1884

MS: Present whereabouts unknown: Holmes Booksellers <u>Catalogue,</u> Philadelphia (1992)

90, Gloucester Place, | Portman Square. W. | 7 March 1884

Summary:
WC "sorry to hear such a melancholy report of" Kent's "health". Is "now between the two houses" and "began the year badly". His "new story[1] is no easy one to write".

Note

1. *I Say No.*

To A.P. Watt, 7 April 1884

MS: Private Possession

[90, Gloucester Place, | Portman Square. W. | 7th April 1884]

Summary:
WC sends Watt copy: "I write in wretchedly bad spirits. My dear old friend Charles Reade was dying when I heard of him yesterday. We had known each other for thirty years."[1]

Note

1. They first became close friends in 1854.

To Paul Hamilton Hayne,[1] 3 May 1884

MS: Present whereabouts unknown. Published Coleman, pp. 290–1; "Some Unpublished Letters of Wilkie Collins," *Bookman* (American ed.), 27 (March 1913), 66.

90, Gloucester Place, | Portman Square. W. | London |
3rd May 1884

My Dear Sir,

I am sure I need not tell you that your kind letter has pleased and encouraged me. You are known to me already by name – and your favourable opinion is one of the rewards of my literary career which I honestly prize.

Your estimate of the value of the last new school of novel writing is my estimate too. We are living in a period of "decline and fall", in the art of writing fiction. To allude to your country alone, when I read for the hundredth time <u>The Deerslayer</u> or <u>The Red Rover</u>[2] – and when I find myself yawning over the last new work of (let us say) Mr Blank, the enormous depth of the literary downfall in which I find myself plunged, does really astonish me. In this country, we have lately lost one of the "last of the Romans" – my dear old friend Charles Reade. I look out for the new writer among us, who is to fill that vacant place – and I fail to see him. Like the hero of old Dumas' magnificent story (Monte Cristo), we must say to each other: "Wait, and hope." Art, as you have no doubt remarked, is above the operation of the ordinary laws of supply and demand. The influences which produce great – and I will even say good – writers, are entirely beyond the reach of human investigation. It may be hundreds of years, before another Fenimore Cooper appears in America, or another Walter Scott[3] in England. I call these two and Balzac – the three Kings of Fiction.

I am sure I need not say that I shall receive your Poems gratefully, as one more proof of your friendly feeling towards me, and towards my stories.

Believe me with esteem and regard,

Most truly yours, | Wilkie Collins

My health varies a great deal. Gout and work and age (I was sixty years old in January last) try to persuade me to lay down my pen, after each new book – but, well or ill, I go on – and I am now publishing (periodically) a new story with the quaint title of "I Say No" which I hope may interest you when it is finished.

Notes

1. Paul Hamilton Hayne (1830–1886), South Carolina poet. A presentation copy of his *Poems* (1882) was in WC's library at his death.
2. James Fenimore Cooper: the 31 vol. New York edition of his novels (1872) in WC's library.
3. The hero, Amelius Goldenheart of *The Fallen Leaves* has Scott's works in his library: "The writings of the one supreme genius who soars above all other novelists as Shakespeare soars above all other dramatists – the writings of Walter Scott – had their place of honour in his library" (Stroud: Sutton, 1994) p. 186.

To A.P. Watt, 14 May 1884
MS: Private Possession

[90, Gloucester Place, | Portman Square. W. | 14th May 1884]

Summary:
WC has made up lost time: "Poor dear Reade! What a wretched bumptious ill-considered tribute to his memory "in the *Contemporary Review*".[1] Asks "Has Tauchnitz died?"[2] WC "must write to his son".

Notes

1. Compton Reade, "Charles Reade," *Contemporary Review* 45 (May 1884), 707–13.
2. The first Baron Tauchnitz died in 1895.

To A.P. Watt, 11 June 1884
MS: Private Possession

[90, Gloucester Place, | Portman Square. W. | 11th June 1884]

Summary:
WC writes "I am beginning to wonder whether 'I Say No' will ever end!"

To A.P. Watt, 25 June 1884
MS: Private Possession

[90, Gloucester Place, | Portman Square. W. |
25th June 1884]

Summary:
WC writes that there are "a few more slips still to come". He is "thoroughly worn out".

To Paul Hamilton Hayne, 16 July 1884

MS: NYPL (Berg): Published: "Some Unpublished Letters of Wilkie Collins", *Bookman* (American ed.), 27 (March 1913), 67–8.

90, Gloucester Place | Portman Square | London. W. | 16 July 1884

Dear Mr Hayne,

In one of her letters or her prefaces, George Sand declares that of all the wretchedest forms of mortal weariness the fatigue produced by hard work of the brain is the most complete. My otherwise unpardonable silence offers to you its only excuse under the protection of George Sand. The last ten or twelve chapters of "I Say No" were written without rest – or intermission (except when I was eating or sleeping). And when the effort was over a more prostrate wretch could hardly have been found in all this great city than your friend. But why work at this headlong rate? you will ask. Because, at sixty years old, I have not yet learnt to control the rage that possesses me under the strong sense of injustice – or, in plain English, under a sense of the robberies committed on me, and on my American publishers, by the [erased word] pirates. Each weekly part of my story was stolen <u>on the day after it appeared</u> in Harper's newspaper – and this is a great country which recognises the rights of literary property, in the case of its own citizens! The one way of "circumventing" these wretches – and of "helping my publishers round to their moves" (in our [erased word] commercial English phrase) was to get in advance of the printed sheets, and to send the conclusion of the story to Messrs Harper in manuscript, so that the republication in book-form might appear in the United States before the last weekly parts were published. By this time, no doubt, the book is stolen also. But, at any rate [the] Harpers have had the first of the market!

I should not have troubled you with this little grievance of mine but for one consideration. It explains the delay that has occurred on my part as one of your readers. I could look at your beautiful volume – I could feel sincerely grateful for the kindness which had made this welcome addition to my library – but I was utterly unworthy of your poems,[1] until my mind had rested a little. Only at the beginning of this week have I begun to read you – confining myself at first to the shorter poems. May I pick out my favourites <u>thus far</u>? They are, "By the Autumn Sea", "The Dryad of the Pine", and "Love's Autumn". These three represent many others in which I find true poetical feeling, expressed delightfully in truly poetical language. To my mind, this is a very rare quality in the present time. Affectation of language, and obscurity of meaning – no matter what popular names may be attached to them – always, produce the same result, in my case. I close the book, and deny that the writer is a poet. He <u>must</u> please me, he <u>must</u> excite some feeling in me, at a first reading, or I will have nothing to do with him. All good poetry, I know, improves on acquaintance – but what I insist on is, a favourable impression at starting. Excepting Tennyson (in his shorter poems) I read hardly any modern poetry with pleasure. What I like in your poetry (so far as I yet know it) is – that it makes me feel, and that it has <u>not</u> stopped me [erased words] with detestable doubts whether I do, or do not, understand what you are saying to me. Shall I astonish you if I confess that I read Walter Scott's poetry with admiration and delight – and shall I add that I believe Byron[2] to be beyond comparison the greatest poet that has sung since Milton? Now you know what my criticism is worth!

While I am thanking you for your Poems, let me add my thanks for your last letter, and for the enclosure. Absence from London until this afternoon – and the near approach of the post hour – have not allowed me to read the "In Memoriam" today.[3] I shall take it with me when I return to the country, and I will with the greatest pleasure offer it to one of the best of <u>our</u> periodicals here, as soon as you write again and give me leave to do you this little service. Let me add that the sooner the permission reaches me the better it may be.

I have never read the story by Reade which you mention. To my knowledge, it has not been published yet in England. It will no doubt appear in the forthcoming volume of Reade's short stories. When he made use, in other cases, of French literature, he always obtained the author's permission, and paid for the right of using his ideas. In my opinion, he would have done better to trust in his own invention. He knew that I disliked the idea of his borrowing from anybody – and we never spoke of his literary relation with French writers.

Looking at the pretty little engraving of your home, I wish I could see the home itself. But I don't like to read of those sufferings and losses which you allude to with such admirable patience – and I will not trust myself even to think of your War. There are people who still write (and even talk of "the <u>God</u> of Battles")]. What a gross injustice done to the Devil![4]

In what you so kindly say of my books, the reference to "Poor Miss Finch" especially pleases me. English readers in general have never done me justice in the case of this story. In Germany, I hear that they go to the other extreme, and rank "Poor Miss Finch" as the best of all my works, with the one exception of "The Woman in White"!

This unmercifully long letter must come to an end somewhere – and my paper suggests that it may be in this place. In saying goodbye for the present, let me beg to be kindly remembered to Mrs Hayne, and believe me,

Always truly yours | Wilkie Collins

Excuse these wretched slips of paper. My desk is left in the country. I take what I can find, and will appear in a more respectable form next time.

It has just occurred to me to send you a really beautiful photograph portrait taken of me by Sarony of New York – <u>ten years since</u>. The more recent portraits, taken in England, (are nothing like so good <u>as works of art</u>.[)]

Notes

1. See 3 May 1884, n.1.
2. An eight-volume 1857 John Murray edition of Byron's *Works* was in WC's library at his death.
3. Probably a reference to Hayne's poem "Charles Reade: In Memoriam", *Independent* 17 July 1884. "Both Wilkie Collins and Richard D. Blackmore were interested in seeing the poem published in England, but the journals approached refused to print a poem already published" (R.S. Moore, ed., *A Man of Letters in the Ninteenth-Century South* [1982] p. 218, n.2).
4. Hayne's home was destroyed during the Civil War, and he lived in poverty.

To Charles Kent, 8 August 1884
MS: Fales Collection, NYU

90, Gloucester Place, | Portman Square. W. |
Friday 8th Augt 1884

My dear Kent,

If you can, by any lucky chance, come here tomorrow (Saturday) at any time before 5. p.m. – I will give you some of my specially-prepared laudanum – a measuring glass – and "fit you out complete". If not, go to Corbyn's 86, New Bond Street (corner of Oxford Street) and present this next page.

As to the dose – nothing but experience will decide <u>that</u>. Begin cautiously with only twenty (20) minims i.e. d<u>rops</u> – taken in a tablespoonful of water, just before you get into bed. Keep your night-light well out of sight – and – go to sleep – !

Yours affly | W.C

But come if you can.

You ought to have a minim measuring glass – to make sure of the number of drops.

To | Messr Corbyn & Co
86, New Bond Street

Dear Sirs,

I have advised my friend Mr Charles Kent, who is troubled with sleeplessness, to try small doses of laudanum – beginning with 20 minims. Will you kindly supply Mr Kent with a small quantity of the same laudanum which you prepare for me – enough to try the experiment for a week or ten days – when he will be able to report the result.

Faithfully yours | Wilkie Collins

90, Gloucester Place. W. | 8th August 1884

To Charles Kent, 17 August 1884
MS: Princeton

90, Gloucester Place, | Portman Square. W. |
17th August 1884

My dear Kent,

Your Report is a severe disappointment to your amateur medical adviser. I shall see our old friend Frank Beard in a day or two, and shall consult him on your case. In the meantime, here is my opinion (right or wrong).

Laudanum has a two fold action on the brain and nervous system – a stimulating and sedative action. It seems but too plain to <u>me</u> – that your[1] nerves are so strongly affected by the stimulating action that they are incapable of feeling the sedative action which ought to follow. Whether a considerably larger dose than any you have taken would have the right effect I dare not ask. Such a risk is not to be run except under competent medical advice.

The other alternative is – to try a smaller dose than any you have yet taken, on the assumption that your nerves are too sensitive to bear the ordinary number of drops. But defer even this safe experiment till I have seen Beard. You are entirely right in dropping the laudanum after such an experience as yours. I am more sorry than I can well say at this utter destruction of all my hopes for you. But I won't despair yet. There are other sedative persuaders to sleep besides opium. I will write again the moment after I have seen B.

Yours affly, | W.C.

Note

1. WC underline "ou" of "your" twice.

To William Winter, 5 October 1884
MS: Private Possession

Ramsgate[1] England | 5th Oct: 1884

Among the "things in Heaven and Earth["] which are not dreamed of in our philosophy, there is one thing, my dear Winter, which goes by the name of "<u>luck</u>". If you had only happened to be in London a little earlier in the latter half of August, your letter would have found me in town – and y<u>ou</u> would have found yourself in Gloucester Place again the next day. As it was, both your letters have been waiting for me here, while I was travelling at sea, wherever the winds and the tides chose to take me – and a fortnight had passed before I opened your first letter telling me that you were about to leave me in "a few days". To say that I was disappointed is not to say enough – I was really distressed, for I had set my heart on spending a happy day with you somewhere – no matter where, so long as you and I were together. Come back again for God's sake as soon as you can – and I will do my best to live long enough to shake hands with you once more. That cruel institution of "the all merciful Creator" which has said Live (in one breath) and Die (in another) has left me very few friends – and I cling to those few with a desperation which you will understand more and more thoroughly with every new year of your life until you are as old (and let us hope) older than I am.

On Tuesday next I go back to London, and to work – infinitely the better for the thorough <u>salting</u> that I have received, mostly on the German Ocean – and provided with a new idea for a story[2] <u>and</u> a play, which occurred to me on board the yacht. The central notion is (between ourselves) – a divorced husband and wife, who (after a lapse of a few years) regret their separation. <u>He</u> finds that the woman who has seduced him is in no sense worth the sacrifice – and becomes a miserable man. She (passing in the world as a widow) has an offer from a sincerely religious man – hesitates (being a good woman) to marry him under false pretences – decides on telling him the truth – and is rejected with horror by her lover, who remembers his New Testament, and dare not marry a divorced woman. But these same religious principles urge him to bring the separated pair together, in the interests of their eternal welfare. He is innocently assisted by the child of the marriage (a little girl in the mother's charge, who has been told that her father has been drowned at sea, by way of accounting harmlessly for her mother's position). The good friend finds out the husband – brings about a meeting – and then discovers that the woman whom he has restored to her husband, and to happiness, is the very woman whom he loved.

This a miserably bald outline – and hardly even suggests the dramatic and pathetic situations which are to be found in this story. So far as I know, the idea is new. The U.S.A. is the land of divorces – and I trouble you with my small Scenario, on the bare chance that you may know, or have heard of something of the same kind which might have happened, and which might help me. Or – if I am wrong here – you might be able to discover what American clergymen would be likely to do in such a case. Would they consent to re-marry the divorced man and wife ? Or would they say as the Roman Catholic would say – "they never were really <u>un</u>married. That sacred connection is not to be broken by any human laws"?

Goodbye my dear friend. I will write a [erased word] letter better worth reading next time. In the meanwhile, Mrs Graves sends you her kindest regards – and regrets that she has lost the opportunity of saying Goodbye.

Always truly yours Wilkie Collins

P.S. – Our good and dear Mary Anderson will be the first person whom I shall call on when I get back. I am eager to hear how the Romeo and Juliet rehearsals promise for the future. It is my earnest hope that there is another triumph in store for her – if she can only be sure of really competent help from her company.

Notes

1. Collins spent much time in Ramsgate – sailing with his friend Pigott, and taking holidays with Caroline Graves and her daughter Harriet and with Martha Rudd and their three children. Caroline and Martha were never there at the same time, though their children and Caroline's grandchildren were regularly there together (Clarke, pp. 169–73). William Winter, a long-standing American friend, called on him regularly on his London visits and introduced him to the American actress, Mary Anderson, with whom Collins struck up a close correspondence in his last five years. He even contemplated writing a play for her, but it was never finished.
2. *The Evil Genius, The Leigh Journal and Times*, 11 December 1885–11 May 1886; *Bolton Weekly Journal*, 12 December 1885–1 May 1886, and other Tillotson syndicated newspapers; 3 vols, Chatto and Windus, 1886.

To A.P. Watt, 22 October 1884
MS: Private Possession

90, Gloucester Place (in bed) | 22nd Oct. 1884

Summary:
"The kindness which takes charge of my anxieties to such good purpose is one of the remedies which is helping me to recover my health, and which thus takes care of <u>me</u> as well as of my interest.

The doctor's reports, yesterday, assured me that the inflammation is steadily subsiding and that I may hope to have 'got over the worst of it'. The pain is becoming intermittent and is less severe, when it does make itself felt. So I may contemplate getting to work again before the end of this month and sending in my MS (if all goes well) by the 12th of November next."

To A.P. Watt, 12 November 1884
MS: Private Possession

[90, Gloucester Place, | Portman Square. W. | 12th Nov 1884]

Summary:
WC is sending most of the story which he needs three more days to complete. "I am damaging the bad eye, it seems, by using the second eye to write – my amanuensis is ill – and I cannot dictate to a stranger."

To Charles Kent, 15 December 1884
MS: Princeton

90, Gloucester Place, | Portman Square. W. |
15th Decr 1884

My dear Kent,

I am indeed sorry to have missed you. Yesterday I was complaining to Beard of being obliged to go out in the middle of the day, and leave my work. He said, "Your eye is right enough now to go out when you like." Today for the first time I used my liberty, and had left the house (only a few minutes as I gather) before you arrived. There's your luck and mine! Don't trust to luck again. One line to propose any day and any hour that may suit you best. I am only in "the fool's paradise" of planning a story. All the hard work is to come.

Yours afftly | W.C

To E.A. Buck, 30 December 1884

MS: Princeton

90, Gloucester Place, | Portman Square. W. | London |
30th December 1884

Dear Buck,

If you call me "Mr" Collins again, I will commit suicide – and there will be an end of my series of "Spirit" Stories.

But this is not business. I ought to have begun by thanking you for the Dft for £50,, ,, – which reached me safely yesterday.

Have I mentioned in my recent letters that I shall be sixty one years old, if I live until the 8th of January next? Never were praises more welcome than the praises of <u>The Girl at the Gate</u>,[1] for this reason:- they tell me that my brains are not affected by the infirmities of three score and one – and that, I can tell you (seeing that I have just signed agreements for a new serial novel next year),[2] is an unutterable relief.

But Harry – our burnt Harry – I send him my love, but I cannot approve of those scars. My forced principles have always forbidden me to become a Freemason, on the grounds that I really could <u>not</u> consent to take down my trousers and sit on a red hot gridiron, while the Perpetual Grand Master harangued me, sitting himself on a cool bottom? What right under these circumstances, has the P.G.M. to a cool bottom? No Masonic Fraternity has ever yet been able to answer that question. Let Harry try. I am partial to <u>him</u> – and I will listen.

Ever yours Wilkie Collins

Corrected – in the interest of The Commentators, reading back-numbers of <u>Free Spirit</u> five hundred years hence. [printed text follows]

It is generally agreed that Mr Wilkie Collins stands quite at the head of novelists of the present day. His works are read wherever the English language is spoken, and several of them[3] have been translated into German.[4] At the time of his death, the late Charles Dickens left an unfinished work entitled "The Mystery of Edwin Drood". It was Wilkie Collins[5] who was selected to finish the novel – no small tribute, by the way, to the ability of Mr Collins. For several years past this distinguished writer has furnished us a Christmas story, and we believe we can claim the distinction of being the only American journal thus favored. "The Girl at the Gate" is the title of Mr Collins' contribution to THE CHRISTMAS SPIRIT, and, after a careful perusal, we have no hesitation in pronouncing it by far the best story with which he has ever favored us, a conclusion which we feel satisfied our readers will share.[6]

Notes

1. "The Girl at the Gate", *The Spirit of the Times*, 6 December 1884; *English Illustrated Magazine*, January 1885.
2. *The Evil Genius*.
3. In the left-hand margin following the printed "of them", indicated by a line, WC writes: "all of them".
4. In the right-hand margin following the printed "German", indicated by a line, WC writes "Also, most of them into French, Italian, Russian, Swedish, Dutch, and Danish. Cock-a-doodle doo!"
5. In the left-hand margin alongside his name WC places two short vertical lines and writes: "No! no! no! I declined to do it."
6. In the right-hand margin WC scores the first sentence relating to "The Girl at the Gate" and writes: "Ah, here the writer is correctly informed!"

To Sebastian Schlesinger, 27 January 1885
MS: Harvard

90, Gloucester Place, | Portman Square. W. | London |
27th January 1885

My dear Sebastian,

I wish you could have <u>heard</u> the shouts of welcome with which those heavenly ducks were received – I wish you could have <u>seen</u> the silent, I had almost said the sacred, sense of enjoyment with which those ducks were eaten. Come with the ducks, next time – receive my thanks in person – and let us drink one more bottle of Old Champagne, with "gout staring us in the face", and you and I staring back again at the gout with defiant eyes and resolute stomachs.

Yes – of course, I am glad to hear of your growing fame as [erased word] a composer, and of course all that I can do to obtain notices shall be most gladly done. But (a word in your ear) <u>some</u> of the musical critics are the most infernal blackguards that ever held a pen. The one amusing point in their characters is the inordinate hatred they bear to one another. A friend of mine being at the theatre the other night, sat next to one critic, and behind another. Critic Number One went out between the Acts. Critic number Two at once cautioned my friend. "For God's sake take care what you say to that man! He is the most abominable &c & &." On the next occasion Number Two went out. And Number one said to my friend, "I was sorry to see you talking to that man. Beware of him. Of all the damned&c &c &c."

Goodbye for the present, dear Sebastian | WC

To Paul Hamilton Hayne, 28 January 1885

MS: Private Possession. Published "Some Unpublished Letters of Wilkie Collins," *Bookman* (American ed.), 27 (March 1913), 69–70.

90, Gloucester Place, | Portman Square. W. | London |
28th January 1885

The bodily part of you, my dear friend, lives at Copse Hill. That I don't deny. But the spiritual part of you, I firmly believe, crossed the Atlantic not long since – discovered that I was sorely in want of some encouragement – and sent me, not only the Kindest of letters, but a tribute of poetry which I receive as one of the memorable events in my literary life – which I read with admiration – and which I shall remember gratefully to the end of my days.

That middle-age oracle had his reasons for not speaking plain. He is one of the men whom I hate most – a discreet man. If he had been bold enough to tell the truth, he would have answered you in these words:

"Look here, Paul Hamilton Hayne! The less you say about your friend Wilkie Collins the better. His stars, for the past three months, have given him up as a bad job. He went to sea with the ridiculous idea (at his age !) of restoring his youth. He left his ship with the animal spirits of five and twenty, and the splendid complexion of the days when he was a truly beautiful baby – he returned to London – and the next morning, when he approached the looking-glass to [erasure] brush his hair and his beard, he perceived a red streak in his left eye. In three days more, his eye was the colour of a (cooked) lobster. The Gout-Fiend had got him. The Gout-Fiend bored holes in his eye with a red-hot needle. Calomel and Colchicum knocked him down, and said (through the medium of the doctor) 'Wilkie, it's all for your good.' Laudanum – divine Laudanum – was his only friend. He got better – then worse again – then better – then worse once more. If you could see him now, writing to you on a foggy London evening, you would find his eye restored at last to its right colour and to its sight, but left so weak that he is obliged to protect it from artificial light (only candlelight) with a patch. There is the sad story of W.C. – and that is why he has not written to you long ago."

The Oracle having spoken, I may end my letter in my own proper person. Let us make believe, as the children say, that it is only the 1st of January – and let me, with all my heart, wish the happiest of new years to you, and to everyone dear to you at home. I could write much more – but I must spare the sound eye (especially after a long day's work on the first chapter of a new novel)[1] and ask you to consider my letter as periodical publications, "to be continued".

Always most truly yours, | Wilkie Collins.

I have just seen your postscript – and have just drunk a whole wine-glass full of weak brandy and water (!) to your health and to a long succession of birthdays. Oh dear! I remember the happy time when it would have been a bottle of dry Champagne.

Note

1. *The Evil Genius.*

To Sebastian Schlesinger, 9 April 1885
MS: Harvard

90, Gloucester Place, | Portman Square. W. | London |
9th April 1885

My dear Sebastian,

Only the old story to tell over again. Ill, once more! Gratefully sensible of your hearty invitation – but without the strength and the resolution to take the pen and say so. We are keeping this illness a secret, so as to prevent reports from flying abroad which might make the case out worse than it is. There is some nervous mischief, in the region of my heart, (the medical name of the region is "<u>cardial plexus</u>") which every now and then produces the most terrific pain – beginning in the under parts of both arms, and then extending across the chest. After one of these attacks, "a washed-out rag" is a feeble emblem of me for the rest of the day. They have yielded to nothing but a last desperate remedy which acts by inhalation. Five drops of this tremendous elixir, on a morsel of cotton wool, put under my nose, produces a furious throbbing at the temples and a burning heat in the face – but[1] kills the pain, <u>literally, in an instant</u>. Those other unpleasant effects vanish in a few minutes. The attacks are diminishing in number – and the doctor has no fear for the future. But I am obliged, for the first time in my life, to "take care of myself" – to submit to strict dieting – to abstain from fatiguing myself in any way, and so on, and so on [erased word]. Whether – abstractedly-speaking – it is worth while to take all this trouble to keep living, when a man has turned sixty, is doubtful in the last degree. But, <u>relative</u>ly. I have books still to write, and children to take care of – and I must go on paying these [erasure] inscrutable American Life Insurance Offices as long as I can.

There is my dreary little story – the one reply I dare send, so far, to your invitation.

Let me (before I close this egotistical letter) acknowledge receipt of your Song. Shall I try if I can find a competent (and honest) man to review it – in a newspaper?

With love to Mrs Sebastian, and all good wishes,

Afftly yours | Wilkie Collins

Note

1. The "bu" of "but" is underlined twice.

To William Lanier Washington,[1] 9 April 1885
MS: Princeton

90, Gloucester Place, | Portman Square. W. |
9th April 1885

Summary:

"You ask me for 'a rule of life'. One of the wisest rules that I know of was laid down by a philosopher many centuries since. He was asked by a personage of exalted rank for an axiom which should be equally useful in restraining his pride, if he remained at the height of prosperity – and in sustaining his courage if he was destined to suffer the worst that adversity could inflict. The philosopher wrote on the palace wall:

'This also shall pass away.'"

Note

1. Unidentified.

To A.P. Watt, 24 June 1885
MS: Private Possession

14, Nelson Crescent, | Ramsgate | 24th June 1885

Summary:

WC is "getting on so well that" he has "arranged to return on Monday next". His "departure is hastened by the infernal noises which make this delightful place a hell on earth. Organs – brass bands – howling coster-mongers selling fish, make day hideous – and night too, up to 10 o'clock. Nobody complains but me."

To Charles Kent, 17 July 1885
MS: Texas: Coleman

Friday, 17 July 1885

My Dear Kent,

My rooms are uninhabitable with – new carpets – staining of floors – stinks – workmen. I fly this house as soon as my work is done (in a bedroom) – and return to sleep. You shall hear from me again the moment this revolution is over – and we will fumigate the newly carpeted premises together.

Yours affectionately | Wilkie Collins

I address to your private residence – not knowing when you may be at the club.

To William Winter, 24 July 1885
MS: Princeton

90, Gloucester Place, | Portman Square. W. |[1]
24th July 1885

My dear Winter,

In what part of the British Islands, I wonder, will these words find you? Not near Ramsgate or we should have heard from you, and have seen you. And not in London, of course. Soon, I shall be the only person left in Gloucester Place. But London <u>empty,</u> means London perfectly [adequate] to such work as now. So I stay at my desk. At 8.30.p.m. there is [blessed] idleness – and something to eat and drink – in this house. You <u>may</u> be popping through London. I say no more.

Mrs Graves joins with me in sending you love.

Always Af Yours | Wilkie Collins

Note

1. Above the printed address and his monogram, WC writes: "<u>In London again</u>".

To A.P. Watt, 4 August 1885
MS: Private Possession

[90, Gloucester Place, | Portman Square. W. |
4th August 1885]

Summary:
WC will let Watt know how it ends with Tillotson[1] when his lawyer returns:
"I envy you your visit to Abbotsford. Last night, in my wakeful hours I was
reading 'A Legend of Montrose' again for the 100th time."

Note

1. William Frederic Tillotson (1844–1889), Northern newspaper proprietor: see Gasson.

To Robert du Pontavice de Heussey, 14 August 1885
MS: Mrs Faith Clarke

90, Gloucester Place, | Portman Square. W. | London |
14th August, 1885

There are some atrocious persons, my dear collaborateur, whose conduct
is too bad to admit of excuses and expressions of penitence. I am one of
those persons. When I remember that I have not even written to congratulate your brother on his marriage, and that I have allowed all this time to
pass without thanking you for your most friendly and most welcome letter,
I become an object of well-merited detestation to myself. I even begin to
think that I must have deserved to suffer the merciless neuralgic pains in
my chest and my arms which have tormented me in this spring and
summer. Slowly, slowly I am getting the better of this new enemy, and, in
that circumstance, I find the courage to trust to your friendly indulgence,
and to write again – on the chance of recommending myself to your mercy.
Whether you will confirm me in my conclusions, by sending me your essay
on Balzac,[1] remains to be seen. I own at once that I don't deserve it – a circumstance which, with such a nature as yours, may actually give me a claim
on you.

If you still think of writing on Charles Dickens, only tell me what sort of
information you want – and it shall be yours with the greatest pleasure.

Of course (like you) I have been working. Ill or well, I must use my
brains and my pen. Later on this month, I hope to send you a short story
which is to appear in many newspapers, here and in America. Later in the
year a new long story will begin to appear in the same form of publication.

Enough, and too much, about myself. Let me "make my exit" as we say on the English stage. The stage reminds me of Dickens's impatience of the long melodramas which I used to take him to see when we were both in Paris. The second act generally exhausted his powers of endurance. I implored him to respect the <u>Developments of Art</u>. He generally answered "You shall tell me the story of the piece, when you get back to the hotel. I'm off for a walk in the streets." I [erasure] firmly believe he never read one of Balzac's novels. There again the developments were too much for him! With kindest remembrances to [Count] du Heussey – always most truly yours.

Wilkie Collins.

Note

1. WC had in his library a copy of Pontavice du Heussey's *Oeuvres Complètes*, 2 vols, Paris, 1887.

To Francis Carr Beard, 31 August 1885
MS: Princeton

90, Gloucester Place, | Portman Square. W. | London |
31th Augst 1885

My dear Frank,

Your letter this morning was a relief and a pleasure, both in one. Only refrain now from walking too far – and I shall expect to see you again a younger man than ever.

I am getting on fairly well – and finding the refuge from myself which I had hoped to find, in my work. How closely that poor little dog had associated himself with every act of my life at home, I only know now. I can go nowhere and do nothing – without missing Tommy.[1]

So far, there has been no return of that familiar fiend who is so good at sharpening his claws on my breast. The cooler temperature is helping me, I suppose. Here we have a drab-coloured sky and a small rain today. May you have sun and cool breezes for tomorrow! Let me hear how the shooting prospers, and how <u>you</u> prosper with it – and give my love to my friends at Southover.

always yours affectionately | Wilkie Collins

Note

1. WC's beloved Scotch terrier Tommy died 28 August 1885 (cf. Clarke pp. 178–9 and 182).

To A.P. Watt, 7 September 1885
MS: Private Possession

[90, Gloucester Place, | Portman Square. W.] |
7th September 1885

[My Dear Watt]
Welcome back again!
My account of myself is a little gloomy this time. I have lost the dear old friend and companion of many years – my dog. I should not acknowledge to many people what I have suffered during his last illness and death. But I think you will understand me. No more of it now! I think of Walter Scott, when <u>his</u> dog died – asking the friends with whom he was to have dined that day to excuse him because "he had lost a dear old friend" – and love and admire him more than ever.
That matter of the title too still worries me – and Tillotson wants his title this week. Out of a dozen at least, I can only (at present) choose two as specimens.
1. Forbidden Kisses.
2. The Evil Genius.
Which do <u>you</u> like best? Or don't you like either of them. I was so desperate yesterday that I actually thought of calling the book:
Blank
A Novel Without a Title.
!!!!
I must wait till my doctor returns from his holiday, before I settle whether to go away from London or not. Are you very busy? The question is selfish. It only means – when can you <u>quite conveniently</u> come and see me?

[Yours affectionately Wilkie Collins]

To Robert Pontavice du Heussey, 19 September 1885
MS: Princeton

90, Gloucester Place, | Portman Square. W. | London |
19th September 1885

My dear Collaborateur,
Neuralgic troubles in my chest and my arms have been serious obstacles in the way of my correspondence lately. I can only now thank you for <u>Le Livre</u>,[1] and for having given me something to read, while I am recovering,

which has interested me in no ordinary degree. You possess a share in that rare gift – the gift of narrating – which has made the reputations of so many admirable writers in your country and in mine. I have read nothing about Balzac which has interested me as your article has interested me – and that wonderful old lady's description of him places the man before my eyes for the first time. May you find more materials – and show us Balzac in other places and among other good friends.

I have made notes for a few pages about Dickens – but the doctor forbids me to write anything (after my working hours are over) – he protests even against work, but the new story is getting into proof, and the first weekly part is to appear late in next month[2] – and I tell him that I shall be writing the novel "<u>in my head</u>" if I don't write it on paper. Before long, I hope to send you my contribution – alas, my small contribution – and I know you will forgive me in the meantime.

There is much more that I should like to say – but that too must wait till I am stronger.

Always your affectionately | W.C

Notes

1. A presentation copy of Heussey's *L'Inimitable Boz* (Paris 1889), in WC's library at his death, is now at Princeton.
2. *The Evil Genius, Leigh Journal and Times*, 11 December 1885–30 April 1886; *Bolton Weekly Journal*, 12 December 1885–1 May 1886; published in 3 vols by Chatto & Windus, 1–15 September 1886.

To William Holman Hunt, 8 October 1885
MS: Huntington

90, Gloucester Place, | Portman Square. W. |
8thOctober 1885

My dear Hunt,

There is but one [erased word] reason why I don't answer your letter in person – I am rowing [erased word] in the same boat with you, and my doctor's orders send me away to Ramsgate to be patched up. <u>My</u> nerves make sketches with red hot needles under the skin of my chest – and some kind friends are reporting that my death from Angina Pectoris may be shortly expected! I too have been stethoscoped and reported weak in the heart – but no organic disease.

It is really and truly a grief to me to hear such melancholy news of you – I had hoped that you were happy healthy and idle. We have both worked too hard – And I should like to know who <u>doesn't</u> work too hard, excepting always the contemptible impostors in your Art and mine.

The three rules of life that I find the right ones, by experience, in the matter of health, are:

1. As much fresh air as possible. (I[1] don't get as much as I ought.)

2. Live well – eat light <u>and</u> nourishing food, eggs, birds, fish, sweet breads – no heavy chops or joints. <u>And</u> find out the wine that agrees with you, and don't be afraid of it. (Here, I set an excellent example!)

3. Empty your mind of your work, before you go to bed – and don't let the work get in again until after breakfast the next morning. (This is a serious struggle – many defeats must be encountered – but the victory <u>may</u> be won at last, as I can personally certify.)

=

One last word – and I have done preaching. If you don't find that you make better progress, under your present medical guidance, try my old friend, <u>F. Carr Beard</u>, <u>44, Welbeck Street</u>, <u>Cavendish Square</u>. He kept Dickens alive, he kept Fechter alive, and he is keeping me alive. The most capable, and the most honest, doctor, I have ever known.

My best thanks (and the best thanks of my girls) for your kindness in sending the cards. They will go either today – or tomorrow, if the light gets worse today – and will see the finest work of sacred Art that modern times have produced. I shut my eyes – and see that wonderful face of the Virgin as plainly as I saw it in your studio.

> Always affectionately yours | Wilkie Collins

I am going to Ramsgate – to what address, I am not yet sure – but all letters will be forwarded.

Note

1. "I" underlined twice.

To A.P. Watt, 23 October 1885
MS: Private Possession

> 14, Nelson Crescent. | Ramsgate | 23rd Oct. 1885

My dear Watt,

In the first place, it is high time we left off "Mistering" each other. I can only account for our having continued that formal practice so long by attributing it to the "force of habit" – a stupid force in nine cases out of ten. Therefore you and I drop "Mr" – and leave him to be [picked] up by newer Friends than we are.

The stick has arrived in perfect safety. I am indeed most heartily obliged to you for this singularly interesting gift. A stick is a familiar friend – and when that friend associates me with Walter Scott's own plantation I am (in some degree at least) associated with the writer of all others whom I love and admire – the greatest of novelists and the kindest and truest of men. My new stick will be my treasured possession as long as I live.

Let me thank you also for having so successfully concluded the negotiations for the American story. The publication day in New York is, this time, December 26<u>th</u>.[1] So we shall be alright here. I will not forget that the MS is wanted by November 10th.

The strain of writing the play as well as the novel was taken off me two days ago – and I have been in better health ever since.

[Yours | WC]

Note

1. *The Evil Genius.*

To A.P. Watt, 29 October 1885
MS: Private Possession

[14, Nelson Crescent | Ramsgate | 29th October 1885]

Summary:
"I am a hunted man. Tillotson hunts me with demands for weekly parts, America hunts me with warnings to send the play (and protect my property) without delay, the Doctor hunts me with unlimited directions relating to exercise and fresh air – and volunteer translators and autography collections fill up the intervals ... I look at the boatmen here, eternally idling with their hands in their pockets, with feelings of ferocious envy." WC glad to let Carl Rosa[1] have the play. Three acts are finished, so far "only sufficiently completed for the <u>formal</u> (a 'bogus') performances in London which secures my rights!" He must consult Tillotson. "<u>My</u> idea is that the play[2] might help the novel. <u>His</u> idea may be that the play will forestall the interest of the novel – published in weekly parts – by telling the whole story at once."

Notes

1. Carl August Nicholas Rosa (1843–1889: *DNB*), impresario, manager of the Carl Rosa Opera Company.
2. The stage version, *The Evil Genius: A Drama in Four Acts* "never produced except for a single afternoon performance at the Vaudeville Theatre, 30 October 1885, purely to establish [WC's] dramatic copyright" (Gasson).

To A.P. Watt 8 November 1885

MS: Private Possession

14, Nelson Crescent. | Ramsgate | 8th November 1885

[My dear Watt]

I am hard at work on the short story.[1] But the time is terribly short – and that blessed institution the British Sunday makes Saturday evening <u>here</u> an evening without post – and so loses me a day in sending to my copyist.

The said copyist is my adopted daughter, Mrs H.P. Bartley, 61 Finchley Road. She is so near your private residence that I have suggested to her sending what she has done to 117 Alexandra Road on Monday evening, so that you can take it with you (if you kindly will) – and send it to Messrs Macmillan, if they <u>must</u> have something on Tuesday – I hope to finish tomorrow (Monday) so that my copyist will finish on Tuesday when she receives my MSS by post. This will make me a day late. I can't help it – being away from Town.

I hope to return on Thursday next. As I have no time to correct the MSS copy, I ought to see proofs. If they will not be ready before Thursday, they had better go to 90 Gloucester Place. I shall try to get away by the 10 am train (to save time) which reaches London at 12. Oh, I am so tired!

[Yours | WC]

Note

1. Probably "The Poetry Did It: an Event in the Life of Major Evergreen", published in *The Spirit of the Times*, 26 December 1885 and in the *English Illustrated Magazine*, January 1886, published by Macmillan.

To Doris Edith Bartley,[1] 13 November 1885
MS: Princeton[2]

90, Gloucester Place, | Portman Square. W. |
13th November 1885

My dear Doris,

I was very glad to receive your letter at Ramsgate, and to see how nicely it was written. We had some very fine weather, and the sea air has done me a great deal of good. Charley[3] was with us. He rowed in a boat in the harbour – and he went to a place called Sandwich on a tricycle – and he eat good dinners – and he enjoyed himself very much. We came home yesterday – and a man ran after our omnibus all the way from the railway station to this house. He was poor, and he wanted to get a little money by carrying our luggage upstairs, and he did it very well, being a strong young man. He was pleased when I paid him, and I think he went away and got some beer. We hope you will come and see us soon. We send our love to you, and to Sissy, and to Bolly,[4] and to your Mamma.

Your affectionate godpapa | Wilkie Collins

To | Miss Doris Bartley

Notes

1. Doris Edith Bartley (b. 1879), daughter of "Carrie": see Clarke, pp. 196–8.
2. "letter in hand of Caroline Graves, signed by W.C", (Peters, p. 476, n.22): date "13th November 1885" also in WC's hand.
3. WC's son William Charles Collins Dawson.
4. "Cissie", Cecile Marguerite, "Carrie's" daughter; "Bolly", Evelyn Beatrice, "Carrie's" daughter (see Clarke, pp. 194–9).

To Paul Hamilton Hayne, 27 December 1885
MS: Present whereabouts unknown. Published "Some Unpublished Letters of Wilkie Collins," *Bookman* (American ed.), 37 (March 1913), 70–1.

90, Gloucester Place, | Portman Square. W. | London |
27th Dec 1885

At last the cloud-battalions through long rifts
Of luminous mists retire ... the strife is done;
And earth once more her wounded beauty lifts,
To meet the healing kisses of the sun.

Exert your imagination, my dear friend, and please see W.C. in his bed, reading your fine poem on the storm among the Georgian Hills, reaching the last verse, admiring the charming image in the last two lines – and then seeing through his window a dense dirty dripping London fog, extinguishing all hope of sunlight, and showing nothing but the dim dingy brick-fronts of the opposite houses. Add the dismal tinkling of church bells in a distant street, and the hoarse screeching of a boy selling Sunday newspapers – and you will be prepared to hear that I heartily wished myself in Georgia with my poet and friend. The next best thing was at least to see him in his photograph, and to feel (as I did) by instinct that it must be a good likeness – a more <u>living</u> likeness, to my mind, than the portrait in the Poems. I have to thank you for consolation as well as poetry, this time – and of myself I have little or nothing more to say. Good days and bad days (in the matter of health) – every week a number of "The Evil Genius" (my new serial story) to be written, whether I am well or ill – with publishers and translators waiting for it, in England and the English colonies, in the United States, in France, Italy, Germany and Holland. "What <u>must</u> be done, sir, <u>will</u> be done", old Doctor Johnson said, and said truly, in the last century. I hope you like Doctor Johnson. He is one of my heroes – Boswell's Life of him is my favourite book – and (to the astonishment of some of the shallow literary men of the present time in England) I persist in thinking his "Vanity of Human Wishes", and his "lines on the death of Robert Levett" two of the grandest poems ever written.

My best love to all at Copse Hill – and my heartiest good wishes for a happy New Year.

Affectionately yours, | Wilkie Collins

In the forefront, the Gout has given up trying to kill me – and fierce neuralgic pains (really "angina", but we keep <u>that</u> a secret in fear of newspaper reports of my death) have succeeded the Gout. My doctor and I, and "Arsenic", and "Amyl", make a good fight of it – and, in spite of the weather, I get better.

Part IX
Letters to "Nannie"
1885–1888

Introduction

We have made an exception to our chronological order in the case of Wilkie's correspondence with Nannie Wynne, which extended from 1885 to 1888, because it forms such a unique exception to all his other letters. We have therefore put these particular letters in a separate section of their own.

Wilkie's letters to eleven-year-old Nannie Wynne (as she was in 1885, when the correspondence began) and her mother, only came to light as late as 1988. Sir John Lawrence, having read William Clarke's biography, *The Secret Life of Wilkie Collins*, got in touch with him to find out whether his wife, Faith, Wilkie's great grand-daughter, might have the other half of the correspondence Wilkie had had with his mother Nannie (or, to give her her full name, Anne Elizabeth le Poer Wynne) when a girl. Sir John had over 40 such letters. The answer to his query was "No".

The fortunate upshot, however, was that Sir Lawrence made the letters available for the first time (they were eventually sold at Sotheby's in 1989).[1] The letters revealed once again Wilkie's open, teasing approach to both women and children. They did far more. They enabled a 60-year-old bachelor, with two mistresses and a morganatic family of three, to live a fantasy marriage through correspondence with a young girl.

Sir John had first learned of his mother's involvement with Wilkie when she found him reading *The Woman in White*. "Did you know Wilkie Collins was very fond of me?", she asked him. Wilkie had apparently first got to know the Wynne family through Dr Frank Beard (their joint medical adviser) and other mutual friends, such as Edward Pigott and Robert Browning. They were also reasonably close neighbours and met each other socially.

Nannie was clearly a friendly child, occasionally bringing Wilkie flowers from the countryside. Wilkie for his part delighted in children, taking them seriously, meeting them on equal terms, and never writing down to them. Polite exchanges over tea and luncheon soon gave way to "thank you" letters from eleven-year old Nannie, as well as intriguing questions about how Wilkie wrote his stories. By the end of 1885, Wilkie was asking Nannie's advice, sharing news of his health, promising to write her special stories, and, finally, treating her as his wife and her mother as his mother-in-law. He showered her with adoration and love and occasionally chided her.

We only have Sir John's account of Nannie's mother's reactions to the "affair". When telling him about Wilkie's friendship, she explained how her mother, though startled by the way things were going between Wilkie and her daughter, quickly came to the conclusion that there was no harm in it. She was probably right. Not only was Wilkie quite open about the corres- pondence and his meetings with Nannie, but as the correspondence shows, he was careful to include her mother in most of his invitations or to seek his "mother-in-law's" permission. Nonetheless, it remains intriguing that a man who all his life had not only deliberately avoided the matrimonial state, but even joked openly about it, should suddenly begin to live out such a fantasy. Perhaps, once again, as in so many other areas, he was openly getting the best of all worlds.

Note

1. Excerpts from the letters were first published in a paper by William Clarke to the Wilkie Collins Centenary Conference in Victoria, British Columbia, September 1989 and in the *Sunday Times*, London, 19 November 1989 (see "A Teasing Marital Correspondence with 12-year-old", Smith and Terry).

To Mrs le Poer Wynne and Anne "Nannie" le Poer Wynne,[1] 12 June 1885
MS: Private Possession

14, Nelson Crescent | Ramsgate | 12th June 1885

Dear Mrs Wynne,

I am ashamed of myself – I ought to have got well long since, having such kind interest as yours to encourage me.

In this air I really think I am beginning to recover my long lost strength – and here I must remain for a little while, in training for the Banquet, and in reliance on your unwearied and most friendly hospitality. The moment I know on what date I return to London, the first letter which mentions that return shall be a letter to you.

Believe me | always truly yours | Wilkie Collins

Note

1. Anne le Poer Wynne, "Nannie", the twelve-year-old "posthumous only child of a promising member of the Indian Civil Service who died of cholera". She and "her widowed mother lived in Delamere Gardens" (Peters, p. 411).

To Anne le Poer Wynne, 12 June 1885
MS: Private Possession

To Miss Nannie Wynne | 12th June 1885[1]

In return for your flowers, dear Nannie, I have written a ghost story[2] for you. It wants – what you never want – correction, and then it will be ready for you.

When I have the pleasure of visiting you, at your Mama's luncheon table, I wish to ask your advice on a matter of serious importance. Everybody tells me I ought to "take care of myself" if I wish to get well. My misfortune is that I don't know how to take care of myself. I should like to hear what your ideas are on this subject, and whether You have ever been in the habit of taking care of yourself and (if yes) how you did it, and whether after all you found it worth your while ? I am – as I take it – not more than fifty two (or three) years older than you are – and your example would therefore be of the utmost value to your faithful | Old Man.

P.S.

No – I have not written about a murder in a cab.[3] But if one of your young men (of whom I am jealous) should get murdered in a cab, I shall be interested in hearing of it.

Notes

1. WC's letter to "Nannie" is enclosed with that to her mother.
2. "Mrs Zant and the Ghost" ("The Ghost's Touch"), *The Irish Fireside*, 30 September–14 October 1885; *Harper's Weekly*, 23 October 1885.
3. Nannie "seems to have had advance knowledge of Fergus Hume's *The Mystery of a Hansom Cab*, eventually to outsell even *The Woman in White*" (Peters, p. 413).

To Anne le Poer Wynne, 15 July 1885

MS: Private Possession

90, Gloucester Place, | Portman Square. W. |
15th July 1885

My lovely funny Lady, don't be angry with me. I only got your nice letter on my return to London last night. It had followed me back from Ramsgate – and I had been idling at Margate and Westgate on Sea on my way home. Ask your Mama, with my kindest remembrances, at what hour I may call tomorrow (Thursday) if I have a chance of seeing you before you[1] go away next.

This afternoon I am engaged to go to Harrow – or I should have taken my chance instead of writing.

Let me have one word to tell me the hour – and may you never have such a number of letters to answer as I now see on my writing desk!

Yours affly | W.C.

Note

1. "ou" of "You" is doubly underlined.

To Anne le Poer Wynne, 12 August 1885

MS: Private Possession

90, Gloucester Place, | Portman Square. W. |
12th Augt 1885

Oh my admirable Nannie, w<u>hy</u>, <u>why</u> did you submit to have those teeth torn out of your nice little mouth? I protest against that cruel and funny system of curing the toothache – and, what is more, I have heard of a dentist – no! not a dentist, An Angel – who refuses to take out teeth and who cures his patients without having their bones out of their jaws.

The next time you have the toothache, let me know – and I will find his address, or get it from the friend[1] who first revealed to me the existence of this glorious creature.

Yes – I received with pride and pleasure the delicious flowers, and I kept them alive as long as they would live, and lamented their untimely death. I am going away for a day or two to rest – and then coming back to work, work, work, harder than ever. Let me know where you are on the 22nd of this month so that I may send you the newspaper with the Ghost Story in it – and remember me most kindly to your Mama. You are both of course away from London. Gloucester Place is a ghastly solitude, and your devoted old man leads the life of a hermit. | W.C

Note

1. Probably Dr Frank Beard.

To Anne le Poer Wynne, 15 September 1885
MS: Private Possession

90, Gloucester Place, | Portman Square. W. |
15th Sept 1885

Dear, and much injured, Nannie,

I have not been well – and the wretched publisher (without telling me of it) has delayed the publication of your Story in the newspaper until the 26th of this month. As soon as it does appear, you shall have it – but it is cut into three weekly parts, so it will not be complete till the 10th of October. By that time you will perhaps be in Delamere Street again – and I shall be able to bring it with me.

In the meanwhile, forgive your old man like a dear good young sweetheart – and give my kindest remembrances to your Mamma.

Ever affly yours, | W.C.

To Mrs le Poer Wynne, 18 September 1885
MS: Private Possession

90, Gloucester Place, | Portman Square. W. |
18th Sept 1885

Dear Mrs Wynne,

I have marked 1, 2, 3, the likenesses which seem to me to be best. No 1. especially is so near to being successful in the matter of expression that it rather exasperates me. But, my little sweetheart is not nicely treated by the photograph. If they try again, suggest powdering her hair (especially over the forehead). It will then "print" lighter, and not look like a wig. My first exclamation (when I saw one of the portraits) was, "Oh Damn!" But I am now patient – and I shall be glad to place No 1. among my treasures, if you "reprint".[1]

My neuralgia is plaguing me again – and I am afraid I shall have to go away again. You are – I hope, suffering this essentially h<u>ea</u>vy weather with better success.

My love to Nannie – and my everlasting gratitude must be added, in remembrance of what she has gone through for my sake. Having a tooth out, having your hair cut, and having your photograph taken are the three great trials of this mortal life. Always truly yours | W.C

Note

1. "re of "reprint" doubly underlined.

To Anne le Poer Wynne, 7 October 1885
MS: Private Possession

90, Gloucester Place, | Portman Square. W. |
Wednesday. 7th Oct: 1885

Alas, my Nannie, this old man is told that he must go again to the seaside, and reform the present state of his health if he can. But he has tomorrow (Thursday) still at his disposal – and at any time between 3 o'Clock and 5 o'Clock will be convenient, he will be proud and happy to receive his young lady, and to have her photograph to comfort him in his Exile.

Signed S.O.M. | (sickly old man)[1]

Note

1. "s" of "sickly", "o" of "old" and "m" of "man" are doubly underlined.

To Anne le Poer Wynne, 5 November 1885
MS: Private Possession

14, Nelson Crescent | Ramsgate | 5th November 1885

Dear and admirable Mrs Collins, I hope to get back to London in a week more. To know that I burnt beautifully without popping is a great consolation to me. I am better – but still so terribly hard at work that I feel an older old man than ever. You will revive me when I see you – with your present. As yet – tell your Mama, with my kindest remembrances, – that we are keeping the Nitro-Glycerine in reserve. When I a<u>m</u> blown up, rely on my bursting in your direction – just at lesson-time.

I send you another newspaper, with the beginning of another story in it – and a portrait[1] which accurately represents me crying over my separation from my young wife.

Goodnight – it is 11 o'Clock – and bed is waiting for your affectionate | W.C

Note

1. The letter contains a newspaper photograph of WC with the sub-head "The Popular Candidate: among all sections and parties of South London", with WC's handwritten note.

To Anne le Poer Wynne, 27 November 1885
MS: Private Possession

90, Gloucester Place, | Portman Square W. | 27th Nov 1885

Mrs Wilkie Collins, if this weather goes on you will change your present position in life – you will be <u>a wid</u>ow. I don't object to your marrying again, but when you order your mourning cap I have to request that you will shorten those long floating streamers which I see in the young widow who is represented in the advertisements of mourning warehouses. I don't like a widow who expresses grief by long streamers and by tight-lacing.[1]

This is Friday. On Sunday (unless there is a sun and a blue sky) I have arranged to pass the day in bed – the agravation of the church bells being unendurable to me in any other than a horizontal position. After Sunday, choose your own day and hour (otherwise your Mama's day and hour) for coming here – after our long separation. If it <u>must</u> be as far off as Thursday your sinking husband submits.

I am steeped in Devilish drugs – arsenic among them. Never, in all your experience of me, has my temper been so vile as it is now.

Je reste, Madame, votre atroce époux [I remain your atrocious husband].

P.S. How are the children?
Vilkie[2]

Notes

1. WC scores his left-hand margin from "warehouses" to "tight-lacing".
2. "ie" of "Vilkie" underlined four times with a flourish.

To Anne le Poer Wynne & Mrs le Poer Wynne, 9 [December] 1885
MS: Private Possession

9th [Dec^r] 1885

The Violets, dearest Mrs, still keep their delicious scent. They are by my desk while I write – and I have been trying to get to Delamere Street, and thank you in a better way than this. But my Evil Genius has got in my way, so I write to my Good Genius. I am getting better as fast as I can – in the hope of being yet worthy of the Bullybase (that is the way to spell it, my dear).

But now I want to know how your Mamma is. Do write me one of your nice little letters and satisfy me about her health, and tell me how she bears the cold. I[1] delight in it – except <u>at night</u> when (if I go out) I find it lays its hands on my chest, and scratches me as if it was a "female", and jealous of your devoted husband. | W.C.

Note

1. "I" doubly underlined.

To Anne le Poer Wynne, 25 December 1885
MS: Private Possession

90, Gloucester Place, | Portman Square. W. |
25th Decr 1885

The prettiest and simplest Christmas Card that I have received is yours, my Nannie. The only card I could send back yesterday was the English Illustrated Magazine containing a little story of mine.[1] When you will receive it – when you get this letter that thanks you – I am afraid to think. The Post Office is overwhelmed. T<u>wo</u> postmen and a boy this morning, in my street, for one delivery of letters. I must come and deliver myself and thank my "Mrs" in that way – on any day at which her Mama will let me come to Delamere Street, after <u>this</u> week. Then I can wish you both a happy New Year. Happy Christmas is impossible on such a day as this. The fog chokes your loving husband. W.C

Note

1. "The Poetry Did It: an Event in the Life of Major Evergreen", *The Spirit of the Times*, 26 December 1885; *The English Illustrated Magazine*, January 1886.

To Anne le Poer Wynne, 15 January 1886
MS: Private Possession

90, Gloucester Place, | Portman Square. W. |
15th January 1886

Dear Mrs Wilkie

Your pretty violets are still alive, and looking at me while I write. If the Evil Genius doesn't finish me first – I shall finish The Evil Genius by the end of next month – and then we will celebrate its conclusion (if your Mamma permits it) at 4. Delamere Street, and at luncheon time. I am so tired when evening comes that I am only fit to sink in my chair – and smoke – and wish I was y<u>ou</u> (with a lovely velvet dress, and a broad sash, and a charming governess to teach me[)]. My only comfort now is that you have gone to Mr Beard – if <u>he</u> doesn't cure your neuralgia I shall be disappointed indeed. For this next twenty years, my angel, ought not to know what neuralgia means.

"The Evil Genius" is waiting. Goodbye sweetheart. Remember me to Mamma. W.C

To Anne le Poer Wynne, 1 February 1886
MS: Private Possession

90, Gloucester Place, | Portman Square. W. |
1st Feby 1886

Si carissima sposa mea, noi pranzeramo nell' Workhouse. What am I about? I am so weary of writing English all day, that I fall into Italian. I mean we have a very nice Workhouse in this neighbourhood and we will dine there. The gruel is said to be strong, and the master won't be hard on us when we are set to breaking stones if we do it badly.

Mark my words! that round tower will tumble down. In these modern days people have lost the art of building round towers. The builder will cheat – he will make it of rubbish and cover it with stucco. But I subscribe – 12 postage stamps enclosed. Oh, you sly little hussy with your persuasive postscript, trying to wheedle me into subscribing five shillings! I regard five shillings for a round tower as ostentation – and even shocking ostentation, considering that it is a sacred question of a church. A pious person subscribes a shilling.

With these sentiments I think it is only right now to go to bed. Having written myself into a state of headache, and finished one of the most interesting chapters in my book, let me say good night and waft you a Kiss in this way[1] till we meet again.

My kindest remembrances to your Mamma. I am dying to see what was bought at the sale.

Always your loving | W.C.

Note

1. WC draws a circle indicating a kiss.

To Anne le Poer Wynne, 1 March 1886
MS: Private Possession

90, Gloucester Place, | Portman Square. W. |
1st March 1886

1st Excuse:

Please refer, very much-injured missus, to the Marriage Service – You will find you took me "for better, for worse". My long silence and my want of punctuality in thanking you for your List of 100 books – exhibit "worse".

I deserve to be divorced – I can only leave it to your mercy.

2nd Excuse

P. and W.

Is it possible that you want to know what this means? Let me hasten to explain:

P. and W.

mean

Pain and Work[1]

or

shall we say

I. and E.G.

Illness and Evil Genius?

=

I begin the last weekly part today. If I live to finish it, you shall see the "better" side of me. If not, my love and goodbye, and kindest remembrances to Mamma from your unfortunate W.C.

Note

1. "Pain" and "Work" written in large, bold letters.

To Anne le Poer Wynne, 19 March 1886
MS: Private Possession

> 90, Gloucester Place, | Portman Square. W. |
> Friday 19th March 1886

Here I am, my darling, – and here I shall be delighted to receive that conjugal embrace at 3 o'clock tomorrow if that hour will be convenient to you. I thought you had long since left me – and was wondering why Mrs Wilkie did not write and tell me how she liked Bath. Now I shall see her! and I am more than satisfied.

> Yours always afftly, | W.C.

To Anne le Poer Wynne, 10 May 1886
MS: Private Possession

> 90, Gloucester Place, | Portman Square. W. | London |
> 10th May 1886

Your pretty flowers, my angel, have not found me an ungrateful husband – they only find me dying under the dreadful English Sirocco – not knowing where to write to you on the first occasion, and doubtful of your figures on the second occasion, when I know that you were at "Circus, Bath", but when I am not quite sure whether "[lg]" (accurately copied from your writing) means:
  [lg]. Circus. Bath
  or
  39. Circus Bath.
  I adopt 39, – but, oh Heavens, what will happen if I am wrong and if it ought to be "[lg]".[1] Will the postman (not finding you at 39) tear up my letter? Or will he show it to his wife, and will she say "what a shame to disrupt the bride and bridegroom!" Do write (there's a dear!) and tell me if it <u>is</u> 39, and let me hear when you are coming back again – and [erased word] where Mamma is, and how she is. My languid love – I can write no more in the exhausted [reserves] in which I am now living – I cannot sign my name – but I can write
  39[2]

> Your grateful | W.C

Notes

1. WC's imitation of "Nannie's" writing, especially the first letter, is difficult to reproduce.
2. The figures are large and boldly written.

To Anne le Poer Wynne, 19 May [1886]

MS: Private Possession

90, Gloucester Place, | Portman Square. W. | 19 May

Dearest Dear, do you ever swear? (you know you may confess anything to your husband). If you wish to enchant me, please swear at the Irish. My poor dear story cannot be published before the autumn, because the public eye is fixed on Home Rule – General Election – and Civil War – and won't look, for the present, at any Evil Genius but Mr Gladstone.

It is not easy to say how much embracing I want. Your Mamma will tell you why it is my hard lot to be obliged to wait till next week – and why I must offer my love, and retire for this week.

W.C

To Anne le Poer Wynne, 24 June 1886

MS: Private Possession

90, Gloucester Place, | Portman Square. W. | 24 June 1886

I write this, my love of loves, in an interval of pain. If I had been well, you would have seen me before today. I am slowly getting better – and I am to go away yachting as soon as I can. But I am not quite well enough to be able to welcome you tomorrow. If next week will be convenient for your Mamma and you – and Mr Thomas[1] (whom I shall be very glad to see again) I will write once more, and report myself in good time. For this time, goodbye my angel! | W.C

The shilling story is only trying to come to me – but the cruel neuralgia gets in the way, and says "I^2 have got him, be off!"

Notes

1. Unidentified; possibly a pet dog or cat!
2. "I" underlined twice.

To Anne le Poer Wynne, 1 July 1886
MS: Private Possession

90, Gloucester Place, | Portman Square. W. | 1st July 1886

No, dearest little wife, Beard says – "Go with another air; I can do nothing while you are in London." I am only waiting to hear from the seaside – and to put off certain engagements with printers and publishers – and then away I go, in search of health, and on the look-out for a friend's yacht. I hope to get away by the end of this week – and I must not venture to make any appointments in the meantime – for I had a bad attack yesterday – and the pain has left me shaken today. Make my excuses to your Mamma, and to Mr Thomas – like a good dear. I am sure they will forgive me – until I come back and can plead for myself. You will still love me – in Suffolk – won't you? And I shall write, from some sea port (the wind will decide which), and report my progress towards recovery. Goodbye darling for the present. | W.C.

To Anne le Poer Wynne, 27 July 1886
MS: Private Possession

27 July 1886 | Ramsgate

I am only now, dearest and best of wives, beginning to get better – and I am ashamed of myself for not having written to my Nannie before this. So far, I am certain of what I say. Everything else is doubtful. I don't know how long I shall stay here – I don't feel sure that I may not accept an invitation to stay with a friend at Santa Barbara, on the coast of California (N.B. He would be glad to see my wife if she would come with me) – I don't know when I shall begin the 1s novel – and I am miserably uncertain about putting in Lady Snagge. My fear is that she might scratch my face if she found it out. Would it be well if I slightly altered the name, and called her Lady Snugge or Lady Snogge ? Doubt! nothing but doubt in my present state of mind and body! I love and adore my Nannie – that alone is certain. Tear up this letter, and I will write another when I know something more about myself. Perhaps my mind will be steadier when I begin to work again. My love to my mother-in-law. And don't show her these lines or she will regret our marriage. Tear up! tear up! | Your loving | W[1]

Note

1. WC writes a large florid "W".

To Anne le Poer Wynne, 20 September 1886
MS: Private Possession

Monday 20th Sept 1886

This,[1] dearest missus is Me. You have heard of "the torture of the D——d". I am just able to announce that the gout attacked my eye in the midst of my sailings and enjoyments of wind and sea.

After weeks of the aforementioned tortures the eye is recovering its colour and its sight – but oh Nannie, I am so[2] weak after the pain and (what the Doctor calls) "the treatment". My nerves are in such a state of ridiculous irritability that I cannot endure the passing of vehicles in the street – and I am going away for a little quiet, to return in a week or so [erasure] – and then to write and tell you the result and to be fit to see my wife and my mother-in-law at last. My love, no more. Yes, one bit more of news – I have got to write a Christmas book!!! Pleasant – my Nannie – isn't it?

Your loving W.C

Notes

1. WC draws a face with an eye patch above the first word.
2. "o" of "so" underlined three times.

To Anne le Poer Wynne, 7 October 1886
MS: Private Possession

90, Gloucester Place, | Portman Square. W. | 7th Oct 1886

Yes – my angel – I thank you with all my heart for the photograph. But I wish the lights had not been so very light – and the shadows so very dark. It will be an excellent likeness of you when you are twenty five years old.

You won't like this opinion – so let me retire and consider my ears boxed (which I richly deserve).

I am half way through my Christmas book – and they are going to print fifty thousand copies of that half to save time. If I break down or die, you will have to finish the story. I must say goodbye – the printers are waiting for me – I have no leisure time till the evening, and then I go to sleep.

Ever miserably, | WC

The gout has gone. I hope you hate weak brandy and water. I do.

To Anne le Poer Wynne, 14 October 1886
MS: Private Possession

Savage Gardens | 14 Oct 1886

Hush! My angel. Don't mention it. I am in hiding at the above address. Your last photograph has been the cause of my dipping my hands in human gore. I have felt much pleasure in murdering two persons – 1st the miscreant who made that frightful dint (or notch) on the top of your head, exactly in the middle (see photograph). 2ndly, the still more merciless enemy who has deprived you of your waist, and has hunched your clothes up about your back that it looks like a bundle instead of a back (see photograph again). And I was the more angered, and the readier to murder, because the face in this last portrait is, beyond all comparison, the best that has been done – soft, and young, and pretty, and [possessing] the right light and shade. And then to go and dent your head and make your figure look like a bundle of old clothes. Look at it! Swear at it! God bless you. I remain, | The Modern Cain

– and go back to "The Guilty River".[1] There's a title! And such a story, if I am not hanged before I finish it.

Note

1. "The Guilty River", published 15 November 1886 by J.W. Arrowsmith of Bristol.

To Anne le Poer Wynne, 23 December 1886
MS: Private Possession

90, Gloucester Place, | Portman Square. W. |
23rd Decr 1886

Yes, dearest, I am glad to hear you are going to do me honour in the character of a Dresden Shepherdess. Bring me back a tender lamb – and I will receive him with gratitude and garlic (stuffing).

I am so glad to hear from you (I also hear from the excellent B.) that Mother-in-law is setting me such a good example of recovery. I try to imitate her with some little success – but that infernal pain comes back again every now and then. I don't want to be obliged to go away suddenly – so I still wait before I show myself in Delamere Street, until I and my familiar devil have parted company. Yesterday I was free. This morning I had some red hot scratches again, and had to sniff at my "Amyl" (N.B. This is not the Christian name of another wife. It is only a glass capsule).

My best thanks for the drawing. When it gets cooler, I shall jump off that bridge and swim in the lovely water and dry myself among those noble ruins.

My love to you both.

Ever affly yours | W.C

To Anne le Poer Wynne, 15 January 1887
MS: Private Possession

Saturday Jan^ry 15 | 1887

My Lamb,

Shall I find you and Mama at home if I call at 3 on Monday next?

If Monday presents a snow storm and a hurricane – then Tuesday at 3, when it is sure to thaw.

Your loving | W.C.

If the answer is Yes, don't trouble to write.

To Anne le Poer Wynne, 10 March 1887
MS: Private Possession

90 Gloucester Place | London. W. | 10th March 1887

I am proud of my wife. Her account of the earthquake is the best that I have read yet. She is also a little angel who thinks of her husband and sends him a nice box of flowers – when other women might have been prostrate under the shock, and have thought of nothing but the state of their nerves. Mia sposa adorata, brava! brava!

But I had heard of you and your mother through Knox.[1] He sent a copy of the earthquake part of Mama's letter to Pigott, and Pigott sent it to me and I sent it back to Pigott with a prophecy – Viz: – that the excitement of being earthquaked would shake you both up and do you good – and that the Riviera air would also do you good if you rushed into the street in the costume of a late Queen of the Sandwich Islands – a hat and feathers and nothing else.

Am I to encourage my wife and my mother-in-law in the vice of gambling? In the name of Hypocricy I protest – and refer you to the next page. Of many gambling superstitions which I once knew, it is the only one that I now remember.

My love (and congratulations on her improved health) to mother-in-law. I adore you. I have no more to say. W.C.

The Numbers-Dodge

Take the three last and highest numbers on the board: (I mean the Roulette table):

34, 35, 36

Add them together 34
$$35$$
$$\underline{36}$$
105

Divide the product by your age:
13/105/ 8 and
$$\underline{/104/}$$
1 over

1st Moral:

Try your luck by dividing your stake and placing it on the two numbers 8 and 1.

2nd Moral:

The chances against the ball stopping on either of those two (or of <u>any</u> two numbers) are, in the case of each number, 37 to 1 against you!

Note

1. Alexander A. Knox, author or *The New Playground, or Wanderings in Algebra* (1881), friend of Edward Pigott – life-long friend of WC.

To Anne le Poer Wynne, 1 June 1887
MS: Private Possession

90, Gloucester Place, | Portman Square. W. | 1st June 1887

Welcome back again, sweet Mrs Wilkie and Mrs Wilkie's mother! Here we have had neuralgia in place of earthquake terrors – I have been taking forced holidays with my excellent friends Opium and Quinine until all my literary work has fallen into arrear – and now I am obliged to perform the detestable act of penance called "making up for lost time". Next week I hope to be able to ask on what day I may come, and hear of your gamblings and gaieties – the more shocking you have been in the poisonous atmosphere (morally, my dear prisoner) of Monaco, the more interested I shall be. This week I am the galley-slave chained to his oar.

Your loving | W.C

I am going out to get some useful information wanted for my new story.

To Mrs le Poer Wynne, 25 June 1887
MS: Private Possession

90, Gloucester Place, | Portman Square. W. |
25th June 1887

Dear Mrs Wynne,

I am only well enough to thank you for your kind letter today. My nerves are still – if I may use the striking American expression – "unscrewed". My temper is vile, and if anybody opens the door suddenly I start as if a cannon has been fired off behind me. The other day, I was "taken out for a drive" – a thing I loathe when I am in health. On this occasion it was remarked that I was "silent and subdued". The truth is that I was frightened out of my wits every time the coachman turned a corner.

Perhaps the idiotic Jubilee has something to do with it. Any way, I am doing my best with my dear friend's medical help, to get better; and to find myself at your table again at last.

I must trust to you to make my peace with my wife. My humility is very great. If she is getting tired of me I will put no difficulties in the way of a divorce. But while I <u>am</u> in a condition to send this message I beg to offer my love, and to make my apologies.

Ever yours | W.C.

To Anne le Poer Wynne, 17 October 1887
MS: Private Possession

90, Gloucester Place, | Portman Square. W. | 17th Oct 1887

I hear, Dearest Nannie, of Mamma's illness. Tell her of my sympathy and my hope that she is already (with the help of the best of Doctors) on the way to recovery. Let me hear about her. Do you know what the word "Seedy" means? The word Seedy means Me.

I must go on with my work. My <u>love</u> offers itself. W.C.

To Anne le Poer Wynne, 28 November 1887

MS: Private Possession

90, Gloucester Place, | Portman Square. W. |
28th Novr 1887

Yes, dearest Nannie, you may well be proud of the new address. Grand! Grand!

I am so hard at work that I don't know whether I have got my head on my shoulders or off. I am strictly shut up from every human being – even my wife. It is dreadful – and this new story is more dreadful still. You shall hear again when I have a spare few minutes – and you shall box <u>my</u> ears at the first opportunity for I[1] gave George those fatal orders. In the meantime I love and adore you. W.C

I hope Mama is in glorious health in the new "flat".

Note

1. "I" is doubly underlined.

To Anne le Poer Wynne, 8 February 1888

MS: Private Possession

90, Gloucester Place, | Portman Square. W. | 8th Feb 1888

Dearest and best of Mrs Wilkie Collinses, I have just got two chairs and a bath – and a desk and pen and ink – and cigars and brandy and water – and plenty of physic – and that is all. I am dieted without mercy – I dare not eat with you or drink with you – my recovery depends on still "taking the greatest care of myself", and my serial story begins on the 18th of this month and is only half done. To complete my wretchedness, my bath is to be taken away from me and set up in the new house – new cistern and paper – and a new "range". In the interval I remain not only your loving and bedevilled, but also your dirty, W.C

My love to Mamma

To Mrs le Poer Wynne, 27 April 1888
MS: Private Possession

82. Wimpole Street | W. | 27th April 1888

My dear Mrs Wynne,

   The horrors of moving (not over yet), and the dire necessity of writing against Time, have been a little too much for me together. And when several thousand patterns of wall-paper (intended to replace a paper in the dining-room which influences my eyes every time I look at it) presenting every variety of hideous ugliness, arrived one after the other in interminable series, my power of endurance gave way, and I became one mass of yellow green Bile from head to foot. I am slowly, slowly getting better under a system of physic and diet (on which I will not dwell) which makes the bare idea of a delicious lunch something maddening to contemplate. Let me thank you for the moment, and engage to write again when my novel[1] is off my mind, and my appetite has returned. In one word, when I am worthy of your hospitality. I must be capable of enjoying my position when I am once more in your house.

Always truly yours | W.C

Note

1. *The Legacy of Cain.*

To Anne le Poer Wynne, 27 April 1888
MS: Private Possession

27th April 1888[1]

Dearest Mrs Wilkie,

   Don't bully me. Mother-in-law will tell you that I am already prostrate. Besides, I don't approve of your conduct since I have been away. I hear you have got tall. Have you forgotten that I am short? News has also reached me that you have got a waist. Have I got a waist? And, greatest disappointment to me of all, I am positively assured that your back hair is on the top of your head. My back hair hangs on my shoulders. I have not had my hair cut for the last four months to please you. A good wife follows her husband's example. What right have you to hide the top of your head from Me. I have a right to see (and, if I like, admire) the top of your head. There may be one excuse for you. Are you getting bald on the top of your head?

If <u>that</u> is the case, I pity and forgive you. When I come to see you, I will bring with me "Mrs Allen's Hair Restorer" and rub it in myself. But don't allude to "Galantine and Truffles" – your mother, your excellent mother, will tell you why. With all your faults, I love and adore you.

W.C

Note

1. WC draws a few lines through the old address, above which he writes the date, using his old monogrammed paper. WC's letter to "Nannie" enclosed with his letter to her Mother. On the last leaf of his letter, he writes in pencil: "For the Mississ".

Part X
Declining Years
1886–1889

Introduction

Wilkie sees his 62nd year in with cases of champagne, not forgetting Martha. Leading the "life of a hermit" [15 January 1886], he strains himself to meet deadlines. *The Evil Genius* is dedicated to Holman Hunt, to whom Wilkie writes of "modern obstructions of conventionality and clap trap" [24 July 1886]. Increasingly time is spent at Ramsgate, attempting to recover from the gout, nervous exhaustion and chest pains. Wilkie's situation is summed up in his words to his New York agent, E.A. Buck, "October: Not dead – not blind – fastened to my desk to make up for lost time" [22 October 1886]. The struggle to complete *The Guilty River* "has something to do with [his] constitutional collapse" [2 February 1887]. The pattern continues of illness, visits to Ramsgate and lengthy letters to Sarony, Schlesinger, Winter, and others. Wilkie's letter on the art of writing, with particular reference to *The Woman in White*, appears in *The Globe* [26 November 1887].

At the end of 1887 Wilkie is seized with a spasm in the street. He becomes a prisoner in his own house, struggling to remain well enough to complete *The Legacy of Cain*. His troubles are compounded by his being forced, on 25 February 1888, to move to Wimpole Street. A letter to Schlesinger [26 August 1888] makes the first mention of Wilkie's family on holiday at 27, Wellington Crescent, Ramsgate, under the name of Dawson. The autumn of 1888 sees him completely unnerved by the London damp and fog.

"The wrong side of sixty" [8 March 1889], confined to his house, Wilkie struggles to get to the half-way stage of *Blind Love*, which will be posthumously completed by Walter Besant. Returning in January from a dinner with Schlesinger, he has a narrow escape from serious injury when his cab is in a collision, but which gives him a severe shake and hardly helps his deteriorating condition. A stroke in June compounds his troubles. Dosed with laudanum and surrounded by his close friends, he struggles on through the summer and early autumn, finally signing off, prophetically, to Schlesinger on 7 September 1889: "Good bye, old friend". On Saturday, September 21, he writes his last letter – a plea to his doctor, Frank Beard: "I am dying, old friend ... Come for God's sake." And at 10 a.m. on Monday, 23 September 1889, he dies. He is buried in Kensal Green Cemetery.

To William Holman Hunt, 15 January 1886
MS: Huntington

90, Gloucester Place, | Portman Square. W. |
15 January 1886

My dear Holman

Your handwriting is always a welcome sight to me – especially when it brings better news of your health. Having relieved me so far, you startle me next by the suggestion of another journey to the East. I believe firmly in the vigour of your constitution – but my doubt is whether the capacity for taking long-journeys and encountering severe changes of climate, successfully, is not dependent on a healthier state of nerves than either you or I can claim to possess just yet.

That is all I have to say on this subject (which interests your old friends almost as strongly as it interests you). It is quite likely that I am wrong – and you know best. Wait a little, and let us see. I say no more.

The post which brought me your letter, brought also one of the many odd letters written to me by strangers. The writer complains of my books, in this case, for not being "sufficiently transcendental"! She [erased word] informs me that the dead are perfectly well aware of everything that goes on in the world which they have left. When I think of our old friend's magnificence and prosperity – after receiving this expression of opinion – I think of old Mrs Millais in Gower Street, and I say to myself, How that excellent woman must be bragging about "Johnny", in the empty air above her son's palace at Kensington!

As for me, I have no reason to complain, and every reason, so far, to feel hopefully. For years past, I have only been able to write, with the printers close behind me as the spur that drives me on. Every week, publishers of newspapers at home and abroad, and translators here there and everywhere, wait for (and swallow up) a weekly part of my new story. I can only be equal to this strain by putting myself, as poor Dickens used to say, "in training". I lead (quite willingly) the life of a hermit – and, so far, I am equal to the work – although I feel it more now, and no wonder, considering that I reached sixty two years of age on the 8th of this month. But I don't feel any drop in the spirits which I inherit from my mother (excepting times of downright pain) – and my invention comes to my call as easily as it ever did. Now and then the "angina" (or in old English "breast-pang") tries to come back, but doesn't succeed of late. There is my report!

You know how glad I shall be to see you and Cyril.[1] There is always something on the table here between 2 and 3 – if you will drop me a line first to choose your day and so ensure my not being out on a constitutional walk. I hope to finish my work towards the end of next month – and I shall come to you, if you don't get to me before that date.

Affectionately Yours | Wilkie Collins

Note

1. Hunt's son Cyril.

To William Winter, 11 February 1886
MS: Princeton

90, Gloucester Place, | Portman Square. W. | London |
11 February 1886

My dear Winter,

I have just received the Tribune[1] – and I know of the death of your son.

In the face of the dreadful misfortune that has fallen on you, I am one of the unfortunate people who have nothing to say. The state of mind which finds relief in the "consolation of religion" is, I am sorry to own it, a state of mind unintelligible to <u>me</u> – and I read with wonder the neatly-arranged figures of speech by means of which Mr Curtis[2] offers consolation, in perfect sincerity of friendship I don't doubt. In my experience, there is no true consolation to be found, except in the lapse of time, and the one "palliative" in the meanwhile is work. But the sore heart does feel some little relief in the sympathy of true friends. I can, in some degree, understand what you are suffering – for I have children of my own – and I feel for you with my whole heart. There is no more to say.

Always affectionately yours | Wilkie Collins

Notes

1. The *New York Tribune* for which Winter was dramatic critic from 1865 until 1909.
2. George William Curtis (1824–1892: *DAB*), American journalist who wrote for the *Tribune* and edior of *Harper's Weekly* from 1863. Winter's *Old Friends* (1909) contains a chapter on Curtis (pp. 223–74).

To Robert du Pontavice de Heussey, 15 March 1886
MS: Princeton

90, Gloucester Place, | Portman Square. W. | London |
15th March

Summary:
"I ought to add that I had not ever thought of the 'Woman In White' in 1855. The book was not published – even in its first serial form – until 1859–60. Some few of my earlier stories had been translated into French at that time – and some of the illustrious French authors had read them – notably <u>Scribe</u> who charmed me by his kind encouragement. But the wide celebrity of the "Woman In White" had not shone on me when I was with Dickens at Paris in 1855. We saw each other every day, and were as fond of each other as men could be. Nobody (my dear mother excepted, of course) felt so positively sure of the future before me in Literature, as Dickens did."

To Mary French Sheldon,[1] 11 April 1886
MS: Library of Congress

90, Gloucester Place, | Portman Square. W. |
11th April 1886

Dear Sir,

My letter must begin with excuses for a long-deferred reply, as well as with thanks. The addition which you have so kindly made to my library reached me at a time when I was very busily occupied, and not very prosperously situated in the matter of health.

When "Salammbô" was first published, I read it – and (I hope it is needless to add) I was deeply impressed by the power and beauty of the work. The one drawback to my enjoyment (as I now remember) was the sense of <u>effort</u>, here and there, which I have found in the writings of all the disciples (English and Foreign) of the unapproachably-great master who wrote "Old Mortality" and "Quentin Durward". Even the admirably easy "narrative" of the elder Dumas does not, to my mind wholly conceal this defect. It is felt, instinctively, by the average reader – and it will be, as I think, the only obstacle in the way of the success of the English "Salammbô".

Whether I am right or wrong in taking this view, of one thing I feel sure. Your translation has honestly met, and has triumphantly conquered, the innumerable difficulties of transforming the language of France into the language of England. From the beginning of the book to the end, I admire without reserve the profound knowledge of the two languages, the delicacy of handling, and the inflexible integrity of interpretation, which you have brought to your task. Your translation of "Salammbô" has given an English book to English readers. I say this honestly, and I need say no more.

Believe me, dear Sir, | Faithfully yours | Wilkie Collins

M. French Sheldon Esq

Note

1. Mary French Sheldon, (1847–1936: *DAB*), translated Flaubert and other French works into English. A presentation copy of her translation of Flaubert's *Salammbô* (1886) was in WC's library at his death.

To A.P. Watt, 28 April 1886
MS: Private Possession

[90, Gloucester Place, | Portman Square. W. | 28th April 1886]

Summary:
WC has forgotten arrangements for promissory note from Tillotson. "As to the republication of 'The Evil Genius' in book form, I am in some doubt. The infernal Irish trouble and the possibility of a general election, suggest delay. And there was some 'understanding' with Tillotson, I think, about deferring the publication ... This is a helpless letter. I am (as the Doctor says) 'smothered in bile' and strictly reduced to weak brandy and water, in fear of the gout."

To William Holman Hunt, 24 July 1886
MS: Huntington

14, Nelson Crescent | Ramsgate | 24 July 1886

My dear Holman,
   A day or two before I came here, I presented your card, and saw your exhibition.
   My first impression, on entering the room, was of such a feast of magnificent colour as I had not seen since I was last at Venice. My next pleasure was to study the pictures in detail. You know so well how

incapable I am of flattering anybody – least of all, a dear old friend – that I shall say freely what is in my mind. As a painter of human expression, the most difficult of all achievements in your Art, there is no man among your living English Colleagues (and not more than two or three among the dead) who is fit to be mentioned in the same breath with you. To my mind, you are a great teacher as well as a great painter.

With obstacles and discouragements which I lament, you are nevertheless steadily doing good in teaching the people to see for themselves the difference between true art and false. Such a reform as this in the popular Taste works, as we both know, insensibly on the popular mind, and clears its way slowly through the thousand modern obstructions of conventionality and claptrap. But the reform does go on. I saw some people silently wondering before the picture of the Christian priest, saved from the Druids. They consulted in whispers, and went on to the next picture. But the Priest had got them. They came back – and had another long look – and consulted again. Slowly and surely that fine work was pleading the good cause with people ignorant of the subtle beauty of it; but insensibly discovering its appeal to their sense of nature and truth. I am absolutely certain that the next Royal Academy Exhibition will not succeed as well as usual in imposing on those innocent strangers.

I must wait till we meet again to speak of the pictures individually. If I attempt to write about them, I shall produce a book instead of a letter. Goodbye then for the present – and let me only add Mrs Graves's thanks to mine. The Exhibition was a revelation to <u>her</u>.

Ever yours affectionately | Wilkie Collins[1]

Note

1. A note possibly in WC's pencilled hand on the blank leaf of the letter reads: "I think this may interest you to read, and you will let me have it back?"

To Wybert Reeve,[1] 29 July 1886
MS: Private Possession

Ramsgate | 29 July 1886

My dear Reeve,

I have been sailing, and have come here for my letters.

The news of my poor dear old friend's death has shocked and distressed me. Another of the very few friends of younger days now left to me has been torn away. No words of mine can sufficiently acknowledge the unremitting devotion of Biers[2] to my literary interests in Australia, for twenty years past and more. Always eager to make the very best possible pecuniary arrangements for me, and always successful in doing so, his labour was throughout – at his own express stipulation – a labour of love. Not very long since, I acknowledged this, most inadequately, by sending him a little present – and I had the happiness of hearing from him that this keepsake was very welcome. When you see his daughters pray tell them that I really share in their sorrow, and feel the sincerest sympathy with them.

Let me thank you heartily for your friendly offers of help. My new novel – now shortly to be published in book-form – has appeared previously in various newspapers, and the speculator, purchasing all serial rights in England and the Colonies (for the largest sum that I have ever received) managed the Australian publication himself. So I have no present interest (of the literary sort) in the book market of our antipodes.[3] If I have any hopeful dramatic work that promises well, it shall be sent to you. In the meantime, let me congratulate you on your success. It has been well merited, I am quite sure – and it will I hope be the predecessor of more triumphs to come.

As for my health, considering that I was 62 years old last birthday – that I have worked hard as a writer – and that gout has tried to blind me first and kill me afterwards, on more than one occasion – I must not complain. Neuralgia, and nervous exhaustion generally, have sent me to the sea to be patched up – and the sea is justifying my confidence in it. I must try and live long enough to welcome you when you return to us.

Pardon a stupid letter, written in a hurry. I will do better next time.

Always truly yours | Wilkie Collins.

Notes

1. Wybert Reeve (1831–1906), actor-manager, close friend of WC. See his *From Life* (1892), and "Recollections of Wilkie Collins" *Chambers's Journal* (9 June 1006), 458–61.
2. WC's Australian representative.
3. For an account of WC's serialization, see Elizabeth Morrison, "Serial Fiction in Australian Colonial Newspapers", *Literature in the Marketplace*, ed. J. O Jordan, R.L. Patten (1995), 313.

To Frederick G. Kitton,[1] 2 August 1886
MS: Princeton

14, Nelson Crescent | Ramsgate | 2nd August 1886

Dear Sir,

Your letter has followed me to this place.

Your kindness will I hope excuse me from contributing to the work on which you are engaged. I abstain from adopting your suggestions, out of consideration for the wishes of Dickens himself. He more than once expressed to me his dislike of being presented to public curiosity by means of "pen-portraits", and his desire to be only known to the great world of readers after his death by his books.

I remain, dear Sir, | Faithfully yours | Wilkie Collins

Frederick G. Kitton Esq

Note

1. Wilkie refused to contribute to Kitton's reminiscences *Charles Dickens by Pen and Pencil* (1890).

To Francis Carr Beard, 10 August 1886
MS: Princeton

14, Nelson Crescent | Ramsgate | 10th Aug 1886

My dear Frank

I had hoped that your letter would tell me you were able to get away from London – if not as far as this, at least to some nearer place. It is sad news indeed to hear that y<u>ou</u> are "feeling prostrate".

As for <u>me</u> I have a contradictory state of things to report. All day long, I feel infinitely better – I sleep far more soundly at night – I have a better appetite – but[1] in the early morning, say from 5 to 7, that damnable pain in the chest returns regularly. I have tried to circumvent it by an early breakfast in bed, without success – and what I have done to provoke it, I don't know. Take yesterday as a sample. I did <u>no</u> <u>work</u> – I went out for a little walk between one and two – I went out again at three for a sail, and was on the water more than three hours – I drank no champagne at dinner – I slept (only waking once for a few minutes) till 5 this morning. At 5:30 the vile gnawing began again – and, required three of those capsules before

I could get rid of it. And here I am writing to you now – at 12:30 without an ache or pain to complain of, and this on the muggiest of muggy days, with the thermometer at 70 close by an open window!!!!! What does your art say to this? And what sort of prescription is "indicated"? To complete this queer "case", let me remind you that while I was in London – half dead for want of fresher air – I was entirely without the chest pain. (N.B. Bowels kept steadily to their duty – and no medicine taken except your pick-me-up to keep my digestion in good order.)

Enough of myself for the present! I wish you had been with us yesterday in the boat. We "dodged" the rain, pouring over Ramsgate, by steering in every direction which showed a morsel of blue sky. It was the funniest chase – the great clouds trying to catch our little boat, and, at one time, a sea fog helping them. But we got back with dry skins nevertheless.

Let me have a line by return of post – and tell me you are feeling better.

Yours ever affly, W.C

Note

1. The "u" of "but" underlined three times.

To E.A. Buck, 22 October 1886
MS: Princeton

90, Gloucester Place, | Portman Square. W. |[1] London |
22nd Oct: 1886

My dear Buck,

Your kind letter received with joy, and the dates duly noted.

Three weeks since I should have asked leave to contribute my epitaph, in place of the customary story – and should have sent for the cremation society to consider the form of my Urn. Now I may hope to send you my story as usual. Here is a chapter in my autobiography:

1886 | August: cruising at sea, and wishing we had Buck and Son on board.

September: In a darkened room. The gout in my right eye.

The tortures of the damned. An engagement to write a new Christmas Book, to be ready by October 30th.

October: Not dead – not blind – fastened to my desk to make up for lost time. With an extra week's allowance I hope to do it, and to be ready for you. If I break down, the best of friends and doctors (F. Carr Beard) shall telegraph. No news is good news. Love to you and Harry – printers waiting – pen ink (beastly ink as you see) and paper waiting. Goodbye.

Yours affly | Wilkie Collins

You invent everything in the U.S. Have you invented ink that will bear the immediate application of blotting paper – and not look like <u>this</u> ink?

Note

1. WC uses printed paper with his monogram, above which he writes "In a tearing hurry".

To Francis Carr Beard, 26 November 1886
MS: Princeton

Friday evening 26th Novr 1886

My dear Frank,

I am obliged again to send to hear about you, instead of coming myself. Between the weather and the work, I am so utterly worn out that I can hardly cross the room. On Sunday I hope to have done at last. In the meantime, I am so eager for better news that I send George with this. A verbal message of course – one word – "Better". Always affly yours | W.C

To Edward Pigott, 10 December 1886
MS: Huntington

90, Gloucester Place, | Portman Square. W. | 10th Dec 1886

Summary:
Arranges to see him. "I am getting better thank you – but certain symptoms in the neighbourhood of the heart, warn me to remember for the future that I am too old for writing against time at the rate of twelve hours a day. There is some damnable perversity in me that won't f<u>ee</u>l old, after years of ill health. I have not even learned to be discreet. 'God help us all, God help me too, I am – God knows as helpless as the devil can wish.' So says Byron."

To A.P. Watt, 15 December 1886
MS: Private Possession

90, Gloucester Place, | Portman Square. W. |
15th December 1886

Summary:

Thanks Watt for *King Solomon's Mines*. "When I saw the 'bloody' map (oh I am not swearing!) which decorates the beginning of the book – I foresaw a day's delight, in spite of the weather. More, when I have read the story ... My congratulations on your 'flitting' to Paternoster Square. I shall certainly, I hope, see the new offices – and make my bow, at the same time, to your neighbour, the finest church in the world (externally speaking)."

To Sebastian Schlesinger, 22 December 1886
MS: Harvard

90, Gloucester Place, | Portman Square. W. | London |
22nd December 1886

My dear Sebastian,

Besides being a thorough good friend, are you by any chance also a Wizard?

I have just written a little book.[1] Yesterday, I was making out a list – a small list of special friends to whom I proposed to send copies, and had put down your name. This led to an unspoken soliloquy. "Does [erasure] S. owe me a letter? or do I owe S. a letter?" If it is my fault (and it well may be) that I have heard nothing of him for some time – then I shall be ashamed to write – the book shall go first as a peace-offering, and my long-due letter shall follow at an auspicious moment. Having arrived at this mean resolution, the servant interrupted me, bearing birds – the birds were canvas-back ducks – and the card was Sebastian's card! Is this a coincidence? or a supernatural proceeding? I rather hope it is the latter, and that I shall see you at table today sitting opposite to me carving the duck – in the spirit – and drinking [erasure] not my Champagne, but yours – the only good dry Champagne I tasted when I was in Boston, Mass. In any case, you know that I am not unworthy of your delicious gift – and you know that I thank you in more than the ordinary sense of those much-abused words.

Here is an end of all that I have to say about myself. Will you write and tell me something about yourself? Are you still true to the Muse of Music?

(I forget her Pagan name). And do you still preserve your rosy complexion? And do you feel any older since we last met, twelve years ago? If I live until the 8th of January next I shall be 63 years of age. After <u>that</u> announcement, the sooner I take my leave the better.

Yours aftly | Wilkie Collins

I take this opportunity of writing to the firm about my insurances in U.S.A.

By the way, I assume that 20 West 26th Street means New York. Personally, as well as commercially you have done with Boston Mass – have you not?

Note

1. *The Guilty River*, published 15 November 1886: see Gasson.

To A.P. Watt, 1 January 1887

MS: Present whereabouts unknown. Published *Letters Addressed to A.P. Watt*, 1894, p. 18.[1]

[90, Gloucester Place, | Portman Square. W.] |
January 1, 1887

I desire that my friend and literary representative, Mr A.P. Watt, of 2 Paternoster Square, may act as my Literary Executor, and that his advice may be accepted as representing my literary interests and wishes in regard to the copyrights of my books which may remain to be sold after my death by my other executors.

Wilkie Collins

Note

1. The published letter is headed "To the intense regret of all lovers of fiction, Mr Wilkie Collins died on the 23rd of September 1889. Attached to his Will was the following memorandum in his own handwriting: –" This letter follows.

To A.P. Watt, 4 January 1887
MS: Private Possession

90, Gloucester Place, | Portman Square. W. |
4th January 1887

Summary:
Reiterates thanks for <u>King Solomon's Mines</u>. "If you ever read the 'notices of the press' attached to advertisements of new novels, you will find that the crop of great geniuses now engaged in writing fiction amounts at a fair average to seven or eight in a week. Of the great work thus produced (owing I suppose to some perversity in me which I am at a loss how to cure) I am a thoroughly unworthy reader. I don't care two straws for the characters to which the great geniuses introduce me – and I see through and through the 'breathless interest' of their stories (when there is any story) before I am at the end of the first volume. Let me honestly confess it, my frame of mind was not hopeful when I opened 'King Solomon's Mines'.[1]

To my wonder and delight the book seized me at once, and held me fast straight through to the end. I found myself reading the work of a man, possessing imagination, invention, sense of dramatic effect, respect for truth to nature, and – in an inferior degree as yet – an eye for character. Here I find room for improvement in Mr Haggard, and I will try to explain myself.

To my mind, our author is strong in the conception, and weak in the development, of character. 'Allan Quatermaine' is, as the lawyers say, a case in point. He is supposed to be the writer of the story, and he begins in his own character. But as he goes on, he is set aside and replaced by Mr Haggard himself.

If you look again at the earlier pages of the book, you will find Q. writing in harmony with his own character, as described by himself – a sensible man whose native good sense has made use of his opportunities, within his limits. Quaint humour and capacity for observation are in him (again within limits) but, by his own confession, he is without literary cultivation. On that side of him an ignorant man.

Now look on to page 72 and you will find this uncultivated elephant hunter exhibiting a highly trained admiration of the beauties of nature – and actually expressing admiration in a skilled and eloquent English style. I will copy one sentence, and you will see what I mean.

' ... we lay down and waited for the moon to rise. At last about nine o'clock up she came in all her chastened glory, flooding the wild country with silver light, and throwing a weird sheen on the vast expanse of rolling desert before us, which looked as solemn and quiet and as alien to man as the star-studded firmament above.'

Here – and in dozens of other places to which I might refer if I had no respect for your time – is merely Mr Haggard's poetical feeling, and Mr Haggard's skilled handling of English, pouring miraculously from Mr Quatermaine's pen. I fancy I hear Q. intent on improving himself, asking for explanations: 'Excuse me sir, but when you say "chastened glory", do I understand you to mean it was a fine bright moon? And would you mind telling me whether "weird sheen", is a thing or a person or a place? I am with you, sir, heart and soul, when you say "alien to man"! That's a cut at the Hottentots and they richly deserve it.'

The defect which I have tried to indicate is the only obstacle that I can now see in Mr Haggard's way. If he will be on his guard against this – and if he will not let publishers tempt him to lead his readers too often over the same ground – I believe he has the ball at his foot, and I shall be rejoiced to see him kicking it to good purpose.

I am still idling, as the doctor bids me. Last night, an idea knocked at my head. Answer: not at home."

Note

1. Published in one volume, Cassell (1886).

To A.P. Watt, 6 January 1887
MS: Private Possession

[90, Gloucester Place, | Portman Square. W. | 6th Jany 1887]

Summary:
WC sending some quill pens as a present: "I tell the Stationer to enclose his card ... The worst ills of life – after rheumatic gout or poverty – are letters."

To A.P. Watt, 25 January 1887
MS: Private Possession

[90, Gloucester Place, | Portman Square. W. | 25th Jany 1887]

Summary:
"If you ever feel inclined to leave me a book again, check the benevolent impulse, and say to yourself. 'I can't trust that man.' The Parcel Post takes

back to you – after a most inexcusable delay – those two books of Mrs Oliphant's[1] which you so kindly trusted to me. I found them this morning buried under heaps of other books ...

I must talk to you about 'She'[2] the next time you give me a look-in ... 'She' is better written than 'Mines' – but it has not got the movement of the story and the variety of situations ... And I doubt the effect on the stupid reader (a most important person, unhappily, to please) of the lady who is 2000 years old.

I have been thriving in my idleness – until I am tired of it. My pen is consequently in my hand again, revising no less than 15 short stories ... for republication! Some of them I had actually forgotten myself."

Notes

1. *The Chronicles of Carlingford.*
2. *She* published by Longman's, serialized in the *Graphic*, October 1886–January 1887.

To Nina Lehmann, 2 February 1887
MS: Princeton

90, Gloucester Place | London. W. | 2nd Feby 1887

Oh what a wretch I am, dearest Padrona, to be only thanking you now for your delightful letter – and for that adorable photograph of the boy. I may tell you what I told his father – when I had the pleasure of meeting him at Berkeley Square – that I must be introduced to your grandson at the earliest possible moment after his arrival in England. I brought away with me after our luncheon such an agreeable impression of Sir Guy Campbell that I must repeat my congratulations to Nina on her marriage.[1] There was but one drawback to my enjoyment when I found myself in those familiar rooms again – the dreadful word "Dead" when I asked after dear little "Buffles".[2]

If you were only at the north of Scotland – say Thurso – I would rush to you by steamer, and become young again in the fine cold air. But when I think of that fearful French railway journey, and of the southern climate of Cannes, I see madness on my way to the Mediterranean, and death in lingering too much on the shores of that celebrated sea. We have had here – after a brief Paradise of frost – the British Sirrocco. Fidgets, aching legs, gloom, vile tempers, neuralgic trembles in the chest – such are the conditions under which I am living, and such the obstacles which have prevented my writing to you long since. "The Guilty River" (I am so glad you like it) has I am afraid had something to do with the sort of constitutional collapse which I have endeavoured to describe. You know well what a fool I am – or shall I put it mildly and say "how indiscreet"? For the last week, while I was finishing the story, I worked for twelve hours a day – and galloped along without feeling it, like the old post horses, while I was hot. Do you remember how the forelegs of those post-horses quivered, and how their heads drooped, when they came to the journey's end? That's me, Padrona – that's me.

Good God! is "<u>me</u>" grammar? Ought it to be "I"? My poor father paid ninety pounds a year for my education – and I give you my sacred word of honour I am not sure whether it is "me" or "I".

After this, the commonest sense of propriety warns me to remove myself from your observation. I have just assurance enough left to send my love to you and Nina and Guy Colin, and to remind you that I am always affectionately yours | Wilkie Collins

Notes

1. Nina and Frederick Lehmann's daughter Nina married the diplomat Sir Guy Campbell. The Lehmanns also had a son, Guy Colin (b. 1884), and a daughter, Pamela, who died in a cholera outbreak when she was two years old. See John Lehmann, *Ancestors and Friends* (1962), pp. 269–70.
2. "Buffles" was the Lehmann's "favourite Skye terrier", R.C. Lehmann, *Memories of Half a Century* (1908), p. 74.

To Robert du Pontavice de Heussey, 4 February 1887
MS: Princeton

90, Gloucester Place | London. W. | 4th Feby 1887

My dear Collaborateur,

I have been away from London, trying to find air that I can breathe. A few days of frost here, at the beginning of January, were succeeded by our damp relaxing British Sirocco. To <u>me</u>, the unnatural mildness of this winter season, all over England, means nervous relaxation of the most intolerable kind – and if I was ten years younger I would go away again, to Greenland this time – and thrive in the Arctic frosts.

So for this bad reason I have been long in thanking you for "Le Livre", and long in reading your article on Goldsmith. I am delighted with it. It is even better than your article on Dickens – more animated, more various, more subtle in treatment. You are the only French Man of Letters – mind, I say this seriously – who understands England and the English. And, because I mean this, you will find on the next morsel of paper, some corrections of trifling slips – to be noted before you <u>re</u>publish your contributions to "Le Livre".

The dramatic end to the article is so good that I don't like to suggest doubts about it. But Forster told me that "Northcote" was not to be depended on – and Forster's account of "She Stoops to Conquer" takes Goldsmith to the Theatre – makes him alarmed by hearing a solitary hiss, and repeats Coleman's abominable insult to Goldsmith: "Don't be afraid of a squib, Doctor, when we have been sitting these two hours on a barrel of gunpowder!"[1]

Yours affectionately | Wilkie Collins

Note

1. John Forster's *The Life and Times of Oliver Goldsmith*, published in 1848; James Northcote's (1746–1831) anecdotes of Goldsmith published *In Memoirs of [G.] Joshua Reynolds*, 2 vols, 1818.

To Robert du Pontavice de Heussey, 14 February 1887
MS: Princeton

90, Gloucester Place, | Portman Square. W. |
14th Feby 1887

My dear Collaborateur,

I have got just five minutes before post time – and I employ them to thank you for your kind letter. I leave the proof of "Magdalen" in perfect confidence to you – and I look forward with true interest to receiving a copy of the play when it has received your last correction and has become a published work.[1]

I most sincerely envy you a first reading of Boswell's wonderful book – the greatest biographical work that has ever been written.[2] I am constantly dipping into it, to this day. As for the great "Taine" we take the liberty of laughing at him in England. I have even heard him called – it is almost too terrible to mention – called:

"An Ass"

Affectionately yours | Wilkie Collins

Have you read an English novel called "King Solomon's Mines"? (Tauchnitz Edition 1. Volume).[3] In its way, a very clever book.

Notes

1. A copy of *Madeleine; pièce en quatre Actes, dont un prologue d'après Wilkie Collins par R. du P. de Heussey*, (Paris, 1887) was in WC's library at his death.
2. A copy of the 5 vol., 7th edition of Boswell's *Life of Johnson* (1811) was in WC's library at his death.
3. Todd and Bowden, 2386, p. 358: published February 1886.

To William Holman Hunt, 14 February 1887
MS: Huntington

90, Gloucester Place | W. | 14th February 1887

My dear Holman,

Come on Wednesday next, as you propose, and you will find us delighted to see you. We have got the surest of all good things – a good ham in the house. So keep an appetite for any hour in the evening that you like best. I should be quite happy in the prospect of seeing you – but for that visit to the doctor. Bring me word that he has dismissed you (professionally speaking), and I shall be quite satisfied. <u>My</u> state of body has come to "a pretty pass" – I rejoice in the easterly winds!!!!

Ever aftl^y yours | Wilkie Collins

To Napoleon Sarony, 19 March 1887
MS: Folger

90, Gloucester Place | London. W | 19^t March 1887

My dear, my wonderful Sarony!

The photographs came here yesterday. If they had arrived a week earlier they would have found me too completely weakened and depressed (by gout and its remedies) to even open the box. As it is, they have arrived exactly at the right time – when I am enjoying another of my intervals (they are never more) of something which is a near approach to health. No more of my infirmities – the subject now is Sarony's triumph.

Other men's hands at sixty six years old are beginning to fail them in the matter of drawing. Y<u>our</u> hand is improved. In your artistic handling of the Nude there is now more firmness, more knowledge, more power. And this development takes place when you are within four years of seventy, and when you have passed the day in the labours, the wearisome worrying [erased word] labours sometimes, of the photographic Studio. Wonderful, and I add, sympathetic man! For I too think the back view of a finely-formed woman the loveliest view – and her hips [several erased words] the most precious parts of that view. The line of beauty in those quarters enchants me, when it is not overladen by fat. Some of the best examples of your capacity as a draughtsman are too strongly developed for my taste. My [beau] ideal is the "Venus Callipyge" – holding up her robe, and looking over her shoulder at her own divine back view. From the small of her back to the end of her thighs, she has escaped the detestable restorers – and my life has been passed in trying to find a living woman who is like her – and in never succeeding. After this, you will understand that my three favourites, of the Nude Series, are the girl with closed eyes floating past the moon – the girl reclining with transparent lace over part of her body, and more lace on her head – and last (and most charming to me) the girl entering her bath-room. She has the fineness of line which approaches my Venus – and the pose of the figure and the drawing of the figure are really admirable. No man but a born artist could have done it. Bravo! bravo! [erased word] carissimo Sarony! And I repeat my cry, in turning to the other drawings – which I call the Series of charmers accommodated with clothes.

The action of the girl who is pouring water out of a bucket. The graceful lady with the [two erased words] nosegay in one hand, and the fingers of the other occupied in the divination by flowers. And the sweet young creature holding a tazza and looking at it seriously and thoughtfully. This last is as graceful as a figure by Stothard[1] – and far better drawn. I must stop somewhere in my catalogue, or you will begin to regret [erased word] having [erased word] sent me this delightful present. But there has been one omission. The ferocious [erased word] profile, with the broad hat and the enormous ruff, meditating schemes of vengeance which make me rejoice in remembering that 3000 miles divide me from the U.S.A. [several erased words] also reminds me that I am without Sarony in the character of Hungarian Count. I ought to be [erased word] satisfied, I know, with the delightful photos of [Mrs] Sarony. But do remember that I have never seen you with decorations, and with a sword by your side.

As for your portraits of me, I dare not ask any more. The glorious photo which I send with this shall be registered – I am in such terror of its being lost. One more copy is all I possess. When ladies find their way in here, and want my photograph, I open my repository, and try to put them off with some of the later photographs done of me in England. They all discover other photos hidden underneath – all say, "What have you got there?" – all snatch out Sarony, and flatly refuse to take any other portrait. I tried to save one copy the other day from a comic actress who was here. She had got the photo face downwards – I seized her hand – and said, "For God's sake don't look at that; it's <u>something indecent</u>!" She instantly answered: "Then, I must certainly look at it!" – and so got the portrait.

I think I must send to you – <u>by book post</u> – the three last portraits done of me in England. If y<u>ou</u> can see any resemblance between them – and, excepting the profile, any vague sort of likeness to me – it is more than I can do. If they prove nothing else, these odd productions do plainly show that photography is <u>not</u> a mechanical art – but does depend like other arts on the man who exercises it.

I make my exit – with a hundred things more to say. My recent illness has left heaps of unanswered letters, and arrears of literary work – and Time flies faster than ever. When you receive the photos by book post, you will discover how damnably sly I am in sending them. "Poor Wilkie! I can <u>not</u> leave him with such wretched portraits as these. Though he <u>is</u> 13 years older since <u>I</u> 'took him', he must have a few more of 'my likenesses'." <u>That</u> is the idea – and the commentary is, "Fie, for shame!" Ever yours (in the Blessed Bonds of Bohemia) Wilkie Collins

Note

1. Thomas Stothard, R.A. (1755–1834: *DNB*), illustrator, historical and portrait painter, noted for his female figures.

To Napoleon Sarony, 4 June 1887
MS: Private Possession

[90,Gloucester Place, | Portman Square,W.] | London |
4 June 1887

My dear Sarony, with this[1] you have my impressions of some of the photographs – sincerely expressed. The only lines in your letters that I don't like are the lines which tell me of your eyes. After what I have suffered in that part of me, my sympathy with you is not easily expressed in words.

With best thanks to Mrs Sarony and with love to you. Ever yours afty |
W.C

I will write to Mrs Brown Potter[2] about sitting for you. She was cruelly treated here, and she is cruelly treated in your newspapers in the U.S. After seeing her in my play, I say she has a decided vocation for the actress's art.

I lead the life of a hermit – see no Society – go to no clubs. For years, I have not met Irving – and I can only describe myself as being "acquainted with him". But I admire him as artist and man.

Note

1. WC's "Catalogue Raisonné" is no longer with this letter but at the Folger Library: see text as follows.
2. Mrs Brown Potter [Cora Urquhart] (1858–1936), actress.

To Napoleon Sarony, 4 June 1887
MS: Folger

90, Gloucester Place | London. W. 4th June 1887

Sarony:

=

(Catalogue Raisonné: Works presented to W.C. Selections only – for want of room and time.)

<u>Preliminary Notice</u>:

This catalogue has been delayed on its way to New York by a shattering of the writer's nerves, accomplished (1) by writing too many books. (2) by taking debilitating remedies for gout. (3) by the unexampled ferocity of the British spring. Result: the malady called (when I was a boy) "tic-doulourou" – described at the present time as "Neuralgia". Remedies: Lauda=num, quinine, and devilish obstinacy inherent in the character of the patient.

=

No I.   <u>Portraits of Mrs Sarony</u>. All admirable specimens of the Art. Three of them simply exquisite: namely (- in their order of merit) – 1. In a dark dress – the right hand holding a fan – the left hand resting on the hip. If I cannot have a portrait by Reynolds or Gainsborough, give me this. 2: In a light dress, with a striped parasol tucked jauntily under the left arm, and a face which says: "Here I am, perfectly dressed to go out – and here is that wretch, Sarony, telling me that it has just begun to rain!" No 3. In another light dress, with trimmings of white fur, and a lovely-left arm. Pose excellent – and drapery most happily arranged. Pray present my compliments and congratulations to Mrs Sarony. And one question to conclude: Say, on your "solemn soul" – will these photographs fade, if they are framed, and hung in a good light?

No II.   <u>Portrait of Field Marshall Sarony in uniform</u>. A faithful likeness – with (to a peaceable man of letters) a terrifying side to it. When we go to war, on the subject of the Fisheries[1] – I don't know anything about the question in dispute – but remember this: <u>I fight on your side.</u> Don't hurt me with that horrid sword, and put me behind you when the battle begins.

=

No III.   <u>The Girl at the Bath</u>. I offer the flattest contradiction that the laws of politeness will permit to what you have written about her in your letter. Down with Diana! – down with the ideal! Titian's Venus has just come <u>out</u> of her bath – and Sarony's Venus is just going <u>into</u> her bath, and is by far the most charming woman of the two.

She is now in her beautiful frame, exhibited in the best light in my front study. [two erased words] Everbody who sees her, admires her. The other day, a professional artist called on me. Mentioning no names, at first, I asked what he thought of it. "Admirably drawn – the action excellent. Who did it?" I put another question before I answered. "The man who did that," I said, "is, as I think, a born-artist. Am I right?" "Of course, you are right – there can be no doubt about it." I then revealed your name. His amazement (judging you of course by photographers in general) was a sight to see. And now, shall I tell you who he was? My dear old friend: | Holman Hunt.

No IV.　The draped darling in Profile. She holds a tazza on a pedestal, and looks at it thoughtfully. Here is another anecdote. A friend of mine, literary agent to me, and to many other English writers, saw Venus entering the bath! "I have got a charming work by Sarony", he said,"sent as a specimen to some publishers here. Let me offer it as a present." Needless to add that I said yes, with enthusiasm. The work arrived in the neatest and nicest of little frames, and proved to be "The draped darling" – an enlarged copy, beautifully printed in light brown tints. In short, looking like a chalk drawing by an old master. Let this anecdote be followed by a confession. F. Carr Beard, the old friend and doctor of Charles Dickens; the old friend and doctor of Charles Fechter; and the old friend and doctor of yours truly, saw my draped darling, placed in a chair opposite to me while I was at work. It literally enchanted him; there was no getting away from it. He wanted to send to New York, and buy a copy of it. I felt that I could hardly allow the devoted friend who keeps me alive to do this – and I made him a present of the smaller duplicate which I possessed – thanks to your kindness. Am I forgiven?

No V.　Miss Rehan.[2] A grand and striking photograph. But – between ourselves – I find I don't love Miss Rehan; Too much jaw, too much mouth, too little nose. Fine eyes I admit – but no gaiety in them, and no delicious depths of tenderness in them. I have seen ugly women – with the charm of expression – whom I should prefer. I ought to add that I never saw Miss Rehan or the other members of Daly's Company when they were in England. The gout had got me at that time.

No VI.　The birth of Venus. Another glorious picture. In respect of the delicious roundness of the limbs, the softness of the flesh, the exquisite "half lights" playing on the figure, a feast for the eyes in the strictest sense of the words.

No VII. <u>Sarah Bernhardt</u>. Most interesting art-records of a great actress. How valuable they will be when you and I and Sarah have taken our departure for that "other world", of which we know nothing, and <u>in</u> which surely there will be not room enough for us all – unless spirits pack easily, like clothes in a big portmanteau. The large portrait of Sarah (front face) seems to me to be sadly suggestive of the wear and tear of her life. You have noticed no doubt, as I do, that there is a suspicion of coming paralysis in one of her eyes which is conspicuously smaller than the other, and over which the upper lid dr[oo]ps lower than in the eye which is in the best state of preservation.

Other Numbers. Must be reserved for another occasion. Let the present Catalogue end with the affectionate expression of the compiler's gratitude.

Notes

1. For the Anglo-American fisheries dispute of 1887, see the London *Times*, 7 January, p. 13a; 31 March, p. 3d; 3 June, p. 5e; 4 June, p. 7d.
2. Ada Rehan (1857–1916), Augustin Daly's leading lady, great Irish-American actress.

To A.P. Watt, 16 June 1887

MS: Private Possession

90, Gloucester Place, | Portman Square. W. | 16 June 1887

Summary:

   "A word to thank you for your kind letter. You are one of the few people who never forgot a duty or a kindness.

   I don't know which I am most weary of – the Jubilee or the heat. I think of going away for a few days to the neighbourhood of Harrow. With the thermometer at 74 in my study literary work is hard work indeed – and the longing to get drunk on champagne checked by the abject fear of gout, represents, as I think, one of the saddest personal grievances of the present time."

To A.P. Watt, 1 July 1887

MS: Private Possession

[90, Gloucester Place, | Portman Square. W. | 1st July 1887]

Summary:

Thanks Watt for new Rider Haggard book.[1] Needs the relief of enjoyment. "My [tonics] – after succeeding at first – have turned traitors, and deserted me – and have to be 'cleared out of me' ... The result is that I cannot work at present ... In the meanwhile I have been reading 'Guy Mannering' again for the 50th time at least. That wonderful book was written in six weeks! What a set of pigmies we are, by comparison with Scott!"

Note

1. *She*, published in the *Graphic*, October 1886–January 1887: Longman, 1887.

To A.P. Watt, 29 July 1887
MS: Private Possession

[90, Gloucester Place, | Portman Square. W. | 29th July 1887]

Summary:
Safe arrival of *Kidnapped*[1] and the *Gazette*. WC unable to work yesterday, so he read *Kidnapped*. "The first half of the story is well imagined, and very strongly and characteristically written. It greatly interested me. But 'The Flight in the Heather' is prolonged to the utmost limits of (my) human endurance. The narration being written by Mr David Balfour in his own proper person, we know[2] positively that he must have escaped – and that seems to me a reason for not prolonging the flight. Mr Balfour ... on board the Brig kept me with my cigar extinct in my mouth. I discovered that it had gone out and lit it again with great deliberation in the early part of 'The Flight'."

Notes

1. R.L. Stevenson's *Kidnapped*, serialized in *Young Folks*, May–July 1886; published in one volume, Cassell, 1886.
2. WC doubly underlines "know".

To William Winter, 30 July 1887
MS: Princeton

90, Gloucester Place, | Portman Square. W. | London | 30th July 1887

My dear William Winter,

When I saw your handwriting, before I opened your letter – I dare not look back at the letter itself, for the date would be a reproach to me that I have not courage enough to encounter – I justfully took it for granted that you were coming to England, and had written to tell me when to expect you. The more gratefully I felt the affectionate terms in which you had written (when I read the letter itself) the more sorry I was to know that the hope of seeing you must be (for the time) given up. After the terrible affliction that has struck at you, the one alleviation that I can believe in is change of place – for this simple reason that it means (in some degree at least) change of mind. In the greatest misery of my life – the death of my mother – sympathy added a pang to the heart-ache, work was only a remedy while the pen was in my hand. Nothing helped me in the smallest degree but travelling. Even if you cannot travel as far as England, I should be relieved about you if I heard that you were travelling too.

As for me, I have been, and I am still, completely unnerved by the heat. I know, my dear friend, what it is to be a coward. The last time I was dining out, I was sick with fright every time the coachman turned a corner. The doctor says "Leave London". When I think of the railway noises, I feel, as I felt on the first occasion (God knows how many years ago!) when I had to make a speech in public. Night-walking in quiet neighbourhoods is the system of treatment that I follow. As for the daytime, I stand committed to work – a new serial story and places engaged for it in the newspapers. "Sir" said the great Sam Johnson, "What must be done will be done." You know that quite as well as I do. If I am well, I work – and, strange to say, I don't find any signs of wear and tear in my imagination, though I was 63 years old on the 8th of January last!

Has anybody told you that "The Jubilee" was an outburst of Loyalty? I tell you that it was an outburst of Fear and Cant. In my neighbourhood, there was a report that we should have our windows broken if we did not illuminate. In the year 1832 when I was 8 years old, my poor father was informed that he would have his windows broken if he failed to illuminate in honour of the passing of the First Reform Bill. He was a "high Tory" and a sincerely religious man – he looked on the Reform bill and the cholera (then prevalent) as similar judgments of an offended Deity punishing social and political "backslidings". And he had to illuminate – and, worse still, he had to see his two boys mad with delight at being allowed to set up the illuminations. Before we were sent to bed, the tramp of the people was heard in the street. They were marching six abreast (the people were in earnest in those days) provided with stones, and with their officers in command. They broke every pane of glass in an unilluminated house, nearly opposite our house, in less than a minute. I ran out to see the fun, and when the sovereign people cheered for the Reform Bill, I cheered too. Fifty five years later, I heard of the windows being in danger again, and illuminated again (on a cheap scale which accurately represented the shabby nature of my loyalty). This time, the people had no interest in the affair. The roadway in this street had been mended with granite fragments, which might have tempted a few mischievous lads here and there to "have a shy" for mischief's sake. In that case, my pictures might have been damaged. Nothing of this sort happened – and nothing could exceed the contemptible ugliness of the draperies in balconies here abouts, and the wretched arrangements of dirty looking flags. Everywhere the people behaved well – and that was the one creditable circumstance in connection with the Jubilee. The "South Kensington Gang" are going to build an Institute on their own ground, if they can get the money – and the parsons want to set up a new club and call it "A Church House". In t<u>hat</u>, the Jubilee has ended. And, like the Jubilee, I come to an end too.

Yours affectionately | Wilkie Collins

Mrs Graves [declares] her Kindest regards. Pigott is out of town. You were quite right about The Guilty River. It was spoilt for want of room.

To Sebastian Schlesinger, 3 August 1887
MS: Harvard

90, Gloucester place, | Portman Square. W. | London |
3rd August 1887

My dear Sebastian,

How many months have passed since I last heard from you? It was a melancholy letter telling me of domestic calamities[1] which are, of all calamities (as I think) the hardest to endure. My reply went back to you at once. I could only offer [to: erased] to you the sympathy of an old and true friend.

But there was a cheering side to your letter. You told me that there was a prospect of seeing you in England in July – and I suggested that you should write again, and let me know at what date to expect you? Early in the month? or late? From that time to this, [erasure] you have been on one side of a gulp[h], and I on the other – the gulph called "Sebastian's Silence".

What cause has left me without news? Not more trouble I hope and trust. Perhaps illness? In that case my sympathy is doubly yours – for I have been, and shall remain, wretchedly out of health. The heat of this summer has completely <u>unnerved</u> me. As one example of what I mean – I am still in London, because I am unable to endure the noises inevitably associated with travelling by railway.

But after all perhaps you are only lazy? In any case, and wherever this letter may find you, let me have a word of news, and let it be good news.

Yours aftly | Wilkie Collins

Sebastian Schlesinger Eqre

Note

1. Schlesinger's "wife had discovered his infidelity" (Smith and Terry, p. 47).

To Rev. George Bainton,[1] 23 September 1887

MS: Princeton. Extract, George Bainton, *The Art of Authorship* (1890), pp. 89–91.

> 90, Gloucester Place, | Portman Square. W. | London |
> September 23rd 1887

Dear Sir,

Let me first acknowledge the debt that I owe to your friendly letter. A reader like you encourages and rewards a writer like me. I gratefully feel that you have a right to all that I can tell you, in relation to the methods which have formed my style.

After some slight preliminary attacks, the mania for writing laid its hold on me definitely when I left school. While I was in training for a commercial life – and afterwards when I was a student at Lincoln's Inn – I suffered under trade and suffered under law with a resignation inspired by my endless engagement in writing poems plays and stories – or to express myself more correctly, by the pleasure that I felt in following an undisciplined imagination wherever it might choose to lead me. I produced, it is needless to say, vast quantities of nonsense, with an occasional – a very occasional – infusion of some literary promise of merit. But I did not think my time was entirely wasted – for I believe I was insensibly preparing myself for the career which I have since followed.

My first conscious effort to write good English was stirred in me by the death of my father – the famous painter of the coast scenery and cottage life of England. I resolved to write a biography of him. It was the best tribute that I could pay to the memory of the kindest of fathers. "The Life of William Collins R.A." was my first published book. From that time to this, my hardest work has been the work that I devote to the improvement of my style. I can claim no merit for this. When I first saw my writing presented to me in a printer's proof, I discovered that I was incapable of letting a carefully constructed sentence escape me without an effort to improve it.

The process by which my style of writing is produced may be easily described.

The day's work having been written, with such corrections as occur to me at the time, is subjected to a first revision on the next day, and is then handed to my copyist. The copyist's manuscript undergoes a second revision, and is then sent to the printer. The proof passes through a third process of correction, and is sent back to have the alterations embodied in, what is called "The Revise". The Revise is carefully looked over for the fourth time, before I allow it to go to "Press", and to preserve what I have written to my readers. My novels are published serially, in the first instance. When they are reprinted in book-form, the book-proofs undergo a fifth, and last revision. Then at length my labour of love comes to an end – and I am always sorry for it. The explanation of this strange state of things I take to be that honest service to Art is always rewarded by Art.

Enough, and more than enough by this time, of me and my writing. I can only hope that this long letter may be of some little use to you in the object that you have in view.

Believe me, Dear Sir, | Vy truly yours | Wilkie Collins

The Revd George Bainton

Note

1. Rev. George Bainton (1847–1925), Congregationalist minister in Coventry.

To Edward Pigott, 20 November 1887
MS: Huntington

90, Gloucester Place, | Portman Square. W. |
Friday | 20th November 1887

My dear Ted,

Just a word to say that I am indeed sorry to hear that the cough has returned. You are quite right to keep at home while this [wind] lasts. So far, Ramsgate air still keeps <u>me</u> in a state of preservation. How long it will last is another matter. Beard seems to think that my destiny is to <u>live</u> at Ramsgate. With two houses to keep going in London, I don't quite see how I am to accommodate myself to this picture.

Let me hear (by a line) how you go on, and what you are doing to get rid of the cough. If you could only take opium! – I say no more.

Caroline's love. | Ever yours afftly | W.C

To a Friend, [26 November 1887]

MS: Huntington. Published with minor variants, *The Globe*, 26 November 1887, pp. 511–14;[1] Appendix C, *The Woman in White*, ed. A. Trodd. Boston, 1969, pp. 511–14; *The Woman in White*, ed. H.P. Sucksmith. Oxford, 1975, pp. 595–98.

My dear Miss –

I

You ask me, Madam, to tell you how I write my books; and you express an opinion that other persons besides yourself may be interested in the result, if I comply with your request. I am not at all sure that I have the honour of agreeing with you. My own impression is that the public cares little how books are written. If the books are easy to get, and if they prove to be interesting, the general reader asks for nothing more. You assert, upon this, that there is but one way of deciding which is the sound opinion, yours or mine; and that way is – to try the experiment. Your will is law. Let the experiment be tried.

II

All my novels are produced by the same literary method. If we take one book as an example, I shall perhaps be able to make myself more readily understood; and I shall certainly occupy less of your time. When I think of the claims of the toilette, the claims of the shops, the claims of conversation, the claims of horse exercise, and the claims of chat – to say nothing of hundreds of other smaller occupations – my respect for the value of your time is part of my respect for yourself. Which book shall we choose as a specimen? Shall it be the most popular book? Very well. I have now to tell you how I wrote "The Woman in White".

III

My first proceeding is to get my central idea – the pivot on which the story turns.

The central idea of "The Woman in White" is the idea of a conspiracy in private life, in which circumstances are so handled as to rob a woman of her identity by confounding her with another woman, sufficiently like her in personal appearance to answer the wicked purpose. The destruction of her identity represents a first division of the story; the recovery of her identity marks a second division.

My central idea suggests some of my chief characters. A clever devil must conduct the conspiracy. Male devil? or female devil? The sort of wickedness wanted seems to be a man's wickedness. Perhaps a foreign man. Count Fosco faintly shows himself to me, before I know his name. I let him wait, and begin to think about the two women. They must be both innocent and both interesting. Lady Glyde dawns on me as one of the innocent victims. I try to discover the other – and fail. I try what a walk will do for me – and fail. I devote the evening to a new effort – and fail. Experience tells me to take no more trouble about it, and leave that other woman to come of her own accord. The next morning, before I have been awake in my bed for more than ten minutes, my perverse brains set to work without consulting me. Poor Anne Catherick comes into the room, and says, "Try me".

I have got my idea; I have got three of my characters. What is there to do now? My next proceeding is to begin building up the story.

Here, my favourite three efforts must be encountered. First effort: to begin at the beginning. Second effort: to keep the story always advancing, without paying the smallest attention to the serial division in parts, or to the book publication in volumes. Third effort: to decide on the end. All this is done, as my father used to paint his skies in his famous sea-pieces, at one heat. As yet, I do not enter into details; I merely set up my landmarks. In doing this the main situations of the story present themselves; and, at the same time I see my characters in all sorts of new aspects. These discoveries lead me nearer and nearer to finding the right end. The end being decided on, I go back again to the beginning, and look at it with a new eye, and fail to be satisfied with it. I have yielded to the worst temptation that besets a novelist – the temptation to begin with a striking incident, without counting the cost in the shape of explanations that must, and will follow. These pests of fiction, to reader and writer alike, can only be eradicated in one way. I have already mentioned the way – to begin at the beginning. In the case of "The Woman in White", I get back (as I vainly believe) to the true starting point of the story. I am now at liberty to set the new novel going; having, let me repeat, no more than an outline of story and characters before me, and leaving the details, in each case to the spur of the moment.

For a week, as well as I can remember, I work for the best part of every day, but not as happily as usual. An unpleasant sense of something wrong worries me. At the beginning of the second week, a disheartening discovery reveals itself. I have not found the right beginning of "The Woman in White", yet.

The scene of my opening chapters is in Cumberland. Miss Fairlie (afterwards Lady Glyde); Mr Fairlie, with his irritable nerves and his art-treasures; Miss Halcombe (discovered suddenly, like Anne Catherick), are all waiting the arrival of the young drawing-master, Walter Hartright. No: this won't do. The person to be first introduced is Anne Catherick. She must be already a familiar figure to the reader, when the reader accompanies me to Cumberland. This is what must be done, but I don't see how to do it; no new idea comes to me; I and my manuscript have quarrelled, and don't speak to each other. One evening, I happen to read of a lunatic who has escaped from an asylum – a paragraph of a few lines only, in a newspaper. Instantly the idea comes to me of Walter Hartright's midnight meeting with Anne Catherick, escaped from the asylum. "The Woman in White" begins again; and nobody will ever be half as much interested in it now, as

I am. From that moment, I have done with my miseries. For the next six months the pen goes on; it is work, hard work; but the harder the better, for this excellent reason: the work is its own exceeding great reward.

As an example of the gradual manner in which I reach the development of character, I may return for a moment to Fosco. The making him fat was an after-thought; his canaries and his white mice were found next; and the most valuable discovery of all, his admiration of Miss Halcombe, took its rise in a conviction that he would not be true to nature unless there was some weak point, somewhere in his character.

My last difficulty tried me, after the story had been finished, and part of it had been set in proof for serial publication in "All the Year Round". Neither I, nor any friend whom I consulted, could find the right title. Literally, at the eleventh hour, I thought of "The Woman in White". In various quarters, this was declared to be a vile melodramatic title that would ruin the book. Among the very few friends who encouraged me, the first and foremost was Charles Dickens. "Are you too disappointed?" I said to him. "Nothing of the sort, Wilkie! A better title there cannot be."

You are kind enough to allude, in terms of approval, to my method of writing English, and to ask if my style comes to me easily. It comes easily, I hope, to you. Let a last word of confession tell you the rest.

The day's writing having been finished, with such corrections of words and such rebalancing of sentences as occur to me at the time, is subjected to a first revision on the next day, and is then handed to my copyist. The copyist's manuscript undergoes a second and a third revision, and is then sent to the printer. The proof passes through a fourth process of correction, and is sent back to have the new alterations embodied in a Revise. When this reaches me, it is looked over once more, before it goes back to press. When the serial publication of the novel is reprinted in book-form, the book-proofs undergo a sixth revision. Then, at last, my labour of correction has come to an end,[2] and (I don't expect you to believe this) I am always sorry for it.

You have enjoyed, Madam, a privilege dear to ladies – you have had your own way. How I write my books, you now know as well as I can tell you. If you have been able to read to the end, show these lines, if you like, to any friends who care to look at them. In the meantime, I make my bow and my exit.

Wilkie Collins.[3]

Notes

1. MS written by an amanuensis, signed by WC, with corrections in his hand. Published with minor variants in *The Globe* under the MS heading "How I Write My Books: Related in a Letter to a Friend".
2. Printed text reads "I have done with the hard labour of writing good English."
3. "k" of "Wilkie" and "n" of Collins underlined twice.

To Nina Lehmann, 28 November 1887
MS: The Heirs of Horace Noble Pym

[90, Gloucester Place, | Portman Square. W.] | 28th Nov 1887

Dear Padrona

I am so hard at work that I don't know whether I stand on my head or my heels.

But I never did – and never will – say No to You.[1] The work shall be cast aside – and I will have a delightful holiday at your luncheon table.

[Ever truly yours] | WC

Note

1. The last two letters of "You" are heavily underscored twice. A note on the blank integral third leaf of the holograph mss reads: "Lunch at 15 Berkeley Sq. | Thursday 1st Dec '87 | 1[30] p.m."

To Horace Noble Pym,[1] 5 December 1887
MS: Present location unknown. Published, Horace N. Pym, *A Tour Round my Book-Shelves* (1891), pp. 40–1.[2]

[90, Gloucester Place, | Portman Square. W.] | London |
5th December 1887

My Dear Mr Pym,

Let me heartily thank you for the kindness which has given me such an admirably clear and complete abstract of that interesting story. My one regret is that I am not able to begin making use of my materials at once. But a new serial story, which is to begin in February next,[3] claims all my working hours, and forces me to make the most of my time before the weekly publication begins.

How the law disposes of the two surviving conspirators – and especially what becomes of the interesting "Julie" – will probably appear in the newspapers. In any case, I shall keep a wary eye on the foreign news in The Times. In the case of the romantic – or I ought to say the dramatic events, your skill in telling (and writing) a story has left nothing wanting.

A visit to your house is, thanks to your friendly invitation, something pleasant to anticipate when I am a little less rigidly chained to my desk. As I get older I find it more and more difficult (in the matter of literary workmanship) to please myself. By comparison with my late "colleague" Anthony Trollope, with his watch on the table, and his capacity for writing a page in every quarter of an hour, I am the slowest coach now on the literary road; and holidays grow more and more like those "angel's visits" recorded by Poet Campbell.

Once more thanking you, believe me, | Always truly yours, | Wilkie Collins

P.S. – When I wrote my Life of my father I was not personally acquainted with Dickens. Determining to make the book pay its expenses beforehand, if the thing could possibly be done, I published by subscription. Dickens (who knew my father personally, as well as by reputation) was one of the first subscribers. So my first book found its way into his library;[4] and I am indeed glad to hear that it has its resting place in your library now.

Notes

1. Horatio (Horace) Noble Pym (1844–1896), lawyer, friend of Dickens, the Lehmanns and others.
2. Letter sold Sotheby's (London), 23 April 1996, lot 32. For the events surrounding this letter see Horace N. Pym, *A Tour Round my Book-Shelves* (1891), pp. 31–44. Pym "told [Collins] of an insurance fraud perpetrated in Germany. A dying man, bearing a sufficient likeness to the perpetrator of the fraud, was substituted for him so that he could collect on a large life-insurance policy ... It was a story of doubling bound to appeal to him" (Peters, p. 428).
3. *The Legacy of Cain.*
4. *Memoirs of the Life of William Collins*, 1848, from Dickens' library, Sotheby's 23 April 1996, lot 31: "The Library of Horace N. Pym" auction.

To A.P. Watt, 20 December 1887
MS: Private Possession

[90, Gloucester Place, | Portman Square. W. | 20th Decr 1887]

Summary:
"On Sunday last, I very nearly put a premature end to 'The Legacy of Cain' ... I went out for a walk – and in two minutes the detestable raw air caught my heart, or my lungs, or both – I staggered back as nearly suffocated as a man could well be. And I am a prisoner at home ... ordered to go upstairs backwards."

To William Holman Hunt, 2 January 1888
MS: Huntington

90, Gloucester Place, | Portman Square. W. |
2nd January 1888

My dear Holman,

For the worst of all possible reasons, I am late in thanking you for your kindest of kind letters. Two weeks' imprisonment in the house, with the doctor for Gaoler, and no certainty yet of a day of deliverance – there is my dismal story, and the hateful obstacles which will prevent me from making my bow to the Majesty of Misrule. Add to this that I must get well enough, later in this month, to move into another house, and you can form an opinion of the auspicious manner in which the New Year is beginning for me. May it be a prosperous and a happy New Year, my dear old friend, to you.

Always yours aftly | Wilkie Collins

To Sebastian Schlesinger, 3 January 1888
MS: Harvard

90, Gloucester Place, | Portman Square. W. | London |
3rd January 1888

My dear Sebastian,

When a man begins the New Year badly, is he justified in [the: erased] wishing prosperity and happiness to one of his best friends? or does he spread the infection of his ill-luck? If you will promise to take the Scotch way of protecting yourself against fatality, I will wish you the happiest possible New Year. Put your right hand, under the table, and knock that under-part of the table three times, with the knuckle of your forefinger. This done, you are a [erasure] safe Sebastian. If you laugh, and don't do it, you may be a Sebastian who will live to repent of his own rashness.

What is the matter? I hear you inquire.

Towards the end of 1887 I went out on a damp day, and was seized with a sort of neuralgic spasm which nearly suffocated me. It all but stopped the payment of my Insurance premiums – and the doctor is [to: erased] afraid to let me go out again just yet. However he won't let me write to the Cremation Society telling them to light my fire and reduce me to harmless ashes – so I suppose I have not done wrong to write a business letter to Messrs Naylor & Co, requesting them to kindly pay my premiums as before.

But I have not done with the list of my misfortunes yet. As soon as the doctor will let me go out, I must move into another house. The lease here has expired, and the terms asked for allowing me to renew it are so [erasure] enormous that I have no choice but to go. Add to this that I am in the middle of a new serial story which will begin [two erased words] in newspapers, published in the English language, all over the world, in February[1] – and there is the story of my life, up to the present time.

And how is music getting on? Are you writing an Opera? Are you going to hear Verdi's "Othello": in the U.S.? An astonishing effort, I am told, for a man of 75. In this barbarous city – the largest in the world – Mr Carl Rosa is hesitating to risk [word erased] six weeks performances of his opera company. In Manchester, Liverpool, Birmingham, and so on, he draws great audiences. Here, they won't come to him. Hallé's[2] experience is the same. When he wants to revive some unfairly neglected music, he tries his experiment at Manchester – not in London.

In Literature and Art there is nothing new [erasure] on this side of the Atlantic. The best novel recently written by a new man is "King Solomon's Mines". [erasure] Have you read it? or don't you care about novels? A very clever book – of its kind – I say.

This is a dull letter – but what can I do, cut off from my walking exercise? Return me Good for Evil, and send me a brilliant letter. In any case, believe me,

Yours affectionately | Wilkie Collins

Notes

1. *The Legacy of Cain*, published New York, Lovell, July 1888: 3 vols; London: Chatto & Windus, 1889 (November 1888): *Leigh Journal and Times*, 17 February–29 June 1888, and other Tillotson syndicated newspapers.
2. Sir Charles Hallé (1819-1895: *DNB*), pianist and conductor who, in 1857, founded the Hallé Orchestra, Manchester.

To J.A. Stewart,[1] 9 January 1888
MS: Fales Collection, NYU

90, Gloucester Place, | Portman Square. W. |
9th January 1888

Summary:
"After more than thirty years' study of the Art, I consider Walter Scott to be the greatest of all novelists, and 'The Antiquary' is, as I think, the most perfect of all novels."

Note

1. Unidentified.

To Frederick Lehmann, 3 March 1888
MS: Princeton: Text, Coleman.

90, Gloucester Place, | Portman Square. W. |
3rd March 1888

My dear Fred,

Are you still in this dismal London? If yes – then be still the best of good fellows and do me a favour. I have received a letter from Germany – handwriting and language impenetrable mysteries, though both the names are known to me. Will you ask the clerk at your office who knows German to translate for me?

After a month's confinement to the house (nervous seizure) – I am soon to be turned out of the house. Half my furniture has gone already – I live in a dressing-room. The new house is at 82 Wimpole Street. On, or before the 25th (when my lease expires) I must be moved – perhaps in the van, unless the weather improves. Don't you "wish you were me?"

My love to the Padrona – wherever she may be | Yours afftly | W.C.

To Elizabeth Harriet Bartley, 14 March 1888

MS: Princeton

90, Gloucester Place, | Portman Square. W. |
14 March 1888

My dearest Carrie,

I only venture to write to you when the worst that affliction can do has been done – and, even now, I ask myself what I can write to you that is worth reading.

With my way of thinking, I cannot honestly suggest topics of "religious consolation". And no <u>man</u>, let him feel for you as he may – (and I have felt for you with all my heart) – is capable of understanding what a woman must suffer who is tried as you have been tried. The fate of that poor little child[1] – after making such a gallant fight for its life – is something that I must not trust myself to write about. My sorrow is yours and my sympathy is yours. For the rest, Time is the only consoler.

When you can leave the other children, do come here. My love to you and my love to them.

Always affectionately yours, | Wilkie Collins

We hope to get to 82 Wimpole St next week.

Note

1. Carrie's youngest daughter who died, a few months old, in the spring of 1888 (Clarke pp. 180, 225).

To Hall Caine,[1] 15 March 1888

MS: Manx National Heritage: Extract Hall Caine, *My Story* (1909), pp. 334–5; A. Sherbo, "From *The Bookman of London*", *Studies in Bibliography*, 46 (1993), p. 351; *The Bookman* (London), 20 (August 1901), 334–5.

90, Gloucester Place, | Portman Square. W. |[2]
15 March 1888

Dear Hall Caine,

(Let us drop the formality of "Mr" and let me set the example because I am the oldest.)

I have waited to thank you for "The Deemsters"[3] until I could command time enough to read the book without interruption. Let me add that the chair in which I enjoyed this pleasure is not the chair of the critic. What I am writing conveys the impressions of a brother in the art.

You have written a remarkable work of fiction – a great advance on "The Shadow of a Crime"[4] (to my mind) – a powerful and pathetic story, the characters vividly conceived, and set in action with a master hand. Within the limits of a letter, I cannot quote a tenth part of the passages which have seized on my interest and admiration. As one example, among many others which I should like to quote, let me mention the chapter that describes the fishermen taking the dead body out to sea in the hope of concealing the murder. The motives assigned to the men and the manner in which they express themselves show a knowledge of human nature which places you among the masters of our craft, and a superiority to temptations to conventional treatment that no words of mine can praise too highly. For a long time past, I have read nothing that approaches what you have done here. I have read the chapters twice, and, if I know anything of our art, I am sure of what I say.

Now let me think of the next book that you will write, and let me own frankly where I see some form for improvement in what the painters call "treatment of the subject".

When you next take up your pen, will you consider a little whether your tendency to dwell on what is grotesque and violent in human character does not require some discipline? Look again at the "The Deemster", and at some of the qualities and modes of thought attributed to "Dan".

Again, your power as a writer sometimes misleads you, as I think, into forgetting the value of contrast. The grand picture which your story presents of terror and grief wants relief. Individually and collectively, there is variety in the human lot. We are no more continuously neglected than we are continuously happy. Next time, I want more of the humour which breaks out so delightfully in old "Quilleash". More breaks of sunshine in your splendidly cloudy sky will be a truer picture of nature, and will certainly enlarge the number of your admiring readers. Look at two of the greatest of tragic stories – Hamlet and the Bride of Lammermoor, and see how Shakespeare and Scott take every opportunity of presenting contrasts, and brightening the picture at the right place.

[Always truly yours | Wilkie Collins]

Notes

1. Sir Thomas Henry Hall Caine (1853–1931: *DNB*), Manx novelist and friend of WC.
2. Alongside the printed address and monogram, WC writes: "early next week: 82, Wimpole Street".
3. Hall Caine, *The Deemster* (1887).
4. *The Shadow of a Crime* (1885).

To W.H. Barnes, 17 March 1888
MS: Princeton

82, Wimpole Street | W. | 17th March 1888

Summary:
Tells unidentified correspondent that when planning <u>The Two Destinies</u> (1876) WC "heard of an unhappy lady suffering from some disease of the blood which produced a terrible deformity in the face. She was invariably veiled – and she uniformly refused to say why (naturally enough as it seems to me). I purposely introduced incidents and surroundings in 'Miss Dunross' which would prevent my fictitious character from presenting any resemblance in details, with the personage who had served me (in the painter's phrase) as a model. The name of the disease, and nature of the deformity, my informant refused to reveal."

To Harry Quilter,[1] 11 April 1888
MS: Huntington

82, Wimpole Street W. | 11th April 1888

"If you please, sir, I don't think the looking glass will fit in above the book-case in this house." – "Your father's lovely little picture can't go above the chimney-piece. The heat will spoil it." "Take down the picture in the next room, and try it there." "But that is the portrait of your grandmother." "Damn my grandmother." "If the side-board is put in the front dining-room, we don't know where the cabinets are to go." "I am sorry to trouble you, but I miss three books out of the library catalogue – Forster's Life of Goldsmith, and Lamb's Essays and Leigh Hunt's Essays.[2] Do you think they have been stolen?" "Here is the man, sir, with the patterns of wall-paper." "What on earth is to be done with the Story of Cupid and Psyche – ten big photographs and no place to hang them in." "How will you have your bed put? against the side of the wall, or standing out from the wall?" "I say, Wilkie! when you told Marian and Harriet[3] that they might help to put the books in their places, did you know that Faublas and Casanova's Memoirs were left out on the drawing-room table?" "I beg your pardon, sir, did I understand that you wanted a lamp in the water-closet?" "Do take some notice of the cat, he's fond of you, and the workmen are frightening him out of his senses." "When will you see Mr Bartley about the dilapidations at Gloucester Place?" "Dear Sir, we are sorry to notice irregularity in the supply of copy lately. Please excuse our writing to you on this subject.

We must not keep the colonial newspapers waiting for their proofs. Yours, &c &c"

=

My dear Quilter,

Do the domestic circumstances reported above excuse me for not having written sooner. Oh, surely, yes?

I have had one happy half hour since I established myself in the new house – and I owe it to You. Your generous review – seen in print – has added to the pride and the gratitude and the delightful sense of encouragement which I felt when I first read it in MSS. I have been inclined to doubt whether it was worth while to have lived to be 64 years old. After reading that article,[4] I am quite satisfied that it <u>was</u> worth while. Childish, isn't it? But it is so, nevertheless.

My workshop is ready to receive you, and eager to receive you. When will you come and tell me how the new Review is getting on – and try another cigar, and some more tea? Don't bother to write more than one line (literally) to choose your day and hour.

Yours affectionately | Wilkie Collins

Notes

1. Harry Quilter (1851–1907), art critic; started the *Universal Review* in 1888.
2. None of these items was among WC's books when he died.
3. Marian and Harriet were WC's daughters by Martha Dawson (Rudd).
4. "A Living Story-Teller: Mr Wilkie Collins", *Contemporary Review*, 53 (April 1888), 572–93.

To Hall Caine, 1 May 1888
MS: Manx National Heritage[1]

82, Wimpole Street, W. | 1 May 1888

Dear Hall Caine,

I am really and truly ashamed of myself for having allowed weeks to pass without thanking you for your friendly and welcome letter. The strain of writing a serial story (with the newspaper's weekly publication not far behind me) I am used to. But when to this is added a fight, in this new house, with every form of decorative bad taste which the average Englishman can stick on the walls and paint on the doors and drag up the staircase – then the test of endurance becomes heavy in the case of a man who numbers four years on the wrong side of sixty, and my old friend the Doctor has been here in his professional as well as his personal capacity. But I am better again now – and my workshop is comfortable and I have my pictures and books around me. Whenever you are in London with time to spare, pray come and see me. <u>You</u> won't interrupt me if you find me at my desk. As to my hours I begin at 10 a.m. and go on sometimes till 3 or 4 in the afternoon. At any time between 3 and 5, you will be welcome with open arms. After this I get out. But if you find yourself free at earlier hours than these, do not hesitate to come in. I want to hear about your play. In my own case when I have had plays produced, I take refuge in the dressing room of one of the actors, and wait for my fate, stupefied with incessant smoking. There is no hope of my being able to take the place in your box which you so kindly offered to me, in my present state of health. And it is fortunate for you that I shall not occupy one of the chairs in the box. A first night – and especially a friend's first night – is no enjoyable occasion to me. The malice of enemies and the stupidity of fools, among the audience, and the stage fright behind the curtain, are tests which my nerves are not strong enough to sustain. When your play is successfully started on a long run, I will try to get well enough to go and enjoy it.

In the meantime, and for the present only, goodbye.

Always truly yours, | Wilkie Collins

If there is any hope of my seeing you this week, I have just remembered that Saturday is the only day on which I shall <u>not</u> be at home.

Note

1. Note on back of letter in Caine's handwriting: "This was Wilkie's answer to my invitation to share my box on the night of the production of the play founded on 'The Deemster'."

To Alexander Gray,[1] 26 May 1888
MS: Donald Whitton (San Francisco)

[82 Wimpole Street | London. W.] | 26 May 1888

My dear Alexander,

Your welcome letter arrived just at the right time to be a relief to me, when the innumerable worries of getting into a new house, and the necessity of feeding the newspapers with [erased word] their [erased word] weekly allowance of "The Legacy of Cain" were trying my powers of endurance together. I finished the last chapter of the story (which will be published in the first week of July) on Whit Monday – and now I am able to attend to my correspondence, and to thank you for your letter.

When I visited the United States in 1873–74 – and met with a reception from friendly readers which I shall remember gratefully as long as I live – I had hoped to see San Francisco and to become personally acquainted with your wife and your children. But I am one of those unfortunate people who are unable to sleep in a railway carriage, and whose nerves suffer under the noise and vibration of railway travelling. I arrived at Chicago (from New York) in such a state of exhaustion that I alarmed the landlord of my hotel. "What <u>can</u> I do for you?" that worthy man asked. I answered, "Let me have a bottle of the driest Champagne you have got in your cellar – and then let me go to bed." How many hours I slept, I don't now remember. I was informed that they opened my door, from time to time, and looked in to make sure that I was alive. After this experience, the terrible journey to San Francisco daunted me – and to the great amusement of my American friends I wasted a whole week in resting at one place and another, on my way back to New York.

Marian[2] often calls here, and is the benevolent fairy of my existence who brings me blessings in the shape of new laid eggs – rarities not always attainable in London, no matter what price you may give for them. Do not let me mislead you into supposing that your sister keeps fowls. Her landlord takes that responsibility, and Marian takes the eggs.

I hear with sincere pleasure that you are happy in your wife and your children. A man who suffers under Domestic misery is, as I think, the most unhappy of men. With good children and a good mother, the other troubles of human life are all more or less endurable.

As for me, I gave up what is called "Society" some years since, in the interests of my health, sadly tried by the reiterated tortures of gout in the eyes. I live in retirement (with a few old friends still left) – Devoted to my Art.

With kindest remembrances to all at home, believe me, | Ever truly yours,
Wilkie Collins

Notes

1. WC's cousin: "His mother's sister, Catherine, had married John Westcott Gray. Their son, Alexander, had grown up in Salisbury but left England in the early 1850s, originally to go to Australia, but later to California" (Clarke, p. 222, n.42).
2. i.e., Alexander's younger sister.

To Robert du Pontavice de Heussey, 12 July 1888

MS: Princeton

82, Wimpole Street | London. W. | 12 July 1888

My dear Collaborateur,

Please notice the above address. I feel penitently that I ought to have written to you weeks since – and there is my excuse!

After 20 years residence in Gloucester Place, I have been driven into encountering the horrors of moving by the expiration of my lease, and by the exorbitant terms asked me for renewing it by the agent of my landlord, an enormously rich nobleman named Lord Portman. He asked me to pay, for the right of continuing to live in the house no less a sum than <u>twelve hundred pound</u>s – to say nothing of other merciless stipulations. In our choice English phrase I determined to "see him damned first" – and here I am in a much quieter situation and in a much nicer house, beginning domestic life again at the age of 64 (alas!). Let me add that the dire necessity of moving presented itself while I was publishing a new serial story in weekly newspapers in Great Britain, Australia, Canada and the United States, and that I had to supply this large public with their weekly allowance of fiction all through the confusions and interruptions and hammerings of workmen incident to shifting from one house to the other. How it is that I am not in a lunatic asylum I don't understand. The excitement and worry have, however, taken another form – they have set my invention <u>boiling</u>. My head is so full of a new story and new characters that I have got what Balzac used to call "a congestion of ideas", and am actually obliged to relieve myself by beginning another book. There is my autobiography presented to my dear and good friend.

There is a sympathy in our destinies as well as in our sentiments. You too have suffered the <u>peine forte et dure</u> of moving, and you too have been working against obstacles – I am sure to good purpose. The prospect of reading your "Dickens" is something that I look forward to with delight. The little that I have read of what is new in contemporary literature <u>here</u> is not encouraging to my tastes. I want to be interested – and I wait for <u>you</u>.[1] I shall follow you in December with the first publication <u>in book-form</u>, of the serial novel to which I have alluded already, "The Legacy of Cain". The first serial issue ended on the 7th of this month. But there is to be a second serial issue – and so the book publication must be deferred.

Pray take care of your health. The one part of your letter which I was sorry to read is the part of it which alludes to your illness. Here, we have had cold weather of which there has been no example for the past sixty years. It strings up my nerves, and keeps me well. But your lungs must be sensitive, after that attack – and distrust of the season (if your summer is like ours) will be the wisest of all distrusts until the warm weather comes.

always your affectionate friend Wilkie Collins

Note

1. The "o" of "you" is doubly underlined.

To Sebastian Schlesinger, 26 August 1888
MS: Harvard

[27, Wellington Crescent | Ramsgate] | 26th August 1888

My dear Sebastian,
    Wilkie Collins, of 82 Wimpole Street has disappeared from this mortal sphere of action, and is replaced by | William Dawson | 27. Wellington Crescent | Ramsgate.

=

In plain English, I am here with my "morganatic family" – and must travel (like the Royal Personages) under an alias – or not be admitted into this respectable house now occupied by my children and their mother. So – if there is any more news from America – address W. Dawson Esq. for the next fortnight. I shall be, after that, in London again, so far as I now know.
    My only excuse for not having written before this, or having "dropped in on you", as they say, at your Chambers, is my new novel.[1] It is a tough job this time. I have been nowhere and have seen nobody and am nothing better than the slave of my pen – the most agreeable slavery that I am acquainted with.

Ever yours | W.C

Note

1. The unfinished *Blind Love*.

To Hall Caine, 25 October 1888
MS: Manx National Heritage

82, Wimpole Street. | W. | 25 October 1888

My dear Hall Caine,

My best thanks for the photograph. The only objection to it that I can discern, no doubt felt by your friends – the likeness is overprinted and the result is a dark-haired man. And perhaps the light was allowed to fall a little too strongly on your face when you sat – and the reflected light in the pupils of your eyes come rather wildly. Making these small allowances the likeness seems to me to be excellent and the position of the figure well managed.

I am not at all surprised to hear of the success of "Ben-my-Chree"[1] in the country. The average London audience is the stupidest in England. In the country towns (especially the great towns) the superiority of intelligence is really remarkable. I heartily congratulate you on the result of your dramatic venture – after your play escaped from its confinement in the hideous Princess's Theatre.

When you are next in London you will find me, as I hope, here and ready to see you again. I was at Ramsgate, not Broadstairs, and so we missed each other. My illness was painful (neuralgia, complicated by an abscess), but never serious.

Shall I make a dreadful confession? I am at work again – hard at work – furiously at work – nearly a third of the way through a new story. I will tell you about it when we meet. In the meantime, an indignant (and devoted) friend has discovered a very good reason for the obstinacy of the ancient novelist in refusing to let go of his pen. "I'll tell you what it is, Wilkie, you are a canny fellow and a clever fellow and you contrive to hide it from most people – but I tell you, seriously and positively, you're mad!" This is my only excuse for being just as incapable (when a story comes to me) of resisting the temptation to write it, as I was forty years since!

Ever yours, | Wilkie Collins

Note

1. The play based on "The Deemster".

To Sebastian Schlesinger, 24 January 1889
MS: Harvard

82, Wimpole Street. | W. | 24 January 1889

My dear Sebastian,

Your copy of "The Legacy of Cain" has been sent to you by today's Parcel Post.

I am again under the doctor's care – indigestion and gouty disturbances, and strict abstinence from all the good things at your table only too necessary. You will forgive my absence, I am sure.

Returning from that delightful dinner of yours I had a narrow escape of some serious consequences. Turning from Weston Place into the Knightsbridge Road, my four-wheel cab collided with some vehicle. A frightful smash of broken glass – a turning round of cab and horse – a twist over of the cab just as I jumped out of it. My coat covered with broken glass – but my face and my hands untouched. I did not feel it much at the time – but I fancy it has given me a shake, and stirred up the gout. But there are no bad symptoms, so far – and the enemy has been met in time. I must however be careful – and alas! – I must be absent from feasts and felicity.

Ever yours | W.C

One line to say if the book has reached you. I think of the lost canvas-back-ducks,[1] and take "a pessimist view" of the fate of parcels.

Note

1. Schlesinger sent WC special ducks which apparently got lost.

To Thomas DeWitt Talmage,[1] 8 March 1889
MS: Princeton

82, Wimpole Street. | London | W. | 8th March 1889

Dear Doctor Talmage

The winter climate of England in the year 1889, has tempted gentlemen of British birth, who have reached the wrong side of sixty, to regret their nationality, and to envy the happy lot of the African savage, who lives under a nice warm sun, and has never heard of bronchitis and neuralgia. In these morbid sentiments pray find my excuse for a shamefully late acknowledgment of your kindness. I should be insensible indeed if I did not take the first opportunity which illness has conceded to me of heartily thanking you for the magnificent addition which you have made to my library. If I fail to feel the compliment to myself which is implied by your gift, I should be travelling blindfold along "The Pathway of Life".

It would be an act of presumption, on my part, if I attempted to write critically of such a book as yours. But I may be allowed to mention the impression produced on me by what I have read, thus far. Your work is especially interesting to me in this respect – that it reveals the secret of the widely-extended influence which you exercise over those who hear you and read you. In the pulpit and out of the pulpit, the man who knows what to say, and how to say it, is a man in a thousand – so far as my experience extends. Turn to what pages I may, I find this rare gift in useful action all through your Volume – and I especially value the frank and friendly tone in which a large-minded and tolerant Christianity addresses itself to readers of all ways of thinking. The wise words which tell married people how to bear with each other, and to help each other, under the trials and troubles of their lives – and, again, the admirable pages which prove that the conditions of happiness do not depend on social position – are among many other examples that I might quote of your value as a teacher of the people who never forgets that he is always the people's friend.

I might well say more than this – but six weeks of imprisonment in the house interfere a little, I find, with the free movement of my old friend the pen. When I have asked you to accept the congratulations on the completion of your work, my letter – such as it is! – reaches its end.

Believe me, very truly yours | Wilkie Collins

The Revd | T. WeWitt Talmage. D.D.

Note

1. Thomas DeWitt Talmage (1832–1902), his *The Pathway of Life. A Book for the Home* was published Richmond, Va.: B.F. Johnson & Co., 1889. Curiously, not in WC's library at his death.

To Sebastian Schlesinger, 27 March 1889
MS: Harvard

82, Wimpole Street. | London | W. | 27 March 1889

S. E. B.
The one gleam of good fortune left to brighten my damnable Destiny is accurately described in those three letters, encircled by a pen and ink halo.

I have never recovered my six weeks of confinement to the house. Saturated with bile – racked by neuralgia (in the face, this time). I am incapable of taking advantage of one more of those many acts of kindness on your part, which I shall remember gratefully to the end of my days. This morning, there is a cloudless sky – a splendid sun – and I have as much chance of "finding the longitude" or "squaring the circle" as I have of going out for a drive. And with a pretty woman too! A handkerchief covers my right [erased word] cheek – an abscess is forming in my [erased word] mouth, [erased word] which contains hot laudanum and water, and is dumb to the utterance of Love. Add to this that I am obliged to put off writing one of my two proposed novels, and to sell my copyrights – and you have me complete, with one subject of consolations, which Ends – as it has begun – my letter

S. E. B.

Let me see you as soon as you return – and let us get drunk together.[2]

Notes

1. The initials are in large Gothic letters encircled by a looped line.
2. WC doesn't sign his letter.

To Sebastian Schlesinger, 2 May 1889

MS: Harvard. Extract, Smith and Terry

82, Wimpole Street. | W. | 2nd May 1889

My dear Sebastian, Welcome back to London! You have had a delightful holiday I am sure – with only one drawback. The dear delightful dirty old houses in the Jews' Street at Frankfurt have been tumbled down by Time and Government in these later years. I say (what nobody ever says) "Alas!"

No – my dear friend – there is nothing surprising in that letter. I have said it to you, I have written it to you – She[1] never has, and never will forgive you. You now have her own acknowledgment of that state of mind in this last letter. I hope and trust you have <u>not</u> answered it. And, what is more, I advise you <u>not</u> to write to her again. Decide on a certain yearly allowance to be made to her – paid quarterly. Write on that occasion to announce your decision – and show the Dft of your letter to your lawyer, before you let me look at it. You will very likely receive a penitent letter – perhaps a "heart-[erased word] rending" letter. Don't answer! If you feel softened, look at the letter which I return herewith – [erasure] and say to yourself – "There's her mind, stripped for my private view."[2] I have had between 40 and 50 years Experience of women of all sorts and sizes. You have the result.

I am afraid I shall not be in the right state of stomach and liver for that supper on the 12th. But pray come here before it, [erased word] if you can. A note or telegram to say when – and I shall not be out trying to walk off Bile, Bile, Bile – when you come here. Your time is my time.

Ever yours | W.C

Notes

1. i.e., Mrs Schlesinger who had discovered her husband's infidelity with Mrs Sherman.
2. Lonoff observes: "Schlesinger followed Collins' advice. He settled £700 a year on his wife" (Smith and Terry, p. 48). See next letter.

To Sebastian Schlesinger, 4 May 1889
MS: Harvard

82, WImpole Street. | W. | 4th May

My dear Sebastian,
    In your place, I should <u>begin</u> my letter with the paragraph on the 2nd [erasure] page: "Hitherto, I have taken Louise into Consideration &–"
    What you have written before that, [erasure] only tells her that she [shall: erased] has succeeded in stinging you. You say yourself, "I don't wish to discuss that." Then why discuss it? Never answer an angry woman – when you do not possess the advantage of being a woman yourself. The rest of the letter seems to me to be excellent – just what was wanted.
    I write <u>giddy with bile</u>. I wrote this time in a hurry.

Ever yours | W.C

The income you propose to settle on her is almost lavish in its generosity – over £700 a year (!) I shall be curious to see in what tone she writes to you, after <u>that</u>.

To A.P. Watt, 26 August 1889
MS: Private Possession

82, Wimpole Street | 26 August 1889

[Dear Watt]
    My daughter's hand[1] thanks you with all my heart for your most welcome and friendly letter. Your good son's help has been rendered to me

in the kindest manner. My good friends encourage me to get better, and the doctor is content with my progress. Pray tell Walter Besant[2] that his ready and valued help has been offered to a grateful brother in the art – and let me sign myself now that I can write a little again.

Yours afftly | Wilkie Collins

Notes

1. Apart from signature, letter written in the hand of Mrs Henry Bartley ("Carrie"). A pencilled note at the top of the letter in A.P. Watt's holograph reads: "The last letter from my friend".
2. Sir Walter Besant (1836–1901: *DNB*), novelist who completed *Blind Love*.

To Frederick Lehmann, 3 September 1889
MS: Princeton. Published, Robinson

82, Wimpole Street. | W. | 3rd Sept 1889

My dear Fred,
    A word to report myself to <u>you</u> with my own hand. I am unable to receive Martin today, for the reason that I have fallen asleep – and the doctor forbids the waking of me. Sleep is my cure he says – and he is really hopeful of me. Don't notice the blots – my dressing-gown sleeve is too large – but my hand is still steady. Goodbye for the present dear old friend – we may really hope for healthier days.
    My grateful love to the best and dearest of Padronas.

Yours ever affly, | Wilkie Collins

To Sebastian Schlesinger, 7 September 1889
MS: Harvard

82, Wimpole Street. | W. | 7th Sept: 1889

My dear Sebastian,
    <u>Where</u> are you? <u>How</u> are you? When shall I hear from you again? When shall I see you again? Here is my report declaring myself with my own hand on the way to recovery, after the calamity that fell on me some time since.[1] I am well looked after. Two good nurses, the doctor who is Curing me –

and my two daughters[2] to see it and help. I want you [erased words] to see my children – <u>Why</u> you will easily guess.[3]

Good bye old friend,[4]

Yours aftly, | Wilkie Collins

Notes

1. Probably a reference to his sudden stroke in June 1889 (see Clarke p.1).
2. i.e., Marian and Harriet.
3. Reference to the insurance policies WC took out during his American trip for the benefit of his children, which Schlesinger helped to arrange.
4. A somewhat prophetic close: WC died the morning of Monday 23 September 1889.

To Francis Carr Beard, 21 September 1889

MS: Princeton. Peters, p. 431; reproduced Clarke, p. 185.

82, Wimpole Street. | W. |[1] Sept 21

I am <u>dying</u> old friend | W.C[2]

[3]I am too wretched to write. They are driving me mad by forbidding the [Hypodermic].[4] Come for God's sake.[5]

Notes

1. Note written in pencil.
2. On one leaf.
3. "On a separate scrap of paper" (Peters, p. 431).
4. "The first letter of this word is clearly 'h', the second probably 'y'; the remainder is indecipherable. [WC] had been taking hypophosphates. 'Hypodermic' is another possibility, or the powerful sedative hyoscine" (Peters, p. 431, n.).
5. "Wilkie died at 10 a.m.", Monday 23 September 1889 (Peters, p. 431; citing Caroline's note in WC's diary).

Appendix:
Unpublished Letters

As indicated in the Preface, letters which have not so far been published in full or in a summarized form, are included in this Appendix, in date order, with an indication of the present source.

Date	Recipient	Topic	Source
1866			
Jan 28	Elizabeth Blakeway-Smith	Unable to accept invitation	N Carolina
Feb 6	Francis Beard	Tell Dickens he will be at Verey's	Dickens Hs
13	F Enoch	Returns illustrations for *Armadale*	PM
20	I Mosceles	Sorry to miss you. Going to Paris	Private
March 14	Alice Ward	Hopes to see her (and the picture)	Bodleian
17	Mrs Harriet Collins	Visit to Paris "put off"	Private
19	Alice Ward	Thanks for return of gloves	Bodleian
25	FV Phillips	On question of foreign reprints	Texas
Apr 15	Unknown	Leaves proof of last number	Private
May 1	Mrs Harriet Collins	Back from Paris: heat frightful	Private
22	Mrs Harriet Collins	Father's painting made £975	Private
23	Miss Doran	Sends autograph	Kansas
31	Mrs Harriet Collins	Arranging next visit	PM
June 14	Smith Elder	Sends proofs of play	Huntington
25	Elliott & Fry	Thanks for photo. Will sit Wed	PM
30	Miss Speed	Sends letters from Dickens etc	Private
July 6	Smith Elder	Thanks for 25 copies of play	Huntington
18	Mrs EM Ward	Declines invitation	Texas
23	WH Wills	Suggests housing for poor author	Jns Hopkins
Aug 16	Stringfield	Can he come to lunch?	Princeton
Sept 12	Palgrave Simpson	Suggests dinner	Shakespeare Lib
16	Unknown	Discusses plays. Suggests sailing trip	Private
28	Lady Goldsmid	Hopes to see her before Italy	Private
Oct 13	John Bullar	Sends autographs	Texas
Dec 14	Mrs Harriet Collins	*W. in White* "the rage in Berlin"	Private
17	Lydia Foote	Congratulates on performance	Brit Theatr Mus
31	Smith Elder	Discusses book copyrights	NLS
1867			
Jan 5	Charles Benham	Wants to talk about copyrights	Glasgow
15	Mrs Harriet Collins	Reports skating accident in Park	Private
16	Smith Elder	Discusses cheap edition of *Armadale*	NLS
29	Mrs Harriet Collins	Discusses dinner with Forster & plays	Private
March 25	FV Phillips		
30	Miss Speed	Sends autographs	Texas
April 1	[Joseph Hogarth]	Requests photographs	Private

Date	Recipient	Topic	Source
8	Smith Elder	Discusses details of copyrights	NLS
20	Smith Elder	Will write again about proposal	NLS
May 2	J Elliott	Introduces his brother Charles	Princeton
8	WH Wills	Requests Christmas number	Jns Hopkins
9	WP Frith	Wants advice on father's pictures	V & A Mus
14	WH Wills	Discusses payment for *No Name*	Illinois
June 18	Harper & Brothers	Offers new novel	Texas
July 7	Mrs Harriet Collins	Asks for father's autograph	PM
20	Harper & Brothers	Accepts 2nd of two proposals	Texas
Aug 30	Smith Elder	Discusses sale of copyrights	NLS
Sept 4	Mrs Harriet Collins	Will see her tomorrow	PM
16	Mrs Harriet Collins	Sends list of books	PM
[Dec '64–			
Sept '67]	Unknown	"Much better"	Private
Oct 18	Charles Kent	Accepts both requests	Huntington
18	Smith Elder	"Inappropriate" offer for copyrights	NLS
22	Charles Kent	Will attend dinner	Huntington
24	Charles Kent	Unable to attend meeting	Huntington
25	Dr Emil Lehmann	Accepts offer for German translation	Private
26	Charles Kent	Sends list for dinner	Huntington
Nov 16	Benjamin Webster	Discusses Miss Le Clercq's role	Unknown
18	Mrs EM Ward	Declines invitation	Texas
26	Mrs Harriet Collins	Correcting *The Moonstone*	Private
Dec 15	WP Frith	No free admission to first night	V & A Mus
23	Mrs Harriet Collins	Hopes to come tomorrow	Private
27	Mrs Harriet Collins	Play "immense success"	Private
28	Mrs EM Ward	Cannot accept Mrs Casella's invite	Texas
28	Mrs Casella	Party same as play's first night	Yale
1868			
Jan 16	Holman Hunt	Invites him to dine and see play	Huntington
21	William Tindell	"Extract to be sent to Australia"	Glasgow
Feb 1	William Tindell	Visit depends on mother's illness	Glasgow
4	William Tindell	Writes to make appointment	Glasgow
5	William Tindell	Cannot make appointment	Glasgow
23	William Tindell	Discusses terms for play	Glasgow
29	Harper & Brothers	Thanks for £500. Sends weekly revision	Texas
[March 18]	Holman Hunt	Mother still holding onto life	Huntington
April 20	GH Lewes	Wishes him to call	Unknown
June 2	Charles Benham	Discusses police court bail	Glasgow
2	Benjamin Webster	Production of *No Thoroughfare*	Unknown
6	William Tinsley	Hopes to finish *Moonstone* at 32/33 part	Texas
16	Charles Benham	Too late to find him or Tindell	Glasgow
28	Charles Benham	Bringing conclusion of *Moonstone*	Glasgow
July 8	Mr Gregson	Wishes to see him [landlord & dentist]	Private
18	Charles Benham	Will call on him	Glasgow
28	Emily Clunes	Mother's legacy to her of £50	Private
Sept 9	Charles Benham	Wishes to discuss Tinsley's proposal	Glasgow
11	Miss Elmore	Has been travelling abroad	Private
12	Harper & Brothers	Just returned from Switzerland	Texas
12	Harry [Leman]	Refuses request to dramatise *Moonstone*	Unknown
Dec 7	Felix Mosceles	Cannot join séance	Private
28	Nina Lehmann	Wants to take them to pantomime	Unknown

Date	Recipient	Topic	Source
1869			
Jan 3	Nina Lehmann	Discusses possible cook	Princeton
4	Nina Lehmann	Not to engage cook	Princeton
25	Charles Ward	Makes request	PM
27	Mrs Brinley Richards	Accepts invitation	Private
29	Mrs WP Frith	Cannot accept invite. Will be in Paris	Brit Lib
Feb 4	John Hollingshead	Admires theatre. Promises play	Huntington
21	Charles Benham	Tinsley not yet paid £50	Glasgow
27	Smith Elder	Cannot accept proposal	NLS
Mar 23	WP Frith	Can they go to see *Black & White*?	Princeton
April 1	Charles Ward	Good reception for *Black & White*	PM
7	Mrs Williams	Sends theatre ticket	Texas
9	T Hyde Hills	Declines invitation	Melbourne
May 6	Charles Benham	Is *Moonstone* registered in Paris?	Glasgow
12	Charles Ward	Encloses cheque for £50	PM
24	John Hollingshead	Has idea for play. Possible for Gaiety	Princeton
June 1	John Hollingshead	Decides to make play into book	Texas
14	Margaret Carpenter	Thanks her for book	Private
17	Joseph Ellis	Thanks for poems	Bodleian
26	Mrs Henry Bullar	Sorry to miss her	Private
July 8	Strahan & Co	Sends Charles' papers/illustrations	Princeton
Aug 10	Thomas Galpin	Promises to write again about story	Texas
10	Harper & Brothers	Asks for offer for *Man & Wife*	Texas
10	G P Putnam	Asks for proposal for *Man & Wife*	Private
13	Thomas Galpin	Promises legal Draft	Texas
16	WP Frith	Asks for opening for actress	V & A Mus
17	Thomas Galpin	Discusses details of legal agreement	Texas
24	Cassell, Petter etc	Is awaiting replies from America	Texas
Sept 6	General [Dik]	Introduces Frederick Lehmann	Unknown
7	Cassell, Petter etc	Gives details American agreement	Texas
7	Harper & Brothers	Accepts proposal	Unknown
21	Cassell, Petter etc	Is finishing 7th weekly part	Texas
22	Editor, Cassell's	Encloses 6th part of *Man & Wife*	Texas
22	Mrs Laura Seymour	Glad she likes beginning of story	Private
25	Cassell, Petter etc	Accepts objection to "damn it", but	Texas
28	Frederick Lehmann	When can they meet?	Bodleian
Oct 5	Holman Hunt	Introduces his friend Parkinson	Huntington
12	Harper & Brothers	Encloses corrections	Unknown
19	Harper & Brothers	Thanks for £500. Bill of Exchange	Private
26	Harper & Brothers	Thanks for duplicate Bill of Exchange	Private
29	Cassell, Petter etc	Sends correction for advert in *Cornhill*	Texas
Nov 5	Cassell, Petter etc	Dishonesty of Dutch publishers	Texas
5	William Tindell	Thanks for draught. Discusses tenant	Glasgow
8	James Payn	Discusses Payn's *The Substitute*	Texas
9	Cassell, Petter etc	Sends copy of letter to Dutch publishers	Texas
10	Charles Ward	Discusses investments	PM
12	Cassell, Petter etc	Discusses letter for *The Echo*	Texas
21	Cassell, Petter etc	Thanks for their activities	Texas
26	James Payn	Suggests form of letter to press	Texas
27	Harper & Brothers	Asks for publication of Dutch dispute	Unknown
29	Cassell, Petter etc	Will they deposit weekly in Berlin?	Texas
30	Editor, *The Echo*	Announces agreement with Dutch	Texas
30	James Payn	"Belafonte Brothers give in !"	Texas
Dec 9	EM Ward	Delighted to dine	Texas
15	William Tindell	Asks advice for Italian friend	Glasgow

Date	Recipient	Topic	Source
1870			
Jan 5	Mrs WP Frith	Declines invitation : gout	V & A Mus
18	TH Hills	Accepts his invitation	Melbourne
19	Charles Ward	Discusses dividends and accounts	PM
31	William Tindell	Discusses tenant's affairs	Glasgow
Feb 3	William Tindell	Still confined to dark room	Glasgow
14	William Tindell	Eye getting better. Suggests dinner	Glasgow
16	William Tindell	Monday will suit for dinner	Glasgow
21	TH Hills	Declines invitation: illness	Melbourne
22	William Tindell	Will be at home from 7 to 9	Glasgow
22	William Tindell	Discusses lease on house	Glasgow
24	Cassell, Petter etc	Is better. Weekly instalments	Texas
Mar 6	William Tindell	Will call to discuss *W in White*	Glasgow
9	CJH Kleinan	Sends set of Cassell's magazines	Princeton
25	William Tindell	Can he see him on Monday?	Glasgow
26	William Tindell	Suggests Tuesday next for meeting	Glasgow
April 1	Mark Lemon	Will he consider Drummond?	Unknown
9	James Payne	Thanks for book dedication	Texas
26	Cassell, Petter etc	Will they republish *Man & Wife*?	Texas
30	Harper & Brothers	*Man & Wife* as book: when?	PM
May 8	William Tindell	Will decline Cassell & Tinsley	Glasgow
10	William Tindell	Will see him tomorrow	Glasgow
17	Mrs EM Ward	Will attend if not in Switzerland	Texas
18	William Tindell	Will see him tomorrow	Glasgow
24	William Tindell	Discusses advertisement	Glasgow
June 1	William Tindell	Suggests papers to take advert	Glasgow
2	Editor, Cassell's	Needs duplicates for Canada	Texas
3	Cassell, Petter etc	Discusses Canadian copyright protection	Texas
4	Harper & Brothers	Sends papers. Canadian piracy	PM
4	Hunter, Rose & Co	Arranging publication prevent piracy	Princeton
9	Charles Ward	Encloses £40 cheque for account	PM
11	Harper & Brothers	Sends conclusion of *Man & Wife*	PM
11	William Tindell	Discusses form of advertising	Glasgow
15	Cassell, Petter etc	Encloses signed receipt : *Man & Wife*	Texas
18	William Tindell	Discusses copy & corrections	Glasgow
21	William Tindell	Thanks him for legal book	Glasgow
23	William Tindell	Discusses press advertisements	Glasgow
23	Hachette & Co	Thanks for registering book in Spain	Private
30	William Tindell	Second edition to be 500 new copies?	Glasgow
July 6	Harper & Brothers	Thanks for £250	PM
12	William Tindell	Just back from cruise off East Coast	Glasgow
23	William Tindell	Needs copies *Man & Wife*. To sea again	Glasgow
27	William Tindell	Has done right to go for 500	Glasgow
Aug 7	William Tindell	Arranges to meet	Glasgow
15	William Tindell	First US performance a publication ?	Glasgow
22	Unknown	Discusses staging of *No Name*	Texas
22	Thomas Galpin	Will consider offer later.	Texas
Sept 10	William Tindell	To discuss *Man & Wife* with manager	Glasgow
20	William D Booth	Daly's alterations to his play	Princeton
22	Dion Boucicault	If problem, can offer play elsewhere	Texas
28	Charles Ward	Asks if box available at Drury Lane	PM
29	Benham & Tindell	Has communicated about *Man & Wife*	Glasgow
Oct 22	Sir Ed Bulwer-Lytton	Discusses Canadian publication	Herts Rec
22	Harper & Brothers	Writing plays. Will offer next book	PM

Date	Recipient	Topic	Source
22	William Tindell	Discusses accounts and rents	Glasgow
25	William Tindell	Sends draft	Glasgow
26	Benjamin Webster	Sends second Act	Private
27	Charles Ward	Asks him to lend a hand on Sunday	PM
Nov 14	George Smith	Agrees suggestion on payments	Nth Car
Dec 21	George Smith	Asks advice on French earnings	NLS
28	Mrs John Forster	Delighted to attend party	Dickens Hse
1871			
Jan 13	William Tindell	Discusses tenants	Glasgow
14	Cassell, Petter etc	Are they interested in his new story?	Texas
14	Charles Ward	Encloses £50	PM
17	Miss [Rushout]	Thanks her for stable rent	Private
19	Editor, *Cassell's*	Can follow Charles Reade's story	Texas
21	William Tindell	Did he receive letter about stables?	Glasgow
23	Charles Ward	Sends £49	PM
30	Cassell, Petter etc	Needs quick response to proposal	Texas
Feb 2	Cassell, Petter etc	Length and payment for next novel	Texas
7	Cassell, Petter etc	Agrees terms. Awaits draft	Texas
7	Harper & Brothers	Offers new serial story	PM
15	William Tindell	Is he free for first night?	Glasgow
23	G Augustus Sala	Sends his reaction to article	Princeton
25	George Smith	Will vote for Mr Shand	NYPL
March 3	William Tindell	Discusses agreements with Cassell's	Glasgow
6	Cassell, Petter etc	Discusses details of agreement	Texas
14	Cassell, Petter etc	Cannot publish earlier	Texas
14	Harper & Brothers	Accepts their "liberal" terms	PM
25	Cassell, Petter etc	Can publish in Colonies, not Canada	Texas
29	Cassell, Petter etc	Sends agreements	Texas
30	George Smith	Thanks for cheque for £173	NLS
30	Charles Ward	Encloses £173 cheque for his account	PM
31	George Smith	*Moonstone* is book to begin with	NLS
April 3	William Tindell	Asks advice on Xmas story translation	Glasgow
5	Cassell, Petter etc	Encloses agreement with signature	Texas
8	Lord Jerviswood	Accepts invite Scott centenary	Scot. Rec
14	Charles Ward	Received 100 guilders from Dutch	PM
16	William Tindell	Suggests accept Smith's terms	Glasgow
22	Mrs WP Frith	Accepts invitation	V & A Mus
26	WR Sheddon-Ralston	Accepts invite to Royal Institution	Yale
May 16	Unidentified lady	Discusses possible Italian translation	Unknown
29	Charles Reade	Missed him at theatre. Play changes	Private
June 10	Charles Ward	Discusses his account	PM
10	Unknown	Thanks for cutting. Personal details	Unknown
19	LS Wingfield	Can't attend. Suggests small meeting	Texas
July 8	Harper & Brothers	Sends first proofs of *Poor Miss Finch*	PM
19	William Tindell	Seeks factual advice	Glasgow
24	Cassell, Petter etc	Seeks illustration for Canada	Texas
26	William Tindell	"Don't forget the Codicil"	Glasgow
Aug 2	Cassell, Petter etc	Advice on Dutch & German publishers	Texas
2	James K Medbury	Not visiting US this year	Private
2	William Tindell	Can he see him tomorrow?	Glasgow
7	Unknown	Discusses US production of "Fosco"	Princeton
12	William Tindell	Wants agreement with Bancroft	Glasgow
14	William Tindell	Can he stop advertisement?	Glasgow
15	William Tindell	Thanks for draft agreement	Glasgow

Date	Recipient	Topic	Source
22	Cassell, Petter etc	Send payment to Coutt's	Texas
Sept 2	TW Satchell	Registration of *Moonstone*	Texas
19	TW Satchell	Copyright of magazine articles	Texas
19	William Tindell	Advice about copyright of plays	Glasgow
21	TW Satchell	Copyright of magazine articles	Unknown
21	Charles Ward	Discusses payment to relative	Private
22	Mrs Laura Seymour	Glad she likes *Poor Miss Finch*	Private
26	Cassell, Petter etc	Apologies for unnecessary parts	Texas
Oct 7	Elliott & Fry	Hopes to give sitting in week's time	Private
10	Cassell, Petter etc	Received cheque for friend's article	Texas
10	George Smith	*W. in White* play: success hoped	NYPL
12	Cassell, Petter etc	Friend wishes keep copyright	Texas
12	Georgina Hogarth	Seeks little subscription	Princeton
15	Charles Ward	Hoped he liked the play	PM
18	Charles Ward	Encloses first cheque *W. in White* play	PM
19	William Tindell	Queries Tinsley's commercial pos'n	Glasgow
23	Charles Ward	Encloses cheque. Can he dine?	PM
25	William Tindell	*Man & Wife*: advice on piracy	Glasgow
Oct 26	William Tindell	Can he keep Tinsley waiting?	Glasgow
30	Cassell, Petter etc	Detailed proposal on *Poor Miss Finch*	Texas
30	Thomas Galpin	Cannot accept publishing proposal	Texas
Nov 2	George Smith	Declined Cassell's proposed new edition	NYPL
2	Charles Ward	Cassell's refuse to come up to his price	PM
6	William Tindell	Seeks advice on Tinsley's references	Glasgow
8	Cassell, Petter etc	Asks for "purchase money"	Texas
8	RB Davy	Proposes to forward an answer	Private
8	William Tindell	Thanks for reference advice	Glasgow
13	William Tindell	Discusses security of money	Glasgow
16	William Tindell	Refuse Tinsley's offer	Glasgow
19	Charles Reade	Offers to introduce him to agent	Private
20	Charles Reade	*W. in White* play doing well	Private
22	EM Ward	Application to Benevolent Fund	Texas
24	EM Ward	Supports petition	Texas
27	William Tindell	Accepted offer from George Bentley	Glasgow
30	George Bentley	Cannot persuade Forster (on Dickens)	NYPL
Dec 2	A Daly	No time to read drama	Harvard
6	Charles Ward	Four more weekly parts: then Paris	PM
9	John Forster	Sends proofs of new story	Nat Art
12	Mrs WP Frith	Accepts invitation	V & A Mus
1872			
Jan 18	William Tindell	Discusses "notice to quit" to tenant	Glasgow
27	John Hollingshead	Gives advice on piracy of play	Huntington
29	William Tindell	Asks about expiry of copyright	Glasgow
Feb 10	Harper & Brothers	Received £200 for *Poor Miss Finch*	PM
19	William Tindell	Back from Ramsgate	Glasgow
22	TW Satchell	Discusses declaration of copyright	Unknown
22	CS Carter	Refusing proposals : Unable visit US	Private
29	TW Satchell	Thanks for copyright advice	Unknown
29	William Tindell	Asks advice on licencing performances	Glasgow
Mar 2	William Tindell	Not necessary to buy US law books	Glasgow
9	John Bonner	Discusses various plays	Private
11	William Tindell	Details of provincial agreement	Glasgow
13	William Tindell	Thanks for agreement	Glasgow
16	Cassell, Petter etc	Will answer Dr Lehmann's letter	Texas

Date	Recipient	Topic	Source
18	TW Satchell	Concerns Customs declaration	Texas
19	Cassell, Petter etc	Informs them of Bentley's edition	Texas
19	BC Tauchnitz	Discusses proposals for *Miss or Mrs?*	Unknown
22	Cassell, Petter etc	Will communicate with Bentley	Texas
April 9	JP Knight	Accepts invite to Royal Academy	Texas
12	TW Satchell	Discusses "notice" to Customs	Unknown
17	William Tindell	Asks advice about Vining	Glasgow
17	Augustus Dunlop	Declines contract for short story	Unknown
17	George Vining	Refuses to alter play. Will release him	Glasgow
20	Harper & Brothers	Offers a short story	PM
23	Harper & Brothers	Further details of short story	PM
May 10	George Smith	Concerning Customs regulations	NYPL
18	Harper & Brothers	Discusses terms for short story	PM
28	Harper & Brothers	Discusses library system	PM
June 10	William Tindell	Come to dinner. Tinsley "imbecile"	Glasgow
July 29	Theodore Michaelis	Regrets unable to meet	Kansas
Aug 5	J Palgrave Simpson	Seeks advice about play in Vienna	Private
16	William Tindell	Returns on Saturday. Then Lowestoft	Glasgow
Sept 20	William Tindell	Asks about registration of books	Glasgow
Nov 1	George Smith	*Man & Wife* play next January	NYPL
1	Sotheran & Co	Subscription for 1st issue only	Private
4	George Bentley	Will bring Tauchnitz edition	Illinois
4	Mrs WP Frith	Accepts invitation	V & A Mus
11	BW Bryant	Cannot accept his services	Texas
11	William Tindell	Sends draft agreement with Bentley	Glasgow
Dec 2	William Tindell	Encloses £51 cheque. Dinner Thursday	Glasgow
4	Charles Reade	Unable to keep dinner engagement	Private
11	J Palgrave Simpson	Cannot accept Clayton's proposal	Illinois
12	G Smith	Sales of novels	NLS
17	TH Hills	Thanks for the portrait	Private
26	Charles Mullar	Already has a German translator	Princeton
26	BC Tauchnitz	Is dedicating *Miss or Mrs?* to him	Unknown
26	William Tindell	May have to alter draft of new Will	Glasgow
28	Harper & Brothers	*New Magdalen*	PM
1873			
Feb 5	Virtue & Co	Cannot accept their proposal	Private
14	Holman Hunt	Confirms seat for play's first night	Huntington
14	EM Ward	Does he want two stalls seats?	Texas
March 2	J Palgrave Simpson	Will Clayton play "Julian Gray"?	Unknown
7	George Smith	Yes. Print the 5s editions	NLS
13	Mrs Cunliffe	Sends photographs. Hard at work	Texas
28	Mr & Mrs WP Frith	Cannot get to Drury Lane	V & A Mus
April 4	George Smith	Thanks for royalty cheque	NYPL
8	SA Hart	About Sir David Salomons' illness	Yale
16	Mrs Laura Seymour	Agrees to offer part elsewhere	Private
19	Charles Ward	Encloses cheque. Offers "pot luck"	Private
22	Dikar	Brother died. Characters in play cast	Texas
22	William Tindell	Proceed with Olympic agreement	Glasgow
May 1	Anthony Trollope	Accepts invitation	Princeton
5	Herbert Watkins	Thanks for the photographs	Texas
5	George Smith	Wants a few presentation copies	NYPL
7	George Smith	Will accept uniform series of books	NYPL
11	George Smith	Apologises for trouble	NYPL
12	Rev GJ Chester	Asks for support for Pigott at R A	Bodleian

Date	Recipient	Topic	Source
13	WP Frith	Offers two seats for *New Magdalen*	V & A Mus
15	George Smith	Thanks for books and cheque	NYPL
20	Royal Academy	Provides reference for Pigott	Huntington
20	Mr & Mrs Frith	Cannot accept dinner invitation	V & A Mus
24	D Booth Eyre	Reports first night reception	Princeton
31	George Smith	Gladly accepts proposal	NYPL
June 5	William Tindell	Friend will ask question on theatre	Glasgow
9	Anthony Trollope	Accepts invitation with pleasure	Princeton
10	Mrs WP Frith	Accepts invitation	V & A Mus
11	Lethbridge	Contact his friend, S Poles	Girton Camb
July 9	Mrs EM Ward	Cannot dine. Has rheumatism	Texas
17	Squire Bancroft	Man & Wife "magnificently acted"	Unknown
17	Edward Pigott	Very sorry he's not chosen by RA	Huntington
29	Lord Lymington	Cannot provide *W. in White* play	Private
Sept 2	William Tindell	Will be with him tomorrow	Glasgow
9	John Elderkin	Leaves for America Saturday	Princeton
11	Stefan Poles	Can act in Europe on *New Magdalen*	Glasgow
Oct 8	Duncan Sherman & Co	Encloses two cheques	Private
25	Unknown	Gives details of readings/travel	PM
30	George M Towle	Cannot accept invitation	Texas
Nov 16	Sebastian Schlesinger	Can Frank Ward help in South?	Private
Dec 13	JG Thompson	His report of trial led to short story	Private
1874			
Jan 17	Louise C Moulton	May be able to meet in Boston Lib.	Congress
17	Sebastian Schlesinger	Plans changed. Boston on Wednesday	Harvard
18	Joseph W Harper	Discusses stories for Library Edition	PM
27	Frank Archer	Discusses possible unauthorised play	Unknown
Feb 1	Joseph W Harper	Discusses three volume edition	PM
2	William Tindell	Gives him power to act in his name	Glasgow
March 2	Joseph W Harper	Sailing on Parthia Sat. Hopes to call	PM
7	Oliver W Holmes	Leaving at 11.00 on Parthia.	Lib Congress
7	William A Seaver	Sails "in snowstorm". Thanks	Yale
16	Cyrus W Field	On board. Gratitude for everything	PM
31	Frank Ward	Hearty congratulations. Meet soon	Princeton
April 10	William Tindell	Seeks legal advice (on Jos. Clow?)	Glasgow
25	William Tindell	Can he see him today?	Glasgow
May 7	George Smith	Introduces US writer to *The Cornhill*	NYPL
12	George Bentley	Accepts his advice	NYPL
16	TD Spain	Explains efforts to help Mr Bellew	BL
18	George Smith	Possible new edition *W. in White*	NYPL
27	George Smith	Will delay suggesting price change	NYPL
29	George Smith	Thanks for royalty cheque	NYPL
June 5	Unknown	Declines invitation	Unknown
8	HO Moore	Acknowledges receipt	Yale
13	Hollingshead	Will support "good cause"	Huntington
20	Joseph W Harper	Sends specimen of next book	PM
23	Mrs WP Frith	Accepts invitation	V & A Mus
25	William Tindell	Asks for *Graphic* agreement	Glasgow
July 3	George Bentley	Thanks for cheque. Will call	NYPL
16	William Tindell	Copyright in Australia and US	Glasgow
21	Joseph W Harper	Accepts proposal for US publication	PM
22	Phelp	Welcome to London. Can he lunch?	Private
Sept 9	James Munnings	Discusses re-publications	Texas

Date	Recipient	Topic	Source
9	Chatto & Windus	Signed *Law and the Lady* memo	Reading
Oct 24	Mrs Laura Seymour	Promises proof of *Law and the Lady*	Private
29	William Gale	Thanks for being elected	Texas
30	Mrs WP Frith	Accepts invitation	V & A Mus
Nov 5	Oliver W Holmes	Has dedicated *Readings* to him	Lib Con
6	William Tindell	Discusses translation & new publishers	Glasg
11	G Holsworth	Acknowledges cheque	Yale
16	Frank Archer	To revive *New Magdalen*. Casting	Unknown
19	Chatto & Windus	Agreement on 13 novels	Reading
23	William Tindell	Discusses agent proposal	Glasgow
30	[Tilford]	Orders several books	Princeton
Dec 18	Harper & Brothers	Acknowledges cheque. Sends proofs	Private
25	Harper & Brothers	Encloses proofs	PM
25	Charles Reade	Discusses his novel *A Hero*	Princeton
1875			
Jan 7	William Tindell	Just finished *Graphic* story	Glasgow
16	Chatto & Windus	Stereoplates of novels	Reading
28	William Tindell	Publication date of *Law & The Lady*	Glasgow
29	William Tindell	Has done right. *Graphic* been warned	Glasgow
29	William Tindell	Has seen *Graphic*. "Satisfied"	Glasgow
29	Henry Herman	Requests theatre tickets	Illinois
Feb 8	Chatto & Windus	£1000 paid for *Law & the Lady*	Reading
11	Charles Reade	Gives advice about *Graphic*	Princeton
27	William Tindell	Off to Paris next Friday	Glasgow
March 4	Thomas Woolner	Just leaving for Paris	Sydney
13	William Tindell	Back from Paris. Discusses actor	Glasgow
15	Mrs WP Frith	Accepts invitation	Princeton
16	William Tindell	Sent *Law & the Lady* yesterday	Glasgow
March 18	William Tindell	Discusses article in *The World*	Glasgow
27	George Bentley	Glad he approves letter in *The World*	NYPL
27	Richard Edgcumbe	Accepts membership of Committee	Unknown
April 9	George Bentley	Glad he accepts suggestion	NYPL
13	George Bentley	Thanks for £200 cheque (*Frozen Deep*)	NYPL
20	William Tindell	Returns corrected proofs	Glasgow
June 21	William Tindell	Discusses Italian copyright	Glasgow
23	William Tindell	Asks him to write direct to Italy	Glasgow
July 3	Hunter Rose & Co	Sends "little story"	Stanford
5	George Bentley	Considering "something new"	NYPL
29	George Bentley	Been ill. Suggests postponement	NYPL
Aug 27	William Tindell	Illness. Will comply with request	Glasgow
Sept 29	William A Seaver	Not well enough for New York	Yale
30	George Bentley	Hopes story to appear in January	NYPL
Oct 4	William Tindell	Going abroad	Glasgow
6	William Tindell	Discusses Will. Contacted Brussels	Glasgow
17	Mrs Sebastian Schlesinger	Declines invitation	Lib Con
Nov 8	Henry Herman	Returns first Act *Miss Gwilt*	Illinois
10	George Bentley	Returned from Continent. Sends copy	NYPL
20	Harper & Brothers	Sends part of *The Two Destinies*	Princeton
Dec 4	Edward Saker	Concerns Liverpool production	Illinois
12	Edward Saker	Thanks to all at Alexandra Theatre	Unknown
14	Moy Thomas	Discusses proposal for US authors	Texas
21	William Tindell	Sends Italian address	Glasgow

Date	Recipient	Topic	Source
1876			
Jan 15	Ford Maddox Brown	Thanks for memoir about his son	M/C Lib
26	Frank Archer	Too fagged to offer him something	Unknown
Feb 28	George Bentley	Thanks for cheque. Is rheumatic	NYPL
March 14	Jesup, Paton & Co	Thanks for Shakespeare as an artist	Princeton
April 19	Mrs Laura Seymour	Discusses first night of *Miss Gwilt*	Private
19	George Bentley	When does *Temple Bar* go to press?	NYPL
28	Mrs Austin	Encloses theatre tickets	Private
May 3	Hunter Rose & Co	Acknowledges £50	Princeton
4	Harper & Brothers	Encloses June part	Princeton
7	J Weekes	Has written no sequel to *Fallen Leaves*	Private
19	Reginald Hanson	Declines invitation from Lord Mayor	Princeton
20	William Seaver	Milburn and son well received	Princeton
June 6	Harper & Brothers	Sends conclusion for July	Princeton
13	Hunter Rose & Co	*Two Destinies* completed September	Princeton
15	Charles Dickens Jnr	Discusses Christmas story	PM
July 2	Unknown	French translation already arranged	Texas
4	Andrew Chatto	Requests two bound editions	Princeton
29	George Bentley	Thanks for cheque. *Destinies* in proof	NYPL
Sept 4	George Bentley	Going away for a month	NYPL
Oct 17	William Tindell	Paris. Starting for Calais next Friday	Glasgow
18	William Tindell	Theatre matter now gone too far	Glasgow
18	Charles Reade	*No Thoroughfare*'s casting	Private
21	Lord Mayor	Declines invitation	Private
24	Andrew Chatto	Apologises for error	Melbourne
25	Andrew Chatto	Has agreed Christmas story for US	Princeton
Nov 10	Mrs Laura Seymour	Explains absence from rehearsal	Private
Dec 7	George Bentley	Arranges meeting	Illinois
29	Mrs Laura Seymour	Declines dinner invitation. Is ill	Private
1877			
Jan 29	Charles Dickens Jnr	Accepts terms for *All The Year Round*	PM
Feb 9	Kate Field	Going to Paris. Gives views on play	Boston
March 10	Kate Field	Has gout. Cannot get to theatre yet	Boston
10	HP Sumter	Rights for German translation gone	Texas
15	Madame Lue	French translation rights bought	Private
17	Latey	Happy to see Mr Ingram	Private
17	Unknown	Repeats facts about translation rights	Texas
22	Frank Archer	Photo received. Recovering from gout	Unknown
May 15	R Monckton Milnes	Declines invitation. Confined to room	Cambridge
25	Mrs Laura Seymour	Rheumatic knees. Discusses casting	Private
June 1	Edwin de Leon	Rheumatism. Hopes to see him.	Princeton
July 4	Mrs Laura Seymour	Caroline left her *Moonstone* first act	Private
7	George Bentley	Has had to defer sitting. Crippled knees	NYPL
Aug 16	Wybert Reeve	Delighted he is in town. Will meet	Princeton
17	Miss Folkard	Gives advice to actress	PM
Sept 8	Fanny Davenport	Encloses "piece". Will write next week	Texas
13	Mrs Laura Seymour	Cannot attend rehearsal. Knees bad	Private
18	Alfred de Stern	Thanks for good wishes	Salomon's
25	Augustin Daly	Ideas for new *Moonstone* play title	NYPL
26	Carlotta Leclerq	Resting [in Brussels]. See on return	Fales NYU
Oct 23	Andrew Chatto	Accepts terms for *Two Destinies*	Princeton
Dec 3	BC Tauchnitz	Alert on *My Lady's Money*	Unknown
4	Norris J Foster	Been travelling in Italy	Yale

Date	Recipient	Topic	Source
1878			
Jan 12	Chatto & Windus	Paid for: article & cheap edition	Reading
25	George Bentley	Please send M/S here	NYPL
Feb 16	Mrs Lancing Thurber	Contributes to autograph collection	Private
March 13	Tom Cullen	Contributes to aurograph collection	Private
16	Andrew Chatto	Thanks. Has written note	Princeton
16	Sampson Low etc	Deliver 209 copies of *Basil*	Princeton
April 1	Andrew Chatto	Timing for setting up monthly part	Princeton
6	Hunter Rose	Encloses first part of *Haunted Hotel*	Private
8	Andrew Chatto	Asks him to write to Australia	Princeton
24	Andrew Chatto	Encloses second part *Haunted Hotel*	Princeton
30	Chatto & Windus	Sends proofs corrections	Princeton
May 1	Andrew Chatto	Corrected proofs of *Haunted Hotel*	Princeton
16	Chatto & Windus	Discusses numbering of chapters	Princeton
23	Mr Oppenheim	Will do his best to get better	Princeton
31	Blanchard Jerrold	Approves his intentions	Fales NYU
June 3	Eduard Hallberger	German version already under way	Fales NYU
10	GF Rowe	Refuses request to perform *No Name*	Harvard
15	Chatto & Windus	Thanks for £50 cheque	Princeton
19	Chatto & Windus	Sends 4th part of *Haunted Hotel*	Princeton
19	Charles Dickens Jnr	Does he object to story reprint?	PM
July 2	WH Steedman	Authorises sending of M/S	Private
14	Charles Reade	Hoped to invite to dinner but ill	Private
24	Chatto & Windus	Sends copy	Princeton
August 5	William Winter	Likes Byron & Scott. Praises Cavendish	Stanford
10	Chatto & Windus	Thanks for £50 cheque	Princeton
12	Chatto & Windus	Sends more copy	Princeton
14	Andrew Chatto	Can he cut last part in half?	Princeton
17	Chatto & Windus	Sends corrected proof	Huntington
31	Andrew Chatto	Got cheque. Breezy days in Ramsgate	Princeton
31	Chatto & Windus	Thanks for £50 cheque	Princeton
Sept 30	Andrew Chatto	Publication dates for *Haunted Hotel*	Princeton
Oct 2	Chatto & Windus	Sends story for *The Belgravia Annual*	Princeton
10	Chatto & Windus	Sends proof corrections	Princeton
11	Georgina Hogarth	Will see her next week	Princeton
12	Chatto & Windus	Title-page & dedications approved	Princeton
15	EJ [Collings]	Sends photograph	Princeton
21	Andrew Chatto	Asks for publishing details for friends	Princeton
21	Robson & Sons	Sends weekly copy of new story	Texas
23	Andrew Chatto	Discusses advertising *Haunted Hotel*	Princeton
Nov 5	Chatto & Windus	Queries "publication" of *Haunted Hotel*	Princeton
6	Chatto & Windus	Pleased with presentation copies	Princeton
15	James Payn	Accepts dinner invitation	Princeton
18	Trubner & Co	Explains his right to copyright	Stanford
19	Trubner & Co	Agrees to English circulation	Stanford
19	Chatto & Windus	Explains his US copyright decision	Princeton
20	Chatto & Windus	Has written to Trubner & Co	Princeton
25	George Bentley	Sends proofs	NYPL
25	Mrs Woolner	Declines dinner invitation	Private
Dec 18	WH Freemantle	Contributes £5 to Poor Fund	Fales NYU
27	George Bentley	Discusses "A Rogue's Life"	NYPL
30	Chatto & Windus	Expects payment punctually for story	Princeton
31	Chatto & Windus	Acknowledges £39 cheque	Princeton

Date	Recipient	Topic	Source
1879			
Jan 11	Alfred de Stern	Concerns luncheon engagement	Salomon's Hse
16	George Bentley	Thanks for copy of "The Rogue"	NYPL
21	Alfred de Stern	Luncheon engagement	Salomon's Hse
23	Hunter Rose & Co	Thanks for cheque. Awaits terms	NYPL
Feb 1	WE Adams	Thanks for cutting	Texas
4	Henry Herman	Suggests changes in play proposal	Princeton
10	George Bentley	Will work on "Rogue" tomorrow	NYPL
13	George Bentley	Encloses corrected "Rogue"	NYPL
15	George Stewart	Terms for Canadian publications	Private
24	Mrs EM Ward	Cannot help with correspondence	Texas
27	Henry Herman	Has written to Miss Davenport	Princeton
March 5	George Bentley	Hopes to send "Rogue" to printers	NYPL
21	Charles Reade	[Unavailable]	Private
24	George Bentley	Agreement. Will remember suggestion	NYPL
25	George Bentley	Thanks for gift of "The Rogue"	NYPL
28	JH Addison	Makes appointment	Private
April 1	George Bentley	Asks advice	NYPL
9	Carlotta Leclerq	Thinks draft play is "such rubbish"	Texas
10	Hunter Rose & Co	Seeks his confirmation of terms	Fales NYU
10	Mrs Olive Logan Sikes	Hopes to visit them shortly	Texas
22	George Bentley	Has he read *Fallen Leaves* proofs?	NYPL
May 21	Andrew Chatto	Has not heard about *Fallen Leaves*	Princeton
28	Chatto & Windus	Sends printed copy. Asks for proofs	Princeton
30	Chatto & Windus	Second volume copy complete	Princeton
June 5	Andrew Chatto	Introduces illustrator	Princeton
11	Chatto & Windus	Sends 3rd volume *Fallen Leaves*	Melbourne
11	C Thomas	Encloses corrected proofs	Private
18	Charles Ward	Caroline and cheques. Courier advice	Princeton
21	C Thomas	Corrections to proof	Princeton
24	Andrew Chatto	Encloses agreement *Fallen Leaves*	Private
25	GA Sala	Discusses recent legal wrangles	Yale
30	Andrew Chatto	Returns proofs. Translation rights	Princeton
July 15	Chatto & Windus	Thanks for copies of *Fallen Leaves*	Princeton
29	Charles Reade	Writes about Laura Seymour [death]	Private
Nov 6	EA Buck	Mending slowly. Suggests title	Texas
7	FD Finlay	Declines invitation. "Rheumatic gout"	Yale
14	Mrs J E Millais	Declines wedding invitation. Away	PM
15	EA Buck	Date for Christmas story	Unknown
Dec 3	AS Barnes & Co	Sends proofs. Asks for terms	Private
18	Paul [Jungling]	Refuses German translation rights	Princeton
18	Unknown	Discusses terms of German translation	Texas
1880			
Jan 1	R Lehmann	Accepts invitation	Unknown
8	Mrs Meredith	Thanks for gift	Princeton
9	Chatto & Windus	New story ready for publication	Unknown
9	Frederick Lehmann	Will willingly sit for his brother	Princeton
Feb 2	Chatto & Windus	Irate at proof mistakes	Princeton
15	Tillotson & Co	Encloses Dickens's letter	Bolton
19	Chatto & Windus	Encloses agreement: *Jezebel*	Princeton
24	Frederick Enoch	Encloses M/S of first *Armadale* play	Huntington
March 2	Chatto & Windus	Asks about early copy of *Jezebel*	Princeton

Date	Recipient	Topic	Source
4	Miss HA Lowe	Contributes autograph	Unknown
13	George Bentley	Sorry to miss him. In good health	Illinois
22	CCB Tauchnitz	Happy to accept arrangement	Unknown
31	Harry	Come [to Ramsgate] for day or two	Princeton
April 12	Carlotta Leclerq	She is right to accept apologies	Princeton
14	Williams & Norgate	Help needed with Customs	Private
16	Rudolph Lehmann	At his service next Monday	BL
20	Andrew Chatto	Has written to Colonel	Princeton
30	Leader & Sons	Gives consent to South London Press	Princeton
May 19	Andrew Chatto	Declines invitation to Caroline	Princeton
20	William Seaver	Welcomes him to London	Yale
June 1	Unknown	Seeks offer for new serial story	Private
1	Rev William Sharman	Thanks for sympathy	Fales NYU
3	Rudolph Lehmann	Come here Sunday: Richmond visit	Princeton
5	Mrs James Payn	Sorry about father's illness	Princeton
9	Unknown	Third attempt to send book	Private
18	Unknown	Glad to receive book	Portsmouth
July 20	Miss Tiny	Thanks: "one of the prettiest presents"	Unknown
Aug 16	Tillotson & Son	May return to writing for stage	Bolton
1881			
Jan 12	William Seaver	Asks advice New York proposal	Princeton
Feb 8	Baroness de Stern	Declines dinner invitation	Salomon's Hse
23	George Maclean Rose	Encloses small correction	Princeton
March 3	Andrew Chatto	Can he look at proofs	Princeton
5	Baroness de Stern	Accepts dinner invitation	Private
10	Alfred de Stern	"Dramatic pilgrimage" to *King Lear*	Salomon's
11	Andrew Chatto	Asks about publication day	Princeton
11	Alexander A Knox	Has heard about him from Pigott	Unknown
29	Charles L Kenney	Will help his daughter on stage	Harvard
30	Andrew Chatto	Legal changes to agreement	Princeton
April 7	Chatto & Windus	Praises presentation copies	Princeton
8	Andrew Chatto	Will bring agreement with him	Princeton
15	Eveline M Burnblum	Sends photograph as thanks	Texas
28	Mr Johnson	Asks him to call about proposition	Unknown
June 22	Kemsley & [Kington]	Nothing by him for new Journal	Princeton
24	J Palgrave Simpson	Asks for support for Charles Kent	Unknown
July 13	Andrew Chatto	Declines invitation: rheumatic gout	Princeton
15	James R Osgood	Has been ill. Hopes to see him	Private
August 5	Chatto & Windus	Asks for details of *Belgravia* stories	Princeton
8	Charles Willis	Writes about *The Fallen Leaves*	Princeton
10	Andrew Chatto	Sending corrections. Mentions new story	Princeton
Sept 2	GM Fenn	Agrees to extracts from his books	Texas
9	Andrew Chatto	Returns proofs. May pick up idea at sea	Princeton
10	Andrew Chatto	Presentation copies arrived safely	Princeton
22	James R Osgood	Promises details about Fechter	Harvard
Oct 8	Richard D'Oyly Carte	Good wishes for the New Theatre	Fales NYU
17	Chatto & Windus	Returns proofs	Melbourne
24	EA Buck	Encloses proof of new work	Unknown
28	R du Pontavice de Heussey	Keep M/S for present	Princeton
Nov 1	WS Johnson	Can he call to discuss proposal?	Private
3	Chatto & Windus	Criticises advertisement	Princeton
8	Andrew Chatto	Asks publication date. Requests proof	Princeton

Date	Recipient	Topic	Source
8	R du Pontavice de Heussey	Delighted to see his brother	Princeton
19	Andrew Chatto	"Here is the new story"	Princeton
21	Chatto & Windus	Could he have proofs Christmas story	Princeton
22	Francis Carr Beard	The new actress won't do	Princeton
28	HJ Nicoll	Provides biographical details	Texas
Dec 3	Chatto & Windus	Thanks for cheque	Princeton
5	James Payn	Ashamed not to have returned it	Private
10	AP Watt	Formal agreement to terms	Private
1882			
Jan 6	Jane Ward	Will see Mr White. Wedding a triumph	Princeton
16	Charles Kent	Has read story. Thanks for present	Princeton
18	JR Osgood	Promises memories of Fechter	Unknown
31	Charles Kent	Has written to Charles Reade	Princeton
Feb 1	Chatto & Windus	Thanks for £100 – *Law and the Lady*	Reading
1	Chatto & Windus	Thanks for £31 cheque	Unknown
4	OH Peck	Contributes an autograph	Private
4	AP Watt	He is to control US interest in story	Private
6	Andrew Chatto	Seeks advice on play copyright	Princeton
9	Andrew Chatto	Returns slip with thanks	Princeton
10	W Holman Hunt	Sends *The Black Robe* by book post	Huntington
10	Charles Kent	Gout in eye. Discusses Society ballot	Texas
10	Alfred Arthur Reade	Explains how tobacco affects his work	Huntington
28	Charles Kent	Says Pigott will give his signature	Princeton
March 10	AP Watt	Has agent in Melbourne already	Private
31	Charles Kent	Sorry to miss him. Correcting play	Princeton
April 11	Robert du Pontavice de Heussey	Asks him to help with play	Private
22	[Frank] Marshall	Declines invitation. Gouty signs	Princeton
24	Andrew Chatto	1st Volume of collected stories ready	Princeton
May 3	JE Smith	Grants rights for *Black & White*	NYPL
13	Charles Kent	Involved in new serial story	Kansas
17	Rosa Kenney	Analyses her performance on stage	Harvard
24	AP Watt	Getting better. Glad to see him	Private
June 1	AP Watt	Sends cutting from proof	Private
2	AP Watt	Regarding proofs	Private
5	Andrew Chatto	Promises more chapters	Princeton
8	Chatto & Windus	Sends copy for four chapters	Princeton
10	Nina Lehmann	Gout in eyes. No hope for tomorrow	Pym
10	GM Rose	Comments on US copyright	Princeton
12	Andrew Chatto	Sends more copy	Princeton
13	Charles Kent	Had gout in eye when he called	Princeton
16	H Biers	Sending weekly parts by book post	Private
20	AP Watt	Sending parts to Australia, Canada & US	Private
July 4	Andrew Chatto	Discusses length of weekly parts	Princeton
13	Dr CA Gordon	Thanks him for medical book & facts	Private
13	Thomas Woolner	Asks him support candidate at Savile Club	PM
13	George Bentley	Asks him support candidate	Private
25	Andrew Chatto	Adds 3 more pages to weekly part	Princeton
26	Kate Field	Discusses Dickens portrait & Fechter	Boston
26	AP Watt	Has had 3 applications for new novel	Private
27	GM Rose	Refers to "morganatic family"	Princeton
Aug 11	AP Watt	Forwarded weekly proofs to Australia	Private
23	Chatto & Windus	Acknowledges cheque for £25	Princeton

Date	Recipient	Topic	Source
23	Andrew Chatto	Sends friend's story for their verdict	Private
25	AP Watt	Forwarded weekly parts to Australia	Private
31	AP Watt	Acknowledges £199	Private
Sept 9	AP Watt	Indicates misprint in revises	Private
12	Carlotta Leclerq	Declines dealing with man about his play	Princeton
Oct 4	Chatto & Windus	Acknowledges £22 cheque	Princeton
26	AP Watt	Payment for *Heart & Science*	Private
27	GM Rose	Glad firm has "risen from its ashes"	Princeton
30	AP Watt	Glad Tauchnitz has outbid opposition	Private
31	Chatto & Windus	Received cheque for £28	Bodleian
31	AP Watt	Proposal for short story agreed	Private
Nov 2	Carlotta Leclerq	Will consult his lawyers	Princeton
21	Chatto & Windus	Is sending rest of *Heart & Science*	Princeton
26	AP Watt	Will be a week late with part	Private
27	Chatto & Windus	Asks for proofs	Princeton
Dec 1	Chatto & Windus	Has received cheque for £26	Princeton
3	Andrew Chatto	Seeks pamphlet for *Heart & Science*	Princeton
4	AP Watt	Needs date when M/S is wanted	Private
6	Andrew Chatto	Story will not end this week	Princeton
8	AP Watt	Sending Xmas story	Private
13	AP Watt	No terms to sever Tauchnitz connection	Private
15	AP Watt	Sends corrected proof Xmas story	Texas
18	AP Watt	"Quite worn out". "Overworked"	Private
19	Unknown	Seeks revisions. Thanks for courtesy	Private
27	AP Watt	Thanks for cheque and his devotion	Unknown
29	Charles Kent	Sore chest; weak heart. Finished book	Unknown
1883			
Jan 4	AP Watt	*Heart & Science* book form in April	Private
23	Rosa Kenney	Not well enough to go to theatre	Private
31	[Andrew Chatto]	Discusses book proofs	Princeton
Feb 1	AP Watt	Acknowledges cheque	Private
9	Chatto & Windus	Thanks for proofs	Princeton
12	Unknown	Thanks for ticket. Attack of gout	Private
16	Roma Le Thière	Thanks for calling. Hopes for future	Fales NYU
19	Chattro & Windus	Acknowledged cheque for £32	Princeton
21	AP Watt	"Gouty eye improving"	Private
23	AP Watt	Discusses American rights new book	Private
24	WM Laffan	US thefts of *Heart & Science*	Texas
March 5	Charles Kent	Discusses comedy *Darnley*	Princeton
8	WF Tillotson	New novel periodical rights sold	Bolton
9	Editor, *Belgravia*	Discusses revisions *Heart & Science*	Texas
9	Andrew Chatto	Delighted to see him Monday	Princeton
13	Andrew Chatto	Value of Heart & Science copyright?	Princeton
19	Andrew Chatto	Decided on 7-year lease	Princeton
24	WM Laffan	Earlier date for *Heart & Science*	Texas
27	Andrew Chatto	Will look over the agreement	Princeton
April 2	Andrew Chatto	Discusses *Black Robe* agreement	Princeton
5	Napoleon Sarony	Portrait arrived. Book sent to him	Fales NYU
7	Andrew Chatto	Signs duplicate agreement	Princeton
10	Chatto & Windus	Acknowledges cheque for £33	Princeton
12	CCB Tauchnitz	Glad his father against vivisection	Unknown
16	[Henry Higgins]	Encloses lines to be inserted	Unknown
19	AP Watt	Contacting Fotheringham	Private
19	AA Reade	Natural champagne is his help	Princeton

Date	Recipient	Topic	Source
19	MJG Fotheringham	Register *Heart & Science* in Paris	Private
20	AP Watt	Sends cheque for books	Private
24	FP Cobb	Mentioned him in preface	Huntington
25	Unknown	Needs copy of Act 4	Texas
29	Henry Higgins	Discusses copying of play	Texas
30	Arthur [?]	Very sorry. He submits	Princeton
[April]	Frank Archer	Miss Lingard to play chief part	Unknown
May 5	Frank Archer	Delightful evening. Analyses play	Unknown
8	Henry Higgins	1st Act of *Rank & Riches* to Bruce	Kansas
10	Henry Pigott	Encloses & discusses *Frozen Deep*	Huntington
11	[Henry Higgins]	Alterations to 4th Act	Unknown
13	[Higgins]	Requests corrected drafts	Unknown
15	Andrew Chatto	Never sees reviews. How is it going?	Princeton
17	[Henry Higgins]	Requests corrected 1st Act	Princeton
17	Unknown	Is returning photograph	Private
19	Andrew Chatto	Discusses two cuttings	Princeton
May	[Chatto & Windus]	Encloses corrections	Princeton
June 4	Chatto & Windus	Thanks for £33 cheque	Princeton
5	Unknown	Cast of play had been completed	Princeton
6	Andrew Chatto	"Splendid" recognition in *The World*	Princeton
8	Andrew Chatto	Encloses two stalls tickets	Princeton
9	Ada Cavendish	How many places for performance?	Bodleian
9	Edmund Yates	Article has claims on his gratitude	Private
16	Charles Sugden	Caught gout in time. Praises his acting	Princeton
17	Henry Higgins	Promises 2nd and 3rd Acts	Princeton
19	Ezra Bower	Obstacles to *Fallen Leaves* sequel	Unknown
25	WM Laffan	AP Watt acts with full authority	Texas
30	GM Rose	Acknowledges £40. See him in London	Princeton
July 1	EA Buck	M/S *Rank & Riches*. Defends his play	Texas
3	Chatto & Windus	Received £20	Princeton
9	Charles Kent	Come today at 4	Princeton
15	Andrew Chatto	Come for lunch tomorrow	Princeton
17	AP Watt	Asks approval of letter to Tillotson	Private
20	AP Watt	Approves advertisement	Private
Aug 13	Henry Higgins	Seeks name of Belgian translator	PM
17	Alberic Iserbyt	Encloses answer to Mr Herman	Princeton
17	Thomas [Stewart]	Is returning signed photograph	Private
18	Fanny	Thanks for pears. Will see Pritchard	PM
22	AP Watt	Testimonial. He is now agent & friend	Private
Oct 1	Alberic Iserbyt	Sends German letter for translation	Princeton
3	Alberic Iserbyt	Thanks for translation. Sends answer	Princeton
9	AP Watt	Has "gout again"	Private
16	AP Watt	French translation of *Heart & Science*	Private
17	Andrew Chatto	Asks for M/S to be read. Gout in eye	Princeton
18	Edward Pritchard	Can he defer appointment?	Princeton
18	Edward Pritchard	Returns proof of circular	Texas
20	Edward Pritchard	Thanks him for proof	Texas
22	[JH] Hamilton	Encloses £35. Discusses payments	Fales NYU
30	AP Watt	Corrects telegram to Watt	Private
Nov 3	JA Rosier	Declines performance of *W. in White*	Princeton
9	John F Phayre	Returns corrected proofs *I Say No*	Texas
12	Andrew Chatto	Proposal for Indian translation	Princeton
25	AP Watt	Concerns timing of Christmas story	Private
29	AP Watt	Consents to transfer of *I Say No*	Private
30	AP Watt	Asks if Watt can act in Melbourne	Private

Date	Recipient	Topic	Source
30	AP Watt	Has not heard from Melbourne agent	Private
Dec 3	AP Watt	*I Say No* for *All The Year Round*?	Private
4	Andrew Chatto	Watt will deliver copy tomorrow	Princeton
7	Charles Kent	Decision right: sacrifice justified	Princeton
14	AP Watt	Refuses consent for story transfer	Private
15	Kelly & Co	Breach of contract. Applies for proofs	Private
15	AP Watt	Encloses copy of Kelly letter	Private
18	Andrew Chatto	Can they print *I Say No*?	Princeton
23	AP Watt	*I Say No* running smoothly again	Private
24	Harper & Brothers	Sends proofs directly	Texas
27	Beechene, Yaxley & Co	Thanks for their gift of sherry	Texas
28	Douglas [?]	Thanks for "token of remembrance"	Fales NYU
[1883]	George H Putnam	Praises book by woman author [AK Green]	Unknown
1884			
Jan 3	AP Watt	Thanks for cheque for *Royal Love*	Private
4	Alberic Iserbyt	Asks for German translation	Princeton
5	AP Watt	Is sending copy	Private
6	FP Cobbe	Discusses reprints of *Heart & Science*	Private
7	Alberic Iserbyt	Translation fees for work	Princeton
10	AP Watt	Alerts him to a piracy	Private
12	AP Watt	Thanks for advice. Accepts it	Private
15	JF Phayre	"Act of audacious literacy robbery"	Texas
16	AP Watt	No sign of proofs yet	Private
17	AP Watt	Sorry to miss him	Private
18	Mr Charles	Asks for private box ticket	Princeton
22	Harper & Brothers	Robbery by Philadelphia publisher	Texas
22	AP Watt	Gives him M/S and list of revises	Private
28	Sebastian Schlesinger	Not received "Minstrel Boy"	Harvard
Feb 7	AP Watt	Sends 5th part of *I Say No*	Private
9	Alberic Iserbyt	Asks for letter translation	Princeton
12	Beechene, Yaxley & Co	Can publish his letter in circular	Texas
12	Unknown	Contributes to autograph collection	Princeton
21	Frederick Kerr	Praises his stage performance	Princeton
21	George F Rowe	Returns newspaper cuttings	Texas
26	Alberic Iserbyt	Thanks for translation	Princeton
March 13	JF Hamilton	Explains transfer of foreign money	Private
13	Alberic Iserbyt	Requests German translation	Princeton
15	Alberic Iserbyt	Thanks for translation. Sends reply	Princeton
17	AP Watt	Drove out and made calls	Private
21	Charles Kent	When will he come?	Unknown
26	Charles Kent	Requests alternative appointment	Princeton
28	AP Watt	If get rid of Kellys will celebrate	Private
April 1	AP Watt	Delays due to Post Office	Private
3	AP Watt	Acknowledges money	Private
3	Edmund Yates	Read law report with sorrow	Kentucky
8	Edward Pigott	Discusses dangers of piracy	Huntington
15	AP Watt	Kellys haven't sent all proofs	Private
18	Mr Charles	Thanks for return of picture	Princeton
19	JF Phayre	Cannot write Charles Reade obit	Texas
21	AP Watt	Sends copy	Private
[April 1884]	Mary Anderson	Praises her performance	Unknown
May 3	George Bentley	Is writing serial story. Cannot comply	NYPL
5	JF Phayre	Use duplicates for *I Say No* reprint	Unknown
11	AP Watt	Sending one chapter of *I Say No*	Private

Date	Recipient	Topic	Source
19	AP Watt	Thanks for relieving mind on Tauchnitz	Private
20	TD Galpin	Will not forget friendly offer	Private
20	Alberic Iserbyt	Thanks for prompt translation	Princeton
20	[J Simpson]	Grateful for registering *I Say No*	PM
21	Harper & Brothers	Hopes to finish *I Say No* with 30th part	Texas
21	AP Watt	Hopes to finish *I Say No* with July 5	Private
22	Alberic Iserbyt	Another letter for translation	Princeton
27	Harper & Brothers	Sends first instalment of conclusion	Texas
27	AP Watt	Has sent copy	Private
28	AP Watt	Likes idea of halfpenny public	Private
30	AP Watt	Will consider Xmas story	Private
June 2	AP Watt	Sending penultimate part	Private
3	Alberic Iserbyt	Another letter from Berlin	Princeton
8	AP Watt	Sending last weekly part	Private
9	JF Phayre	Concerns revisions to *I Say No*	Unknown
17	Harper & Brothers	Sends proofs direct to them	Unknown
23	AP Watt	Last part so long may need cutting	Private
July 3	AP Watt	This artist thinks for himself	Private
4	Alberic Iserbyt	More letters from Berlin: translate	Princeton
8	WF Tillotson	Short stories already purchased	Bolton
11	FH Biers	Appoints Australian representative	PM
21	Elliott & Fry	Not availed himself of proposal	Private
21	Charles Kent	Book finished	Private
22	Alberic Iserbyt	Is he still in London?	Princeton
22	Jane Ward	Gives advice about family trust fund	Princeton
23	Charles Kent	Suggests meeting on Friday	Princeton
24	Alberic Iserbyt	Thanks for quick response	Princeton
27	AP Watt	Looking forward to friend's yacht	Private
Aug 3	Andrew Chatto	When will they make printing decision	Princeton
18	P Hamilton Hayne	Has sent poem to Mr Chatto	Philadelphia
26	George Evans	No letters of John Leech	Harvard
30	Miss Mairs	Answers her personal questions	Unknown
Sep 15	P Hamilton Hayne	Chatto cannot print poem. Off to sea	Unknown
Oct 13	AP Watt	Back after "salting" on friend's yacht	Private
15	Alberic Iserbyt	Thanks for translation. Sends reply	Princeton
17	AP Watt	Gout in eye. Been re-thinking story	Private
30	Viscount Portman	Not his intention to renew lease	Preston
30	AP Watt	Had relapse. Will he see Tillotson?	Private
30	John R Whitley	Can put name on Council of Welcome	Holborn
31	AP Watt	Better. Encloses letter to Tillotson	Private
Nov 14	AP Watt	Sending more of "Girl at the Gate"	Private
15	AP Watt	Elliott is an old friend	Private
17	Williams & Norgate	Authority for delivery of 6 novels	Princeton
26	Emily Clunes	Sends his portrait	Texas
27	Perry Mason & Co	AP Watt is his representative	Yale
27	AP Watt	Explains mistake about father's picture	Private
Dec 2	JM Russell	Declines proposals	Stanford
6	Charles Kent	Getting over gout attack	Princeton
11	Beechene, Yaxley & Co	Thanks for cheque	Texas
12	AP Watt	Thanks for his help	Private
15	Andrew Chatto	Asks for details of bookbinder	Princeton
17	AP Watt	Encloses request for a syndicated novel	Private
19	AP Watt	Regrets missing him	Private
21	Charles Kent	Call on Dr Beard before Xmas	Princeton
24	Andrew Chatto	Thanks for presentation copies	Melbourne

Date	Recipient	Topic	Source
24	Ernest March	The work he mentions is *Man & Wife*	Texas
30	Mr & Mrs GW Childs	Good wishes for New Year	Princeton
30	Mrs Williams	Good wishes for New Year	Private
1885			
Jan 5	Manager, Mutual Insurance	Requests reminder	Princeton
6	George Bentley	Impact of foreign parcels post	NYPL
9	Charles Kent	Caught cold in the chest	Princeton
10	Alberic Iserbyt	Two letters to translate	Princeton
14	Henry Bartley	Beauty of their birthday present	Princeton
15	Harry D Waller	Encloses a letter from Charles Dickens	Princeton
18	JA Rosier	Glad to him on Tuesday	Princeton
19	Charles Kent	Views on Dr Beard's stomach illness	Princeton
27	Sebastian Schlesinger	Thanks for ducks. Will help him	Harvard
30	Holman Hunt	Will be at Studio on Sunday	Huntington
Feb 16	Holman Hunt	M/S received. Will send advice	Huntington
19	Andrew Chatto	Comments on novel he received	Princeton
20	Holman Hunt	Comments on M/S of picture	Princeton
March 7	Rev JA Jennings	Unable to give permission to republish	Princeton
10	Edmund Yates	"Hoorah"	Queensland
11	Mary Anderson	Heart running down. Ghost story	Unknown
16	Charles Kent	Wants to report on Ramsgate. Beard ill	Princeton
April 5	Charles Kent	Has been ill. Can he come Tuesday?	Princeton
9	AP Watt	Had neuralgia. Tillotson story complete	Private
14	Mary Anderson	Wants to find subject for play	Unknown
18	Charles Kent	Will next Friday suit him?	Princeton
23	Harriet Bartley	Bring last 6 pages. Has just seen children	Texas
23	Beechene, Yaxley & Co	Wishes to try case of port	Texas
24	AP Watt	Will send M/S [*Evil Genius*] next week	Texas
27	Mrs GL Dickinson	Contributes to her collection	Huntington
28	P Hamilton Hayne	Got printed sonnet. Had neuralgia	Unknown
28	AP Watt	Sends M/S Tillotson story	Private
May 2	AP Watt	Sorry servant did not let him in	Private
7	TH Sweet Escott	Will comply with request. Needs time	BL
10	AP Watt	Ramsgate landlady has let her house	Private
13	AP Watt	Seaside trip put off	Private
20	Ada Cavendish	Encloses note concerning Miss Melon	Private
20	AP Watt	Has had 6 revises of "The Ghost's Touch"	Private
21	AP Watt	About Tillotson and Perry Mason	Private
21	William Winter	Come for lunch	Private
June 7	Mrs Holman Hunt	Declines invitation. About to try sea air	Huntington
11	Charles J Davis	Agrees to be Honorary Steward	Princeton
12	Charles Kent	Has run away to sea air	Princeton
14	AP Watt	Is at Ramsgate. Discusses Tillotson	Private
19	Andrew Chatto	Asks if he wants a little sea air	Princeton
20	Andrew Chatto	Thanks for £38	Princeton
24	AP Watt	Returning Monday. Infernal noises	Private
26	Charles Kent	Come to see him after Monday	Princeton
July 2	AP Watt	Delighted to see you tomorrow	Private
3	Beechene, Yaxley & Co	Orders half bottles champagne	Texas
4	AP Watt	Lawyer says Tillotson in the wrong	Private
13	Beechene, Yaxley & Co	Champagne not dry enough	Texas
22	AP Watt	Will he look in tomorrow	Private
24	AP Watt	Tillotson not to advertise book until ...	Private

Date	Recipient	Topic	Source
25	AP Watt	Counsel says title to be abandoned	Private
Aug 7	WF Tillotson	Encloses receipt for cheque	Bolton
7	AP Watt	Tillotson has sent £300 cheque	Private
10	AP Watt	Is sending commission to his clerk	Private
11	Beechene, Yaxley & Co	Champagne dry but not old enough	Texas
17	P Hamilton Hayne	Encloses short story. Is better again	Unknown
25	Alberic Iserbyt	Another German translation	Princeton
Sept 13	AP Watt	Tillotson annoying. Write to him	Private
14	AP Watt	*Bolton Journal* announcing *Evil Genius*	Private
16	AP Watt	Glad there is grace in Tillotson	Private
17	Beechene, Yaxley & Co	Got through champagne. Orders more	Texas
21	AP Watt	Difficulty with revises for abroad	Private
29	AP Watt	Pamphlet story copies will be "curiosity"	Private
Oct 7	AP Watt	Going Ramsgate. Query on "Royal Love"	Private
13	Henry Pigott	Starting for Ramsgate. Piracy robs him	Huntington
16	AP Watt	Ramsgate doing its good work	Private
17	AP Watt	Discusses illustrations	Private
23	Edward Pigott	Thanks for help. Charlie "joins" him	Huntington
23	AP Watt	Thanks for gift of stick & US agreement	Private
24	Mary Anderson	Has not forgotten possible play	Texas
25	Charles Kent	Is getting better	Princeton
30	A [Pappritz]	Last novel already translated into German	Princeton
Nov 4	AP Watt	Leaves decision on *Evil Genius* to him	Private
5	Leopold Katscher	Translation rights already purchased	Princeton
9	AP Watt	End of stay in Ramsgate	Private
12	AP Watt	Back at the "old work shop again"	Private
16	Charles Kent	Asks him to call to hear about Ramsgate	Princeton
16	Eleanor Selfe	Obstacles to Fallen Leaves sequel	Private
19	AP Watt	Another specimen of Tillotson	Private
22	AP Watt	"Here he is again." Write to Tillotson	Private
24	AP Watt	Deal with T's letter as think fit	Private
Dec 1	AP Watt	Translators of *Evil Genius* "enthusiastic"	Private
2	AP Watt	Revises of *Evil Genius* missing	Private
2	AP Watt	More proofs by evening post	Private
3	J Saunders	Obstacles to *Fallen Leaves* sequel	Private
5	AP Watt	More annoyance from Tillotson	Private
13	AP Watt	Boswell's *Life of Johnson* favourite	Private
28	AP Watt	Horrid Xmas is over. Live on champagne	Private

IX : Letters to 'Nannie' 1885–1888

1885

July 16	Mrs le Poer Wynne	Accepts invitation	Private
21	Mrs le Poer Wynne	Sends two portraits of himself	Private
Aug 12	Anne le Poer Wynne	Thanks for flowers. Promises ghost story	Private
22	Mrs le Poer Wynne	Sends story proofs	Private
Oct 7	Mrs le Poer Wynne	Neuralgia returned. See them tomorrow ?	Private
Dec 19	Mrs le Poer Wynne	He is "most ungrateful of husbands"	Private
28	Mrs le Poer Wynne	Trying to see "poor dear wife"	Private

1886

| May 28 | Mrs le Poer Wynne | Accepts invite. "Love to his wife" | Private |

Date	Recipient	Topic	Source
1887			
Aug 5	Mrs le Poer Wynne	Is wife "taking care of the children?"	Private
Dec 22	Mrs le Poer Wynne	Neuralgia. Is moving. "Love to Mrs Wilkie"	Private
1886			
Jan 12	Beechene,Yaxley & Co	Orders champagne; 3 to "Mrs Dawson"	Texas
18	Harriet Bartley	Because of your gum will delay copy	Texas
27	AP Watt	Perry Mason angels not publishers	Private
29	William Yaxley	Will certainly get the book	Princeton
Feb 2	AP Watt	Trouble again from Tillotson	Private
8	Chatto & Windus	Summary of agreement *Evil Genius*	Reading
8	William Yaxley	Orders book on Mary Qn Of Scots	Princeton
21	Henry Pigott	Thanks for asparagus. Come for "pot luck"	Huntington
23	CH Ross [Ally Sloper]	Proud to sign 'FOS' (Friend of Sloper)	Stanford
March 7	Holman Hunt	Wishes prosperous trip to the East	Huntington
9	Charles Kent	Rejoices in his recovery. Come Thursday	Princeton
9	AP Watt	Last chapter *Evil Genius* in post	Private
12	WS Withers	Declines proposal. Gives details of story	M/Clib
14	Lillie Langtry	Congratulations on performance	Princeton
15	Henry Pigott	Caroline called on Uncle Ted	Huntington
16	JF Gluck	Promises M/S for Buffalo Library	Princeton
16	AP Watt	Thanks for copy of book and cheque	Private
19	Edward Pigott	Beware railway draughts	Huntington
30	Unknown	He arranges to visit	Princeton
31	David Stott	Asks him to procure books	Princeton
April 2	AP Watt	Glad of recognition of his father	Private
3	Edward Pigott	Mrs Langtry's acting. Caroline at theatre	Huntington
8	Edward Pigott	Wants to stop piracy of *New Magdalen*	Huntington
9	Harriet Bartley	Reports success with producers of his play	Texas
9	Edward Pigott	Authors rights have been asserted	Huntington
9	AP Watt	Delighted to see tomorrow	Private
12	Percy	Invites to dinner Saturday	Princeton
22	Alberic Iserbyt	Berlin correspondence has ended	Princeton
May 5	AP Watt	Has had last of money from Tillotson	Private
7	S Weeks	Obstacles to *Fallen Leaves* sequel	Private
7	Thomas Woolner	Appreciated estimate of father's genius	Bodleian
9	Peter Cunningham	Unable to undertake journalism	Princeton
11	Emily Clunes	Sends sympathy to aunt	Private
11	Charles Kent	*Evil Genius* as book in autumn	Texas
June 3	AP Watt	Sends second story for Perry Mason	Private
6	Alberic Iserbyt	Requests help in copying plays	Princeton
6	AP Watt	Getting new copyist	Private
10	AP Watt	Third story. He needs copy again	Private
11	Georgina Hogarth	Sorry she has been ill	Trinity Coll
16	AP Watt	Received request for short serial	Private
17	Alberic Iserbyt	Sends 4th Act	Princeton
17	JR Scarlett	Thanks for approval. Sends catalogue	Princeton
18	AP Watt	Right to ask the price he did	Private
21	AP Watt	Encloses play	Private
24	[JF Gluck]	M/S *Two Destinies* sent to Buffalo	Yale
July 6	AP Watt	Perry Mason pleasant. Tillotson mad	Private
8	AP Watt	Would like to kick Tillotson	Private
11	Holman Hunt	Delighted see tomorrow. Then Ramsgate	Private
13	Andrew Chatto	Wants to discuss new novel	Princeton
13	AP Watt	Tillotson has "excelled himself"	Private

Date	Recipient	Topic	Source
16	Andrew Chatto	Here is *Evil Genius* printed copy	Princeton
16	AP Watt	Bogus item to preserve *Guilty River*	Private
18	Andrew Chatto	Foreign translations. Come smell the sea	Princeton
21	Mr Coleman	Sends excuses. Ramsgate with Mrs Graves	Private
26	Francis Carr Beard	Ramsgate. Children "in and out".	Princeton
Aug 1	ES Robertson	Not yet returning to London	Princeton
4	Alberic Iserbyt	Congratulations	Princeton
16	AP Watt	Harper's offer "impudent". Returning early	Private
18	AP Watt	Home again. New story : *Guilty River*	Private
19	AP Watt	Returns signed document	Private
29	Chatto & Windus	Send dedication to printers	Private
30	Andrew Chatto	Will he look at M/S from Frank Archer	Princeton
30	AP Watt	"Old tortures in the eye"	Private
Sept 2	George Bentley	Intermission of pain	NYPL
9	Andrew Chatto	Thanks for £500. Admires binding	Princeton
11	Holman Hunt	Is dedicating *Evil Genius* to him	Huntington
14	AP Watt	Criticises complaint from Perry Mason	Private
16	AP Watt	Has exactly interpreted his wishes	Private
22	Andrew Chatto	Payments	Princeton
24	Unknown	*Evil Genius* idea occurred while yachting	Princeton
Oct 2	AP Watt	Writing at 11 pm with proofs to correct	Private
6	AP Watt	Congratulations son's birth. Patch off eye.	Private
10	Harper & Brothers	Discusses royalty arrangements	Unknown
10	AP Watt	Posts first part of *The Guilty River*	Private
11	AP Watt	Will he take on Australian literary business.	Private
27	Harriet Bartley	Thanks for US copy. Love to children	Texas
27	Beechene, Yaxley & Co	Sends cheque. Cruise followed by gout	Texas
30	Harper & Brothers	Publishing *The Guilty River* Monday	Unknown
30	AP Watt	Sends letter asking for short story	Private
Nov 3	Sir Henry Thompson	Declines invitation. Lives hermit's life	Private
6	Harper & Brothers	Duplicates of *Guilty River* being sent	Princeton
8	AP Watt	No time for him to receive proof	Private
10	FG Kitton	Thanks for addition to portrait collection	Princeton
10	AP Watt	Wants terms, price etc of M/S	Private
12	AP Watt	Hopes his illness not serious	Private
21	AP Watt	"Brains addled with work"	Private
28	FR Osgood	Has made blunder. Discusses terms	Unknown
Dec 4	Andrew Chatto	Here is new short story	Princeton
7	Frederick Lehmann	Athenaeum Club. Dead friends haunt it	Princeton
7	AP Watt	Should have got jury exemption	Private
12	Frederick Lehmann	Can he call next Sunday?	Unknown
14	Frederick Lehmann	Accepts. Can drink 2 glasses champagne	Princeton
15	AP Watt	Thanks for *King Solomon's Mines*	Private
21	Mrs Henry Dickens	Declines dinner	Canterbury
21	AP Watt	Returns amended agreements.	Private
22	WH Rideing	US publishing problems with P. Mason	Princeton
23	King, Baillie & Co	Birds arrived in excellent condition	Private
26	Unknown	Looks forward to literary association	Texas
27	AP Watt	Domestic establishment in "crisis"	Private
20	Miss Le Thiere	Requests a little delay	Princeton
1887			
Jan 5	AP Watt	Thanks for *She*. Meanness of Harper's	Private
18	Frederick Lehmann	Wants to lunch again	Princeton
19	Frederick Lehmann	Next Sunday will do	Princeton

Date	Recipient	Topic	Source
28	Harry Quilter	His letter "event in my literary life"	Huntington
Feb 21	Frederick Lehmann	Gout threatening. Has he been elected?	Princeton
21	Mrs Wagg	Encloses his autograph	Unknown
23	Mrs Walter Besant	Declines invitation. Neuralgia in chest	Texas
25	AP Watt	Managed half hour walk yesterday	Private
March 1	AP Watt	Thanks for Security of Literary Property	Private
2	AP Watt	Returns & discusses magazines	Private
3	AP Watt	Acknowledges cheque for £21	Private
9	Andrew Chatto	Will he republish stories in book form?	Private
11	AP Watt	Stallion in US called "Wilkie Collins"	Private
12	Andrew Chatto	Discusses lease of short stories	Princeton
15	Harry Quilter	Delighted to see him on Thursday	Princeton
15	AP Watt	Asks him to write to Harry Dickens	Private
21	Andrew Chatto	Grumbles about title copyright	Princeton
21	AP Watt	Affair brought to courteous conclusion	Private
22	Andrew Chatto	Suggests several titles for book	Princeton
22	AP Watt	Offers seats for revival *Man & Wife*	Private
23	Andrew Chatto	Let us decide on "Little Novels"	Princeton
28	FP Cobbe	Thanks for ticket. Driven from London	Princeton
29	AP Watt	Offers theatre tickets. Thanks for book	Private
30	EW Bok	Unable to contribute to memorial	Princeton
April 5	Beechene, Yaxley & Co	Orders six dozen Ribera Sherry	Texas
5	Mrs Hepworth	Thanks for newspaper cutting	Princeton
7	R du Pontavice de Heussey	Thanks for dedication and poems	Princeton
7	Harry Quilter	Not dared to see the play yet	Huntington
10	Mrs OL Sykes	Declines invitation	Private
14	CT Palmer	Writes to arrange visit	Princeton
21	N Sarony	Photographs	Iowa
26	AP Watt	Tillotson's story is far off	Private
28	Andrew Chatto	No preface or dedication for stories	Princeton
28	AP Watt	Starting story tomorrow	Private
29	Andrew Chatto	Thanks for *Evil Genius*	Kansas
May 7	Isaac [Tarras]	Encloses photographic portrait	Princeton
8	AP Watt	Can he look in with estimate of story?	Private
16	AP Watt	Thanks for picture	Private
19	Andrew Chatto	Thanks for presentation copies	Princeton
20	AP Watt	Doubts about Tillotson	Private
June 2	Andrew Chatto	Thanks for drafts for "Little Novels"	Princeton
3	Mr Bigelow	Cannot see anyone.Neuralgia returned	Princeton
8	Chatto & Windus	Will not be in London on 21st	Princeton
23	Dixon-Spain	Returns tickets : Temperance Soc	BL
28	AP Watt	Nerves "unscrewed". Agrees try Scribner.	Private
July 4	J Jenkinson	Declines invitation to Birmingham	Princeton
18	Pierre Berton	Is ill. Admired his father as artist	Fales NYU
21	Frederick Lehmann	Cannot vote at Club. Gout threatening	Princeton
27	AP Watt	Half way through story	Private
Aug 6	Harriet Bartley	When is she leaving for seaside	Princeton
8	AP Watt	Hoping to go to Margate in a week	Private
22	AP Watt	Sorry about "Glasgow savages"	Private
Sept 14	Edward Bok	Cruising at sea. Hopes to send article	Private
14	LS Metcalf	Will write for *The Forum*	Princeton
23	[?] Smith	Has not written essay on *Simple Story*	Texas
24	AP Watt	Back after Margate and some cruising	Private
28	AP Watt	Offers at 600; if Tillotson 750	Private
30	AP Watt	Thanks for article on Scott	Private

Date	Recipient	Topic	Source
Oct 7	R du Pontavice de Heussey	Will try to get music for him	Princeton
10	Beechene, Yaxley & Co	Orders "Vin Brut", dry and before 1880	Princeton
11	Andrew Chatto	Discusses theft of book title	Princeton
13	Andrew Chatto	Encloses letter from publisher	Princeton
13	AP Watt	Delighted to see him tomorrow	Private
20	Beechene, Yaxley & Co	Champagne delicious. Orders more	Texas
20	Andrew Chatto	Has written to Leng about title	Princeton
23	Andrew Chatto	Unsatisfactory answer. Consulting lawyer	Princeton
24	AP Watt	Mentions a story	Private
25	Andrew Chatto	Register *Evil Genius* tomorrow	Princeton
26	AP Watt	'No' to Tillotson. Going to law	Private
26	AP Watt	Sends him a book	Private
27	Beechene, Yaxley & Co	Thanks for champagne opportunity	Private
27	Andrew Chatto	Thanks for advice. Taking legal opinion	Princeton
28	Tillotson & Sons	Discusses French & Italian translations	Princeton
Nov 2	Edward Bok	Thanks for £50 cheque	Princeton
4	AP Watt	Not capricious in refusing Leng	Private
8	AP Watt	Has found nice upper part of capital house	Private
9	AP Watt	Encloses proposal from *Bow Bells*	Private
17	AP Watt	Proof of article	Private
21	Andrew Chatto	*Evil Genius* piracy ends with submission	Princeton
Dec 2	AP Watt	Sending story to *Bow Bells*	Private
5	Frank Archer	Can he look in next Wednesday	Unknown
5	James Payn	Sorry not to have returned book	Private
10	Edward Pigott	Unable to see him before he travels	Huntington
28	AP Watt	Confined to house. Needs advice	Private
30	Mary Anderson	Ill. But still hopes to see her on stage	Fales NYU
1888			
Jan 2	Henry Pigott	Prisoner in house. Heart. Gout	Huntington
8	Harry Quilter	Appreciates article on his writing methods	Huntington
10	AP Watt	Has been wretchedly ill. Trying to work	Private
19	Editor, *The Critic*	Thanks for remarkable story	Unknown
20	Mary Anderson	Is Romeo. When can he see Juliet?	Unknown
25	AC Alexander	Agreeable to name on Committee	Princeton
25	Sebastian Schlesinger	Introduces secretary. Asks about insurance	Harvard
26	Henry Pigott	Suggests "pot luck" next Saturday	Huntington
Feb 4	AP Watt	In troubles with moving	Private
4	Unknown	Fees for German translation	Unknown
6	WM Thomas	Discusses piracy of *New Magdalen* play	Texas
6	AP Watt	Discusses his story in *Weekly Scotsman*	Private
8	Hall Caine	Delighted to discuss copyright problems	Manx
8	AP Watt	Discusses Hall Caine's proposed visit	Private
10	EH [Barnstock]	Cannot find wall space in new house	Princeton
19	M Thomas	Glad he proposes to use his experience	Texas
March 7	Charles Kent	Hopes to see him at 82 Wimpole St	Unknown
7	Mrs Cornelia Strong	Is moving. Cannot think of a "sentiment"	Princeton
7	AP Watt	Tillotson has sent cheque	Private
22	A F Maitland	Sends last rent. Will send keys Saturday	Princeton
[March 1888]	Mary Anderson	Can he call and praise her acting	Unknown
April 8	AP Watt	Is he well again?	Private
12	PW Bunting	Blinded with dust. Hopes to contribute	Princeton
12	AP Watt	Refusing to give title/synopsis new story	Private
19	AP Watt	Chatto made offer to buy books	Private

Date	Recipient	Topic	Source
23	Chatto & Windus	Received £250 for 5 novels until 1895	Reading
25	AP Watt	Describes Chatto's visit and offer	Private
26	Andrew Chatto	Thanks for 3 interesting novels	Princeton
May 1	Hall Caine	Cannot share box on night of his play	Manx
9	Henry Pigott	Suggests lunch. Is finishing story	Huntington
9	AP Watt	*Legacy of Cain* will run to 21 parts	Private
16	William Winter	Invites him and son to lunch	Folger
18	Harry Quilter	Promises articles	Huntington
29	Harry Quilter	Promises short article on Saturday	Huntington
30	Tillotson	New house a "haven of rest"	Bolton
30	AP Watt	Finished last part of *Cain*. Rec'd £250	Private
31	AP Watt	Accepts invitation to dine at Club	Private
June 2	Harry Quilter	Will try, but don't count on it	Huntington
2	Harry Quilter	Copy gone by registered post	Huntington
6	Hall Caine	Sorry to miss him. Come to lunch	Manx
9	Benjamin Bryan	Declines invitation from Committee	Private
9	Miriam F Leslie	Is she staying in London longer?	Fales NYU
12	[Mr Bennock]	Offers excuses of moving. Hopes to call	Huntington
12	AP Watt	Thanks him for a book	Private
13	Henry Bartley	Has paid for dilapidations	Private
15	Rev George Bainton	Thanks for factual advice	Illinois
15	AP Watt	Father's picture Barmouth Sands	Private
16	Edwin Ashworth	*Men of the Time* corrected by him	Texas
22	Hall Caine	Cannot see him. Will he be in London	Manx
27	Unknown	Contributes his autograph	NYPL
27	William Winter	Sorry to miss him. Come tomorrow	Folger
29	AP Watt	Is going to Crystal Palace Tuesday	Private
30	Holman Hunt	Glad to see Theodore Watt	Private
July 3	Harry Quilter	Just got back. Wishes to see tomorrow	Huntington
4	Chatto & Windus	Serialisation ended July 7	Reading
5	Harry Quilter	Letter received?	Huntington
7	SS McClure	Returns cheque. Refers to AP Watt	Princeton
10	AP Watt	Acknowledges cheque £301	Private
12	Andrew Chatto	Can he see General Mitchell & M/S	Princeton
13	John Turner	Gives details of some of his articles	Unknown
18	AP Watt	Irish nature is only in Prologue	Private
25	AP Watt	Thanks him for gift of stick	Private
27	Sebastian Schlesinger	Taking morganatic family to seaside	Harvard
30	AP Watt	Every book translated into German	Private
30	Unknown	Payment to the Slade fund	Unknown
30	Mrs M [Flint?]	Letter writing	Private
Aug 7	Chatto & Windus	Requests £500 for *Legacy of Cain*	Reading
7	LS Metcalf	Thanks for *The Forum*	Princeton
8	Andrew Chatto	Sends printed copy of *Legacy of Cain*	Princeton
9	Chatto & Windus	Discusses proofs	Princeton
Sept 10	Sebastian Schlesinger	Better for sea air. Now neuralgia	Harvard
12	AP Watt	Send copy for Dicks	Private
13	Chatto & Windus	When will he receive proofs?	Princeton
13	AP Watt	Ill since returning from Ramsgate	Private
14	Annie Carpenter	Sympathy on death of her mother	Texas
14	Unknown	Neuralgia in face. Abscess in mouth	Princeton
24	Unknown	Plot of *No Name* entirely imaginary	Fales NYU
Oct 5	AP Watt	Recovery. Back at work	Private
6	Sebastian Schlesinger	Wants to present the children to him	Harvard
[9]	AP Watt	Glad to dine with him & Rider Haggard	Princeton

Date	Recipient	Topic	Source
Nov 13	AP Watt	Has achieved masterly success	Private
23	Mrs Linsell	Thanks for quinces	Unknown
30	James Payn	No need to dress tomorrow	Texas
Dec 7	Andrew Chatto	Thanks for presentation copies	Princeton
11	Walter Michel	Declines proposal	Private
12	AP Watt	Sly hint – hope of meeting Haggard	Private
14	Andrew Chatto	Thanks for cheque and cutting	Private
17	AP Watt	Accepts dinner invitation	Private
18	Henry Pigott	Arranges time for dinner	Private
22	CB Tauchnitz	Thanks for receipt of *Legacy of Cain*	Unknown
29	Rev George Bainton	Sends him *Legacy of Cain*	Yale
29	Unknown	Sends copy *Legacy of Cain*	Princeton
1889			
Jan 1	Henry Pigott	Out for first time	Huntington
9	Sebastian Schlesinger	No box of game delivered	Harvard
15	Edward Bok	No reminiscences of his life written	Private
15	Sebastian Schlesinger	Ducks just arrived. What time dinner?	Harvard
23	AP Watt	Collision in cab. "Without a bruise"	Private
24	Sebastian Schlesinger	Describes cab accident. Stirred up gout	Harvard
28	James Payn	Will he be massing on Sunday?	Private
28	Sebastian Schlesinger	Thanks for delicious bird	Harvard
Feb 1	AP Watt	Returns novel with observations	Private
7	William Tillotson	Sends excuses. Confined to room	Unknown
7	AP Watt	Piracy of *Legacy of Cain* in Hungary	Private
10	Hall Caine	Good luck on first night	Manx
11	Beechene, Yaxley & Co	Orders 6 dozen pints champagne	Texas
11	AP Watt	Don't write to "Hungarian vagabond"	Private
12	AP Watt	Found Ingram agreement	Private
14	AP Watt	Attack of angina	Private
19	Edward Bok	Thanks for and comments on Book Buyer	Private
19	AP Watt	Better but not well enough to write	Private
20	AP Watt	Able to write. Is Tillotson dead?	Private
25	Sebastian Schlesinger	Hasn't seen him	Private
25	AP Watt	Servants away. Can he send messenger	Private
26	AP Watt	Letter from New York. Makes offer	Private
March 1	AP Watt	Thanks for cheque	Private
3	AP Watt	Can't work. Admirable idea new book	Private
7	AP Watt	Has eased his mind	Private
9	AP Watt	Smart practice by late Mr Tillotson	Private
12	Mr Nunn	Is ill. Would have voted for friend	Norfolk
19	AP Watt	Better. Working hard at revision	Private
April 2	Chatto & Windus	Agreement. Rights 24 novels: £1800	Reading
2	Georgina Hogarth	Advises her consult Watt: Dickens letter	Illinois
5	AP Watt	Thanks for success on copyrights	Private
12	Walter Besant	Gladly signs petition	Private
12	AP Watt	Taking time off. Dining on oysters	Private
25	Beechene, Yaxley & Co	Encloses cheque: excellent champagne	Texas
25	Walter Besant	Sends him letter meant for him	Texas
25	AP Watt	Discusses money for French translation	Private
May 2	Andrew Chatto	Discusses offers of translations	Princeton
20	Hall Caine	Do come when in London. Asks for news	Manx
20	WG Collings	Relief from dry champagne when weary	Illinois
24	Sebastian Schlesinger	Sorry to disappoint. Will try for dinner	Harvard
[May 1889]	Sebastian Schlesinger	His daughters determined. Is unnerved	Harvard

Date	Recipient	Topic	Source
June 13	Henry Pigott	Will see them Tuesday. Lobsters arrived	Huntington
15	AP Watt	Thanks for setting mind at rest	Private
21	Mrs Beit	Accepts dinner invitation	Princeton
27	William Winter	Sorry to miss him. Come tomorrow	Folger
28	Holman Hunt	Longing to see picture. Cannot dine	Huntington

Letters of Uncertain Date

Sept 1856– Spring 1859	Mrs WH Wills	Little better today	Yale
[1860s]	Charles Ward	Letter delay. Gave details viva voce	PM
[1860s]	Charles Ward	Come by all means at six	PM
[1860s]	EM Ward	Sure of legal hearings. Lawyer consulted	Texas
[1870s-1880s]	Unknown	Can he see the picture if he calls now?	NSW
[Date uncertain]	Hachette & Cie	Gives details of story in *After Dark*	Private

Index of Correspondents

Note: Only the first page number of each letter is given; a range of pages (e.g. 234-7) indicates two or more consecutive letters to the same recipient.
Volume 1 ends on page 260; Volume 2 begins on page 273

Index

LaVergne, TN USA
21 January 2011
213490LV00003B/53/A